DEATH COMES FOR THE POETS

Matthew Sweeney
&
John Hartley Williams

Death Comes for the Poets

© 2012 Matthew Sweeney & John Hartley Williams

Published by The Muswell Press Ltd

ISBN 978-0-9572136-0-9

A CIP record of this book is available from the British Library.

Design by Barney Beech
Front Cover by Chris Hamilton-Emery
Printed and Bound by Short Run Press Ltd.

Muswell Press Ltd
www.muswell-press.co.uk

I had now met all those who were to make the nineties of the last century tragic in the history of literature, but as yet, we were all seemingly equal whether in talent or luck, and scarce even personalities to one another. I remember saying one night at the Cheshire Cheese when more poets than usual had come: None of us can say who will succeed or even who has or has not talent. The only thing certain about us is that we are too many.

W.B Yeats

To the memory of Ern Malley
Liverpool, UK 1918 – Sydney, Australia 1940

Rise from the wrist, O kestrel

Chapter 1: *The Siege of Lucknow*

Fergus Diver eased his bulk into an ornate chair and blinked at five-headed and four-armed Shiva in lotus pose on the embossed wallpaper. He had been glad of the anonymous tip-off – the town of Maidstone did not feature on any culinary map he had ever looked at – but the extremely baroque décor made him apprehensive. Shiva was the destroyer as well as the benefactor, was he not? It was a benefactor Diver needed at the moment; the poetry reading he had just given to an audience of about twenty two comatose members of the Kent Marshes Poetry Society had been a clunker. Thank God for this Indian restaurant, its agreeably perfumed air and promise of good food.

And thank God he had managed to dodge the octogenarian chairman of the society, Herbert bloody Ludlow. Diver should have been warned off by the gushing enthusiasm of the man's voice on the telephone. Why on earth had he agreed to the gig? He had caved in to the man's boundless, gibbering persistence, that was why.

At the start to the reading, Ludlow had delivered the longest, most rambling and redundant introduction to a guest reader that Diver had ever had. And each of the very few facts mentioned had been wrong. Titles of books scrambled. Prizes awarded that Diver hadn't won; prizes he *had* won neglected. Worst of all, the old man kept getting the name wrong, even though he'd been instructed beforehand: 'Diver pronounced Divver,' the poet had said with the modest smile he used to convey vital information. Ludlow had kept calling him Fergal Diver, deaf to the poet's hissed corrections.

Christ, what a way to spend a Sunday evening! The trains had all been fucked up on the way down from London; biblical floods of rain had ruined his second best jacket, and he'd signed only one book afterwards. Many of the members of the Kent Marshes Poetry Society, thought Diver, were well into the territory where they should have been giving serious thought to euthanasia. And they were mean as peasants to boot; the only book he had signed had been a long out of print copy of his second collection, *The Tram to Nowhere*. He took a deep breath.

Was it the four beers he had had at the reading that were making him dizzy, or was it Shiva's five heads?

Diver tried to blank out the discreet pinging that Indians called music. He allowed the plashing of a fountain at the end of the room to soothe him. A tolerable background, if you had to have noise at all. *Not much in Maidstone to satisfy the gourmet,* the message had read, *but you might find* The Siege of Lucknow *pleasing.* The mystery informant had signed himself: *An aficionado of your column.*

He rather liked that use of the word 'aficionado'. Diver's restaurant column in *The Observer* brought him more praise and good wishes (and followers) than anything he had ever done in the poetry line. He was used to being approached by diners who had enjoyed places he had written about, and also those who had shared his experiences of gastronomic hell. If there was one thing that united all peoples of the world, it was food – the most universal language of all, more accessible than music, more lyrical than poetry.

Apart from a group of four people at a distant table, he was alone in the restaurant. There were no signs of any staff. He waited. He was beginning to think the waiters had absconded but a sudden yelp and a loud crash from a direction he presumed to be the kitchen reassured him that cookery was in process. A tall Sikh in a turban appeared, handed him a menu, and walked over to the party at the other table. As he studied the menu, Diver became aware of a slight altercation, voices raised. A dispute? He looked up and watched the waiter, who seemed to be putting decorous pressure on the other diners to settle the bill. In no time at all they were being shooed out into the rain, accompanied by much respectful bowing from the Sikh, his hands put together as if in prayer. One of the departing guests said something loud, possibly insulting – a parting shot? Diver took out his notebook and scribbled in it. He always made a point of noticing the behaviour of restaurant staff. The dining experience had many aspects to it; there was a lot more to consider than whether or not one's steak was perfectly *à point*. Or one's rice *al dente*.

The main restaurant door closed, a heavy curtain fell across it, and the waiter vanished back into the precincts of the kitchen. Diver looked around. He was now completely alone. Why would they chivvy people out of the restaurant when there were so many free tables? Nothing attracted customers more than seeing that places were well patronised. That was what restaurateurs wanted more than anything else; it was a sign of good things. But perhaps a coach party was expected later. Diver looked at his watch. Ten already! Maybe they just wanted to close up.

He opened the opulent menu and began to study it. Diver knew from experience that surprising gastronomic delights were to be found in the most unlikely places and the dishes on offer were far from the usual Indian restaurant fare. Perhaps the evening was going to end well after all; he deserved it. Passing over the starters, he decided to opt for the main course. When the turbaned waiter reappeared, he asked for Murgh Bhogar, Alu Badam Dum, Sagh, pilau rice and a stuffed paratha. "Yes, Sir, the chicken with scrambled eggs, a very good choice, Sir. Smothered potatoes with almonds, excellent. You have picked some of the best things our chef does. Anything to drink, Sir?"

"This 2005 Rioja looks good. Bring me a bottle of that."

"Yes, Sir."

In very short time the man had returned with the Rioja, used a proper corkscrew in the professional manner (Diver was pleased to see this in an Indian restaurant), sniffed the cork, poured a finger for Diver to taste and then, on Diver's nod of approval, half filled the red wine glass and retreated.

The wine was excellent. Diver noted down the price, the year and the name of the producer. Aromas of raspberry and plum, and a hint of mown grass. This was obviously a good place. He settled back in his chair.

They'd started the reading late of course. Why did it always have to be 'of course'? He'd been liberally supplied with Guinness from the moment he'd walked through the door of the pub and once upstairs in the room designated for the reading he had quaffed a third pint while the venerable chairman hovered at the door as if his entreating eyes would suck more people into the room. From time to time, Ludlow had glanced back at the visiting poet as if to make sure Diver was not about to metamorphose into a roaring drunk - a possible side effect of readings given to the Kent Marshes Poetry Society?

Diver, surveying the uncrowded room, had noticed that one woman had brought a child of eight years or less. Well, he was not going to delete any expletives on that account. A number of very elderly people were having difficulty finding parking space for their walking sticks and other more cumbersome paraphernalia. Two nuns had stared at him from the end of a row. Had his reputation as one of England's most famous atheists not reached Maidstone? He had directed an anti-clerical scowl at them and they had smiled and nodded back. He ought to have got up and left then, but of course old troupers keep trouping, the show has to go on, all that rot.

He brooded, staring towards the kitchen. The waiter emerged through waistcoat swing doors, bringing poppadums and pickles, placed them on the table, beamed at Diver and vanished back into the inner precincts.

The poet cracked some slivers and refilled his wine glass. Perhaps it had been a mistake to begin his reading with that poem about the skeleton of a giraffe? It ended with what Diver considered an apocalyptic flourish, possibly a rather too demanding trope for an out-of-town audience, and during the silence afterwards – not so much awe and astonishment, perhaps, as bafflement - he had raked his gaze along the rows of seats as if defying the audience not to applaud. One acne-ridden student-type had indeed started to put his hands together, but stopped when he realised he was alone. That was when Diver's attention had been caught by the two latecomers. One of them, a tall heavily bearded man, was wearing a deerstalker. The other was von Zitzewitz, the Bavarian-born haikuist.

What was Manfred von Zitzewitz doing at a reading by Fergus Diver? The poet crumbled more poppadum, and chewed thoughtfully. Manfred and he had ceased speaking to each other years ago, after a ferocious argument on a train about the Auden Prize. Diver had won of course. Manfred had been a very bad loser.

The waiter returned and offloaded a tray of sumptuously bubbling pots on to the table, enquired if everything was to Diver's satisfaction, and went, leaving the poet surrounded by little dishes perched on candle warmers. The poet began to eat with relish, belching between forkfuls, and wishing he had company, anyone at all, with whom he could share appreciation of the excellently prepared food.

Even von Zitzewitz?

No. Diver had drawn a line under that one. He thought back to the reading. There'd been a hum on the mike that had distracted him for a while but the total fiasco had occurred when he had given his new villanelle an outing. After the fourth stanza, with the same two lines repeating in slightly altered contexts down through the poem, he was stopped in his tracks by a piping child's voice: 'You've said that already.' Members of the audience had laughed aloud, including von Zitzewitz, who had risen to his feet and with a sardonic nod to Diver quit the room. Yeah, get lost, thought Diver, as he watched him leave. The other latecomer had not even removed his deerstalker, and he was gazing at the poet with a broad smile on his face.

Diver sighed. The Murgh Bogar was a dream. He'd never tasted the dish prepared so brilliantly. *The Siege of Lucknow* must have engaged a Michelin-starred chef. After such humiliation, what forgiveness? He merited this, didn't he? Diver emptied and refilled his glass again and recalled how only a week ago an audience of three thousand Columbians had got to their feet and shouted 'Maestro! Maestro!' after that same villanelle. Oh to be back at the festival in Medellin, dancing late at night in the tango bar with those sinuous Colombian women.

But this was Maidstone. Utterly Maidstone.

There was always a tipping point when you knew you'd lost your audience, and the villanelle had been it.

At the end of the reading, ignoring the feeble applause and Ludlow's announcement that Fergal would now be willing to respond to questions, he had made for the door at great speed. The upstairs room of *The Spotted Dog* in which the reading had taken place was connected to the lounge bar by some twisting, ill-carpeted stairs, and Diver descended these in a rush only to find himself walking towards von Zitzewitz, who was sitting at a far table, grinning in his direction. Turning on his heel, Diver had fetched up by a small bar in the so-called Snug, aware that he was ahead of his audience and would, if he wasn't careful, end up paying for his own drink. In a state of mortal indecision, he had stood staring at the price list on the wall until a barman had placed a pint glass in front of him, smiled, and vanished. With what gratitude had he downed that Guinness!

He closed his eyes and tried to erase the Kent Marshes Poetry Society from his consciousness by making careful tasting notes in his notebook. Waves of retrospective ignominy halted his pen. He leaned back in his chair, emitting a resonant and prolonged belch. Phew! He was sweating. Looking up from his unhelpful notebook, he observed Shiva's five heads staring back. Did they all bear a resemblance to von Zitzewitz?

He took a deep breath. A trip into the restaurant's basement would also have to go into his report. The beers he'd had earlier, together with the wine and the highly spiced food were beginning to create their own karma. What you needed were the suavely-carpeted stairs, the non-kitsch sex-signalling on the lavatory doors, the subdued lighting the big mirrors with their roseate flush, the plentiful soap and hot water, the warm towels...excellent! He felt refreshed as he padded back to his table and found an unasked-for dish of mushrooms, liberally sprinkled with a curious herb, placed on his table mat. He concluded the waiter had seen him making entries in his notebook. This, then, had to be *the* speciality of the house. He was always gratified to have his connoisseurship appealed to.

He emptied the last drops of Rioja into his glass. The mushrooms were indeed very good, if curiously astringent – a taste he knew he could learn to acquire. He would have to find out from the waiter what the herb was. Somehow or other, he would also have to track down the benefactor who had recommended this place and thank him properly.

"Splendid reading" a Welsh voice had said. "Pity about the audience. What can I get you to drink?" Diver had turned to see the man in the deerstalker behind him.

"Thank you. I've just had a Guinness, but I could use another."

"Did you get my message this morning?"

............"Message?"

"I'm devoted to your poetry Mr Diver. It's a real privilege to hear you read."

"Thank you."

"But I very much enjoy your restaurant column in *The Observer* as well. I suppose poets can't make a living from poetry alone?"

"Indeed, they can't. So you are my cryptic intelligencer?"

"Guilty," said the Welshman. "*The Siege of Lucknow* is truly exceptional for a provincial restaurant. But here comes the audience. I'll leave you to their tender mercies."

And then the fellow had gone. Diver had not even learned his name. No doubt Ludlow would know it. The Kent Marshes Poetry Society was obviously a cabal of deviously intimate conspirators who would all know each other's names. What a piece of luck he'd managed to dodge them at the end. They had actually had the temerity to suggest taking him to the Wimpy bar round the corner.

"Does anyone know *The Siege of Lucknow*?" he'd asked, downing a beer he had bought himself.

"It's just down the street," a lady standing next to him had said- Not wishing to give unforgivable offence, and searching the room for a deerstalker that appeared to have gone, Diver had enquired: "Perhaps some of you would care to join me there?"

"It's too late for me, Mr Diver," said Ludlow with an odious chuckle. "We're really rather modest here as regards our eating habits. A man of your gourmandising sensibilities would probably prefer dining alone anyway."

Diver had hefted the empty beer glass in his hand, and thought about bringing it down hard on the octogenarian's bony skull. No, if he could have chosen he would have elected to dine with his Welsh well-wisher. He had thrown a glance across the bar at a known ill-wisher. What had brought von Zitzewitz to his reading, and why was he still sitting there, grinning? Deciding that offence was what he wanted to give after all, Diver had said with venom:

"Actually, I would prefer to eat in discerning company, but if there's none to be had, I'll do without." And he had headed out into the dripping street.

The fountain plopped. The sitar plonked. Diver tried out a few more descriptive arabesques to capture the flavour of the mushrooms. Then, scraping the bowl clean, he sank back in his chair, glugging the last of his Rioja. Another day in the life of a poet. He checked the time, saw it was after eleven, remembered he had put the key for his hotel in a pocket, searched for it in a state of anxiety, and then found it. His room number was 101. He leaned back. He would have liked to have fallen asleep where he was, but suddenly the Sikh waiter was there presenting the bill.

"Was everything OK, Sir? "

Diver tried to express his complete approval but found himself somehow tongue-tied. He struggled to his feet to gain access to his pocket, and in doing so, embarrassed himself by farting. The waiter ignored this, smiling, and when Diver had counted out enough notes to cover the amount plus a generous tip, spun round and vanished back into the kitchen with the little pile of crumpled notes on a silver tray. Diver picked up the receipt left on the table, folded it into his wallet, reclaimed his overcoat, and walked a mite unsteadily out into the night. Behind him he heard the door being bolted.

Which way was it to that damned hotel, and what was it called again? Only a hundred yards or so? More like a hundred miles. As he made his way down the main street he noticed how cold he felt. Stepping off the kerb to cross the road, he nearly lost his balance and fell. Surely he hadn't drunk that much. A searing pain in his gut left him gasping for air. Christ, maybe it was that chicken with scrambled egg dish. Could it be salmonella? Surely it didn't act this fast? He stopped and looked up at a flickering sign. *The Rudyard Kipling*. Yeah. That was it. What a stupid name for a hotel. He crossed the road, realising he couldn't feel his feet and his hands anymore. This made it extremely difficult for him to locate the key in his pocket. He managed, however, but then the keyhole kept moving around in the door. He stabbed at it, cursing, and finally lurched into the foyer. He dragged himself up the stairs to his first floor room.

Shiva was waiting for him, seated demurely on the edge of the bed. All his heads were smiling, showing terrible, stained teeth, and snakes were uncoiling slowly from five dark throats.

Four arms beckoned him in. At the extremities of each arm were hands as big as shovels, holding knives. The arms elongated and reached caressingly towards him, then slit open Diver's belly from groin to navel. Shiva was laughing, extricating Diver's guts, unwinding them and coiling them on the floor.

Diver tried to remonstrate but his vocal cords were suddenly stopped up with some thick, black, bituminous stuff. He turned and staggered away from this monstrosity towards the bathroom, feeling a hand insert itself into his rectum, a whole arm, and then there was Shiva's hand emerging from Diver's own mouth, appearing in front of his own eyes, and wagging a 'naughty boy' finger at him.

Diver twisted round, impaled like a puppet on this infinitely extensible arm, and sank backwards as he saw a frightful apparition appear in the doorway of the bathroom. The pain was something beyond pain. It was the cosmos exploding. The face no longer looked demure. Not friendly. It was the implacable, dark, frowning face of the destroyer, Shiva, and it murmured his name with the relish of one savouring a victim, Diver, Diver, Diver. Come to me, Fergus Diver.

Chapter 2: *The Poetry Wars*

Despite heavy traffic on the road from Deal to Lewes, a red Porsche flew past the slowly forward moving column of cars as if there had been no traffic at all. It slipped through gaps most ordinary motorists would barely have considered large enough for a motorbike and flashed onward in the morning sunlight before left-behind drivers had time to be startled. It wasn't that Victor Priest was late, although he was a bit. He was good at driving fast, and relished doing it.

Two solid lanes of jammed vehicles at the entrance to Lewes obliged him to come to a dead stop. He sat, fretting, his gloved fingers drumming on the steering wheel. Were they all going to the funeral? Hardly likely. Poets didn't attract large followings, even poets as prominent in the literary world as Fergus Diver. The words of the critic Stanislaus Green, which he'd read that morning in *The Daily Tele-graph,* came back to him: 'Few poets have ever managed to describe with such forensic acuity the death-haunted human condition.' Or something like that. It was a fair enough assessment, Priest thought, recalling Diver's work as the car inched forward. The obituary had sent him to his bookshelf, to the *Selected Poems*, and he'd turned to the famous piece, 'The Poisoned', that imagined a series of violent ends in renaissance Italy. It was a poem he was very familiar with. Surely the Telegraph could have reprinted it, or at least a section of it, for the occasion.

The newspaper had not omitted the details of Diver's excruciating end. A chambermaid had found him sitting naked and stiff on the toilet. His huge bulk was set in a slouching pose, and his lips were drawn back above his teeth which had bitten through his tongue. He had soiled himself on the bed and there was excrement everywhere.

An undignified exit, thought Priest, for one of Britain's finest poets.

Eventually, parking the Porsche on Western Road at some distance from St Anne's Church and striding past the hearse and the mourners' black Daimler, Priest went up the heavy flagstones of the path and reached the front door of the church. The strains of a recording of Count John McCormick singing 'Oft in the Stilly Night' came floating from the interior. Faces turned to study his arrival. He found an empty pew halfway to the front and sat down. There were fewer in the congregation than he'd expected but he recognised a number of eminent poets, including some foreign ones, among them the most recent Nobel Prize-winner for Literature, the Mexican poet Pedro Velasquez. An extremely attractive woman in black stood by his side. McCormick's lament concluded, and the Orcadian poet Ruarí Mac-Leod climbed the steps of the pulpit with the aid of a blackthorn stick, placed reading glasses on the end of his nose, peered at his notes, and launched into a eulogy for his dear friend Fergus Diver.

This ended with a reading of Diver's poem 'Skua Attack', then four hefty mourners hoisted the coffin to shoulder height, staggering slightly, before moving forward at a stately pace, with the congregation following, out into the bright sunshine, round two ancient yew trees into the churchyard where a hole awaited. Priest walked at the back of the procession and listened as the last rites were read. As the coffin was lowered into the grave, he watched a bright yellow butterfly follow the coffin down, flutter along its polished length and then rise into the light breeze and veer away. Diver's soul would not flutter, thought Priest. There had been no lightness about him. The sight and sound of each member of the congregation dropping a handful of earth on to the coffin brought his attention back to the sombre charade in progress. He went forward, added his crumbly contribution, and walked on to where the woman in black was standing on the arm of Pedro Velasquez. She studied him with a smile of puzzlement.

"Please allow me to express my sincerest condolences for your loss, Mrs Diver. I wasn't invited but I hoped you wouldn't mind my paying my respects. Victor Priest."

He took her hand.

"Very good of you to come, Mr Priest. Did you know Fergus well?"

"We corresponded a few years ago, regarding his archive. I'm very aware of his work and his reputation."

"He had many followers."

Pedro Velasquez nodded vigorously and put his arm around the widow's shoulder. She gave the Mexican a half-smile and looked at Priest.

"Are you a poet?"

"A collector, Mrs Diver. I collect and deal in literary manuscripts. But my day job, so to speak, is investigating art crimes."

"Art crimes?" said Velasquez with a laugh. "We poets are all guilty of those, Señor. How do you investigate such things?"

"I investigate forgeries and thefts in the art world. But I also handle literary deceptions, plagiarism, unauthorised translation, pirate publication. *Artcrimes* is the name of my company."

"Oh,' said the widow. "Was it you who recovered that stolen Van Eyck? I thought you looked familiar. I saw you on TV in that documentary. It was clever detective work."

"I merely put two and two together, Mrs Diver."

"You must come to Mexico," said Velasquez. "You can put two and two together in my country and still they do not make four."

"Is that bad? Or good?"

"It is exhilarating, Mr Priest."

"Perhaps you'd like to join us?" said Mrs Diver. "We're having a small reception at our house."

"That's very kind of you."

His first impression of a very attractive woman, had now been doubly confirmed by proximity. He also became aware that her composure was being maintained with effort; there was a look in her eyes that suggested anxiety more than grief. He turned to follow her and Velasquez, as the mourners leaving the grave straggled across the grass back towards their cars.

* * *

The narrow street containing the Diver residence was already full of vehicles when Priest got there. He reversed and parked his Porsche some distance away. It began to hail suddenly and he decided to sit where he was till the shower had passed. The hailstones hit the bonnet of the car with such force he expected to see dents appear and yet people were still making their way towards the Diver's mock-Tudor house. He turned on the radio, catching an item of news to which he listened intently. When the weather forecast began, he switched to Radio 3. Mozart came floating out of the speakers with a counterpoint of drumming hail. He leaned back. What was that accent of hers? It wasn't German, that was for sure. Thinking of her slender shapeliness and her late husband's corpulence, he reflected on what an unlikely pairing the Diver marriage had been.

The hailstorm ceased abruptly. He walked through the white gravel on the pavement and entered the open front door of the house. The hallway was crammed with people holding wine glasses in one hand and plates of food in the other. As Priest stood looking round for Mrs Diver, a voice with an Indian intonation asked:

"You're not a publisher, by any chance?"

"No, I'm not."

"What a pity! I'm fed up with my publisher and I'm looking for a new one."

Priest contemplated a small, plump man wearing blue-tinted glasses.

"You must be a writer."

"I'm a poet. Tambi Kumar. Are you also a maker of verses?"

"Let us say I am an admirer of the late Mr Diver."

"Yes. What a global talent!"

Priest raised his eyebrows. "Can poetry be global, Mr Kumar? Poems are bound to the language they're written in, aren't they?"

"Well, English is global, don't you think? I divide my time between London and Bombay. Have done for a number of years."

"I thought it was now called Mumbai?"

"Oh I'm completely traditional. If you ever want to visit I can set up contacts for you. Do you have a card? What is your name?"

"Victor Priest."

"Not *the* Victor Priest?"

"That would be too much to expect," said Priest with a smile.

"What a pity! We need someone to investigate this. The matter of Fergus's death...Very strange. I'm sure you've read the papers." The Indian lowered his voice and was about to add something conspiratorial when a pretty young woman holding a plate of food joined them. Kumar took in her presence, while at the same time ignoring her, and changed the subject. "Have you been to India, Mr Priest? Do you know Indian poetry?"

"I'm afraid I'm not up to date. Rabindranath Tagore?"

"Oh dear, yes, we've moved on since then. I'll have to bring you up to speed!"

"That's very kind." Priest smiled at the young woman. "What's that you're eating?"

"Your national dish!" cried Kumar. "Delivery boys were carrying in boxes of the stuff earlier."

"Pizza?"

Priest gazed at the woman's plate. The woman looked apologetic. Tambi Kumar giggled, spilling a few drops of wine, then looked down, concerned.,

"How clumsy of me. I hope I didn't ruin your shoes. Well, as you see, there is wine. Would you like a glass? It's not as good as the Indian wine I like to drink."

"I do know a little about Indian wine. Do you drink Château Indage from the Ghats Valley, perhaps?"

"Good heavens, you know it? You're the first English person I've met who's heard of it."

"Wine is a passion of mine."

"A passion? I don't really associate the English with passion." This put Kumar into such a fit of giggling that Priest stepped back to avoid the wobbling wineglass.

"Oh Tambi!" said the young woman. A waiter passed carrying a tray and the Indian pounced like a crow on a pizza slice and took a big bite out of it. With his mouth full he asked:

"Are you quite sure you don't want some? You haven't even had a glass of wine yet."

"I'll go in search of one."

Priest went in the direction of the wine table, poured himself a glass and looked around again, still hoping to locate Mrs Diver. A babble of sound in the next room attracted his attention. Taking his glass with him, he investigated and came upon an altercation under a birdcage. Raised voices had excited a green parrot whose squawks were alternating with scraps of vehement conversation:

"Writing poetry for children – for God's sake! – it's such a waste of intellectual space!"

The parrot screeched.

"The trouble with you, Anita, is that you stick philosophy into your poems without even understanding it!" Another screech echoed the rising tone of indignation with which this was said. Then Tambi Kumar appeared carrying a large white towel which he threw over the birdcage. The two women who were talking stared at the towel as if a dog turd had been flung past their ears and moved away to continue their dispute. The parrot went quiet and Priest appraised the Indian, who turned to him beaming with triumph.

"Very niftily done, Mr Kumar."

"We Indians know all about parrots. It's not as easy to silence quarrelling poets, though, is it? I'm afraid there'll never be an end to these poetry wars!"

"Poetry wars?"

"Were you expecting decorum and civility, Mr Priest? A dignified convocation of poets mourning the departure of one of their own?" Tambi Kumar lowered his voice to a whisper. "Eavesdrop, Mr Priest! I command you to eavesdrop! Many in this room are secretly celebrating the departure of Fergus Diver!"

Priest glanced around. There was a skull on the wall, decorated with small turquoise mosaics. Under it another bad-tempered conversation seemed to be in progress.

"Are they verbal wars, Mr Kumar, or do they ever get physical? *The Times* considered Fergus Diver's demise to be a matter of bad restaurant hygiene, nothing more or less, I did hear a report that suggested...well...murder."

Kumar emitted his squeaky laugh.

"That would be a most unfortunate escalation."

"Indeed it would. Good parrot husbandry, Mr Kumar. Well done!" Priest moved away, keeping his eye out for the graceful Mrs Diver. His height was an advantage here, and he manoeuvred through the crowd, eavesdropping.

"Horace Venables doesn't rhyme, Elsbeth, he positively clunks."

"Did you see von Zitzewitz's latest haiku in *The Independent*?"

"Saw it, Laurie. Just didn't have time to read it all."

"I'm afraid Gerard-Wright is ineluctably wedded to his ampersands."

"Oh, Gerard-Wright. Totally dated! He's still living in the sixties!" Over the top of this a woman's voice exclaimed:

"Brown only got the award because Krapp was one of the judges!"

* * *

"Mr Priest? Could I have a word in private?" It was Mrs Diver.

Something in her tone, he was encouraged to notice, suggested she was not going to talk to him about poetry. He smiled at her.

"That accent, Mrs Diver. Where is it from? I've tried but can't place it."

"I've lived in England many years, Mr Priest. Many people don't notice. I was brought up in Belgrade."

"To speak English with a hint of an accent gives our language a gloss. I always notice such things."

She thought for a moment. "Are you married, Mr Priest?"

"No, why do you ask?"

"Fergus spent a long time trying to improve my accent to the point where I could pass for English. He felt it was his husbandly duty, but I'm afraid he didn't quite succeed."

He looked at her and nodded.

"You shouldn't consider that a failure on your part."

"I don't."

He smiled. "Fergus will be much missed." Mrs Diver hesitated, then seemed to make up her mind. "Do you ever investigate crimes other than forgeries and thefts, Mr Priest?"

"What kind of crimes?"

"Murder."

"Murder? I hope you're not talking about your husband?"

"The police performed an autopsy."

"That's usual in an unexpected death of an otherwise healthy person."

"We don't know what went on in that restaurant he ate in. I expect you've heard that the staff were found tied up and gagged in the kitchen."

"It was on the radio just now. What did the autopsy reveal?"

"Glyceryl trinitrate, Mr Priest. Do you know what that is?"

"I do. A very explosive poison."

"They found a massive amount. Please come with me, there's something I want to show you."

She led him into the hall, up the stairs and into what clearly had been Diver's study, went to a desk drawer and took out a photocopy of a letter which she thrust into Priest's hand. It read:

DIVER
IT WOULD BE FUN TO TORCH
THE AUTHOR OF THE ARSONISTS
BUT I'VE SOMETHING FUNNIER IN
MIND!

Jokerman.

W

The words were composed of uppercase letters cut from news-papers, the signature was in lower case.

"Was your husband not disturbed by this, Mrs Diver?"

"Fergus? No, he laughed it off. Anyone in the public eye, Mr Priest, gets used to being a target for weirdos. He was used to it. The original is with the police, of course."

"But if they're involved why are you consulting me?"

"To be honest, Mr Priest, I wasn't at all impressed by the investigating officer. Besides, the police haven't done very well lately in solving murders, have they? I remember how you tracked down that stolen painting. Someone with your specialist knowledge of the arts might have an angle on this that would not occur to the police."

Priest reflected.

"What kind of motive could anyone have for murdering your husband?"

She said nothing. He tapped the letter in his hand.

"I've been hearing about the poetry wars. Is it possible that could be
more than just a metaphor?"

"The poetry world, Mr Priest, is something of a ... of a snake-pit. Jealousy, back-biting. You'd be surprised."

"Jealousy? An aesthetic motive?"

"Someone has to win the prizes, Mr Priest. My husband did, and a lot of people didn't. If you see what I mean?"

"I do see what you mean. Tell me about this investigating officer. Why does he not impress you?"

"Dobson is his name, Chief Inspector Dobson. Horrible lech-erous man."

"Lecherous? Has he made advances to you?"

"It's the way he looks at me. Do you know what I mean, Mr

Priest, when I say that some people are just primitive?"

"Murder is a primitive act, Mrs Diver. Perhaps for the solving of such crimes a little primitivism of character is required in a sleuth."

"It seems to me that you would have more fitting qualities for this case than Inspector Dobson."

He smiled and she blushed.

"No, no, I mean...I just thought that a man like you...You have the kind of artistic background that would enable you to understand the poetry world. How could a policeman understand that? If you feel you could get involved, Mr Priest, I'd be happy to offer you access to my husband's archive by way of recompense. You did say you were a dealer?"

"I am. Yes."

Priest stroked his temple with the palm of his hand.

"Quite frankly," he said, "I think there is very little that I can do. However..."

He frowned.

"I suppose I could pursue a line of enquiry. I'd be more than happy to take on the task of finding a buyer for your husband's archive. Naturally, I would not expect any kind of reimbursement...except..."

He studied her face.

"Perhaps the pleasure of meeting you from time to time."

A flush of colour on high cheekbones accentuated the paleness of her face.

"Thank you," she said.

He followed her down the stairs, and indicated he would prefer not to return to the reception. She opened the front door for him, and he walked briskly away down the path. Reaching his car, he got in but did not drive away. Instead he took a notebook from the glove compartment and began writing, scoring things out, writing more, then putting a line through what he had written and turning to a new page. He looked up as the first guests began to leave. A shaft of sunlight sliced through a cloud and struck the tinted windscreen, illuminating the left half of his face, leaving the right in shadow. After a while no further guests emerged. He sat quite still for a further ten minutes or so, started the engine, and steered the Porsche through the streets of Lewes.

Chapter 3: The Submerged Village

Daniel Crane alighted from the 68 bus on Waterloo Bridge. A few days of icy weather had made the steps down to the river very slippery, so he took it slowly, holding onto the handrail all the way. A freezing wind came off the Thames and his thin jacket was not at all efficient in deflecting it.

He hurried under the bridge. A blind busker was playing 'Summertime' on a mouth organ. Exhaling ghostly breath, Daniel hurried into the warmth of the Festival Hall. He felt in his pocket to see if he had enough money for a coffee. He had – he could even afford a croissant. He took his breakfast to a table by the window.

Croissants always made him think of France. They had to taste even better there. He'd promised himself for a year or more that he'd spend his next birthday in France, picking grapes somewhere south of Avignon. Then, on the proceeds, he'd find a room for a few weeks in Paris. He'd sit in a room overlooking the Seine and write poems. To think that Rimbaud had been only a year younger than Daniel when he'd written *Le Bateáu Ivre*!

He drained the last of his coffee, brushed the crumbs from his jacket, and headed for the lift. He was here for the Poetry Workshop to be given by the Irish poet, Barnaby Brown. That was still an hour away, but he would make good use of the time in the Poetry Library. He loved the rolling bookcases that could be moved apart from one another by turning a wheel. It had often occurred to him that by spinning the wheel hard an opportunistic assassin could easily crush someone between them. What a way to go – crushed by poetry! He had once asked the librarian what chances there were of getting a job in the library, but the young woman had begun to talk about qualifications and certificates, and he had sighed, thanked her, and left.

When he reached the library door, it was locked. A notice said it wouldn't open until eleven, which was when the workshop was scheduled to start. What could he do now? He didn't want another coffee. He prodded at the broken spectacles he had repaired that morning with elastoplast, and stood looking at the notice-board of lost quotations, identifying none as usual. Then he wandered to a chair by the window that looked out onto the river.

How many people had drowned in the Thames, since the

city of London had formed around it? And how many of those were suicides? He thought of the American poet John Berryman – that terrible jump into a different river. And Berryman had missed the water. Daniel shivered. The Thames looked cold and grey. It felt appropriate for Barnaby to be giving a workshop on its south bank, as there was so much water in his poems. So much about drowning too.

He remembered the impact the poems had made on him when he'd first encountered them. It had been here, in this building, an event in *Poetry International* – a joint reading with Fergus Diver. He hadn't known either poet's work but Diver's name was everywhere, and it was this that had drawn him to the reading. Brown had read first. He had walked out onto the platform in a black leather jacket, black cords and a light green shirt. His long black hair tumbled over his collar. He took a sip of water and raised his glance to the back of the hall. Then the audience had become aware of a noise filling the room. It was hard at first to identify what it was. As a muted chorus of seagulls became distinct over the crashing of waves, Brown began, in a powerful Irish voice, to read a poem called 'To Ash Again'.

> *The urn turned upside down,*
> *emptied out the ashes*
> *and rolled away. The wind*
> *grabbed each ash flake,*
> *swooped it into the sky,*
> *swirled it across the sea,*
> *over fish, through gulls,*
> *and on the other side*
> *the ashes came together*
> *to form the reborn man*
> *who stole a bicycle,*
> *pedalled up a mountain*
> *and into a rushy tarn*
> *where he drowned,*
> *while the urn floated*
> *across that same sea,*
> *rolled across sand, fields,*
> *then up that mountain, as trout*

heaved the corpse out,
lightning bolts blasted it
to ash, which the urn ate,
then turned upside down...

Daniel had shivered. He knew those feelings of death and
rebirth. He sat entranced as Brown continued with a poem about attempts to rescue a stranded whale. It was followed by a poem about a
ghost U-boat which led to a priest's love-song for a mermaid. In the
background, the gulls whooped. There were poems about wrecks, a
tsunami that missed the Aran Islands and the reading concluded with a
sequence of haiku about seashells. The seagull cries died down. There
was silence followed by great applause.

It had been a terrific performance, and the poems had brought
back Daniel's childhood on the Cornish coast. He had realised that,
like Rimbaud, the sea should be in his poems too. The French poet had
gone instinctively to the sea for his subject matter, even if – most probably – he hadn't even seen it when he wrote *The Drunken Boat*. Why
was Daniel working so hard to create a long poem about London? He
hated London. He longed to get out.

During the interval, he had admired Barnaby's most recent
collection, and watched a queue form for book-signing. He noticed
that everyone had a little exchange of words with the poet. Daniel was
envious. What did they have to say? He couldn't think of anything
intelligent enough. He would just stammer. He couldn't afford to buy
the book and it wouldn't have looked good if he'd presented his library
copy of a much earlier collection.

In the second half of the reading he had been unable to concentrate. Fergus Diver, an older man than Barnaby, had the look of an
overweight football coach. Before commencing the reading, he had
chuckled patronisingly and apologised to the audience for the lack
of sound effects in the second half. As he read, he sweated under the
lights and had to keep taking his spectacles off to wipe them. Each
poem seemed to require a lengthy introduction, about Italian history,
Scandinavian folklore, and such like. They didn't speak to Daniel
about the world he lived in: "My final poem," Diver announced, "will
adumbrate the political and environmental implications of rainfall in
ways I trust you will find unexpected."

Daniel had been outraged. *Adumbrate!* What did that mean?
He had sat through the rest of the reading in a fever of detestation.

A Welsh-accented voice broke into his thoughts.

"You wouldn't happen to be waiting for the poetry workshop,
would you?"

"I'm sorry? Oh. Yes, I am, actually."

He was looking at a man with red hair and a red beard – a big,
round-shouldered man.

"Me too. Robert Rees is the name. I've come all the way from
Aberystwyth for this. Let's hope it's good."

The man pulled up a chair, sat down and held his hand out
to Daniel. Was this another of those people who bothered him in the
Roundhouse bar? The young man took the proffered hand.

"Daniel Crane."

"I'm a recidivist workshop-attender. Are you?"

"What?"

"Are you a regular at these events?"

"It's my first."

"Oh, you're a workshop virgin?"

Not just a *workshop*-virgin, thought Daniel, but he said nothing. The man continued:

"I expect you know the work of Barnaby Brown?"

"Yes, I think it's brilliant."

"Good. Good. Where do you come from?"

"St Ives."

"Wonderful! I edit a magazine called *Storm*. Coming from
St Ives, you'll know what it's like to be blown away by one. Perhaps
you'd like to send me something?"

Daniel was cautious. People didn't offer you the chance of
publication on a moment's impulse, did they? Especially if they knew
nothing about you. After a moment's thought, he said: "I could send
you a section or two from a long poem."

"What's it called?"

"Buried Rivers'. It's a London poem."

But Rees was looking the other way. A small group of workshop participants had gathered by the front door of the Voice Box,
which was being opened by an attendant.

"I think they're going in. Shall we join them?"

Daniel was glad he had Robert Rees to sit next to, particularly as all the others in the workshop were women, and there was nobody of his age there. Barnaby came in, smiling. After a warm-up exercise – a surrealist game Barnaby called *The Exquisite Corpse*, which got everyone laughing – they were given more complex writing challenges, ending with a final, more time-consuming task. They were instructed to wander away to any part of the South Bank Centre in order to complete it. Daniel discovered an unlocked door into the empty Festival Hall and sat in a seat in the very back row, scribbling hard. When an hour had elapsed he rejoined the workshop.

Although he found that the exercise had given him abundant ideas, he felt too shy to share his efforts. He became irritated by his new friend, Rees, whose questions at the end seemed to have little to do with the workshop, and were – or so Daniel thought – too personal, and not relevant.

"Do you teach workshops often, Mr Brown? You do? How interesting? The Tamlyn Trust, yes I've heard of them. I suppose these workshops remunerate you very well and help you to polish up your craft?"

Daniel had the feeling Rees was having some kind of joke at Barnaby's expense. The poet seemed to reach Daniel's conclusion. He put an end to the proceedings, exhorted them all to carry on writing, and left the room.

Afterwards, the red-haired man accompanied Daniel down the stairs.

"Rather an abrupt departure that. Was I getting on his nerves, d'you think? Perhaps you'll join me in a glass of wine?"

"I'm afraid I'm skint."

"No problem. The University of Aberystwyth pays me very well."

Despite the fact that Rees had revealed himself as an editor who might possibly want to publish something he had written, Daniel was anxious to get away, but the Welshman took his arm and steered him to the bar, where he surveyed the wine list, and looked at Daniel interrogatively.

"They have some quite interesting bottles here. Look. Quite a respectable little Bordeaux. We'll get a bottle, shall we?"

Daniel was embarrassed at being treated in such an extravagant manner. What was the man after? Could he be gay after all? They went to a table and sat down. Rees poured two glasses.

"A *votre santé*."

"Thankyou."

"Not bad vino for a snack bar is it? Time they did something about the décor though. It looks like a venue for a provincial beauty contest."

Daniel hadn't noticed.

"May I ask what you teach at the university?"

"Well, now…My speciality is Jacobean Tragedy. The purest form of poetry is drama, don't you think? The core subject of the Jacobeans was death. In whatever guise it comes. This long poem you say you're working on – how much death is in it?"

Daniel went over in his mind what he had written so far of the poem. There was a scene in which he had described a delivery boy being crushed by a Young's beer lorry.

"Just one."

"One? Well, that's a start," said Rees with a smile, and drank.

Daniel drank too. He'd actually been thinking of taking that scene out. The bloody corpse in Kentish Town Road, even though he'd witnessed it himself, had felt like an exaggeration.

Barnaby Brown, in earnest conversation with a young woman from the workshop, came round the corner and went to the bar. Daniel remembered how the poet had said during the workshop that the purest form of poetry was the love-poem. Whatever he and the young woman were discussing, it was probably not death. Barnaby had declared he wanted to write more love poems; the world didn't have enough of them. And he was focussed on the woman in such a way that Daniel could imagine he was already experiencing the gestation of a new love-poem. How confident he looked!

Rees noticed the direction of Daniel's glance and shook his head.

"A bit of a disappointment, your Barnaby Brown."

"Why? I thought he was great! "

"All that emphasis on clarity? Likening poetry to film! You can't write poetry in the 21st century as if language was transparent. The language we use in our daily discourse is full of clichés, stereotypes and commonplaces. It's up to the poet to transform language."

Daniel wondered why Rees had bothered to come. The poems that the Welshman had written in the workshop had seemed deliberately goofy. Barnaby had been very good natured about them. And surely the editor of a literary magazine didn't need to attend a workshop for tyro poets?

Rees refilled both their glasses and set the bottle down with a thump.

"In a sense, the language the poet uses has to die and come back to life."

"The poet has to die and come back to life?"

Rees nodded.

"Yes, that in a way has to happen too. Look at the way death reinvigorates a poet's work."

"What do you mean?"

"Sales. Reputation. Obituaries are great publicity."

Daniel reflected that in order to have an obituary one had to have a reputation first.

"Doesn't reinvigorate the poet though, does it?"

Rees roared with laughter.

"Excellent! Excellent!"

Did reputation matter? Rimbaud hadn't given a toss for it. Daniel watched Rees, who was rummaging in his briefcase. He handed a brochure to Daniel.

"I picked this up earlier. It's a list of Tamlyn Trust writing courses. Mr Brown will be teaching one quite soon. Did you enjoy today's workshop?"

"Absolutely."

"Why not spend a week in Mr Brown's company doing more writing exercises?"

"A whole week?"

"I fear that is correct."

"I expect it costs money. Anyway I couldn't afford the time."

Rees frowned:

"Why didn't you read your efforts out, Daniel? Could I see what you did?"

Daniel thought for a minute, then fished in the pocket of his jacket for the two handwritten sheets. He unfolded them and started to read out what he had done. Rees plucked them from his hand and perused them, chuckling.

"A monologue by a hedgehog, what a brilliant idea!"

"Well, I only did what he asked us to do. I picked an animal and tried to imagine what it might say."

"Why does your hedgehog speak with a Scottish accent?"

"There was a thing in the paper the other day about the culling of hedgehogs on Uist in the Outer Hebrides. They've been going round giving them lethal injections. My hedgehog has something to say about that."

"Indeed he does! A protest poem! Very good! Let me look at the other one."

Rees studied it. Daniel watched nervously.

"Sex with an alien?"

"I was trying to get that fresh angle he was asking for."

"Sex and death are very closely related, of course."

Rees observed the young man with one eye half-closed.

"Do you have sex often?"

Here it comes, thought Daniel.

"No," he said,

"I'm sure I don't have to remind you that the French expression for orgasm is *petit mort*? A little death. The great French poets, of course, Baudelaire in particular..."

No, he was wrong. Rees was an academic after all. Daniel stopped listening and watched Barnaby leave the bar with the young woman. Despite the wine, which was beginning to make him feel fuzzy, he felt suddenly disenchanted by everything. He would never get a woman. Rees's monologue on French poetry was boring, his praises didn't ring true and if he *was* after something else, Daniel wasn't going to provide it. He wanted to escape back to Kentish Town, to his bedsit. When Rees offered to replenish his glass with the last of the wine Daniel refused politely, made his excuses and left.

He took the bus home, lay down on his bed and slept.

Waking up later that evening, groggy and hungry, he took his emergency ten pound note from under the alabaster duck his grandmother had given him and went to the chippie on Prince of Wales Road. He took back with him rock salmon and a large chips, then ate them out of the paper, which he spread on a chair. He'd slung his binoculars round his neck so he could keep an eye on the girl across the street. It was about her bedtime, and he had been lucky enough once or twice to catch her undressing. She wasn't too bothered about drawing the curtains. Seeing that nothing was happening, he went back to his fish and chips, and looked again at the poems he'd written that morning. Even if Rees hadn't been sincere in his compliments, he would submit the poems to *Storm* anyway.

Having eaten, he took off the binoculars, and went to the nearby internet café. He could find no mention of *Storm* magazine. Then he went on to the Aberystwyth University website but could find no mention of any Robert Rees under the staff listings. That was strange. He pondered this for a bit, then went home and keyed in the two new pieces, making small improvements as he did so, and finding titles for them: 'Bristles' and 'Thwuqq'.

They went well together, he thought. He plugged in his printer to the laptop he had built himself from cheap components and printed the poems out. He put them in an envelope and addressed it to Robert Rees, editor, *Storm* magazine, English Department, University of Aberystwyth, Wales. He would post it the following day.

He aimed his binoculars back at the window. She was undressing. He grabbed his sketch book and began to draw her. Yes! He went to bed happy.

*   *   *

Over the next few weeks his submissions to *Storm* came back, addressee unknown; the girl opposite moved out, and an extremely thin man moved in; he resisted the advances of the Round House manager and was fired at a week's notice; he tried very hard to put more death into his long poem about London – but somehow it didn't seem to work; finally he sent 'Bristles' and 'Thwuqq' to *The Boot* magazine and within a week, received a rejection which read 'These poems are juvenile, whimsical and inconsiderable. I have no time to waste on someone who seems to me to have no poetical talent whatsoever. Yours sincerely, Damian Krapp.' Even the welcome news that he'd got the last place on Barnaby's writing course, and that his mother was willing to finance it, failed to lift his spirits. He felt as if he was being pushed out of the world.

With no job to keep him busy, he decided to hitchhike to Suffolk to check out the Tamlyn Trust a few days before the course was due to begin. He took with him his binoculars and a sleeping bag, also his poems and the invitation letter to the course. He was sure he could find a barn and some hay to sleep in – or at the very least a bus station. It was miserable weather, rainy and windy, but at least it wasn't as cold as it had been. He got a lift with a commercial traveller from Yorkshire who cackled when he found out where Daniel was going.

"You're going to write poems for a whole week? Nobody reads poems any more. What are you writing *them* for?"

Daniel did not reply. There was no point in arguing with these people. He was dropped off past Ipswich and rode the rest of the way in a milk tanker. From the security of nearby woodland and outbuildings, he spent the next day observing what went on at the Trust through his binoculars. It looked very busy – people crossing the courtyard with notebooks and manuscripts, or huddled together, discussing things animatedly, or meeting in a big group, everybody talking and laughing. How would he be able to join in something like that? He slept in a ruined church, looking up at the stars. At least it had stopped raining. The following morning he watched the course-members leave. There was a lot of hugging and kissing. He felt as though he'd become a professional spy, and he wasn't sure he liked what he was looking at. What had he let himself in for?

He gathered his stuff, got on the road again and waited for a lift to Dunwich. He'd heard that a whole village had fallen into the sea when a portion of the cliff had collapsed through erosion. He wanted to go up on the cliff and look down on that village.

He had to wait two hours for a lift, but eventually a vicar took pity on him and brought him all the way to Dunwich.

"Are you hungry, young man?" he asked on the way. "You look as if you could do with a square meal."

"I am actually."

"Then I'll treat you to lunch."

The vicar pulled up his Renault Twingo outside a café attached to a petrol station and they went inside. The clergyman bought two hamburgers and two fizzy drinks.

"Where are you going?"

"Dunwich cliff."

"Be careful up there. It's easy to fall off. Do you know the way? Just turn right, keep straight on and you can't miss it."

Daniel parried the vicar's further questions as to his purposes in coming to Dunwich. He hardly knew himself but that village under the sea was on his mind. He thanked the man, and started on his way up to the cliff. It was late afternoon and the light was beginning to fade. He met a few people who greeted him as they passed. He nodded and said nothing.

When he reached the cliff-top, the wind off the sea was very cold. He looked down, searching for a glimpse of the submerged village, the tip of a spire, anything, but the light was poor and he saw nothing. Maybe in the morning it would be possible. He suddenly had an idea as to how he could write about this village – he could imagine being one of the inhabitants. All kinds of images flashed into his mind. He rummaged in his rucksack and extricated his notebook and pen from underneath his folder of poems and the invitation letter. Sitting down on the edge of the cliff, he willed his thoughts down onto the sunken streets. There was no one about to see him writing. For a long time he sat working by torchlight as darkness fell.

The excitement of the workshop was back, intensified this time. He knew every inch of that village, its cobblestones, its winding streets, the little houses, the inn, the church.

His rucksack was still there on the edge of the cliff the following morning, rocking slightly in the wind. A man exercising his dog saw it ahead, and wondered what it was. A seagull perched on the rucksack flew off with a shriek as the dog ran barking towards it.

Chapter 4: *Zum Wohl*

Van Ackroyd pulled the review section of *The Observer* aside to avoid it being drenched by the spray from Victor Priest's vigorous butterfly stroke in the pool beside him. Of all the strokes Priest did this was the one that irritated him the most. It was hard to concentrate on the notice of the new Schneider production at *The Royal Court* with a noise going on that resembled a school of whales having a panic attack. He was always impressed by Priest's level of proficiency and fitness, but was glad when the amplified splashing ceased and Priest climbed out, dripping, pulled off his goggles and began to towel himself dry.

"Sauna, Van?" asked Priest.

"Natürlich, Victor."

The two men walked to the pine door of the sauna and picked up two neatly folded white towels. Ackroyd hung his bathrobe on a hook whilst Priest divested himself of his bathing trunks and both men stepped naked into the resinous heat. Priest climbed nimbly to the top shelf, spread his towel, and sat in the lotus position. Ackroyd contented himself with a lower bench.

"Are you never going to be tempted by the pool, Van?"

"Never."

They both laughed.

"How's business in *The Odic Force*? Are you still selling any books, or has the Internet completely taken away your custom?"

"Well, *you* still come in and buy the odd book."

"What's the latest limited edition?"

"A translation of a 15th century French manuscript by the Abbé Charles Ladru- Mouffetard. They accused him of demonic possession and burned him at the stake. His diary makes breathtaking reading. He also drew countless pictures of his visions. Needless to say, they're exceedingly dirty pictures."

"Sounds completely fascinating, Van. What's it called?"

"*The Demon Monologues.*"

"Reserve me a copy. Throw a ladleful on the coals, will you, Van? I think we could stand a little more heat in here."

Ackroyd did as he was told. A sizzle of steam arose, which he flapped at with his towel, making it circulate. He went back and this time lay on the boards.

"I have news of my own," said Priest. "I've been asked to investigate a murder."

"A murder?" said Ackroyd.

"I *was* a bit surprised to be asked. Yes. A murder."

"The murder of whom, may I ask?"

"The poet, Fergus Diver."

Ackroyd, now encased in a sheen of sweat, considered this. "How on earth did you get talked into taking that on?"

"I went to the funeral and his widow asked me if I would."

"Diver. Wasn't that one of the archives you were sniffing after?"

"I don't sniff, Van. I make direct, above-board approaches."

"I know you do, Victor, but it doesn't always work, does it?" Ackroyd rolled over onto his ample belly.

"So, who murdered him? Have you found out? Will you ever find out?"

"Give me time. I have a feeling this won't be the last poet to be murdered."

"Oh, come on, Victor. Who'd want to go round murdering poets?"

"The widow Diver showed me a letter her husband received before he was killed. I think the murderer may have had aesthetic motives."

"Was Diver that bad?"

Priest laughed. "You might equally well have asked 'Was he that good?'"

"I can just about see that someone with a bad case of demonic possession might want to murder a poet he'd taken a dislike to, but that's hardly a rational act of criticism."

"How about Salieri? Did he murder Mozart or not? And if he did, was he demonically possessed?"

"Your average citizen is often provoked by the prodigality of genius, and geniuses in turn can sometimes display homicidal contempt for their inferiors. Didn't Caravaggio commit a few murders?"

Priest came down to the cooler level and sat beside Ackroyd. He had put on a sauna glove with small rubber studs in its palm and began to move it in long lateral strokes up and down his legs, arms and torso.

"I'm sweating enough without doing that," said Ackroyd.

"Yes, Van. It's time for the ice bath. Then I can put the finishing touches to our lunch. Hose yourself down first. That water's very cold. You don't want to give yourself a coronary."

The two men walked across the tiled floor to a coiled hosepipe attached to a tap. Ackroyd picked up the end of the hosepipe, turned on the tap, and when the water came gushing out, he hosed himself down. Then it was Priest's turn. They made their way to the ice bath which Ackroyd eyed doubtfully. As usual, he went first down the ladder, into the water, a two second immersion, then up the ladder and out again, as fast as he could. Priest took his turn and leapt about in the water like a porpoise. Ackroyd was always amazed at how long Priest could stand the freezing temperature. He had the blood of a lizard, obviously.

Priest emerged, spluttering and gasping, and led the way to the foot bath. They sat side by side on a bench, plunging their feet first into cold, then into hot water.

"Hungry?" asked Priest.

"Ravenous, Victor. What have you got for me today?"

"Think Normandy."

Ackroyd pondered.

"*Sole Dieppoise*," he suggested.

"Wrong."

They began to put on their clothes. "If I thought you'd serve me tripe I'd say *Tripes á la mode de Caen*."

"I just might serve you tripe, but you're wrong again. It's *Faisan á la Normande*."

"Wonderful, Victor. If I were a pheasant that's just how I'd want to be finished off – with calvados and cream. What's coming with it?"

"Julienne of celeriac and potatoes. For starters, crab-cakes with chilli and lime. Not quite Normandy, obviously, but they do eat crab there. And as I found an excellent Sauternes I didn't know I had in my cellar, and as I was thinking of your sweet tooth, Van..."

"I know, *Tarte Normande aux Pommes*."

"Correct."

They entered Priest's kitchen, where Maddy had laid the table for two. A smell of slow-braising pheasant filled the air. Priest splashed out two glasses of white wine and began to busy himself at the stove.

Ackroyd stooped to read the label on the wine bottle.

"When are you going to let me auction that manuscript you showed me?"

"The Eliot translation, you mean?"

"Yes. That canto of *The Inferno*."

"I'd like to stir up a little controversy first. Is it a forgery, or isn't it?"

"Well, is it?" Priest took a glass of wine and handed Ackroyd the other.

"Zum Wohl."

"Zum Wohl."

The crab-cakes had started to splutter in the hot oil, and as he turned to attend to them, Priest called back over his shoulder: "Is the wine OK?"

"Delectable."

Ackroyd seated himself at the table to await the crab-cakes and took an olive, gazing around the kitchen. Priest's house was built high up on cliffs and the big kitchen windows provided a vista of the sea, and a distant steamer. It had been the Edwardian folly of a successful novelist of the period and had been rebuilt to Priest's own specification by a prizewinning London architect. Ackroyd liked coming here. He took another olive.

Priest slid a fish-slice under the crab-cakes, deftly transferred them to Ackroyd's plate and his own, and carried them to the table.

"No. It isn't a forgery. It's kosher."

He put a plate in front of Ackroyd. "There you are. The limes are in that bowl. What do you think of my theory?"

"Theory?"

"That someone out there might have a hit list of writers and be preparing to bump them off."

"This is twenty first century Britain, Victor, not Cinquecento Italy."

Priest took a magazine from a side table and slid it across to Ackroyd.

"Take a look at that."

Ackroyd peered at it. "Oh God," he said, "*The Boot*."

"They publish a quarterly league table of the top poets in Britain and Ireland. If you were on the bottom rung of the ladder, each time you murdered one of the poets above you, you'd move up one rung."

"Nobody takes poetry that seriously."

Ackroyd found the page, and chewed crab cakes while he studied it.

I've never heard of these people, he said. Alexander Duthie, Barnaby Brown, Horace Venables, Melinda Speling, Anita Bellows, who are they? These are absolutely delicious."

"The chilli is the magic touch, don't you think?"

Ackroyd nodded, squeezed a wedge of lime on the last remaining crab-cake, and forked it into his mouth.

"How can you be sure the Eliot is genuine?"

"It's been authenticated by someone I trust. From a dealer's standpoint, that's the most important bit. But wait until people get wind of what I'm going to acquire next."

"And what might that be?"

"A lost cache of Kafka manuscripts that were left with his last lover, Dora Diamant, in Berlin, and confiscated by the Gestapo in 1933."

"Good God, Victor, how did you come by those?"

"They were in the hands of a senior officer of the Stasi. He claims to have found them in a bomb-proof archive in Potsdam. He foresaw the collapse of the regime and hung onto them as an insurance. After the fall of the Wall, he was arrested and served a term of imprisonment. Now he's decided it's time to sell them, and we've come to a discreet agreement."

Priest had finished his crab cakes, and he got up and returned to the stove, half-filling a small frying pan with groundnut oil and raising the intensity of the gas-flame under it. While the oil was heating, he took the casserole out of the oven and basted the pheasants. The celeriac and potatoes had been neatly cut into matchsticks, and Priest grabbed a handful and dropped the vegetables into the hot oil.

"Tell me more, Victor. What's supposed to be in these manuscripts?"

"There's a Berlin diary, a couple of unknown short stories, the beginnings of an abandoned novel, and a few attempted poems in Hebrew."

"I didn't know Kafka could speak Hebrew."

"He took to learning Hebrew with great passion. He and Dora were planning to emigrate to Palestine and open a little restaurant in Tel Aviv, with Dora in the kitchen and Kafka waiting on tables, if you can imagine that."

"He'd have been a disaster," said Ackroyd, draining his glass. By now the white wine was finished, and Priest brought to the table a bottle of red wine which he'd uncorked and decanted a couple of hours previously. He placed two large claret glasses next to the decanter and motioned Ackroyd to pour while he ferried the food to the table. As he carved the first pheasant he was irritated to see Ackroyd picking at the julienne of celeriac and potatoes. He smacked Ackroyd's pudgy fingers lightly with the knife, then resumed his dissecting.

"You remind me of my Granny."

"Try the wine, Van."

Ackroyd swirled the wine around in its glass and knocked some back.

"Well, well, well. Where did you get this one? What is it?"

"*Château Larrivet Haut-Brion.* That's a 1982 *Pessac-Leognan.* A former client of mine in Bordeaux gave me a case as a thank-you present. It's pretty good, isn't it?"

"It's amazing, Victor. Have you many bottles left?"

Priest smiled and put a leg and sliver of breast onto Ackroyd's plate, then spooned some of the aromatic gravy over it, inviting Ackroyd to help himself to the vegetables. The two men ate in silence for a while.

After the second pheasant had been distributed and devoured, and Priest had laid down his knife and fork, Ackroyd reached into the casserole, removed the carcass of the first pheasant and began picking at it diligently until the bones were clean. Then, with a wary glance across the table, he proceeded to do the same to the second carcass. Priest watched all this with amusement, leaning across to scrutinise the pile of bones on Ackroyd's plate.

"Should I have braised a third pheasant, Van?"

"You could have, Victor. You know me."

Ackroyd laughed.

"What makes you think this Kafka stuff is genuine?"

Priest nodded.

"I was sent an extract from one of the stories. On the basis of textual evidence, I'd say it's Kafka. Or else it's a very clever parody. Obviously, I'm not going to put down any money until I've inspected the originals."

"And how are you going to investigate a murder on top of all the other things you're doing? Won't you have to go to Germany?"

"I'll only be away for a couple of days."

"Yes, but what about that stolen Lucien Freud miniature you were telling me about that's supposed to have turned up in Moscow? That's one of your cases, isn't it? And what about those Conrad letters you were supposed to check for the British Museum? You're going to have to take on an assistant."

Priest snorted.

"An assistant! That would be more of a hindrance than a help. I'd have to train one first."

"It wouldn't take that long. You can't delegate, that's your problem."

Priest got up, looking thoughtful, and removed the debris from the table, returning with a large board on which three cheeses nestled under a glass dome – a Roquefort, a wedge-shaped goats' cheese from the Auvergne, and a ripe-smelling *lait cru* Camembert. Ackroyd immediately removed the dome and took large chunks of all three cheeses, spurning the bread that Priest offered him. Helping himself to smaller cheese portions, and sipping his wine, Priest came back to the subject of the assistant. "I suppose it might be quite entertaining to educate an apprentice, if the right one were to present himself."

"Or herself?"

"Out of the question, Van. Women get in the way."

"Get in the way of what, Victor? I assume the widow Diver is not without her charms? What else would have persuaded you to take on a murder investigation?"

"Mrs Diver is an alluring woman, I grant you. But that wasn't why I took the case on."

"Why did you then?"

"Call it a challenge."

"Oh yeah? Bring on the *Tarte aux Pommes*."

With a smile Priest served the dessert, uncorked the chilled Sauternes and half-filled two small glasses.

"Now that we've reached the dessert," said Ackroyd, "and it's no longer crude – your dictum – to talk about poetry, you can put me out of my misery and read me your latest. You have got one, haven't you?"

"Just about, Van. I thought for a week or two I wouldn't have it ready for today. It's in my study, I'll fetch it."

While Priest was out of the room Ackroyd swigged his glass of Sauternes and poured himself another, then sliced off a second thin portion of *Tarte aux Pommes* which he crammed into his mouth with his fingers. He got up and began to wander round the kitchen, inspecting the contents of some of the wall cupboards. He found herbs, spices, asiatic aromatics, stocks of exotic looking flour and oils. Then he opened a cupboard full of tablets of dark chocolate and ginger biscuits. He stared at them, then returned to his place as he heard Priest returning. His friend came in clutching a file. He sat down, opened the file, took out a single sheet of paper and read:

LUNAR CONSPIRACIES

The throbbing leveret of my hand
tenses toward your glacial hair.
What grudge shall bear my tide onward
to the amphora filled with kisses -
be-silvered oracles of syllables,
the spoors of aristocratic snails?
I am building my church in your shadow.
Crazed mosaic of trouble,
bewildered pledge of the last explorer,
scythed prophecies, lunar conspiracies –
the god is swimming to shore.

There was silence in the kitchen. After a while, Ackroyd said: "Very prismatic, Victor. A portrait of a lady? Who?"

Priest had gone to the window and was standing with his hands in his pockets, looking out at the sea. He turned and went back to his seat, giving Van a rueful smile. "Always these requests for information, Van. Poetry isn't about information."

Ackroyd tapped the single sheet of paper with his finger.

"It's a marvellous poem. Three more like that and we'll have a limited edition. Why can't I persuade you to break your embargo on sending things out to magazines?"

"Where to? *The Boot*?"

"Why not?"

Priest held out his hand across the table for the poem, and replaced it in the file.

"What is the point of submitting my work to judgement when there are no standards left? I'm not saying that everything that appears in *The Boot* is garbage, but enough of it is to taint by association the few decent things that do get through."

"Well, the editor has a magazine to fill every three months. There isn't that much good stuff around."

Priest sighed.

"The fact is, Van, I think I belong to an era that hasn't arrived yet."

Ackroyd said nothing. Then he started to laugh.

"What's so funny?"

I'm sure I don't have to remind you of what you did to the editor of the school magazine who rejected your poems?"

"I added some protein to his lunch."

"I'll say. He puked like a geyser when you told him you'd mashed a wasp into his banana sandwich."

"It was two wasps, actually."

Priest put away the file of poems.

"I see the Sauternes is finished."

He got up and left the kitchen again. Ackroyd sat with a smile on his face, recalling the time they had been pupils together at the International School in Hamburg. Priest had had to start up a broadsheet to get his own poems published, and Ackroyd had been his publicity agent, manager, and typist. It had been difficult work to sell.

Priest returned clutching a bottle by the neck.

"Would you like an Armagnac, Van? This is a 1954 vintage."

"You know me, Victor. Pour away."

Chapter 5: *The Drowned Man*

Barnaby Brown could have flown Ryanair from Cork to Stansted to co-tutor the week-long poetry writing course at the Tamlyn Trust's centre in Suffolk, but he never got on planes. The car ferry from Rosslare to Fishguard had seesawed alarmingly in a force five gale. He had sat in the bar trying to write a poem, drinking whisky, and wondering whether the boat was about to sink. His poem was about a drowning – why was he drawn to these subjects? Then the putrid coffee he had drunk in a service station near Cardiff had given him heartburn that only a bag of marshmallows had alleviated. A serious accident on the M4 had caused a tailback that delayed him for an hour. He sipped at a bottle of *Jameson* as he sat in the queue of cars, averted his eyes from the floodlit wreck firemen were cutting open, and trod hard on the accelerator when the logjam broke.

A reluctance to fly was actually a serious professional hindrance. He'd recently had to pass up an invitation to the Adelaide Writers' Week, and when his friend Bill Gerard-Wright had put him forward for the world famous poetry festival in Medellin, Colombia, he'd had to turn that down, too. When Bill arrived in a couple of days, the subject of Barnaby's not flying would doubtless generate some genial guffaws. How could Melinda be so nonchalant in the matter? She had boarded the flight to Reykjavik at a morning's notice.

He'd accepted the invitation to teach the course because Melinda was to have been his co-tutor, and he'd been looking forward to renewing the dalliance of Sicily. What's more the Tamlyn Trust had upped its fee to fifteen hundred pounds, plus travel, making the prospect of having to teach the writing of poetry to sixteen novice poets almost palatable. Then Melinda had telephoned him last week saying she was very sorry, she had to pull out, she'd been offered Ruari McLeod's slot at the Northern Lights Poetry Festival, and she couldn't pass up an opportunity like that, could she? What had that rumbunctious sex on Sicily all been about then? He'd now have to put up with a co-tutor he'd never met, and whose poetry did nothing for him.

It was dark by the time he piloted the dented Ford Fiesta over the cattle grids on the approach road to the Trust. He steered the car under the lee wall of an imposing brick barn and crunched to a halt. Plucking his bag from the back seat, he crossed the gravel and went into the kitchen, banging his head on a beam. He cursed and rubbed his head. There was a hubbub of conversation and a clinking of cutlery coming from the next room and the kitchen reeked of fried onions. He turned towards the door and dislodged a pagoda of saucepans by the edge of the table, which came crashing down, causing a huge white cat to bolt out and fly, screeching, into the night. Immediately, a man in a red waistcoat and tie, and a younger woman in a yellow dress came into the kitchen. They apologized for the clutter and the man bent down to pick up the saucepans.

"That's Ned. I'm Sandy. We're the new couple running the place. You must be Barnaby Brown."

"That's me."

"I hope you're hungry," said Ned.

"Starving."

A short, close-cropped, bespectacled woman had followed the couple into the kitchen. Barnaby stared at two tiny white jade monkeys hanging from her earlobes.

"We were beginning to think you weren't coming," she said. "I am Anita Bellows, your co-tutor."

He held out his hand but she turned away to rummage in a cupboard, asking with a note of complaint:

"Surely we have some green tea somewhere, Sandy?"

Ned smiled at Barnaby and led him into the dining room, where fifteen or so people were seated around a long table. Barnaby was introduced, and he sat down next to a young man with a tooth-brace, who handed him a plate and pushed over a flat dish containing the dried remnants of a lasagne.

"I'm Phil," he said.

"Barnaby Brown."

"Fraid I haven't read your work."

Barnaby poked at the lasagne with a spatula and scooped some out of the dish. He helped himself to a glass of wine and asked for the salad. As he began to eat, the course participants, who had all finished, made their excuses and disappeared to their rooms, leaving him alone with Anita and the Course Managers. He filled his glass again.

Sandy slid over a piece of paper with a list of names.

"All present and correct except for one – a Daniel Crane. I expect he'll arrive tomorrow."

"Daniel Crane?" said Barnaby.

The name sounded faintly familiar.

"He's a young fan of yours, judging from what he said in his application."

"You'd think he'd be eager to get here," said Anita. "What else do fans have to think about except reducing the distance between themselves and their idol? Do you have many?"

"I can't place this one, I'm afraid," said Barnaby, chewing a very crispy piece of lasagne. He finally pushed the plate away and yawned.

"I'll show you to your room," said Sandy. "You must be tired."

She led him across the courtyard, underneath a full moon, to the converted stable where the tutors' rooms were situated, and wished him goodnight. He opened his bag and rooted in it till he found the three quarters empty bottle of *Jameson*, dislodging a packet of condoms in the process. He stared at this for a moment, brushing back his mane of long black hair, then with a grunt flung it deep into the recesses of a drawer and piled underpants and socks on top. He poured himself a drink. "Here's to you Melinda," he thought. "Have a good fucking time in Reykjavik." A vision of jade monkey earrings came into his mind. He shook his head and flung himself on to the creaky divan.

He slept badly and was extremely irritable when he sat down at the long table in the Oak Room, waiting for the course participants to straggle in. All of them did, except for Daniel Crane who had still not arrived. Anita Bellows sat at the far end of the table, sipping coffee and reading a book.

Barnaby was to run the first part of that morning's workshop. He surveyed the fifteen faces looking in his direction and noted that, as instructed, they had all written their first names on pieces of paper or card and were displaying these in front of them. He dealt out photocopies of a poem called 'Bust' by A.D. Penfold, and then read it aloud.

"Comments?" he invited.

"Something odd about the repetitions," said a rather formally dressed man called Hector. "Ah. Now I get it. The same six words go all down the poem I don't really get the title though."

"It's a sestina," said an intense young man in a beret, whose name was Jason. "Six stanzas of six lines each. Same six words ending all the lines of the poem. Different order of words for each stanza."

"I couldn't have put it better myself," said Barnaby.

"The title," continued Jason, "obviously refers to the economic collapse we owe to the monstrous greed of the bankers."

His eyes swept the faces round the table, defying them to contradict his interpretation.

Barnaby nodded.

"I want you to take this poem as a model and write your own sestina. We'll suggest some words in the group, then we'll take a vote to find the ones we like best and everyone will use the same six words as end words."

Once this procedure had been gone through, the group sat in silence studying the random items of vocabulary they had collected.

"This is impossible," said a woman called Gudrun. "I can't do it."

"It's a straitjacket," said Hector. "Poetry is about freedom and self-discovery, not about old fashioned verse forms."

"What's wrong with verse forms?" asked Barnaby. "Is the sonnet old hat?"

"Who cares if a poem has thirteen lines or fourteen?" asked Hector, fingering his tie.

Barnaby shook his head.

"If you're serious about becoming a poet you'll need to learn technique."

There was a groan from the back of the room that he identified as coming from his co-tutor. He ignored this.

"What about the imagination?" asked Jason.

"I assume you have that already," said Barnaby.

"Tell you what," said Jason. "I'll write a sestina with the same six words *beginning* every line, not ending them."

Barnaby smiled.

"Fine," he said.

"Typical of male poets to emphasise technique," said Anita's clear voice from the end of the table. "I've never felt the urge to write a sestina myself."

"I only write in free verse," said a woman called Patricia.

Barnaby gripped the end of the table with both hands.

"There's no such thing as free verse," he said.

"What I find," said a young woman sitting next to Phil, "is that if I use a rhyme scheme, and so on, I have to think so much about solving the problem of what to rhyme with what that I find out what I wanted to say almost by accident."

She blushed.

"Does that make sense?"

"Very much so," said Barnaby. "When they asked Yeats where he got his ideas, he said 'from the rhymes'. What's your name? You didn't put up a card or anything."

"Alice."

He smiled.

"Those of you who want to do the exercise," he said, "should come back here after lunch. Two o'clock. I will be here."

And with a nod to Anita Bellows he left the room. Striding through the kitchen, he bumped into Ned and Sandy, who looked serious and upset.

"Ah, Barnaby," said Ned. "We need to talk to you and Anita urgently. Can you come to the office?"

"Where's Anita?" asked Sandy.

Barnaby pointed back to the room he had just left.

"We'll have to interrupt the workshop," said Sandy.

Barnaby watched her go. He was curious and a little bit apprehensive as he crossed the courtyard to the Course Managers' office. What now? When Anita and Sandy joined the two men in the somewhat cluttered office, Ned got straight to the point.

Daniel Crane will not be coming. I'm afraid it looks as though he has committed suicide. At least that's what the police are suggesting."

"Suicide?" said Anita.

"When? Where did this happen?" asked Barnaby.

"You know the cliff at Dunwich? It's the local jumping-off spot. They found his rucksack on the top of the cliff. The police found the invitation letter from us telling him how to get here. It was in the rucksack."

After a pause, he added:

"They haven't found a body or anything. They're searching. The vicar of Dunwich has come forward to say he gave a lift to the young man, who seemed disturbed."

"Now what?" asked Anita.

Ned looked at the two tutors.

"Well. Should the course continue?"

"What's the protocol in a situation like this?" asked Barnaby.

"It's never happened before, or at least, not as far as we know."

"If he was your fan, Barnaby, he was obviously coming here for you," said Anita. "Maybe it's up to you to decide."

"I've already told you I have no memory of Daniel Crane."

"What do our Course Managers think?"

"Anita, we'll all take the decision together," said Ned.

Barnaby's immediate thought was to cancel the course, and escape back to Galway, but he was in sore need of the money, and he felt he'd already earned a substantial portion of that by getting here.

"It's a shame that Barnaby can't remember. You should keep in touch with your fans on Facebook, as most of us do."

"I wish you wouldn't use that word. I don't have fans. I have readers."

"Oh? Is that what they are? Good for you. I'll be happy to go with the majority decision."

Barnaby said nothing. Sandy looked at Ned.

"Well, the other course participants have not met Daniel Crane," she said. "And there's no reason why they should need to know about this. Shall we agree not to mention it to any of them? One never knows how people will react. Ned and I feel it's all very sad but we think the course should go on."

"That's settled then," said Anita.

"You'd better get back to your students," said Sandy.

Anita moved briskly towards the door and went out. Barnaby stood looking at Ned and Sandy. Both Course Managers seemed unhappy.

"The show must go on," said Ned

Barnaby trudged across the gravel to his room. A light rain was falling. He poured the last of the *Jameson*, lay down on the bed and tried to imagine what Daniel Crane had looked like. Perhaps, if he really had been an admirer, he'd come to one of Barnaby's readings, possibly even had a book signed. Or maybe he'd been at an earlier workshop. But it was just a name – no face would attach itself.

He looked at his watch. This was about as bad a start to a course as he could remember. Not time to meet the students yet, but he would escape his general feeling of discomfort by going over to the library and glancing through the latest issue of *The Boot*, if it was there. He swigged back the whisky and quit his room.

There was one person in the library. Alice was reading his *Selected Poems*, her chair pulled up to a small green table with a lamp. Flat on the table beside her, there was an A4 sheet bearing the text of a poem in a small neat hand.

"Hello. Did you find it difficult?"

"Yes, but I did it. It was useful to read some of yours in here first."

"My editor hates sestinas. You're lucky to find any."

"Your poems are a bit on the grim side, aren't they? I mean, take this poem about a suicide. Or this one. Or this about a drowned fisherman."

He shrugged. How old was she? Twenty two, twenty three?

"What's *your* sestina about?"

"Love, and other matters."

"Good," he said.

He noticed that she was wearing a grey skirt of some silky material. Above it a light blue sweater was tight over her breasts.

One of the words the group picked was 'ostrich. How did you get an ostrich into a love poem?"

She grinned.

"That was easy."

"Mmm. Has everybody else done theirs? Have you seen what Jason has done?"

"I think one or two people went on strike. Yes. I've seen his backwards sestina. It's very funny. Jason is terribly avant-garde. We're all much too traditional for him."

"Lunchtime," said Barnaby, looking at his watch. "I'm looking forward to hear you read your poem out."

*   *   *

It turned out that seven participants, eight if Jason were included, had managed to come up with a sestina. Only Anita managed to sit through the feedback session without laughing once. The seven became Barnaby's loyal followers, and this set the pattern for the rest of the week. On the Tuesday evening, Barnaby took his group to the pub. He bought a bottle of whisky over the counter and put it in his bag for later, then ferried drinks to his students, and drank beer and wine with the others till closing time. After Alice had drunk three glasses of wine, he suggested that he would be happy to look at any work she might have brought with her. She might come over to his room one evening after supper...?

She looked flattered. Her face was flushed and vivacious. The jokes and anecdotes flew back and forth.

Ned and Sandy commented to him at lunch on Wednesday that they had noticed the course had split itself into two, half preferring to attend only Anita's workshops, the other half attending Barnaby's. He shrugged. People voted with their feet, didn't they? He pointed out that there were a few, like Jason, who continued to attend all the workshops.

The Course Managers nodded.

Late on Wednesday afternoon, Barnaby was delighted to find his old friend, the poet and guest-reader for the course, Bill Gerard-Wright, sitting in the kitchen, drinking tea with Alice. The smell of marijuana hung in the air. Bill got up with a beam and the two men embraced.

"Great to see you, Barnaby. How's the course going?"

"Perhaps you should ask Alice here, not me."

Alice gave an uncertain smile. Gerard-Wright looked at her.

"Well, actually, there seem to be two courses going on," she said. "Barnaby's and Anita Bellows'. They're very different."

"Anita Bellows? I thought you were doing the course with Melinda Speling?"

"So did I till a week ago. Get your bag, I'll bring you to your room. Then we can have a drink."

Gerard-Wright picked up a battered trilby from the kitchen dresser, clapped it on his head, and hoisted the strap of a leather bag over his right shoulder. With his grey Buffalo Bill moustache and his long trenchcoat with a squirrel fur collar, he looked like a hired gun from a Peckinpah Western.

"See you later, Alice," he said, and followed Barnaby out.

Over the whisky, Barnaby explained the situation.

"Doesn't surprise me. I know Anita Bellows. I'd rather teach a course with Lucrezia Borghia."

Barnaby raised his eyebrows.

"Keep an eye on her, Barnaby. She won't come to my reading. Nor will any of her gang. I'll keep the reading short, so we can skedaddle up to the pub. Incidentally, what happened to Melinda? I was expecting to have to prise the two of you out of bed."

"She stood me up for a poetry shindig in Iceland."

"Is that so?"

"Yeah. That is fucking so.You heard about Fergus Diver?"

"I did hear, yes. Who'd want to murder Diver? I take it this was more than just a curry that was a bit off? Wasn't he with you and Melinda on Sicily just recently?"

"He was."

"Perhaps you did it."

"I came pretty close."

Gerard-Wright gave a violent laugh.

"Time I rolled a joint."

His practised fingers began to fashion a spliff and Barnaby told him about the apparent suicide of the student who hadn't turned up. Bill shook his head, lit up and took a deep drag.

"Death and decay everywhere," he said.

He handed the joint to Barnaby.

By the time they went over for the reading both men were tipsy and stoned. Though Bill had predicted that none of Anita's hardcore followers would come, a couple did in fact show up. Jason was there, and the presence of Ned and Sandy swelled the rather meagre audience. Gerard-Wright read with force and conviction and was warmly and vocally appreciated by the listeners. The guest-reader's meandering introductions, however, meant the reading was not over as quickly as he'd promised. By the time they reached *The Dick Turpin,* Anita Bellows, surrounded by her coterie, had occupied the far corner of the lounge bar. The newcomers took seats in the public bar, and the two male poets bought drinks for their group.

Gerard-Wright gestured towards the lounge, then leaned towards Barnaby and murmured:

"Wanna hear about La Signora Bellows?"

"Tell me."

"Ever wondered why I'm not with Dolan & Swainson any more?"

"I don't have anything to do with UK publishers."

"Anita Bellows and Mark Dolan are an item. He's crazy about her, and he does everything she says."

"She got him to drop you?"

She made sure that asshole Von Zitzewitz was given my *Selected Poems* to rubbish in *The Times Literary Supplement*. She used that as ammunition to get Dolan to dump me."

"Why would she do that?"

Gerard-Wright took a long pull on his beer.

"Come on, Bill. No secrets."

"It was a long time ago. I was teaching a course in Spain. The money was crap but I went there to catch some bullfights and drink some *tinto*. And what did I get? Young Miss Anita Bellows sitting in bra and panties in my room."

"What did you do?"

"I threw her out. It was bulls I wanted, not virgin brides."

Gerard-Wright made a face and drained his glass.

"She's made it her life's work to be a power in the world of poetry, so if you're on her A list you're OK. If not, well..."

He stood up, apologised to the other students sitting around the table for having neglected them, and announced his intention of buying another round. One of the students tried to protest, saying it was their turn but Gerard-Wright was having none of it. He took orders from the group, went to the bar, ferried the beers and glasses of wine back to the table, then turned to the students.

"Very rude of Barnaby and me to carry on a private conversation. Now it's your turn. What do you people like most about the course apart from the brilliance of this man's teaching?"

He put his arm around Barnaby's shoulders.

"The discovery of the sestina," said Hector. "My masochism was getting a bit stale."

They all laughed, including Barnaby. Then Alice leaned forward and addressed the guest poet.

"Mr Gerard-Wright..."

"Call me Bill, please."

"Ok, Bill. I want to ask you about where your poetry has taken you. I mean, you've obviously travelled a whole lot. What countries have you visited or lived in?"

"Whauw, that's a question! Where do I start? Well..."

His loud drawling voice had attracted looks from drinkers at the other tables and as he registered the fact of a wider audience, Anita Bellows walked past, returning from the ladies toilet, and stared straight through him. He fell silent, watching her rejoin her little throng of admirers.

"Excuse me one minute," he said. "There's something I have to do."

He got up, walked through to the lounge bar, and dragged an empty chair to Anita's table. She looked at him without expression. He gazed at her intently for a moment, stroking his moustache. The members of her student group glanced at one another. He pulled a creased copy of *Trainsmoke* from the back pocket of his jeans and said:

"I came here to do a reading to the *whole* group, Anita. That's what I'm paid for and that's what I propose to do. Here's my poem:

A SINGLE FEATHER

That Apache headdress suits you.
I like the way the fire haunts your tepee,
I like the yellow glow in your eyes.
Think of me as gone, think of me as gone,
down to the bottom of the canyon.
You'll never hear the wind as close as this.
You'll never taste moonshine mescal.
A single feather, that's all –
the ghost of an eagle in the sky,
and blood on the agave's leaves.

His declamation was powerful enough to quieten the entire pub. Closing the book with a slap, he thrust it back into his pocket, stared at Anita on whose throat a reddish rash had started to spread, and repeated the poem's last line: '*and blood on the agave's leaves*'. He held fierce eye contact with her for a moment, then nodded once and began to walk through the continuing silence back to the public bar. Before he got there unrestrained applause broke out. Most of the drinkers, including the bulk of Anita's students, were clapping, but the loudest clapper of all was Barnaby, standing in the doorway between the public and the lounge bar.

* * *

The next morning, after Gerard-Wright had departed with Sandy in the car for the station, Barnaby headed into the kitchen to make himself some fresh coffee. Anita was standing by the table. Behind her Jason was making a pot of tea.

That was a clever little show we had last night. It was your idea, wasn't it? Your cowboy friend and his country and western shit really wowed them in the stalls."

"It did, didn't it?"

Anita turned away.

"Is that tea ready, Jason?"

Jason grinned at Barnaby and followed her through the door into the workshop room, carrying a tea tray. Barnaby took his coffee out of the kitchen, into the wide yard, and stood looking up at the clouds. More rain on its way. He stood tasting the coffee and heard Sandy calling to him from the Manager's Office.

"Barnaby, there's a phone call for you."

He went over to the office and took the receiver.

"Melinda!"

"Oh Barnaby, how are you? Sandy was saying things aren't all that harmonious in the course."

"You can say that again. Why did you land me with someone like Anita Bellows? Is she a friend of yours?"

"I've never met her actually. She was recommended. Is she that bad?"

"She's difficult. Why did you have to go to Iceland?"

"It was too good an opportunity to pass up. In my place, you'd have gone too."

He said nothing.

"Sandy told me about that poor young man who drowned. How awful."

"Yeah. Did she tell you about Fergus Diver?"

"What about him?"

"He's been murdered."

"Fergus Diver! Murdered? You're joking! How? Where? Why?"

"He dropped dead in *The Rudyard Kipling Hotel*. In Maidstone. Apparently someone poisoned him."

There was a silence.

"Are you making this up?"

"Don't they have newspapers in Iceland?"

Another long silence.

"No time for newspapers, Barnaby. Oh my God, this is awful. Why would anyone...? Barnaby, I know I should be there."

"You certainly bloody should."

She gave a long sigh.

"I'll find a way to make it up to you. I'll invent some story for David and come over to Ireland when you get back."

"Yeah."

"That's just terrible about Fergus. I can't believe it."

"Better start trying."

In a very subdued voice, she said: "Barnaby, there'll be the usual party tomorrow. Ignore Anita Bellows. Enjoy yourself."

"Yeah. Maybe I will. Maybe I will."

He put down the phone.

That afternoon he did his sex and death exercise with the students. He gave them an hour to do the exercise and they acquitted themselves well. After the evening's reading, in which the students read their own choice of favourite poems in the library, he invited Alice to his room to discuss her work. She went to find her scripts and he went to his room, poured himself a hefty whisky and gulped it down. He fished the condoms out of the drawer and laid them, handy but unobtrusive, by the bed. He stood contemplating himself in the bathroom mirror.

There was a discreet tap at the door. When he opened it, he saw that she had put on make up and changed into a red blouse that wasn't buttoned all the way up. She wore a slender chain round her neck with a pendant filigree brooch. She came in, hesitantly, clutching a big file of manuscripts. He smiled at her, took the file and laid it on the table. She had put on perfume as well. Christ, she looked good.

He reached out, took her hand, then pulled her to him and kissed her, thrusting his tongue into her mouth and sliding his hands under the blouse, cupping her breasts.

Her body went stiff and she recoiled from him, trying to escape his embrace. He held her fast, but she had turned her face away from his kiss and was pushing at his chest with her arms.

"You're drunk!" she cried. "You stink of whisky!"

He was so surprised by her resistance that he let go. She grabbed her file from the table and ran out of the door, leaving it open. He sank down on the bed, staring out into the night. It was starting to rain, and he could feel a cold wind blowing in. He stared after her for a long while then got up and slammed the door shut with his foot. Drunk? He was never drunk. Stupid bitch. He could have given her such a good time.

He poured out a glass and lay on the bed. Just one more day of this hell and then he could take his cheque and escape.

* * *

The following morning, Alice did not appear at his final workshop and the other students commented, and offered to go in search of her, but he shook his head and said she had told him she was not feeling well. He had a headache, a general feeling of malaise, and a definite stomach disturbance that liver salts had not alleviated. His presentation of the final writing exercises was without conviction. The students seemed to absorb his mood and their own efforts, when they read them back, were uninspired. He kept his eye on the Oak Room clock as the morning dragged by.

After lunch, despite a very fine drizzle, he went for a solitary walk and crossing the field behind the farmhouse, he plunged a foot into a cowpat, ruining one of his suede shoes. He wiped it on grass as best he could, went back to his room, and did some more wiping with an old newspaper. Was stepping in cow dung going to improve his luck? Or the opposite? He went over to the Course Managers' office towards teatime and collected his envelope from Ned and Sandy. They smiled and were polite, but he knew what they were thinking. How much did they know? He was supposed to have three consultations with students about their work, but wasn't able to find the things to say that should have been said. On his way back to his room afterwards, he heard loud laughter from Anita Bellows' workshop. The afternoon was vacant, endless. He didn't go over for supper but lay on the bed in his room, drinking, and listening to the rain fall heavily.

Had he fallen asleep? He sat up and looked at his watch. He'd have to put in an appearance at the farewell party. They'd all be there. Pulling his jacket over his head, he slouched across the gravel to the illuminated barn. Phil was thumping the out-of-tune piano and Patricia, was singing early Beatles songs, off-key. Barnaby sat down next to Hector and Phil, noticing Alice at a distant table. He had arrived late. As far as he could see the whole course was present. Gudrun brought him a can of beer and he raised it to Anita who was sitting by a window, and she reciprocated with unexpected cordiality. Perhaps she was feeling the warm glow of the cheque Sandy had handed out that afternoon. One student plugged in an electric guitar and started tuning up. Another student improvised a drum kit out of paint cans and wooden spoons. Soon a couple of women were jigging about in the centre of the barn.

"Everyone seems to be having a good time," said Barnaby.

Hector nodded.

"It's been great. Such a nice bunch of people."

Patricia, who had stopped singing, came over, sat down with them, and took a large swig of wine.

"Hello Barnaby. We looked at one of your poems today in Anita's workshop. A free verse poem. I really liked it."

He became aware that Gudrun was signalling something urgent to Patricia.

"One of *my* poems? What poem?"

"'Bone Mockery'. It reminded me of some passage from Shakespeare I did at school."

"'Bone Mockery'! Were you there, Gudrun? Is this true?"

"Yes."

"Did my co-tutor hand it out?"

"Not exactly."

"What does that mean?"

"Jason did."

"Jason? Did he say why he picked it?"

"Because of the student who didn't turn up," said Patricia.

Barnaby stood up. He ran the fingers of his left hand through his hair, and walked directly across the room to where Anita was sitting. Over the noise of paint-cans being bashed and the whine of the electric guitar, the anger in his voice made itself heard.

"Didn't we have an agreement at the beginning of the course that a certain subject wouldn't be raised, Anita? Yet you've clearly told your students. Not only that, you've used a poem of mine about a drowning man, and the students tell me it was discussed in your last session."

"I thought it would be interesting. I wanted to see their reactions. You must have had some dealings with that young man. He was a *fan* of yours. Wasn't he?"

"What's that got to do with it? What connection does my poem have with Daniel Crane? I wrote that poem five years ago. Why are you trying to link me to this young man I know nothing about?"

"Know nothing and care nothing. You showed that when you let this course go ahead, as if you had nothing to do with what happened."

"What the fuck are you talking about? We took a collective decision, and you were party to it. This is betrayal, Anita. I had absolutely nothing to do with what happened. I have no recollection of any dealings with that young man. This is not about poetry, Anita. This has to do with ethics, morality. This has to do with bad faith!"

By now the band had stopped completely, and everyone's attention was focussed on the tutors, but all eyes swivelled to the back as the door crashed open and an obviously drunken Jason staggered in. He was dripping wet, and his head and shoulders were festooned with wet twigs and leaves. Laughing like a maniac, he was chanting '*Make way, make way for the drowned man*' and performing a kind of zombie pirouette as he waltzed through the room. Dilating his eyes in a mad stare, he thrust his face into Barnaby's, then collapsed laughing into a chair. No one else in the room was laughing, not even Anita Bellows. Barnaby gave no reaction at first. Then he walked over to where he had been sitting, collected his jacket, stared briefly at Alice, and walked out into the night. She ran to the door after him, calling:

"Barnaby, Barnaby, come back!"

But he wasn't coming back.

Chapter 6: *White Vinyl*

Joe Biggs piloted his Lambretta one-handed through the Wapping traffic, munching a hamburger at the same time. The mobile phone in his parka pocket began to ring and he lobbed a half-eaten burger at a passing bin, missed it, and grabbed at the phone. It was his mother, asking him if he'd be in for supper that evening, and reminding him her friend Carol would be coming round. He had been planning to be in that evening, but the mention of Carol made him change his mind.

"No, Mum, I'm going round to Frank's, to practise."

He'd better let Frank know this. He wouldn't want to arrive there and find Frank out.

He was on his way to Holborn, to his favourite record shop, *White Vinyl*, which had a wider selection of 60s records than any other store in England. Not that he had much money at the moment, having been unemployed for a month. It had been a good number, working for Thos H. Smerdon & Son. He'd liked the look of himself in the black suit, and over the course of two years he had developed a real talent for dealing with people's distress. He did regret not being there to assist the grieving families as they entered the funeral parlour. Having to display calm and dignity made him feel calm and dignified, and of course there was often the bonus of a tearful young woman to be a comfort to.

There was a sudden screech of brakes, a blowing of horns and a bus driver cursing at him. He gave the driver two royal fingers, and cruised around a corner.

The way he'd lost the job at Smerdon & Son had been unfortunate. Mozart's clarinet quintet had been playing in the Chapel of Rest where a young man who'd died in a motorbike accident had been laid out for viewing by the family. The father had been a wealthy local businessman, and when Biggs had flicked a wrong switch on the control panel of the sound system, sending the Who very loudly into the Chapel of Rest, with Roger Daltrey shrieking 'I hope I die before I get old', the father had been enraged. There had been a pretty curt interview with Thos H. Smerdon Senior himself the following morning, and Biggs was out of work.

He bounded over the speed bumps at the entrance to Lambs Conduit Street and came to a halt outside *White Vinyl*. He padlocked the scooter, wrapped the strap of his helmet round his wrist, and went down to the cavernous basement where boxes of brilliantly illustrated 1960s LP covers were laid out on display.

As he entered, the Rolling Stones' 'Sympathy for the Devil' was playing. He liked the Stones – he'd have loved to hear them in their prime. He browsed for an hour, up and down the aisles, making mental notes of records he'd come back for and acquire when he had money again. Then he began to feel hungry. Half a burger hadn't been enough.

He went upstairs, out onto the street, and headed towards a newsagent's that he knew also sold ham and cheese rolls. At the door he stopped to peruse the advertisements on cards that were sellotaped to the window. One of them read:

Young man wanted for part-time work – chauffeuring, telephone duties, general assistance. Knowledge of the art world useful. Contact Victor Priest, Artcrimes, 47 Lambs Conduit Street. Telephone: 74056622.

The art world – that really interested him. He turned around. Number 47 was almost immediately across the street. It was worth checking out. He bought a ham roll and walked up and down, munching it, considering what kind of approach he'd take to meeting Mr Priest, if indeed the man was there. A few doors away, he noticed a funeral parlour – a venerable establishment by the name of A. France & Sons. He read in the window that they'd buried Nelson. Wow. That made Thos H. Smerdon a Johnny-come-lately. If Mr Priest wasn't interested, perhaps he could get a job with A. France?

Straightening his shirt collar by looking at its reflection in the glass, he wondered if, for the interview, he should adopt his old funeral parlour manner but he decided against this. He rang the bell, a voice in the entry phone said 'yes'? and Biggs stated his name. There was silence and he wondered if he should have said more. After a long time, he heard footsteps coming down stairs, and the door opened to reveal a tall man, about forty perhaps, with close-cropped blonde hair. The man's suit looked more like Saville Row than Cecil's Suits. And his yellow silk tie would have interested a bee.

"Oh. Hello. I've come about your advertisement in the newsagent's window."

"Really? I only put the card in the window this morning. Please come upstairs."

Biggs followed the man up into the brightly lit office of *Artcrimes*. The walls were covered in paintings – originals, from the look of them – by a variety of artists. A full bookshelf lined one wall. In the corner, Biggs saw, was the latest Mac computer with a huge flat screen. If he played his cards right he might get the chance to try it out.

The man sat down at a desk and motioned that Biggs should take the chair opposite. In the feeble winter sunlight which came through the window, the man's face shone. But for the hair, he looked like *The Astronomer* in the Vermeer portrait old Smerdon had had in his office.

"Do you have a name, young man?"

"Yeah. Sure. Joe Biggs."

He half rose from his chair and extended his hand across the desk. With a smile, the man reciprocated.

"I am Victor Priest. You are sitting in the office of *Artcrimes*. Let me tell you something about what goes on here, and what exactly I'm looking for. I'm an investigator in the art world. People employ me to authenticate paintings, check for forgeries, and track down stolen artworks. My business takes me abroad a lot, and I've decided I need a part-time assistant to look after the office when I'm away. Also I will need a chauffeur occasionally."

He looked at Biggs's crash-helmet.

"Do you also drive a car, Mr Biggs?"

"Yes, sir."

"Good. And are you interested in art?"

"I did art at A-level, Mr Priest. I'm sort of an art collector."

"You are?"

"I collect 60s album covers. You know, like the Cream's *Disraeli Gears*, the Beatles' *Sergeant Pepper*, the Stones' *Satanic Majesties*."

"That is indeed an art form. Where do you get these album covers?"

"Well, there's a shop right across the street, Mr Priest. I go round the markets. You gotta keep your eyes open."

"You do indeed. *White Vinyl*. Yes. I can't say I've been in there. And do you paint?"

"I did a bit. I do photography now."

"What do you do with the album covers you've collected?"

"I put them on the walls of my room."

Priest nodded.

"In a sense, everything becomes art if you put it on a wall. If you collect record album covers, you're probably interested in music?"

"Yes sir."

"Do you play an instrument?"

"Electric guitar."

"Tell me, what is your line on poetry? Do you read any?"

Poetry! Biggs hadn't read any poetry since he couldn't remember when. He decided the safest strategy was honesty.

"To be honest, Mr Priest, I don't. Unless you count song lyrics."

Priest smiled.

"I specialise in authenticating manuscripts and documents pertaining to 20th century poetry. Recently, for example, I detected that letters purporting to be from WB Yeats to Rabindranath Tagore were, in fact, forgeries."

Biggs endeavoured to look serious.

"I can see from your expression that these are unfamiliar names. Sometimes my investigations bring me in contact with living poets or their estates. It would be helpful to find someone who is acquainted with the field, but it's not essential. Anyway, to your previous experience, Mr Biggs? I'm agog to hear about it."

"Er. I was working till recently as a funeral parlour assistant in East Ham, Thos H Smerdon & Son. I worked there for two years."

"Did you indeed? Honour the dead, I say, and comfort the bereaved. Perhaps you noticed that a few doors up can be found the august establishment of Mr A. France. Why did you terminate your employment?"

Biggs hesitated. He was in honesty mode and it seemed to be going down well. Should he continue?

"Song lyrics got me the sack."

Biggs told the story, and Priest laughed.

"Do you regret your dismissal?"

"It was a good job for a few years, Mr Priest, but I suppose it was time for a change."

"And you think, perhaps, you'd like livelier work? Well. Can I show you around?"

Biggs followed Priest into a tiny kitchen which was surprisingly well- equipped for the space it occupied.

"Are you domestically trained, Mr Biggs?"

"What?"

"You can't make espresso, can you, by any chance?"

"Sorry, Mr Priest, but I can make tea."

"I'm more an espresso man."

Priest opened the fridge, took out a tightly sealed bag, and emptied a measured quantity of coffee beans into a hand-grinder that was affixed to the wall. He proceeded to turn the handle vigorously.

This grinds the beans properly, Joe. It doesn't pulverise them like those electric things."

Biggs watched. Priest filled the bottom of a small espresso machine with cold water, showing the young man that the water must not go above a little bolt screwed into the side.

"Otherwise, the coffee won't taste right."

"Why's that, Mr Priest."

"Because the grains will be wet before the steam hits them."

Priest tipped in coffee, tamped it down with a spoon and lowered the coffee holder into the base. He screwed on the top, and placed the octagonal percolator on a hotplate

"What else would you like to learn, Mr Biggs?"

"I've been thinking I'd like to learn Russian."

"Why's that?"

"I like the look of that alphabet, Mr Priest. Ours is boring.

"Is it? Yes, I suppose it is."

"I was in a club not long ago, and there was two Russian girls sitting next to me. And one of them was a stunner, Mr Priest – a real stunner – but she couldn't speak English. So that was that."

"That's a good reason for wanting to learn a language."

Biggs was startled by a violent hissing that came from the coffee-pot, and he backed away.

"Don't worry, it won't explode. When the hissing stops we drink."

Priest took two tiny black cups and saucers from a cupboard.

"How are you going to set about learning Russian?"

"Night school, Mr Priest. The City Lit. I've already enrolled."

"I see. I admire your resolve. You were not speaking lightly."

Priest poured coffee into the cups, and handed one to Biggs who accepted it very cautiously. Without adding milk or sugar, Victor Priest began sipping at the froth. Joe Biggs did likewise, finding the taste very bitter.

"This is my mini-dishwasher. Neat, isn't it? And here's the half-sized fridge. And the gas-hob, the eye-level grill. I don't have an oven, I'm afraid. Not enough room."

Biggs watched as Priest opened and closed doors, and demonstrated how everything worked.

"Next door is the bedroom. I'm rather cramped for space but this is a nifty German solution to that problem. I don't, of course, live here but sometimes an overnight stay in London is called for."

Biggs observed a bed elevated to within a few feet of the ceiling, and a wooden ladder to gain access to it. Under the bed was a black leather sofa facing a compact television and hi-fi system. In the corner was a well-stocked wine rack. It was the small canvas of a nude woman walking a tightrope strung across a ravine that most struck him, however.

"By a French artist, Jacques Delport. Ever heard of him?"

"Can't say I have. I like the painting, though."

"Yes, she looks completely at home up there, doesn't she?"

Priest pointed out the shower and the toilet, and they went back to the kitchen, where they deposited their empty cups and saucers in the dishwasher.

"It's good to meet a young person with intellectual interests. Have you ever thought of becoming a detective?"

"Never wanted to be a copper, Mr Priest. Where I live they ain't popular."

"I see. I'm not a copper, though you could call me a sort of detective. Occasionally I need to know facts about people's whereabouts, their movements, that sort of thing. Do you think you'd be good at tracking down such information?"

"Reckon I might be, Mr Priest."

"Mmm. I sense you might have aptitude."

"Oh, thanks very much."

"I can't match what Mr Smerdon must have paid you, but the work will be light. The weekly figure I had in mind was £300, but of course it will depend on the level of, er, activity. The hours will vary. Can you start tomorrow? 10am?"

Joe Biggs hadn't been prepared for this. He stared at Mr Priest for a moment, then collected himself. This was a great result.

"Absolutely. No problem."

"And tomorrow really is convenient?"

"Totally."

"Do you mind if I call you Joe?"

"Sure, Mr Priest."

It was Priest who extended his hand this time.

"Tomorrow it is then."

He shepherded Biggs to the steep flight of stairs, went down and opened the door onto Lambs Conduit Street.

"What kind of bike do you ride, Joe?"

"It's a Lambretta."

"I go for big bikes myself. See you at ten, Joe."

The door closed behind him. Sunlight brightened the façade of the shop over the way.

All he had to do was cross the narrow street.

Chapter 7: *The Cheerful Pirate*

A lone cow outside Barnaby's window greeted the dawn with a moo. At 5.37, he dressed, packed, and went out to his car in the half light. There was a slight drizzle. He turned the key in the ignition, and heard the battery strain to turn the motor over. He realised he had meant to get it charged. As the repeated coughs of the starter reverberated round the courtyard, he imagined faces being drawn to windows to witness his getaway. Then the engine took and he accelerated over the cattle grids, past the stares of munching cattle.

It was a long drive to Fishguard. There was heavy traffic on the M11 towards London, and the M25 orbital was the stretch of motorway that most gave him the feeling that driving was a series of near misses. He was glad to get onto the relative calm of the M4. He realised he was starving and he had a stiff neck from the tension of concentration. He stopped for a fry-up and a coffee.

The headline in a discarded newspaper on his table attracted his attention. *Poisoner Targeted Poet Victim* he read. An Inspector Dobson had described to a press conference how Fergus Diver's murder had been executed. The killer was apparently an Asian man, bearded, and turbanned. He had entered the restaurant through a back window. The cook and the waiter had been assaulted, tied up, blindfolded and gagged. Then it was the manager's turn. Entering the kitchen to discover the source of the commotion, the manager had encountered a man with 'staring eyes' and exceptional physical strength. Inspector Dobson, struggling with the logistics of the murder, had many unanswered questions. How could the killer have known that Diver would be in the restaurant? Why had the killer chosen such a roundabout way to commit murder? And why Diver? Had he made enemies on his last reading tour of India? Dobson assured the press that Scotland Yard was making every effort to elucidate the matter.

Barnaby could imagine that Diver made enemies everywhere he went. Nor did he care much for the man's poetry, but that was all irrelevant now. Diver had joined the select company of poets who'd been murdered. Surely it couldn't have been poetry that had got him killed? It was politics that had got Christopher Marlowe stabbed to death in Deptford, but Diver hadn't been that kind of an intriguer. Or had he? Barnaby slapped the paper down, abandoned his coffee and went out to his car. He opened the whisky bottle that was in the bag on the passenger seat, poured some into a small steel tumbler and drank it down. That was better. If he was lucky with the traffic he would get to Fishguard in good time for the night ferry.

The traffic had thinned out a bit, but it had begun to rain again, and his windscreen wipers were producing the most annoying squeak. Driving over the Severn Bridge he could barely make out the car in front of him. He was glad to reach the end of the bridge, and was happy to reflect, as he crossed the border into Wales, that two thirds of his journey were over. The other drivers were annoying him, hooting and flashing at him. What was the matter with these people? Why was there always some busybody beeping at you and not minding his own fucking business? A huge jeep overtook him with a roar, coming much too close, its horn blaring. His car was drenched in the maniac's spray and he swerved; he was almost blinded. He decided to get off the M4. He had made good time and would be early for the boat. He drove towards the town, planning to buy a present for his god-daughter.

He found a car park, drank another measure of whisky to celebrate his safe arrival, and wandered into what seemed to be the main shopping street. In the distance, above the low houses, he could see the bulk of the moored ferry, with the words STENA LINE in large letters. He stopped at a gift shop and went inside. A wooden puppet of a cheerful pirate hanging from a hook caught his eye, and the Welsh salesgirl made the pirate dance on the counter when Barnaby brought it to her. She was bored he could tell. Not many customers at this time of the year or day. She responded to his flirtatious line of chat and he looked towards the back of the shop and wondered if there was a room there where two people could have some quick, anonymous fun. He laid his hand over hers on the counter, smiling, and she smiled back. Then the shop doorbell clonked and two women came in, talking Welsh, and the salesgirl switched languages. Barnaby paid and walked back towards his car holding the pirate. The rain had turned into a soft, pestiferous drizzle.

His car was one of the first in the queue to board. Once he had locked the vehicle, he went straight to his cabin, which was without portholes, took out the whisky and filled his tumbler. He lay down on the bed, and closed his eyes, trying to summon up an image of Melinda, but Fergus Diver marched unwanted into his thoughts again.

In Milan, Diver and Duthie had begun to argue. The Scotsman talked incessantly of politics, of independence for Scotland, and the need for a new revolutionary movement. Diver was an old-fashioned socialist, an anti-devolution militant, and was having none of it. Scotland belonged to the Union. They sniped at each other in Rome, and continued to snipe on the last leg of the tour in Sicily. Jemima Lee, twitchy throughout the itinerary, had not helped matters by siding now with Duthie, now with Diver. It was Melinda's great sense of humour which prevented the flare up that might have brought the whole trip to a premature end.

He remembered seeing her for the first time, petite, dark-haired, in over-large trousers and a shapeless brown pullover. He remembered the taut feeling of her body beneath the baggy clothes. She hadn't even told him she was married until day three. She told him she had decided not to wear her ring the moment she met him. Her candour startled him. Would a ring, had he noticed it, have made a difference? Christ, he needed a woman.

A loud drumming from the engines told him they had begun to move. He sat up, took his *Selected Poems* from the overnight bag, and flicked through the book until he found the poem that Anita had handed out to her group: 'Bone Mockery'. It was an early poem that he had not included in readings for ages.

The poem described a drowning. Pearls glittered in the eyeholes of skeletons as they watched the man's lungs fill with water. It was a vision of the life of the dead beneath the sea, surrounded by flickering fish, dark, weedy fronds, deeper abysses. The narrator had told the story of his own death, watching his own corpse roll away with the currents along the seabed, where pirate treasure, diamonds and pearls spilled from rusted caskets:

> *Some sat in the eyeholes of skulls,*
> *as if to taunt the eyes that once had been,*
> *and glittered at the slimy sea-bed,*
> *in mockery of the bones scattered there.*

Not bad lines, he thought, but in what possible way could the poem be construed as an inducement to drown oneself? He sat up and downed the whisky. Then, closing the book, he took the pirate out of its plastic bag, and hung it from a hook on the back of the door.

"Maybe I should christen you," he said. "How'd you like to be Christopher Marlowe? Yeah. I'll call you Christopher."

There was a bump and a shudder as the boat hit a large wave, and the pirate performed a brief hornpipe.

"Dance you Welsh bandit!" said Barnaby.

The ship continued to roll, telling him they were on the open sea. He took a paperback from his bag and left the cabin. It was time to get something decent to eat.

The ferry was not full and he sat in the half empty restaurant reading. He'd opted for the steak, onion and horseradish suet pudding, and had ordered a bottle of red wine to go with it. The food, when it came, was good and he began to relax, glad to have put a week's hard tutoring behind him, not to mention the social difficulties that went with it.

As he turned the pages of the book and ate, he became aware of being under surveillance. He looked up, expecting to see the waiter, but there was no one. He read on. Finishing the meal, he sat back and surveyed the room and his gaze was arrested by a blonde woman in the far corner who was looking his way. He ran his fingers through his hair. He thought he'd glimpsed her coming out of a cabin earlier. She was sitting alone at a distant table and he had the distinct impression she was studying him, but he couldn't be sure. Maybe she'd seen someone at the door into the restaurant? He half turned to see if anyone was coming in, but there wasn't. He turned back and gave her a gentle smile. She made no indication that she'd noticed this, and continued to look his way. Was this promising, or wasn't it? He concluded for the moment that she was merely trying to attract the waiter's attention and went back to his book.

When he looked up again she was coming towards him. There was a lustrous amber insect on the left breast of her dark purple dress. A scorpion? Her blonde hair was wound up into a bun. For a moment he thought she was going to come and sit at his table but of course she was merely heading for the exit. She gave him a quick smile as she went by.

The lady certainly knew how to use make-up – the long lashes, the dark lipstick, the highlighted cheekbones. She looked like the tall, aloof star of a Hitchcock movie.

Barnaby finished the wine and ordered a whisky, frowning over the semiotics of the brooch. What did that mean? The hell with blondes, he thought. He was going to give up women. He was going to give up sex. He finished the chapter he was reading, downed the whisky, slid the paperback into his pocket, and settled the bill.

Across the corridor from the restaurant, was a lounge bar with a white grand piano. A dinner jacketed pianist was playing 'Autumn Leaves'. Barnaby hesitated. It was much too early to retire to his cabin. He wondered if the blonde woman had perhaps decided to have an after dinner drink. He went in and saw her sitting on a barstool, turning the pages of a book, an espresso at her right elbow. Standing by the bar, waiting for the barman to finish decanting a large glass of olives into smaller bowls, he tried to see what she was reading. She looked up and raised the book so that he could see the title. It was a copy of his own *Selected Poems*.

"Would you mind signing it for me? I recognised you in the restaurant. Your author photo is an unusually good likeness."

"It'll be a pleasure. What name will I write?"

"Viola."

Barnaby scribbled in the book, and handed it back to her. The last thing he'd expected to find on a ferry across the Irish Sea was someone reading one of his books. Someone very attractive, what's more.

"Not often you find people reading poetry."

"I prefer it. It's more succinct. And this? Would you mind signing this?"

She handed him a folded sheet of pristine A4 paper. He looked at her, puzzled.

"It's for my autograph collection."

Her voice was breathy and rather deep. He scribbled his signature again, gave her the paper and stared at her brooch.

"Is it amber?"

"Yes. Bernstein. From the Baltic. Do you like it? It's a scorpion."

"It's certainly succinct. I had a book published in Latvia once. Plenty of amber to be found there. I believe I bought a necklace."

She laughed.

"I hope the lady liked amber."

"Well, it was a bit of a disaster, actually. I couldn't persuade her it wasn't plastic. Would you like a drink?"

"I'll have a vermouth, thank you."

He ordered a whisky for himself and a vermouth, and they carried their drinks to comfortable armchairs in a corner of the bar.

"How come you're reading my *Selected Poems*? Did someone recommend it?"

"Oh, I've known your work for a long time. I bought *The Absence of Trees* when it came out. I thought it was a wonderful first book."

Was Viola what Anita Bellows would have described as a fan? He gave her what he hoped would be taken for a grateful look. They clinked glasses and drank. She leaned back in her chair, smiling at him. How had she known he would go into the bar? He realised that by ignoring him in the restaurant, she had stirred his curiosity.

"Are you a poet yourself?" he asked.

"I make my living by journalism, but I also write poems, which I don't publish."

"Why not?"

"The world isn't ready for them yet."

They both laughed.

"And what kind of journalism do you write?"

"I'm freelance. I do lots of things. Just lately I seem to have been writing obituaries."

"Obituaries?"

"Someone has to."

"Yes. I suppose they do."

"I cover people in the arts world. I research pretty hard, track down long unspoken names – the public has a way of forgetting, Mr Brown."

"Do call me Barnaby." He thought for a moment. "Did you see that the poet Fergus Diver was murdered the other day? You didn't happen to write *his* obituary, I suppose?"

"I did, as a matter of fact. For *The Times*. Did you not see it?"

"Hah! I've been cloistered away all week on a writing course. Nuclear war could have started. Is it true these obituaries are written in advance?"

She nodded.

"Well you wouldn't have written Diver's in advance. He was comparatively young."

"Someone as much in the public eye as Fergus Diver always has an obit on file. It gets updated from time to time, of course. But newspapers like to have them ready for when they're needed."

"Have you written mine?"

"Guess."

He made a face and drank his whisky. She said: "A bit more will have to be added to *your* obituary before anyone reads it."

"I hope so."

"Now then. Look into my eyes and tell me you know what my favourite Barnaby Brown poem is?"

He laughed.

"I haven't the faintest idea."

"Come on. Try."

He looked into her brown eyes.

"I've no idea. 'Bone Mockery'?"

"No, no. It's 'Full Moon Over the Atlantic'."

He caught the note of suggestion in her voice and wondered what she was leading up to. She drank the last drops of her vermouth, savouring them, watching him over her glass. Contemplating the lean ranginess of her figure, he knew that he was aroused. Then she leaned towards him, placed her long-fingernailed hand on his knee, and applied a slight squeeze.

"I know it's the Irish Sea out there and not the Atlantic, but maybe there is moonlight up there."

Should he remind her it was probably pissing down rain, and even if it wasn't, the sky would be so overcast there would be no moon? She was looking at him with an expression he couldn't define.

"Shall we go on deck and have a look?"

"OK," he said.

Things had gone so badly during the week that he didn't entirely trust his luck, but he took her arm anyway and they went up the wide central staircase of the ship. A gang of boys and girls was rushing up and down, shouting and laughing. One freckle-faced redhead precipitating himself down the stairs lost his balance and came tumbling with a scream towards them but Viola caught him, righted him and wagged a reproving finger. The other teenagers fell silent.

"You should have been a goalkeeper," said Barnaby.

"Squash is more my game."

She's strong, he thought. He liked strong women.

They went through the heavy steel door into the wind. It was dark and there was, indeed, no moonlight, but the rain was holding off. He could smell her perfumed warmth close to him.

"Aren't you cold?" he asked. "Here, take my leather jacket."

He draped it round her shoulders and they moved towards the stern. There was a heavy swell and the ferry was pitching enough to make it difficult to walk. No one else had ventured out into the wind. Reaching the stern rail they looked down at the white wake of the vessel in the water. Barnaby put his arm around Viola's waist and pulled her towards him. As he did so, she took his arm in a powerful grip, twisted it behind his back, and pushed him hard against the rail, winding him. The next thing he knew was that she had grabbed his legs, lifted them high, and he was going over the rail. His cry was heard by no one except the single figure standing in the stern who took the jacket from her shoulders, went through its pockets, then flung it down after him. She watched it float and then sink into the churning water, turned from the rail and walked back into the ship.

Chapter 8: *The Boot*

Damian Krapp sighed as he initialised the thirteenth rejection slip of the morning. Where were the British poets? After licking and shutting the last envelope, he took a bottle of *Grey Goose* out of his bottom drawer, poured himself a couple of inches, took a single typed sheet of A4 from the top of his in-tray and threaded his way through stacks of books to the half-open window. He stood sipping his drink and looking down onto the gardens in Tavistock Square. Three red-suited elves were gambolling about in a flower bed, cart-wheeling and leap-frogging each other, and laughing. Some parents apparently thought it was OK to let their kids trample the daffodils. He looked down at the poem in his hand.

It had arrived two days ago on the very day the newspapers had been full of the news that the Irish poet, Barnaby Brown had boarded a ferry to Ireland and then vanished. Two newspapers had displayed large pictures of Anita Bellows, who had been, so she claimed, the last person who knew him to see him alive. In her opinion, Barnaby Brown was a very disturbed soul. Her new book dealt with inner conflict and sexual distress and she recommended people wishing to understand the dilemmas of a man like Brown to read it. Damian had been incensed at such flagrant publicity seeking.

He had only glanced at Brown's poem before, but now he read it closely. It held all the usual ingredients: waves, clouds, seagulls and a drowning. At the end of the poem Barnaby Brown had signed it in ink, a small, neat hand.

Krapp looked back at the elves, who were now picking the daffodils and hurling them at one another. Carry on destroying the environment, he thought. Did the tiny tot hooligans not have minders? He looked quizzically across the gardens, then his eyes wandered back to the poem. What on earth could have happened to Brown? His car had been the last remaining vehicle in the hold of the ferry boat and when crew members went in search of the missing passenger, they had found his cabin empty, the bunk unused, an overnight bag still opened on the floor. A small puppet of a pirate had been laid out neatly on Brown's pillow, with all its strings severed, its limbs disconnected, and pinned to its chest a note saying: *I made him walk the plank*. It appeared that Brown had had been seen in the company of a blonde woman on the evening of his disappearance and the police were trying to trace her. Scotland Yard, in the persona of a not very photogenic Inspector Dobson, was on the case.

I made him walk the plank. What could that mean? One thing Krapp felt sure of was that Barnaby Brown had not been the suicidal type. He sighed and fingered the bow-tie that Ron had picked out. It was in honour of the board-meeting today but it wasn't making him feel any better about the agenda for the afternoon. He went back to his desk and tossed the poem down. Who was Sydney Ross and what did *he* know about the art of poetry? What, come to that, did the Arts Council know about the art of poetry? What had *they* to say to the board members of *The Boot?* He leaned back in his rickety office chair. The upcoming issue was more or less ready to go to print, but he had been planning to publish a long lead review by Fergus Diver which would never arrive now, and the magazine would be the worse for it. Who on earth would want to murder Fergus Diver? And was this Barnaby Brown business in some way connected? In the circumstances he couldn't publish the new Brown poem either. At least, not without comment. Of course, he could publish the poem with a black border around the edge. His reflection in the blank computer monitor gave him back a sarcastic smile.

What had those boys been up to? He drank some more vodka and put his empty glass down on the desk top with a bang.

Eric Lemmon, the student on work experience, came in from the board room.

"Damian, I have to bring up the subject of the mice again. When I got in at nine this morning there were mice absolutely everywhere. I put the remains of yesterday's lunch into a plastic bag, tied it firmly and put it in the waste basket but they gnawed their way in. There were crumbs and mice droppings all over the place. I'm fed up trying to get the Camden pest control people in, but they keep repeating there's a waiting list. What are we supposed to do – make pets of the creatures? You saw me bring my cat in but it just sat and watched them. I've tried mousetraps and poison, but nothing seems to work. I can't bear it, how can I be expected to work with these filthy squeaking vermin everywhere. We have to do something, Damian!"

Krapp listened to this with irritation. What did the young man expect? This was an old and listed building. How could there not be mice? Krapp was used to them and they'd never bothered him.

He looked at the gold loop on Eric's right lobe, and at the blatant words on his teeshirt: MEMBERS ONLY! Why must young people be so in-your-face about their sexuality? It was surely a private matter. And now this hysteria on top.

"Why don't you get the yellow pages and look up some private pest-control firms. Then ring around and get some quotes."

A heavily mascara'd woman in a bright checked coat and what looked like red ballet slippers came into the room. She wrestled off her coat as if it was a creature trying to strangle her and looked round for a chair to throw it on, but Eric draped it over his arm and left the room.

"Jemima, so good to see you. How was your journey down? Did you have a bad journey? What happened?"

Her highlighted eyes, dilated in her pale face, regarded him. "We were all there together."

"Who was? All where together?"

"In Italy. We were a whole week in Sicily – Barnaby, Fergus, Melinda, Alex, Duthie and me. It was a British Council trip. First Fergus and now Barnaby. Damian, we're all going to die, all five of us. I just know it!"

Her flat-toned north-eastern voice swooped.

"No, no, Jemima. Fergus must have acquired a real enemy. He was always a confrontational character. Too much so. And Barnaby is probably on board a yacht with a blonde."

"He's gone, Damian. The ocean has him."

"Don't be silly. No one could have it in for you, Jemima. You're a national treasure."

He held up the bottle of *Grey Goose*.

"Maybe a drop of this would make you feel better?"

Jemima nodded and took the glass he proffered her, as Eric came back into the room.

"Tambi's arrived. I've laid out the sandwiches and opened the wine. Would you like Tambi to come in here or are you two coming out?"

"Oh, send him in. We're having a drink. I'm sure he'll want to join us."

The Indian poet came bounding into the room.

"Damian, Damian, have you read about the murders? They're

killing us off!"

"Calm down, Tambi. Jemima's had a rough trip getting here."

"Oh hello, Jemima. Isn't this frightful? We'll be next!"

Damian got up, went over to *The Boot*'s adviser on south east Asian poetry, and handed him a vodka.

"Cool it, Tambi," he hissed. Then in a louder voice, he said: "You can always hide out in Bombay."

"I need to be in London, for my sanity. And for my poems. Don't you feel endangered too, Damian?"

"Don't be absurd. Who'd want to murder the editor of a poetry magazine?"

"You'd be surprised," said Jemima.

There was silence.

"Did you get those proofs I sent you? I haven't had your reply."

The Indian slurped some vodka, hiccupped, and said: "Sorry, Damian, there are no mistakes in them. I should have emailed you."

"Indeed you should have."

"What about that second batch of poems I sent? You made no comment on them."

"I liked the one about the Indian names on gravestones in Highgate cemetery."

Tambi giggled, took off what Krapp thought was an extremely pretentious pair of spectacles, and began polishing them vigorously with the end of his tie.

"I always feel most alive in cemeteries."

He adjusted his spectacles, looked around the room as if seeing the world afresh, and saw the poem on the editorial desk. He snatched it up.

"A new Barnaby Brown poem! When did you receive it?"

He scanned it with little gasps of astonishment, then smacked the paper with the fingers of his right hand.

"Totally bonkers! Wonderful! I love poems about rebirth. I must do one soon."

"A new poem from Barnaby?" asked Jemima. "Could I see it?"

Kumar handed it to her.

"Hell is having to repeat yourself without it ever getting better," he said with a titter of delighted *Schadenfreude*. "That's what Barnaby's telling us."

"Is it?" said Krapp.

He picked up a copy of the agenda for the meeting which he handed to Kumar.

"As you see, we have an important visitor coming today, Sydney Ross from the Arts Council."

"Goody! More money!"

Damian was about to start an explanation of how arts funding worked when Eric appeared at the door again.

"Poppy, Manfred and Mark have just arrived."

"Ok, coming."

They all went through into the boardroom and Damian greeted the newcomers:

"Glad you could make it, Manfred. I know you're very busy with your moth book."

"I have become a moth, Damian. I work all through the night."

"I prefer butterflies," said Tambi, joining them. "Why have you chosen to write about moths?"

Von Zitzewitz regarded the Indian with disdain, and took a cucumber sandwich from a plate on the table.

"Very Oscar Wilde, Damian, to have cucumber sandwiches," he said.

Krapp turned to Poppy Irving.

"Hello, Poppy. Is the semester over?"

"I wish. Look at those piles of marking."

She gestured to her bulging briefcase on the floor:

"That's what I've been doing on the train."

"How are you, Mark? What's happening at Dolan & Swainson?"

"We're just doing a big reprint of Fergus Diver's *Selected*. It's amazing how many orders are coming in."

It's amazing, thought Krapp to himself, how few scruples these publishers had about cashing in on death. Poet dead. Reprint! That was the motto. He shooed his visitors towards the wine and food. Tambi Kumar had already piled his plate high, swept up a glass of red wine and was bearing his booty away to a window. Von Zitzewitz, nibbling a salmon sandwich, tapped his publisher's lapel with a finger of the hand that held the sandwich:

"More of your poets should die."

"Oblige us then, Manfred," said Mark Dolan, brushing crumbs off his jacket.

From the window came Tambi's cackling laugh.

Krapp downed the last of the vodka, thinking that this wasn't an auspicious prologue to what was promising to be a difficult meeting.

* * *

"I'd like to introduce you all to Sydney Ross from Arts Council England. He's here to talk about the renewal of our funding."

The board members of *The Boot* all regarded the self-assured young man in a dark suit who was sitting on Damian's left. He could have been an investment banker. He had puffy red cheeks and looked determined.

"Maybe I could present our board to you," continued Krapp. "On my right is Eric Lemmon, our assistant. Next to Eric is Jemima Lee. One of our finest poets. We're very glad she could come down from Newcastle today. Sitting next to Jemima is Poppy Irving, Professor of English Literature at Reading University. She is also a poet in her own right, and author of *Aimed at Nobody*, the celebrated biography of the Manx poet Amelia Quirk."

"Quite simply the best British poet of the second half of the 20th century," said Poppy, with quiet challenge in her voice.

Ross met her gaze without changing his expression. Krapp went on: "Then we come to Mark Dolan of the esteemed publishing house, Dolan & Swainson. Though Mark is on our board, I must add that *The Boot* is not their quarterly organ. We cherish our independence."

"Fiercely," said Mark Dolan.

"And next to Mark is Manfred von Zitzewitz, the well-known haikuist, and *The Boot*'s lead reviewer. Last but not least is the Indian poet and our advisor on south east Asian poetry, Tambi Kumar."

"Happy to be reaping the harvest the Empire has sown," said Tambi, beaming.

Von Zitzewitz groaned and buried his head in his hands.

"I have to apologise for the absence of the distinguished critic,

Stanislaus Green," said Krapp. "He's in Canada, giving a series of lectures."

Damian looked at Sydney Ross to indicate that he'd finished. Ross cleared his throat, and without hesitation began:

"I wasn't expecting to meet so many literary *illuminati* at once. It is indeed a privilege to have this opportunity. We at Arts Council England are only too well aware of the work you do individually, both creatively and in organisational support, through teaching and committee work, for the cause of poetry, no, not just poetry, literature in general, throughout the United Kingdom. Believe you me, we do not underestimate your contribution. And of course your work on *The Boot* magazine has assured its status as one of our most widely respected journals, recognised both here and abroad. On behalf of ACE, may I say thank you now."

Get on with it man, thought Krapp.

"As you all know," continued Ross, "your grant application is up for renewal. I have to remind you that ACE has generously funded this magazine for the last five years. Indeed we increased the grant by twenty five percent in the last round. Unfortunately present economic circumstances have made it necessary to implement considerable reductions in our funding programme. This is news I assume you were all expecting. You are all readers of newspapers as well as poems, no doubt."

Ross scanned the faces that were turned towards him, allowing a measure of time for his joke, if joke it was, to produce assenting smiles from his listeners. It did not.

"Yes. Well. In the present *extremely* difficult economic circumstances, we are not simply discussing the allocation of resources. The critical question we are asking is not just *who* deserves support but in what *way* does the enterprise we support benefit the wider community."

He looked at Krapp.

"A succession of dedicated and talented editors has assured *The Boot* of a very wide circulation among serious lovers of poetry. I would go so far as to say it has played a pivotal role in the promotion of the art..."

Why, thought Krapp, do these people always speak in clichés. 'Played a pivotal role' – Christ!

"At the end of the day, however," said Ross, "a balance has to be struck between traditional traditions and the vigour of young enterprise, keen to establish *new* traditions."

He had raised his head to address the ceiling in the manner of one happy to be announcing a discovery. Damian Krapp scribbled the phrase 'new traditions' on a piece of paper, underlined it twice, drew a circle around it, and looked at it as if it was dog shit.

At a meeting last week here in London – and I have to say it gives me no pleasure to tell you this - it was decided that we could no longer continue to support this magazine. Your grant will therefore cease from next January."

There was silence.

"Other established magazines and publishers will also be affected. *The Boot* is not the only magazine that will be obliged to..."

"You mean the grant is to be cut completely?" asked Krapp.

"I'm afraid so."

"Why?"

Krapp's voice was croaky and the question came out with a slight squawk. He had been expecting a reduction but not this.

"It is the new policy of Arts Council England to ensure that the ventures we fund are beneficial to as wide a section of the community as possible. We are looking to subsidise only those artistic projects that are making use of new media, projects that are proactive and conscious of the vital necessity of outreach."

"What do new media have to do with an old, established print magazine? Are we expected to start a radio station?"

"ACE has had thorough oversight of your entire operation," said Ross. "You have no website. You are taking no steps to extend your readership. You play no educational role – you do not encourage younger writers. You don't even run a poetry competition."

"I take it from the drift of your remarks," said Poppy Irving, "that you think we are elitist. You probably think poetry is elitist."

Sydney Ross shook his head. He began to say something but was interrupted by a vehement Tambi Kumar.

"Is the high hall of poetry to be ransacked by the money men? Vandalism! Vandalism! When I was starting out as a poet in India, *The Boot* was *the* magazine. And despite my long association with it, it still is!"

Kumar gave a high-pitched cackle in illustration of his modesty and the endurance of art, and demanded:

"How can this be allowed to happen?"

The Arts Council representative shrugged:

"You may, of course, appeal against this decision. I am sorry to be the bringer of bad news. I hope *The Boot* can find some other source of funding."

"From where?" asked Mark Dolan. "From a private benefactor? One of those Russian football millionaires? They're always looking to diversify into poetry."

The board members sat in silence, focussed on Sydney Ross at the head of the table. If the power of their collective gaze could have had physical force, the Arts Council representative would have detonated like a bomb. But it was the silence that began to explode in a slow-accumulating eruption:

"What is this talk of *outreach*, Mr Ross? What does it mean? *Proactive*? What is *proactive* and how does it behave? Are these *English* words? You speak of *oversight*. In my book that means a mistake or an omission. The word you need is *overview*. I have to conclude that *you* are a mistake. You are obviously not an omission, unfortunately. Do we speak the same language, Mr Mistake? Does the Arts Council know what language it speaks? Is this English – the language I learned to love? I think not."

Von Zitzewitz raised his voice even louder:

"We need a land of poets and thinkers! What we don't need is a land of celebrity poetasters, and poetry sweepstake punters! Why, Mr Ross, does the Arts Council fund nonentity antheaps? Is art now to become a branch of the self-development industry?"

He thumped the table hard. A wine glass jumped, skittered to the table edge, fell on the wooden floor and smashed.

An even longer silence followed this outburst. The board members continued to fix Sydney Ross with a collective evil eye and he was clearly at a loss to know how to respond. He pushed back his chair, muttering something that no one could hear. Eventually, with a nod to Damian Krapp, he gathered his papers, made his excuses, and hurried towards the exit.

The editor escorted him out and returned, looking agitated.

"I need another vodka. Anyone else?"

The board members milled round von Zitzewitz, patting him on the back.

Krapp joined the group:

"Well said, Manfred. 'Nonentity antheaps'. I liked that. Did you think of it on the spur of the moment, or had you been saving it up?"

"Anger makes you free, Damian. I will write about this stupidity in *The Times*."

Krapp nodded. Noticing Jemima Lee standing at the window, he realised she had said nothing during the meeting. He went over.

"It's bitter news, isn't it, Jemima? I've been editing this magazine for fifteen years. How can they say I haven't tried to find new readers? I have actually built up our subscription list. Is all this work going to go down the plughole? I'm not going to start running poetry competitions."

He gulped his drink.

"Yes, Damian, but fuck it there's worse stuff happening."

She waved Barnaby's poem, which she'd kept with her all through the meeting.

"Don't you see? He knew he was going to die."

He put his arm around her.

"That poem's just one of Barnaby's seascapes. Let me have it now."

Taking the poem gently from her hand, he turned to face his board members:

"I'm so sorry you came all this way to hear what you've just heard. There are other things I'd hoped to discuss today, but under the circumstances I think I'd like to declare this meeting over."

There was a murmur of assent and fellow feeling, followed by the sound of glasses being put down on the table.

You will get a petition out for people to sign, won't you? We need to campaign vigorously against this," said Poppy.

"Yes I will."

As Damian saw them out, Eric collected the plates and glasses and stacked them into the dish-washer. He put on his Lacoste jacket and called back from the stairs, on his way out:.

"Just saw another mouse in the kitchen!"

Von Zitzewitz, who had lingered in the doorway, said: "I

think, perhaps, a mice issue is called for, Damian."

Then they were all gone, and Krapp was alone in the darkening office. He wondered whether he should have another vodka. He decided against it, took a couple of back issues of *The Boot* from the shelf and sat down in the scruffy armchair, leafing through them and recalling the excitement he'd felt as he'd put the issues together. Surely his own contribution to British literary culture was not to be snuffed out on the whim of some doltish bureaucrat?

The ringing of the telephone interrupted his thoughts. Ron, he thought! He'd be wondering what had happened at the meeting.

"That you, Ron?"

There was silence for a moment, followed by a chuckle, and a distinctly Welsh voice said:

"What do you think of the Olympic Games?"

"I do not wish to participate in a survey, thank you," said Krapp and was about to put down the receiver when the voice continued: "No, no, not a survey. I'm aware that *The Boot* is a poetry magazine, and I'm aware you have received some very bad news today. Government money is being channelled into funding the Olympic Games. The arts are suffering."

"Who are you? What's all this about?"

Robert Rees is the name. I think I have the remedy for your problems."

Then the phone went dead, leaving Damian Krapp staring at the uncurtained windows, listening to the traffic noises cut through by police sirens outside. Behind it all he thought he heard an owl hooting in one of the trees of Tavistock Square.

Chapter 9: *A Special Hat*

Victor Priest stood reading a letter in his office above Lamb's Conduit Street. Occasionally he glanced down at the passers-by, then returned to the letter. It was a letter from an American publisher, rejecting a collection of his poems. There were two pages to the letter, seven paragraphs in all, and the editor, with whom Priest was acquainted, had taken great pains to explain why he felt he had to refuse an offer of publication.

He read the letter twice and then laid it down. Raising his eyes, he observed Joe Biggs parking his motor scooter on the far side of the road. The young man locked the bike and removed his crash helmet. Beneath a raincoat, he was wearing a mustard suit and a green tie. He started across the street towards number 47, a stockily-built young man, with short dark hair, almost militarily short.

Biggs stopped to watch a traffic warden stalk towards a red Porsche that was parked on a double yellow line in front of the building. Priest smiled, watching him. Biggs hesitated, then continued and rang the doorbell.

"Yes?

"Joe Biggs reporting for duty, sir."

Priest pressed the buzzer on the wall, the door below clicked open, and Biggs went up the narrow flight of stairs. He found his new employer standing before the computer, which was shutting down.

"Morning, Joe. You're looking very smart."

"That's not your car is it, Mr Priest? The Porsche in front of the door?"

"It is."

"Well, you're about to get a parking ticket."

"I don't think so, Joe. Did you not notice the disabled badge on the window?"

"You got a disabled badge, Mr Priest?"

"It's my mother's. I'm afraid she's now in a home and can't drive anymore. But I still renew her badge every year. After all, I might have to drive her somewhere."

"Oh. Yeah. I see."

"Put your helmet in the corner, by the squash racket."

Priest led the way into the office, picked up a newspaper that was lying on the desk, and held up a large photograph of a fat man with a beard.

"Do you know who this is, Joe?"

Biggs shook his head.

"It's Fergus Diver, the eminent English poet. Did you, perhaps, read about his demise in the press?"

"No."

"Do take a seat? Coffee?"

"No thanks, Mr Priest."

"Here. You can read the report. The kinds of crimes I investigate don't normally have anything to do with murder. However, since Fergus Diver died an unnatural death two weeks ago, his wife has asked me to take the case on, and to my own surprise, I have agreed."

"Murder, Mr Priest? Blimey!"

"Mmm. It's not my usual line at all. I have to go down to Maidstone to interview people. If you'd like to come with me, you might learn something about my methods that could be useful later on."

"I'm up for it, Mr Priest."

"Good. And while I'm at it I'd better tell you there seems to have been a further tragedy in the poetry world. I don't suppose you will have heard of the Irish poet Barnaby Brown...?"

"Can't say I have."

"He was on a ferry crossing the Irish Sea but when the ferry reached port he was no longer on it. How would you explain that, Joe?"

"He might have fallen off? Somebody might have pushed him? He might have jumped? Perhaps a helicopter lifted him off?"

"Scotland Yard is of the opinion he was the victim of a homicide."

"Somebody out there bumping off poets? That'd be a funny thing to do. I mean poets are harmless, ain't they? If it was politicians you could see the point."

"Quite. Apparently a puppet was found in Mr Brown's cabin, with all its strings cut."

"One of them psychopaths, I bet."

Priest indicated that his new employee should take a seat and walked over to the crammed book shelf, running an index finger along the spines of the books. Joe Biggs sat down. There was a scent of coffee in the air. Priest's tiny black coffee cup was perched on the arm of the settee.

"What happened to this Diver guy?"

"He was poisoned."

Priest drew two volumes from the book shelf and handed them to Biggs.

"The curious thing is that Fergus Diver's most famous poem is an epic about renaissance Italian poisoners and their ilk, and Barnaby Brown's poems dwell on drownings. There you are. Read for yourself."

Biggs leafed through a couple of poems from each book. Priest watched him encounter Diver's poems, full of cultural bric à brac, foreign words in italics, and reader-unfriendly titles. He observed the frown on the young man's face, and murmured:

"He doesn't go in much for rhymes."

"No, Mr Priest."

Biggs looked up, laid Diver's book down and took up Barnaby Brown,

pausing over one poem in particular. He was nodding his head and Priest leaned over to see which poem had captured his attention.

"Ah yes. The love-song of a priest for a mermaid."

"Makes you wonder what the priest could have been hoping for, Mr Priest. Needs music to go with it. Maybe me and my mate Frank could have a go."

Priest held out his hand for the book, closed it and put both volumes back in their place.

"Have you ever been to Maidstone?"

"Can't say I have. Are we going in your Porsche?"

"Indeed we are. You can leave your crash helmet where it is. You won't be needing it."

*   *   *

As Priest made his way out of London, Joe Biggs reminded his employer of the speed cameras but Priest took no notice.

"Do you know what kind of car this is?"

"Yeah. It's a Porsche."

"To be exact, it's a Porsche 911 Carrera GTS. It really doesn't like speed cameras."

Biggs closed his eyes as they overtook a long line of cars just before a bend.

"Diver's last hours on earth," continued Priest, "consisted of a reading at the Kent Marshes Poetry Society and a meal in an Indian restaurant. He was found dead on the toilet of his hotel room, apparently having suffered a seizure during the course of an unusually violent bowel movement that caused his rectum to explode."

"Explode!"

"Yes. The poison was related to nitroglycerine, and you know what that is."

"Couldn't have been plain old food poisoning, could it? My mum had a meal in *The Bombay Duck* in Wapping the other night and..."

"I think not, Joe. Anyway, I've been in touch with the chairman of this poetry organisation, a man called Herbert Ludlow, and arranged for us to meet him. We need to establish who was present at the reading."

On a two-lane stretch, Priest pulled out to overtake a tour bus and performed a swift S movement to avoid an articulated truck that had been concealed in a dip in the road. Biggs gave a low whistle and Priest laughed.

"Don't you like driving fast, Joe?"

"You're good, Mr Priest. You know how to drive, I'll say that."

Ludlow did not live in Maidstone itself but in a converted oast house in the countryside. Priest parked on a grass verge and Biggs stood staring at the roof of the house, which resembled a lopsided funnel. The old man came out to greet them and noticed that Biggs was staring.

"It was used for drying the hops," said Ludlow. "Not any more. Another country craft disappeared."

Priest extended his hand.

"Victor Priest is the name. We spoke on the phone. And this is my assistant, Joe Biggs."

"You're very welcome."

The old man beckoned them to follow him into the house and they walked up a gravel drive into Ludlow's house and entered a book-lined room.

"Terrible thing about Mr Diver. It was a wonderful reading, too! Imagine! No audience will ever be privileged to hear him read again."

"Indeed," said Priest, peering at a photograph. "Is that you and W H Auden on the wall?"

"It is, Mr Priest. I've been very active in the poetry world. It all started when Rabindranath Tagore came to speak to the 6th form. He was very interested later on when my wife and I started the Fresh Air Movement, and he even came out to visit one of our camps."

He pointed to another photo showing Ludlow beside a white-bearded, longhaired, eastern gentleman. Adjacent to this picture was one of a young and completely naked Ludlow standing next to a naked woman.

"My late wife," Ludlow said, noticing the focus of Biggs' attention. "We were very free in those days. She herself was not interested in poetry. It was the only thing we ever disagreed about."
He hobbled rapidly to a bookshelf and took down a copy of *The Arsonists*.

"It's the last copy of this book Diver ever signed."

Priest studied the looping scrawl with interest.

"I suppose you don't have a record of who was at the reading, do you, Mr Ludlow?" he asked.

"Not really. We do have a signing in book, though not everyone signs in. Shall I get it?"

"That would be useful."

"The Kent Marshes Poetry Society is a small group of about fifty poetry lovers. People don't come to all the meetings. Of course we are open to the wider public. I suppose our membership is rather elderly. I am eighty five, Mr Priest."

Priest nodded and waited. The old man remembered the task he had set himself and left the room. The detective watched as Biggs roved along the library shelves, taking down an old book of photographs that had the word LOVE on the spine. Each page held a black and white print of a male and female nude. Under the tissue paper covers, each print had captured imaginative variations on the act of love.

"That was how it was in the nineteen twenties," said Priest.

Biggs looked at the octogenarian with renewed interest as Ludlow came back into the room holding a leather-bound exercise book and a membership file.

"Here you are, Mr Priest."

"Did everyone who attended the reading sign here?"

Ludlow thought for a moment.

"Pretty much. We don't get many strangers attending our events. There were a couple of latecomers that evening. One of them was no stranger to us, though he's not a member. In fact, he's read here on two occasions. The poet Manfred von Zitzewitz."

"Really?"

"I remember being pleasantly surprised to see him slip in. Von Zitzewitz lives in London. I don't know what he was doing in Maidstone that evening."

"Were they friends, von Zitzewitz and Diver?"

"I don't know. I did notice, however, that they didn't speak in the bar afterwards."

"You said there were two latecomers? What about the other one?"

"I remember a tall man, with a deerstalker and a full red beard."

"Did he say anything?"

"Yes, I believe he spoke to Fergus Diver in the bar. He was Welsh."

"Did this man accompany Diver to the restaurant?"

"No, he left earlier. Diver went alone."

"Did you get the man's name?"

"I'm afraid not."

Priest handed the signing in book to his assistant and asked Biggs to copy down the names from the book and the addresses from the membership file.

Herbert Ludlow asked with a note of anxiety in his voice:

"Are you going to talk to all of these people?"

"That's the idea," said Priest.

"Ailsa and Loretta might get into trouble."

"Oh?"

"They're at the Sacred Heart Convent in Maidstone. The Mother Superior is not very understanding. She disapproves of poetry. She thinks it's an irregularity."

Priest laughed.

"She's probably right. I'll see what I can do. Maybe we don't have to bother them. Hurry up with that, Joe. It's lunchtime."

*   *   *

Maidstone was a busy place, and crowded, but Priest found a sidestreet near his destination and parked on the pavement.

"Cross the street here."

They traversed the street to stand outside a restaurant called *The Siege of Lucknow.*

"Indian?"

"Yes. This is where Mr Diver met his sticky end."

Biggs pulled a face.

"Must we?"

"We don't have to, but by doing so we can eat *and* continue our investigation."

They went in. The only other customers were two young women who were arguing loudly. Priest led Biggs to a quiet table, as far away as possible from the babble, and they sat down. Two menus were laid on the table and while Priest studied one of them, his assistant took in the layout of the restaurant. There was a fountain at the far end of the room. The jet soared up from a basin into the mouth of a fish suspended in the ceiling and then poured back down into the basin again out of the fish's tail. It looked as though anyone sitting close to it might run the risk of a soaking.

"Getting the lie of the land, I see," said Priest with approval. "That's the right approach."

"Quite a fish," said Biggs, pointing.

"Hindu baroque," said Priest. "I suggest you have the tandoori chicken. The curry might be too much of a good thing in view of the ground we have to cover this afternoon."

As they ate, Priest expanded on the idea that the scene of a crime always held some trace of what happened there, and that a good detective had to be alert to this. Biggs listened, and Priest watched him take in the accoutrements of the table, then the representations of Shiva on the wallpaper, then the light fittings and the over elaborate décor, and the counter and cash register behind which the manager stood.

"Eat up, Joe. When you've finished, we will question the manager. That's to say you will."

"Me?"

"Never too early to start practising the trade."

As he was paying the bill, Priest added an extra twenty pound note to the tip, held it down on the silver plate with his forefinger, and looked at the waiter.

"We would like to ask your manager some questions."

"Certainly sir. Thank you sir."

"The twenty pound note worked wonders. Instead of creeping about like undertakers at a funeral, the staff seemed electrocuted. In no time at all, a bespectacled man in a dark suit was standing by the table and bowing. Priest nudged his assistant.

"We would like to ask some questions," said Biggs, "about this murder two weeks ago."

"You police?"

"Yeah. Sort of," said Biggs. "When Mr Diver was poisoned was you on shift? I mean, was you working that evening?"

"Yes, sir. Rajiv, that is the cook, sir, the waiter, Aziz, and I. What kind of police are you?"

"We're like plain clothes police."

"Plain clothes is it?"

"Yeah. So tell us what happened."

"We were assaulted in the kitchen. We were beaten up, sir."

"Did you get a look at him? What was he like?"

"You official plain clothes, yes? Detectives?"

"Scotland Yard."

"Scotland? OK. Very good."

"So what did this guy look like?"

"Sikh. He was a Sikh. I think he was a wrestler."

"A Sikh wrestler?"

"We get tied up, sir. Real professional."

The manager circled his head with his arm.

"He got scarf round mouth, like that, sir, so you can't see his face."

"If he was a Sikh he'd have one round his head too?"

"Yes sir."

"Pretty scarfed up then? And you was in the kitchen when this happened?"

"Yes sir. We see him cooking mushrooms."

"Do what? He cooked mushrooms? Musta been hungry."

"I think he was preparing Mr Diver's poison," interjected Priest.

"Yes, yes! Poisoned in this restaurant. With our mushrooms!"

"Right," said Biggs. "Remind me not to order any."

The manager made a self-exculpating gesture, shrugging his shoulders and spreading the palms of his hands.

"So what about the other customers? What was they doing?"

"No customers, sir. Just your friend, sir."

Biggs looked at his employer who was watching him with an encouraging smile.

"My friend? Right. My friend was alone, then? What time was this?"

"Quarter to ten, sir. Sunday evening."

"Not a busy time, then?"

"Very busy time, sir. Normally we are full on a Sunday evening!"

The manager clapped his brow and looked distressed:

"A gentleman come in about nine fifteen and ask if we got table for eight people, then he go out and never come back. Never come back! Table for eight, you see? Reserved!"

Both men looked to where the manager was pointing and saw a big round table designed for a large party of diners.

"Does that happen often? I mean do people come in and book a table and then never come back?"

"It happens, sir. Quite possible eight people come back and not get in. Who knows?"

"Not get in? Why not?"

"Rajiv help me free, sir, and we calling police. We see someone turn sign round in the door. 'Closed' sign, not 'Open' sign. Maybe this Sikh man do that."

"What did this bloke who reserved a table look like?"

"Distinguish man, sir. Red-haired man. Full beard. Special hat."

"Special hat?"

"Yes sir. Special hat."

Biggs looked at Priest and then back at the manager.

"OK. Special hat. What did it look like? Did it have a feather in it?"

"No sir. Like a cap, sir. Cover your ears. Good for cold weather hat."

"Anything else special about this guy?"

"He was Welshman, sir."

"You'd know a Welshman if you saw one?"

"I live one time in Cardiff, sir."

Biggs looked at his employer, who nodded and pushed another twenty pound note across the table.

"Thank you Mr Bhagat," said Priest, reading the man's name off the name tag. "You've been very helpful."

* * *

Back at the car, they found a parking ticket fluttering under the windscreen wiper. Priest tore it up and stuffed it into a waste bin attached to a lamp post. They climbed into the Porsche.

"Well done, Joe. Good questions."

"Special hat must be that deerstalker Mr Ludlow was going on about."

"Do we have a suspect?"

"Well, Sikhs wear turbans, not deerstalkers."

"Two suspects, then?"

"Maybe. You could put a deerstalker over a turban, couldn't you? Bet you the murderer turned the sign round in the door to keep people out."

"Why would that not have kept Fergus Diver out?"

"Musta turned it round after Diver went in to the restaurant."

"Very plausible, Joe. Now then. Let us talk to some nuns."

Priest typed a destination into the satnav, started the motor, revved it, and the Porsche swept into Maidstone High Street with a squeal of tyres.

"Didn't Herbert Ludlow ask you...?"

"He did, but I've never been in a convent, Joe. Always assuming they will let us in, we have a new experience to look forward to. Or are you familiar with convents?"

"No, Mr Priest."

At the imposing front door of the Convent of the Sacred Heart, Priest yanked a bell rope and bowed to the elderly nun who opened the door, introducing himself and Biggs, and explaining their wish to talk to Ailsa and Loretta on 'police business'. They were shown into a small room and after a lengthy wait, the two nuns appeared.

They had not enjoyed Fergus Diver's last reading one bit. 'A nasty, sneering man,' was their verdict. They could remember nothing significant happening before or after the reading, and had not noticed a man in a deerstalker. Afterwards, Priest paid his respects to the Mother Superior. They stood in the open cloisters of the convent and Priest questioned her on why she viewed poetry as 'an irregularity'. The Mother Superior was at first surprised, perhaps, to be interrogated on such matters by a policeman, but then she became voluble. Priest and Biggs stood listening to her views on the modern world, what had gone wrong, and her opinion that the writing of secular poetry was an attempt to enter into the spiritual life without God, and was therefore a sin.

"I do like people with clear opinions," said Priest as they drove away.

"Bit of a sermon, though."

"Sermons are good for people, Joe. Keeps them in line. Now then. We can't interview all the names on that list, but we should talk to a wide cross section."

The poetry society membership was widely scattered. In a few hours, they covered most of the geography of Kent, passing through Sittingbourne, Faversham, Canterbury, Ashford and Dover. Those members of the Kent Marshes Poetry Society who had been at the poetry reading all had the same story to tell, and nobody could remember any interesting detail that was different.

After they had listened to yet another similar tale, Biggs thought to ask who'd bought Diver all the drinks. The old woman they were talking to didn't know, but didn't remember anyone leaving the table to go to the bar. The barman had brought the drinks. Apart from the poet, none of them had drunk more than a pint.

Afterwards, Priest was complimentary.

"A telling question, Joe. You're getting the hang of this."

"I'm thinking, guv, that someone who wasn't at the table was buying him drinks."

"And I'm thinking we have omitted to talk to the barman at *The Spotted Dog*. On the way back, we'll call in at Maidstone again."

The barman in Maidstone who had been serving on the evening in question confirmed that a customer had left a fifty pound note and the instruction that Fergus Diver was to be supplied with Guinness until he left the pub. The barman had been only too happy to oblige. The generous admirer had a Welsh accent and wore a deerstalker. The barman had made a tidy profit. On the way back to London, Priest asked:

"And what do we conclude from all this?"

"We need to speak to this Welsh bloke in the deerstalker. And this von Zitzewitz character."

"Von Zitzewitz is almost certainly in the phone book. As for the Welshman...? Who knows?"

Priest flicked on the radio and the sound of classical music filled the car. He glanced at the young man in the passenger seat.

"Probably not to your taste, Joe?"

"It's soothing, guv."

"Is it?"

Priest laughed.

"I have a great deal of other business to attend to at the moment and you've shown such aptitude this afternoon, Joe, I think I can entrust you with making enquiries on your own. I'll get a key cut for the office, then you can come and go as you need. This investigation will involve quite a lot of travel. I'll advance you some cash. Will that be satisfactory?"

Joe Biggs stared at the road in front of him and then at the speedometer. Cash. Travel. Keys to the office. Enquiries. He realised he was gripping the sides of the seat so hard his fingers hurt.

"Should I talk to this von Zitzewitz on my own?"

"Yes. And there's a further matter you will have to look into. The more I think about it, the more I am persuaded that the disappearance of Barnaby Brown is connected to the Diver case. I think we must get the full story on what happened to Brown. Do you think you're up to that, Joe?"

"I'll do my level best, Mr Priest."

"Very good. Keep all receipts, won't you?"

"Yes, Mr Priest."

The Porsche came up fast behind a small green builder's van hogging the outside lane. A few inches from the van's back bumper, Priest braked sharply, flashed his lights and muttered in a foreign language. The van in front wobbled, the intimidated driver almost seemed to lose control, but moved over, and as they flashed past they saw a man waving his fist and shouting.

Priest said calmly:

"Some people should never go in the fast lane, Joe. They are at serious risk to themselves and others."

Chapter 10: *Klinge, Kleines Frühlingslied*

Vesna Diver stood in the middle of her husband's study, a room she had not entered for fifteen years. Until recently. Her husband had prohibited anyone from entering his sanctum. It had been kept meticulously tidy and dust-free. She had often heard the old vacuum cleaner roaring at midnight when she was trying to sleep. Fergus Diver had been an insomniac.

Between two bookcases a large space had been allotted to pictures of her husband meeting great personages, a kind of wall of fame. The most prominent photograph, a large colour print, showed Fergus Diver clinking a champagne glass with the politician most responsible, as she saw it, for the criminal bombing of her country. The man wore a monstrous grin. She lifted the heavy frame and turned the picture to the wall. Some of the other pictures, according to the captions, were Fergus with Octavio Paz in Oaxaca, Fergus with Ern Malley in Adelaide, Fergus with Robert Lowell in Boston. She stared at a newspaper clipping of Fergus in audience with the Pope. Her husband had been militantly anti-ecclesiastical. What was he doing talking to the Vatican? The only picture that included her was a photo of Fergus and herself on the trip to Cuba. Since that long-ago tour, Fergus had never taken his wife on any of his reading jaunts. You don't travel well, he used to say. She had always suspected there were other reasons for his solo departures.

She picked up the framed original artwork of the cover of *The Arsonists*. Although it had been his first book, it had remained the one that critics never stopped talking about, and was the only collection he had ever dedicated to her. She went to the shelf that held his various works, and took the volume out. There were love-poems for her in the book, and in subsequent books there hadn't been any.

She selected one of them and read the first lines:

> *Ah my dear, my Balkan love,*
> *Let's jebemo the livelong night*
> *In the soft, dootsy waves*

She had accepted the poem from him with grace though, and believed his assurance that it had been written from the bottom of his heart. It was always a problem that, English not being her first language, she had felt confused and baffled by the things her husband and his friends wrote. For a while she had taken to reading poems in Serbian. She had even tried to persuade Fergus to translate Serbian poetry into English, offering to provide him with literal versions, but he had refused. It was a long time since he'd called her his Balkan love.

Vesna and Fergus Diver had first met in Belgrade in the *Znak Pitanje*. He had always made a joke of the fact that they'd met in a restaurant called The Question Mark. She remembered the occasion very well. He had entered as if the entire restaurant had been reserved for him, an authority in no way diminished by the fact that there were no free tables. He had spoken English to the uncomprehending waiter, and pointed to her table, where there was a free stool. The waiter had looked interrogatively at her, and she had nodded and smiled.

"I'm Fergus Diver," he'd said. "I hope you speak English."

"Yes," she said. "Vesna Pavlovic. I am a student of English."

"What luck. Then you can translate these symbols for me."

The menu had been in Cyrillic, of course, and he had needed her guidance to order.

She had only gone in to eat a *baklava* but had stayed to watch him devour a vast plate of grilled meats from the barbecue, washed down with *Niksicko* beer, which he proclaimed to be very good. As his food arrived, she had been about to leave, but he'd smiled at her and entreated her to stay.

"It's not everyday you get a chance to sit with an English poet," he'd said.

She hadn't just sat with an English poet, she'd married him. Twenty years it had lasted. She had become practised in the art of being a poet's wife, and apart from his often long absences abroad, she had always been at Fergus's side. Whenever he requested her support at important readings, anywhere in the British Isles, she had gone along. She knew every rainy provincial city there was to know. The night he'd won the WH Auden Award, and had got drunk, she'd been there to take him home. She'd put up with his moods when he got rejections or couldn't write, and indeed had hidden his bad reviews. She'd delicately tried to bring him down when he got above himself. She'd dealt with the sycophants and admirers. She'd coped with and supported him over the matter of the stalker, who'd later killed herself. And then, of course, there had been the lovers, to whom she had tried to turn a blind eye. It wasn't once or twice that her friends told her she deserved a medal.

She opened a filing cabinet and looked at the masses of paper crammed in there. How on earth was she going to sort all this out? She knew that Fergus had kept every single draft of every poem, because he'd told her so. When she'd criticised him for attaching undue importance to his own work, he'd replied that this was going to be her life insurance. Perhaps this was true – she'd already received phone-calls from the British Library, and from a university in Atlanta, inquiring about Fergus's archive. And hadn't Mr Priest told her he'd been in communication with Fergus about it? He'd phoned to say he was coming to report on the investigation later that day. She would have to ask him about archives, how they were organised, what they were potentially worth, etc.

What could Mr Priest have found out? He'd been very brief on the phone. She picked up the folder with all the letters Fergus had received in the last year and opened it. The first letter she read was from Ruari McLeod, describing a festival in Antwerp he'd attended. It appeared that Manfred von Zitzewitz had been in Antwerp, spreading bile and rubbishing Fergus's reputation – which Ruari had, of course, defended. The Antwerp people had wanted to give their festival prize to Fergus the following year but von Zitzewitz had scuppered that. In his scrawl, under the text of the letter, Fergus had written *'The enemy increaseth every day...'*

She flicked on through the letters, and stopped at one that began, Hi Panda, how you? Shaking her head, she glanced down to the end of the text to find the words 'Yr little baboon misses you' and felt cold. She put the letter back firmly in its file. The third letter she looked at was from the customer services manager of Aer Blaskett, refusing to reimburse the cost of a squashed laptop. Diagonally across the text of this, Fergus had scribbled in blue pen *Wankers!* She'd have to be vigilant if it came to an edition of Fergus's letters.

She looked around the room. The large house they lived in had been inherited from Fergus's mother, and although they had no mortgage, it was still very expensive to keep up. Despite Fergus's readings, workshops, regular newspaper column and restaurant reviews (which had been only a recent development), coupled with her own teacher's salary, they had found it difficult to make ends meet. Reputations didn't put money in the bank. Each of his widely-acclaimed books had achieved only the most modest sales. 'Wait,' Fergus, would say. 'Wait till I get the Nobel Prize. That'll change things.'

Her eye caught the voodoo mask which was partly out of sight on a high shelf. That thing! She remembered him bringing it back from Africa, and placing it prominently in the living room. Wherever she'd walked, its eyes had seemed to be on her. She'd asked Fergus to take it away but he'd laughed at her, and said she was being superstitious and silly. In the following months, however, terrible things had happened. She'd had a minor car accident. Their dog, Bran, had been run over by a coal lorry, and she'd had a miscarriage – and had never got pregnant again. The mask had begun to invade her dreams and it was only when she'd threatened to leave that he'd moved it into his study.

She realised she did not like being there. He was too much here, and yet he wasn't. She went out, closing the door quietly, and began to go down the stairs. The grandfather clock on the landing began to chime, and then over the top of it, she heard the doorbell. Mr Priest was very punctual.

She was struck again, as she had been at the funeral, by the man's elegance. He was wearing a silvery suit and a cobweb-patterned tie that trapped the eyes.

"Would you like a cup of tea, Mr Priest?"

"Actually, I prefer coffee. Would an espresso be possible?"

"I can offer you Turkish coffee."

"Wonderful!"

She took down the copper *jezvah* from a high shelf, pleased that Priest was willing to try her own favourite brew. As she prepared the coffee, she realised she was trembling – that love-letter, the voodoo mask, Fergus's brooding aura still somehow in the room, and now this man at her elbow, watching her make the coffee...

"It's been a long time since I have had real Turkish coffee. I always thought the Serbs were not friends to the Turks."

"Everyone in my country drinks Turkish coffee. And I am not a nationalist."

She added the water to the coffee and sugar in the *jezvah*, placed it on a tray with two small cups and two glasses of water, added a small glass bowl of *slatko,* and carried the tray through to the living room, followed by Priest. They sat down and he took the spoon she gave him to taste the *slatko.*

"Very sweet," he said.

"Another tradition we have from the Turks."

She poured out two cups of coffee.

"Frothy mud," he said appreciatively, sipping.

"Have you managed to find out anything?"

"I have some news. Have you heard about Barnaby Brown?"

"The Irish poet? I did hear something on the radio. He's disappeared, hasn't he?"

"It seems he too has been murdered. Or he has very cleverly engineered his own disappearance – but why would he want to do that?"

"My God! What happened?"

"All we know is he was travelling on a ferry to Ireland and he didn't reach the other side. The police have ruled out accident or suicide because of something they found in Brown's cabin."

"Oh?"

"A string puppet with its strings carefully cut through and the detached limbs laid out on the pillow."

Vesna Diver looked at Priest over her coffee cup.

"Does this mean you think there's a connection between this and my husband's murder?"

"It sounds like Jokerman, doesn't it?"

She shivered.

"Is it too cold in here for you, Mr Priest? The French window is slightly open."

"Allow me," he said.

He got up and closed the door to the garden, turning to observe the parrot that was standing on its perch in a cage, unmoving. Priest took his pen from an inside pocket and drew it along the bars:

"Speak, parrot," he said

The parrot put its head on one side, regarded Priest and said nothing.

"A beautiful bird," he said.

He returned to the sofa, stretched his long legs, and crossed them.

"Mr Priest, I know there are stupid rivalries in the poetry world, but surely that can't lead to murder?"

"It does seem unlikely, I grant you. Were there any poets that your husband might have described as enemies?"

"He had a very bad relationship with Manfred von Zitzewitz."

"Really? Then why did Manfred von Zitzewitz attend your husband's last reading?"

"Did he?"

"Yes, it was a long way to travel to see a rival perform."

"I can't believe Manfred von Zitzewitz can have had anything to do with my husband's death."

Priest drank down the last of his coffee, got up again, and went to stand by the window, gazing out at the lawn. He turned to look back at Vesna:

"There's a red squirrel out there burying a nut."

"Fergus loved the red squirrels, but not the grey ones. He was trying to shoot the greys from an upstairs room with a rifle."

She went and stood beside Priest at the window. A second squirrel had joined the first one. It too had a nut to bury.

"They are preparing for hard times," said Priest. "We should all do that."

Vesna nodded.

"What kind of rifle did your husband have? Did he acquire it recently?"

"He did as a matter of fact. He had to get a permit."

"Did he acquire it solely for the purpose of shooting squirrels?"

"That's what he said."

"Interesting."

Priest said nothing further, but continued to watch the antics of the squirrels, one of which appeared to be doing a dance of triumph over its buried nut.

"What else have you found out, Mr Priest?"

"There was one other person present at the reading whom we've been unable to account for. A tall, bearded man in a deerstalker. Do you know anyone who affects a deerstalker?"

"No."

"We know that your husband's murderer took over an Indian restaurant and served Mr Diver a dish of poisoned mushrooms. It could have been the man in the deerstalker, or von Zitzewitz, or someone else from the reading, or a Sikh wrestler. Anybody at all."

"A Sikh wrestler?"

"This is how the manager described his assailant."

"So you've really nothing to tell me?"

Priest sighed.

"I'm sorry, not yet. Can you tell me more about the animosity between your husband and Manfred von Zitzewitz?"

She had brought her coffee cup with her, and now she drank the last of the coffee, and placed the cup on a low table.

"They were on a train together, going to a poetry festival in York, and they went to the dining car together. Mr von Zitzewitz always wore a white suit to readings in those days and Fergus found this pretentious. Anyway, my husband had reviewed a new book of Mr von Zitzewitz's haiku, and had been scathing about it. On the train Fergus asked him when he was going to write a real poem. Naturally, Mr von Zitzewitz was very annoyed. He accused Fergus of writing baggy and unmelodious poems."

"Oh dear."

"Fergus threw red wine all over Mr von Zitzewitz's white suit."

"Was the prize reading given in stained regalia?"

"The stain never came out. Mr von Zitzewitz tried to get Fergus to pay for a new suit but my husband refused. Then there was the Auden prize."

"They were the two favoured candidates, were they not?"

"Mr von Zitzewitz accused my husband of having had undue influence with the judges. Fergus took two of the judges out to dinner in Soho the week before the result was announced and this was reported in *Private Eye*. I'll be honest with you Mr Priest, I'm not such a great poetry reader. I don't really see what all the fuss is about."

"I sympathise with your point of view, Mrs Diver."

"There was a terrible scene after the prize-giving at the Auden award. I was there. It was awful."

"What happened?"

"Well, it was stupid really. Mr Kumar – do you know him? - was kind enough to try and bring the two rival candidates together to shake hands, saying a prize was a lottery, but Mr von Zitzewitz disagreed. I think he was terribly disappointed not to have won. Fergus said he'd have to start writing haiku, so there would be a level playing field, and Mr von Zitzewitz poured whisky into Fergus's pocket. We almost didn't get into the restaurant afterwards. Fergus smelled as if he was drunk, but of course he was not."

"I'm very sad to hear all this."

"But I still don't see Mr von Zitzewitz having anything to do with Fergus's murder, do you?"

Behind them the parrot croaked:

"*Trick or treat!*"

"I don't know," said Priest, turning to scrutinise the bird.

"Perhaps you'd like to see my husband's papers?"

"Of course."

She beckoned him to follow her up the stairs to the poet's study. As they entered the room, she noticed that his attention fell on the voodoo mask. He walked straight towards it, reached up for it, and ran his thumb over the smooth wood.

"Remarkable," he said. "This is a Benin mask."

"If that interests you, Mr Priest, you can take it away. I've always hated it. I should warn you it does bring bad luck."

"Thank you, but I'm not superstitious."

"You don't have to be superstitious for bad things to happen."

He looked at her, a long look. She gestured at the desk.

"These are my husband's papers."

He immersed himself for a while, making a cursory inventory. He opened drawers, looked into folders, flicked through numbered drafts of poems.

"I think this archive should fetch a very good price," he said.

"How much?"

"We might be looking at several hundred thousand, if it's dealt with properly."

"I've spoken to someone from the British Library, and from an American university."

"They move fast after a death. Did they make you an offer?"

"No, they both want to come and assess the material."

"You really need an agent to deal with this for you. Otherwise they will pay you less than the market value."

"Oh, Yes. Of course."

"It must be painful for you to stand here in your husband's study, discussing the disposal of his papers."

"It has to be done, Mr Priest. You manage people's literary estates, don't you? Would you be willing to act for me in this matter?"

"Would you like me to?"

"I would."

He bowed: "Nothing would please me more than to please you."

She looked at him a bit surprised. The way he had said that wasn't entirely business-like. But she liked his clarity. He seemed to be a man who was absolutely clear about the direction he was headed in. It inspired confidence.

They returned to the living room, Priest carrying the voodoo mask. The parrot shifted sideways on its perch, and made a hoarse, throaty noise.

"He doesn't seem to like your mask. Does he speak any of your husband's lines?"

"It's a she. My husband spent hours trying to teach her. I think there's one that stuck. If you say 'Ah' she will speak."

Priest studied the parrot.

"Ah," he said

Amalia, the fatal courtesan! " the parrot declaimed.

"Brilliant! From 'The Poisoned'. One of my favourite Fergus Diver poems."

He sat down again on the sofa.

"Amalia..." he murmured. "Perhaps we have been too fixated on the probability of the murderer being a man. Were there any women that might have cause to be angry with your husband?"

"Not that I know of, but Fergus was away a lot."

"I hesitate to ask this, Mrs Diver....how should I put it?.... were there any other relationships. With women, I mean?"

Vesna Diver pressed her hands together and bit her lip.

"There have been some that I know about."

"Could he have severely disappointed any of these?"

"I hope so," she said.

She got up and went to an antique cabinet of bottles and glasses, pulling down a flap at the front.

"You're not in a hurry, I hope. I'd like to offer you a glass of home made *slivovica*."

"Thank you very much."

She took a decanter from the cabinet, took out the glass stopper, and poured two glasses. Would it be right for her to tell Mr Priest? He seemed the kind of man who was willing to listen, and the dream had bothered her for three nights now. Fergus had always dismissed her nightmares as Balkan gobbledygook. She turned back and saw that Priest was standing in front of the parrot's cage and whispering to it in a language she recognised as German.

"What are you doing?"

"I'm teaching her some Heine. I think German might be easier for a parrot to pronounce. *Klinge, kleines Frühlingslied.*"

"I've poured your drink."

As she handed him the glass she thought that Victor Priest was a very unexpected fellow. She felt emboldened to speak

"May I tell you about something that is on my mind, Mr Priest?"

"Please call me Victor."

"In that case, I'm Vesna."

They clinked glasses and drank.

"I've been having some terrible dreams. I keep seeing a person I know is Fergus's killer."

"What does he look like?"

"He's shrivelled, horrible. Almost a dwarf. Then he sees me and he starts to swell up. All the wrinkles vanish and he becomes smoothfaced."

A tremor ran through her body which she quickly controlled.

"Just a dream," he said. "Who does smoothface look like?"

"Nobody I know," she said. "But he looks at me as if...as if..."

"You're next?"

"Yes."

He took her hand.

"Listen, you've had a bereavement. All kinds of things are stirred up in your mind. Dreams are a way of releasing tension."

"I know that," she said.

This man had a soothing aura about him. She was glad of his visit.

"I'm afraid, I have to be going," he said. "Thank you for the hooch."

111

"It was a pleasure."

He picked up the voodoo mask and walked over to the parrot's cage again.

"*Klinge, kleines Frühlingslied,*" he said twice.

He waited, then said it again.

The parrot put her head on one side. With his free hand, Priest took out his pen and drew it once more across the bars of the cage. The parrot followed this movement with her eyes. Priest said the phrase again, this time with a little more volume, and the parrot repeated it:

"*Klinge, kleines Frühlingslied!*"

"See? I told you German was easier to pronounce."

Picking up the voodoo mask and tucking it under his arm, he went out of the room. Vesna followed him to the front door and opened it. He turned, took her hand, folding it into his own, and held her in a comforting grip.

"We will get to the bottom of this mystery," he said.

She watched the car drive away. What had made her blurt out that dream? She went back into the living room and contemplated the two empty coffee cups. Placing her own cup back on the table in front of the sofa, she upturned it in a swift movement so that the last remnants of liquid drained out, then righted it and peered in, studying the pattern the grounds had made, reading her own fortune.

'You will meet a tall stranger.' She began to laugh. Then she was crying.

Behind her the parrot repeated the phrase of German again.

"*Klinge, kleines Frühlingslied .*"

She had no idea what it meant.

* * *

Through the blackness, the light in the round tower could be seen far out to sea. It was high up on the cliffs, a steady, incandescent, white glow. The light did not come from a lighthouse but from a circular room that surmounted the otherwise opaque bulk of an Edwardian folly. Within the room itself, the light was not dazzling but intense, emanating from two ten thousand lux light boxes placed on diametrically opposed tables in the circular room. White reflectors in the ceiling dispersed the light, reducing the glare.

Seated on a high stool before a lectern in the middle of the room, like an old-fashioned clerk, Victor Priest, in the handwriting of someone who had long practised calligraphy, had written across an A5 sheet of artist's paper:

My sensual equerry knows
blood is the rain of lost adventure

Two lines. He sat studying them for minutes, then got up and paced back and forth. He was wearing an old denim shirt, jogging trainers and blue canvas shoes. Two thirds of the room were enclosed by window. A door led out to a circular staircase and beside the door was a mirror. Next to one of the trestle stands that supported the light boxes was a steel-framed folding bed onto which Priest had thrown blankets and pillows. Beside the bed was a coffee pot on a small electric hotplate, an open tin of ginger biscuits, and several tablets of black chocolate in a neat pile.

He lay down on the bed and stared up at the ceiling, reaching for a biscuit with his right hand. Had it been the right thing to do to employ this assistant? He had stuck the advertisement in the shop window without expecting any response, and the unexpected had happened. Priest could imagine the perfect assistant. Was Joe Biggs it?

The breakthrough renegades

He uncoiled from the bed, went to the lectern, added the line beneath what he had written, stood looking at it for ten seconds, and added one more:

have crashed the orifex in veils of doubt.

He closed his eyes, The beneficent effects of the light were irradiating him. He could feel it like a weight on his retina. It made him euphoric.

He went into a boxing crouch, and began to move around the lectern throwing short, jabbing punches at the air as if bearing down on an opponent in the ring who was forced to retreat before the onslaught.

Then he stopped, taking deep breaths, and returned to the sheet of paper:

Under the leaping hounds of storm
I set up demon stalls,
lounge on tilted shadows.

There was a calmness about her. He liked that. He had been eruptive; she had stayed equable. That was the way he was and she didn't seem to have minded.

He stood up, picked up a tablet of chocolate, snapped it in half, then went back to sit in front of his lectern, nibbling the chocolate. He took the fountain pen from the ledge it rested on and wrote with slow, deliberate care:

I roam as blind as jasmine dust beneath
the coloured breath of fortune.

For nearly twenty minutes he did not move. At one point he drew up his legs somewhat, so that his feet rested on one of the lower rungs of the stool. He bent his back forward and pressed his knees together, trapping his hands. He closed his eyes and then opened them again. There was no sound in the room except the far off crash of the sea, and that too was muted by the double glazed windows. He got down off the stool.

Even assuming he would finish this poem, who would publish it apart from Ackroyd? What was more to the point: who would read it? Readers didn't want difficulty. They wanted something that would give them the impression they understood it. If they didn't get that, they wanted someone to give them a key – a kindly critic, a painstaking teacher, anybody really with the gift of the gab. Which was what it was: Gab. It all boiled down to gab.

He went back to his pile of comestibles on the floor and debated: biscuit or chocolate? He took neither and poured himself a cup of coffee and reclined on the truckle bed, hugging the cup to his chest.

This Joe Biggs fellow. Had it been unfair to engage him? What was the point? Vesna Diver had requested Victor Priest's assistance in the matter, and to please her he had agreed. No. He had agreed to please himself. He dwelt for a moment on an image of her pale face. His own intrusion into the affair was, if anything, an unnecessary complication. The murderer would be caught sooner or later and stand in the glare of the spotlight; the game would be up. But now he had employed Biggs he would have to try and point the young man in the right direction.

He thought of her again.

Let me hunt down lanes of disconnection.

Putting down his coffee cup, he got up. He paced up and down, loosing off occasional boxing jabs in any direction, he caught a glimpse of his face in the mirror as he shadow-boxed past it. Two more lines and he would complete it. Outside the window, the night was loosing its hold. Dawn was coming up:

> *Let me wrest these bones from stillness*
> *and kiss the shudders of my meaning.*

Chapter 11: *A Bolt from the Blue*

When Joe Biggs arrived back at Liverpool Street, after two days of travelling across country, the poster read *Poet Killed by Lightning!* He had been planning to hurry home and put his feet up, but he bought a paper first and read the report. He tried calling the *Artcrimes* office, but his mobile phone had run out of battery, making a trip to Lambs Conduit Street necessary. He took a tube to Euston and walked along Woburn Place towards Russell Square and along Guilford Street, savouring the London air. The red Porsche was parked where his employer usually left it, and Priest was sitting in his kitchen, eating oysters and drinking white wine. He greeted Biggs with a smile.

"Joe! I wasn't expecting to see you just yet. Do you like oysters?"

"Can't say as I ever tried them, guv."

Priest drew a box of shells from the refrigerator, tipped them into the sink, and allowed the cold tap to run over them. He drew a metal glove onto his right hand, took a stubby knife with a broad hilt, and began to open the oysters, dropping the opened shells onto a plate.

"Didn't mean you to go to no trouble," said Biggs.

"No trouble at all. There is lemon and pepper on the bar. Tabasco's in the cupboard, though I consider that a heresy. Get a plate for yourself and a fork."

Biggs did as he was told and sat down on a bar stool studying a wooden board that held slices of some very dark, stiff looking material.

"Pumpernickel, Joe. That's German bread. I'm afraid the English have completely lost the art of bread-making. All you can get from an English baker these days is pap. Put a little of that churn butter on the Pumpernickel. You'll find it goes well with the oysters."

"They raw, guv?"

"They are alive, Joe. Watch."

Priest put pepper and lemon on an oyster, tipped the shell, and slid the contents into his mouth.

"Make sure you chew it, Joe. Some people think it correct to swallow them without tasting them. The world is full of idiots."

Biggs tried the oyster and found it good. It tasted of the sea, and he liked the texture. The nutty bread tasted good alongside it. He was hungry.

"This is white *Chteauneuf du Pape,* Joe. You do drink wine, don't you? Most people are familiar with the red, but the white, I think, is exceptional; this particular year merits a gold medal. Now then, what have you found out?"

"Not much, guv. Have you seen the news? Some poet's been hit by lightning, or a meteor or something."

Priest raised his eyebrows, turned to a tiny television set on a shelf and flicked on the news. They had to wait for the passage of the football results till a photograph appeared of a long-faced man with a wart on his left cheek and grey hair. Alexander Duthie, the popular Scots poet, had been killed by an object which had fallen from the sky. He had been walking in his garden at the time. There was speculation that something had fallen from an aircraft taking off from Glasgow airport, however this was unconfirmed. It did not appear to be the result of a lightning strike.

"Sounds like an accident," said Biggs. "Bit of a coincidence, though. Him being a poet and all."

"Accidents have a way of turning out to be more than just the operations of fortune," said Priest, draining his glass. "I fear you'll have to be off on your travels again tomorrow. But I want to hear about Wales. Tell me."

Biggs had not managed to add much to the information they already had about the disappearance of Barnaby Brown, but he took out a notebook and glanced at what he had written. He had tracked down the barman on the Stena Line ferry who had served Brown and his partner drinks. The barman had described Brown's blonde companion as 'a right piece of stuff'. For some reason this very much amused Priest, and he poured himself another glass of white wine. Biggs had managed to get the woman's name: Viola Walsh. He had noted some details of her appearance: blonde hair in a bun, tall, wearing an amber scorpion brooch. The police had made their enquiries long before he got there, and they too had established that Viola Walsh had paid cash for her ticket at the Fishguard office, and that she had been a foot passenger, as far as anybody could tell. This didn't rule out that she might have been a passenger in someone else's vehicle.

After spending a night in Fishguard, Biggs had returned eastwards to Suffolk and visited the Tamlyn Trust, where Brown had been teaching prior to his disappearance. It seemed that Brown had had a bit of a misunderstanding with his co-tutor, a poet called Anita Bellows. Some students had played a prank on Brown at a party and he had left in a huff without saying goodbye to anyone.

"Anita Bellows?" said Priest. "Perhaps we shall need to talk to her. You've done well, Joe. This is all very useful. But I'm afraid tomorrow you will have to go to Scotland."

He got up, went into the other room, and came back with a book of poems. Studying the contents page for a moment, he leafed through the book, found what he had been searching for, chuckled in appreciation, and looked at Joe.

"This is a poem by Alex Duthie," he said. "I think you might find it interesting."

*   *   *

Biggs sat in the prow of the lobster boat peering through the mist at the vague outline of Inishron. There was a raw wind and he was glad he'd thought to buy a coat – an item of clothing most Londoners considered unnecessary. Scotland had always sounded to him like a country you needed to wear a coat in, and now he had verified this for himself. The boat rolled, and he felt queasy. It wasn't just the movement of the boat that induced nausea, but also the fish-smell. He hoped it wouldn't impregnate his new tweed. News reports had given him the disappointing information that Duthie lived on an island close to the west coast of Scotland; he'd been hoping a train ride to Glasgow would be enough. Also, getting to Inishron had not only been difficult, it had considerably diminished the pile of cash Priest had given him.

"Is that it?" he asked the bearded man at the wheel.

"D'ye see any other island, laddie?"

"I can hardly see anything in this murk."

"Mind yourself now. There's a strong current here."

Biggs grabbed the gunwale as the lobster boat lurched alarmingly to the right.

A cliff reared up out of the mist. The lobsterman took the boat along the side of the cliff which opened up very soon into a small harbour. Biggs saw with relief that there was a pier, and moored to it, a sleek white launch. It looked like the kind of expensive kit a millionaire would have. The news reports had said the entire island belonged to a James Renfrew – no, *Sir* James Renfrew.

"I'll call my cousin now," said the lobsterman, bringing the boat in alongside the pier, and lassoing a bollard. He took out his mobile phone, thumbed it vigorously and held it against his ear.

"Murdo, I've got that detective from London with me. We're at the pier. Can you come down?"

Biggs wondered if Murdo would be as suspicious as the lobsterman. From the drawling way in which his ferryman said the word 'detective' it was clear that he thought Joe was a complete impostor. The lobsterman had been very reluctant to take Biggs as a passenger. He had questioned Biggs' youth, his complete ignorance of Scottish geography, his urban attire, and his lack of identifying papers. Nor had he seemed to believe Joe's assertion that he was a lover of the poetry of Alexander Duthie – not, at any rate, until fifty pounds had been produced. What would Murdo's reaction be? Would he have to fork out another fifty quid?

Through the fog, a bearded man in a blue security uniform became visible. But for the uniform, it could have been the lobsterman's twin. He stood above the boat on the pier, an impassive, lanky figure.

"Shall I talk to the boat or are you going to come up?"

Biggs clambered up a ladder, followed by the lobsterman.

"This is Mr Biggs, Murdo."

"Is it, Robbie?"

Murdo did not extend a hand of greeting, and his face showed no expression.

There was an uncomfortable silence until he spoke again.

"This is a private island. Sir James does not welcome uninvited visitors."

"I know," said Biggs. "I'm investigating a murder."

"Well, the police have been here. Are you the police?"

"I'm a private investigator."

" On whose behalf would you be doing this investigating?"

" My employer. He is a great admirer of the work of Alexander Duthie."

"He is, is he? Do you have some form of identification, laddie?" said Murdo.

Biggs produced one of Priest's impressive business cards. Murdo took a pair of broken reading glasses from his pocket and held them to his eyes.

"*Artcrimes*," he read out, "*Victor Priest Investigations*."

He looked at Biggs as if he was a rotten herring.

"But this doesn't identify your good self, does it? And anyway, what makes you think I'd want to speak to the likes of you?"

"Murdo, there's no harm in talking to him," said the lobster-man. "He says he loves Alex's poetry. We want to find out who did that terrible thing to Alex, don't we?"

"Aye, we do. But what makes you think laddie here cares a whit for our Alex?"

Murdo handed back Priest's card and turned away, calling over his shoulder: "Let the police take care of it. They'll get to the bottom of it."

Joe reached into his coat pocket and took out the wallet he had bought to hold Priest's stack of money.

"Half a mo'," he said. "Maybe this'll help?"

Murdo turned and came back, glancing at the notes Joe had half-extracted from the wallet.

"Bribery is it now? You know laddie, I think our local police would be very interested in you and what you're up to."

He took out his mobile phone and began to dial a number.

"What makes you think your local police care about poetry?" said Biggs. "They don't give a fuck about poetry. All the fuzz cares about is clumping around in their big boots and pushing people around. You want to hear from someone who cares about poetry? You talk to my boss."

He extricated the mobile phone he had had the good sense to charge up overnight, turned on the loudspeaker and called a number. Murdo stopped dialling and stared. A cultured voice echoed into the mist.

"Priest, Victor Priest speaking."

"Morning, Guv, could you read me that Duthie poem again. Gotta coupla geezers here don't believe I've ever heard of Alexander Duthie."

There was a pause:

"Just a minute."

In the silence, broken only by the plops of waves against the pier, the two bearded cousins looked at each other. Then out of the phone, in a powerful declamatory tone, came:

THE STUPENDOUS QUESTION

I write to unclog the pure fount of omnipotence
And release into the sky the radiant awareness
The white barge on the rive rof Egypt bearing the queen of victory
Beyond the main deep, beyond the continental shelf
Towards the abyss where questions lurk.

I see the woman from elfland who tantalises me
Stripping herself naked for her living-death lover
With his belching braces and his glowing face and his stained vest
Let her hold to him as eternity clung to Boethius!
Man's extinction is next...! We must not flinch.

I hear them still, the men gathering at the pit head,
Low-voiced in the dark, the glow of their fags, their helmet lit,
Waiting for the lift that will carry them down, down
Like sweat-stained Persephones into the coaly vaults of Dis!
And they interest me not - only the higher brain centres are real!

The mist swirled around the group on the jetty. A seagull screeched from somewhere high above the cliff.

"I'd never have thought I'd hear an English voice read that poem," said Murdo. "And out of a telephone too."

"D'ye remember," said his cousin, "when we were drinking in the *Argyle*, and we noticed he was there, Alex Duthie in our pub, and we bought him a drink, then another, then another, and we asked him to give us that very poem, and he did, from memory. I'll remember that day all my life."

"Aye," said Murdo.

Priest's voice on the phone enquired:

"What's this all about, Joe?"

"Two Scots blokes wanted to hear a poem by Alex Duthie."

"Well, they just did. Would you like another?"

"No thanks, guv."

The phone clicked off and Biggs contemplated the two cousins.

"I was hoping," he said, "you could help me with some enquiries."

*   *   *

Murdo led the way up a slight incline from the pier. The mist
was lifting and a ray of watery sunlight revealed a large white house
at the summit of the island. The building was extensive with a few
smaller outbuildings. It was surrounded by sloping grassland that ran
down to the cliff edge. Biggs saw a patch of tarmac with a circle drawn
on it that he took to be a helicopter launching pad. A weird animal
noise stopped him in his tracks, and the lobsterman coming behind
bumped into his back.

"Blimey," said Biggs. "What was that?"

"Och, it's only the seals. They're all round this island. That's
how it gets its name."

"Inishron?"

"Aye, 'rón' is the Gaelic for seal."

Biggs gazed down at a number of whiskered faces bobbing in
the water. They were staring at him as if they were wondering what he
was doing there. Good question.

"We'll show you where Alex lived. I'm sure that'll be interesting for you."

Murdo brought them to the door of a stone cottage, took out a
ring of keys, and opened up with a flourish.

"This is where he wrote his poems. That's his desk. Everything
here is as he left it."

"Bit of a mess ain't it?" said Biggs.

"The police for you," said Robbie. "They've been through the
lot about ten times."

"They have," said Murdo with a sigh. "Yer right about the big
boots, laddie. At least they didn't go through the whisky. I put it in the
fireplace. See?"

Murdo bent down, scrabbled under some old kindling in the
fireplace and held up a three quarters full bottle of Oban.

"Shall we toast the great man?"

Biggs looked around. Apart from the disorder, he could see

that the cottage was luxuriously furnished. A set of capacious buttoned leather armchairs was grouped around the fireplace. A huge flatscreen TV was attached to the wall at an elevation. The polished cabinet which Robbie was opening held crystal glasses, decanters. Next to it was an expensive looking stereo with a futuristic looking turntable. Heavy woven rugs covered the tiled floor and a pleasant warmth came from the radiators.

Biggs was handed half a tumbler of whisky, a measure that rendered the moistened glass he and Frank stood each other sometimes in the *Earl of Leominster* a total racket. He sipped it with care and let his gaze wander up the circular oaken staircase that led to the upper storey.

"Quite a gaff," he said.

"Nothing but the best would do for Alex," said Murdo. "He only had to ask and Sir James gave it to him."

"Why don't we all sit down?" suggested Robbie. "Tell Mr Biggs what happened, Murdo."

They found places to sit. Biggs put a notebook on his knee and checked to see that his pen worked. The security man took a hefty draught from his glass.

"So you know who Alex Duthie was then, laddie? Do you know how he began?"

Biggs shook his head.

"He was the son of a janitor who worked at the town hall in Dumfries. That's how he had free run of the library, to read all those thousands of books. The best kind of education is the one you find for yourself. But his father had an accident and lost his leg, couldn't work any more and his mother had to take care of the household. He grew up in terrible poverty, and that's what made him a communist. Och, he was radical, was Alex Duthie. He was in and out of Moscow. All his work was translated into Russian, including the hymn to Brezhnev. When he built his house, he flew the red flag over it. And of course he had that famous gate made, the one with the hammer and sickle. Wrought iron. Beautiful workmanship."

Joe scratched his head and wondered what to write. Was this important? His mother's neighbour was a communist. Miserable git.

"Did he stand for election and stuff?"

"No, laddie. He had a lot of good things to say about Stalin and that didn't go down too well with people in Scotland. Alex thought nothing of the new Scottish parliament. Said they were all English lackeys, the politicians, and it was all jobs for the boys. Oh he was militant was our Alex. He wanted independence for Scotland, and a bit less democracy. Said democracy was an English invention. Everything he wrote had one aim – to better the lot of the workingman. Well, hard times came along. His wife left him. He couldn't afford to live in his own house anymore. She had the dayjob, see?"

Murdo emptied his glass, refilled it and passed the bottle to his cousin.

"Scotland's national poet had to abandon his own house," said Robbie. "A crying disgrace. It was the politics of course."

"So how did he get to live on this island?"

"He was doing a reading at the Edinburgh Festival," said Murdo, "and Sir James came up to him and said he really liked the way Alex had put his poems across. Didn't like his politics but he loved the poems. Alex didn't know who Sir James was, see, but when he found out, he went over to him in the bar and says: 'd'ye like my poems enough to become my patron?'"

"That's what he did, alright," cackled Robbie.

"Aye. And Sir James took him seriously. Offered him this cottage and a generous stipend. Lots of people accused Alex of selling out. But he kept on writing great poems."

"It's a bit lonely on this island. isn't it?" Biggs asked. "Did he go back to the mainland a lot? What about his friends? Women?"

"He did have women friends, but not lately. Alex didn't leave the island often. He was too busy writing."

Biggs took another cautious sip of whisky.

"So how exactly did he die? The newspapers don't seem to know."

"We don't talk to newspapers," said Murdo. "And we don't let those TV people on the island. Yer a handpicked man, laddie."

He picked up the bottle of *Oban* and poured another generous measure for Biggs, who tried, too late, to refuse it.

"It's just a wee drop, son," said Murdo.

Biggs appraised the three quarters full glass. He hoped he'd be able to get back down that ladder into Robbie's boat.

"I saw Alex that morning," said Murdo. "He was going for

one of his inspiration-walks like he so often did, and he was wearing a
yellow beret. He collected them, you know, Alex did. He had all kinds
of berets. Anyhow, I was up on the roof about midday straightening
the TV aerial - I often have to do that here because of the wind - and
I noticed a helicopter going round in circles over the ocean. I thought
maybe a boat had gone down and they were looking for survivors.
I knew it wasn't Sir James, because he'd gone to Dublin for a meeting, and I certainly wasn't expecting him before evening. Anyway he
wouldn't buzz around like that, he'd come straight in and land. It was
a black helicopter, smaller than the one Sir James uses. After a while,
Alex comes back across the lawn and the helicopter turns and comes
towards us. I could see there was what looked like a big metal thing
swaying beneath it, attached by cables. I thought it might be a sculpture or something. I could see the pilot plain. He's wearing goggles and
a leather helmet, like one of those old-fashioned airmen. Alex didn't
see it at first until the helicopter comes round in a wide circle and hov-
ers over him. I could see Alex looking up, staring. Then the helicopter
begins to go down and Alex begins to run. By God, man, he's running like a rabbit from a fox, and the helicopter, it's going after him. I
couldn't believe it when I realised it was a gate hanging down underneath it, a bloody big gate. And when the pilot gets over Alex again, he
lets it go, and it falls smack on top of the poor man, crushes him flat."

"Blimey," muttered Biggs, scribbling.

"Well, I go down that ladder quicker than a squirrel. I'm looking up at the helicopter and the pilot gives me the thumbs up, does a
big circle and buzzes off over the open sea. I run to Alex but there's
nothing I can do. Stone dead. Squashed. A great big pool of red blood."

"What was it then?"

"What was what, laddie?"

"Well. this gate thing."

"It was *his own gate*, laddie! Made my hair stand on end.
Alex's gate from the house he'd had to leave, the gate he'd had made.
Crushed with his own hammer and sickle!"

It was getting tiresome, the laddie stuff, thought Biggs.

"Fancy flying. Who would do such a thing?"

"He was popular with the people in Russia," said Murdo. "He
kept on writing about the Soviet Union. He thought it was terrible that
that had all gone. Mr Putin didn't like that of course."

"You think the Russians had him killed?"

"Maybe."

"Yeh," said Biggs, "maybe. Don't think it was Russians murdered Fergus Diver, though."

Murdo and Robbie exchanged glances.

"Fergus Diver?" said Murdo. "Alex talked a lot about him. They were on a poets' trip to Sicily together."

"Oh yeah? Did he mention a guy called Barnaby Brown by any chance?"

"He did. He was in Sicily too. Alex liked him."

"Someone pushed him off a boat. Missing presumed drowned."

"*Three* murders? *Three* poets!"

Murdo was registering astonishment and disbelief.

"Yeah."

Biggs closed his notebook. The glass of whisky was still by his side. He picked up the glass, and eyed the two Scotsmen. He was sitting close to the right side of the fireplace, and he moved his hand away slowly, still holding the glass, and tipped it so the whisky trickled into a copper wood holder beside him. A fume of whisky reached his nose. He got up, holding his now empty glass, and walked to the window.

"Were there any other poets on this trip to Sicily?"

"A couple of women I believe," said Murdo. "Alex didn't have much to do with them but he said the Irish poet did."

The two bearded men laughed.

"D'you remember their names?"

Neither Murdo nor Robbie could recall. Biggs stood contemplating the sloping lawn on which Duthie had been flattened. This new information about Sicily…Mr Priest was going to find that very interesting. He felt suddenly confirmed in his new role as a detective.

"This has been extremely useful gentlemen."

He turned back from the window.

"I don't think I need to take up your time any longer. There's a train back to London I'd like to catch…If I can."

"Aye laddie. I'll take you back across the sound."

*   *   *

Having furnished himself with a fourpack of Triple X and a hamburger, Biggs threaded his way down a platform of Glasgow Central Station, peering through the carriage windows of the London-bound train, hoping to see an empty seat, preferably with a pretty girl sitting opposite.

Spotting what he was looking for, he jumped aboard, knowing how quickly someone could come from the opposite direction and claim the seat. He threw himself into it, depositing his bag, and took up most of the shared table with his food and drink. The young woman lifted her head from a magazine and stared pointedly at the table till Biggs pulled everything back behind an imaginary middle line.

"Sorry," he said with a grin.

She went back to her magazine, giving him the chance to study her. She was more than alright. She could be a mod, he thought, with her hair cut in that bob. He hoped she would be travelling all the way to London. He was in a good mood. He felt he'd handled things pretty well, all things considered. He looked forward to sharing the fascinating details of his investigation with this young lady.

He opened a beercan, took a swig, and then proceeded to un-wrap his burger and fries. The smell wafted though the compartment, and before he'd taken the first bite – before the train had even thought about moving – the young woman jumped to her feet, grabbed her bag from the overhead rack and disappeared in the direction of another carriage. Why couldn't he develop a taste for prawn sandwiches, like Priest? He took a huge bite from his bun, just as a punk in a tartan miniskirt slid into the seat that had just been vacated.

Chewing slowly, he contemplated the two nose-rings and the staples in her ears.

"Emdy's seat?"

"Sorry?"

"Ah says is there embdy sittin here?"

Not only did she have a broader accent than anyone else he'd met up here, but she also had a large stud in her tongue. What would it be like to kiss someone with a thing like that? If it hadn't been for the self-mutilation, she would have been a bit of a looker, he thought. He wondered if he should say yes, but thought better of it. Five minutes later, as the train trundled slowly out of the station, he regretted this as she asked him if she could have one of his beers. He slid one her way, put the debris from his lunch into the bin behind his seat and corralled the two remaining beers close to his edge of the table.

Typical of a Scot, Biggs thought, to get rigged up in a style that had died with Johnny Rotten. She sat quite still, sipping his beer and staring at him, and he found this extremely disconcerting. Moving to another seat was out of the question. He'd spotted this one first, after all, and anyway the train had pretty well filled up. To deter her from making any attempts to initiate a conversation, he took out his mobile phone and dialled Priest's number.

"It's me, Guv. Thought you might like an advance report."

"Have you solved the case, Biggs?"

"No guv. Course not. Turns out Duthie lived on a millionaire's island. Lived like a millionaire too, I'd say. I went out there and talked to the security guard. The thing that killed Duthie was his own gate, from a house he used to live in. A helicopter dropped it on him."

"Jokerman again one must presume. Any theories?"

"Well, the gate had a hammer and sickle on it. Guys on the island think it might be Russians. Duthie was a big fan of the old Soviet Union. He was very popular in Russia. But why would the Russians want to murder Diver, or Brown? They didn't have any connections to communism, did they? I've got another theory."

"Let's hear it."

"Duthie, Diver and Brown were all on Sicily together. Some kinda poets' holiday. There was some women there as well. I reckon they got cheeky and rubbed the Mafia up the wrong way. Maybe they insulted some Mafia boss's daughter."

"Why would they do that?"

"Without realising it, I mean."

"This is all very speculative, Joe. Where is it getting us?"

"Dunno, Guv."

He drank from his can and noticed that the punk, who had drained her can, was straining to catch the half of the conversation she could hear.

"Well, did you examine the gate?"

"The police took it. But the security man got a pretty close look at it."

"What did he say about it?"

"Said there was a blood everywhere, a big red stain of it,

and in the middle the hammer and sickle. Be a bit like the Soviet flag, wouldn't it?"

"That's a very interesting comparison, Joe."

There was a silence on the line. The punk was staring at him.

"I have to go now, I'm afraid. An acupuncture appointment. I'll see you here at the usual time tomorrow. Have a good journey back to London."

"Thanks, guv."

The punk girl had been waiting for Biggs to switch off the phone. As he put it in his pocket, she said:

"Gie's yin o they cans. Wance we've finished these wans ah'll go to the buffet and get us some mair."

Joe pushed a beercan across the table. She snapped the ring open and drank.

"Whit was aw that aboot somdy getting killed wi' a gate?"

Chapter 12: *The Odic Force*

Victor Priest pushed open the door of Deal's most secretive bookshop (it was down a side street and then down another side street), inhaling a familiar fragrance of old volumes overlaid with the perfume of a smouldering joss stick. He ducked his head to avoid a large print of the Third Eye suspended from the ceiling and bowed to a lifesized and lifelike effigy of WB Yeats standing near the window to welcome browsers. He was greeted from the inner gloom of the shop by Van Ackroyd, who was on the phone but came forward to thrust a glass of white wine at Priest.

Priest was wearing motor cycle leathers, and holding a brown paper parcel. He laid the parcel on a window ledge, took the glass that was handed to him, and raised it in a gesture. Van indicated a table piled high with new books and periodicals, then retreated into his office to continue his telephone conversation. Priest went over to the table, put down his glass, and perused what was there. A finely crafted and expensive looking hardback with a shiny jetblack cover announced: *The Demon Monologues* in fiery gothic lettering. He put down his glass and turned the pages, contemplating the erotic detail of the mad Abbé's illustrations. No wonder the Abbé had been burned at the stake.

He closed the book. Next to it was a new collection by Horace Venables, called *Stray*. Venables had been published hitherto by a rather undistinguished imprint called Midland, based in Birmingham, but his new collection had been brought out by Dolan & Swainson. Priest had to admit to himself that Venables had struck unusual gold. The poet's ventriloquising of the voice of a dog was remarkable.

On another table was a pile of unsold copies of *The Boot*, and Priest scanned a long retrospective review of the work of Anita Bellows, ending with her latest: *Eros in Handcuffs*. Priest tossed the magazine back on to its pile and turned to confront a cuckoo clock he was sure had not been there before. Below it, hanging on the wall, were the weights and chains that had once driven it. The clock hands were at midnight. Or at noon.

Suddenly the bird popped out of its housing and cuckooed at him. He stepped back in surprise.

"Pretty good that," said Ackroyd, coming out of his office.

"This bookshop isn't called *The Odic Force* for nothing."

"Batteries, I suppose," said Priest. "The weights and chains are a good red herring, though."

"No batteries. Just the usual Thursday morning miracle."

"Mmm," said Priest, eyeing the little doors behind which the wooden bird had retreated.

"I see you're wearing the kit," said Ackroyd.

"It's a nice day, almost Spring. I thought the Harley needed an airing."

Ackroyd nodded.

"Have you heard this amazing story about Alexander Duthie?"

"A cartoon death," said Priest. "Rather like his agit-prop poems."

"I have the impression," said Ackroyd, "that someone is trying to wipe out poets. Don't you feel your life endangered?"

Priest laughed.

"I only publish in your little limited editions."

"You are nevertheless published, Victor. Somebody out there might be hating you."

Priest nodded:

"I brought you a present, Van. Also a cartoon, in its way."

He indicated the parcel he had left by the window, and Van went over and picked it up, tearing off the wrapping. He liked getting presents, and Priest had the knack of giving you things you didn't know you wanted. He unveiled the mask and gave a cry.

"Victor! It's Benin, isn't it?"

He held it at arm's length with both hands:

"This is a valuable thing. Where did you get it?"

"Let's say I found it."

"Are you really giving it to me?"

"Where are you going to put it?"

Ackroyd laid the object down and scurried to the back of the shop, returning with a small stepladder, a hammer, and a box of nails. He mounted the ladder, stood on the top rung, removed two dusty pictures from the wall, hammered in two nails, and held out his hand to signal that Priest should pass him the mask.

"Does it look straight to you?"

"Ever so slightly askew, Van. It looks even more menacing

like that."

Sunlight through the dusty shop window imparted a glow to the mask.

Ackroyd came down off the ladder, puffing, and stepped back to regard it.

"The perfect symbol," he said, "for a poetry world that is being decimated by an insane poet-killer."

"That's not why I gave it to you," said Priest. "I gave it to you because it's a beautiful thing. And also because I still covet that book."

Ackroyd smiled.

"Ah," he said. "Excuse me. I must answer that."

He trotted off to the telephone and Priest, noticing that the eyes of the mask seemed focussed on the occult books section, wandered over and looked at the titles: *The Order of the Bright Midnight; The Tantric Guide to Sex; Stinkhorn Transcendentalism; The Hermetic Alchemist.*

How was it that in Deal of all places Ackroyd could find customers who shared his obsessions? But he did. At the end of a shelf of books on and by the occultist Aleister Crowley, he found a collection of Crowley's poems called *The Book of Lies,* and read a poem called 'Hymn to Pan'. The lines: 'I am numb / with the lonely lust of devildom' jumped out at him. Priest had a vision of Ackroyd's portly form capering around at a black Mass with a naked woman lying on the flat stone slab of a grave.

Ackroyd called from the back office:

"I think it's time I sorted out our lunch, Victor. I'll call *Mother Purdy's Larder* and have them bring some food round. I have plenty of wine."

"Good. I've eaten nothing today except half a grapefruit."

"We'll order their leek quiche, it's excellent."

Priest took off his leathers and stowed them on a convenient chair. After a while, a boy with acne and a red check shirt swaggered in carrying a cardboard box, deposited it in Ackroyd's office, and swaggered out, calling 'Enjoy your meal!' The two men sat in the tiny office at the back of the shop, eating their lunch off cardboard plates, and drinking white wine. Priest was curious to know what Ackroyd thought of *Stray.*

"Lively stuff. Won't win any prizes though. Not bumptious

enough."

"Not enough ego, perhaps?"

"Since when did poets not have enough ego? Did you know I published two chapbooks of his that Midland didn't want to do?"

"No, I didn't."

"I'm very annoyed he didn't come to me with the new collection."

"But you only do little books, Van."

"Nothing says I can't do a big one."

Priest eyed his friend with an ironic half-smile on his face.

"Where did you unearth those *Demon Monologues*?"

Ackroyd thrust a wodge of leek quiche into his mouth and chewed very slowly. With his mouth full, he said:

"From Jean-Claude Vrain, the Paris bookseller."

"I take it he has the original?"

"No, I bought it from him. Not quite a knock down price. However, I have already recouped the investment from my subscribers."

Priest wiped his fingers with a napkin, got up, went into the shop and returned with the copy from the book table. He sat down again, turning the pages.

"I see you did the translations into English?"

"Yes."

"This is more sexually alarming than the Marquis de Sade. You'll be getting a visit from the police next."

"It reveals the bounds of the possible, does it not Victor?"

"I notice that he uses the tarot pack to classify his perversions."

"Yes. Look at what the Wheel of Fortune and Justice represent – the opposite of what the poor victim might have hoped for."

Priest turned more pages.

"Do you think the Abbé acted out these rapes?"

Ackroyd put a fat thumb on one picture, arresting Priest's turning of the pages:

"If he did, it puts the Abbé in a class with Gilles de Rais or Elizabeth Batory."

"Or Jack the Ripper? I take it this is about the enjoyment of murder, not the enjoyment of sex?"

"Don't you think murder could be quite enjoyable, Victor?"

Priest reached for the bottle and refilled his glass, watching Ackroyd.

"It would depend how much the person had annoyed me."

The book dealer laughed:

"To answer your first question. I don't think the police will be interested. They are too busy chasing drug dealers. Deal is aptly named."

Priest slid the heavy book under his chair, and retrieved his plate. He was about to take another forkful of quiche when he stopped, scrutinised his forkful, and removed something from the pastry with two fingers. He held it up to the light, squinted at it, then displayed it to Ackroyd. Van threw up his hands:

"I'm so sorry, Victor. Mother Purdy's has excelled herself again."

Folding the rest of his quiche into its wrapping paper, Priest dropped it in a bin. He sat back in his chair, finishing the wine in his glass.

"I shall enjoy dinner this evening all the better for not having eaten that."

Ackroyd looked embarrassed:

"Appalling. I don't know what this country's coming to. How is the acquisition of those Kafka papers coming along?"

"I fly to Berlin next weekend."

"I wish you luck."

"It's not a matter of luck, Van. It's a matter of waiting, watching and pouncing. I imagine that was how you found the Abbé."

Ackroyd laughed

"No. It was pure luck, Victor. I came out of *La Grille* in the rue Mabillon, turned up past Saint Sulpice and there was the Abbé's face on a book cover, ogling me from a window."

He got up and took a small plate of cheese from a refrigerator, placing it together with some crackers on a corner of the table. Priest leaned forward:

"What do you think of the idea that some unconscious urge directed your feet into the rue Saint Sulpice?"

"Victor. You know me. I have an excellent astrologer."

"Do you believe what she tells you?"

Ackroyd laughed.

"You're out of date. It isn't a matter of an old woman with big ear rings telling you a beautiful stranger will cross your path. It's always a matter of psychological conjunctions. Also, my astrologer is a man."

Ackroyd examined his friend's face with a look of amusement.

"Something's bothering you, Victor, I can tell. Have you done any writing lately?"

Priest leaned back in his chair, contemplated Ackroyd for a moment, then withdrew a folded page from his breast pocket, announced the title of a sonnet, 'A Rococco Jump', and proceeded to read it aloud. His friend sat in silence for a moment, drank some wine, and then said:

"None of your illustrious contemporaries could match that."

"I know."

"Do I detect a hint of emotional entanglement?"

"No."

"Come, Victor. I remember those poems you wrote to Renate. This has the same force."

"That was a long time ago."

Ackroyd reached out for the poem, indicating that he wanted to read it, but Priest folded the sheet and slipped it back into his breast pocket.

"Do you remember the broadsheet we brought out because they wouldn't publish your poems in the school magazine?"

"I prefer to forget."

Van, with his mouth full of cheese, continued:

"That launch reading we had? You were really crazy about that girl. I can see you now, reading your poems, aiming them at her in the front row. My God, she was a beauty! And you didn't understand why the audience was laughing. The more they laughed, the more passionate you got."

"I said I don't need to be reminded, Van."

"When you turned round and saw those two football players behind you, strip-teasing down to their jockstraps...! The look on your face!"

Ackroyd slapped his knee and roared with laughter. Priest got to his feet and walked over to gather up his motorcycle gear.

"Why are you bringing up this detritus from the past?"

"Don't take it so seriously."

"I do take things seriously, Van. That's the difference between us. I must be going. Thank you for the hairy quiche."

"I'm sorry, Victor.There's another bottle of wine in the fridge. Wouldn't you like to ...?"

The book dealer followed Priest, who had stopped halfway through the shop to put on his motor cycle gear.

"Things to do this afternoon, Van. I shouldn't drink any more anyway. Are you going to give me that book?"

Ackroyd went back into his office and came back with a plastic bag. He handed it to Priest.

"I'm afraid I got the better of the deal," he said. "Your mask is worth a lot more than the book."

"Oh? What's the book worth then?"

"Three hundred, maybe. It's the British edition. Now if he'd *signed* it..."

Priest nodded and headed for the door. Ackroyd called after him:

"Make sure you call on the Muse! Keep those creative juices flowing!"

*   *   *

Early in the afternoon, the doorbell rang, and Vesna Diver opened her front door, not expecting to find Victor Priest in a biker's suit. She took a step back, and bright Spring sunlight illuminated her white trouser suit, yellow blouse, and filigree necklace.

"Victor!"

"I thought I'd drop by."

She ushered him into the hall, where he divested himself of his leathers. She took in the faded blue denims, white T-shirt, and elegant sports jacket he was wearing, and led the way into the drawing room.

"Would you like to try some more of that slivovica?"

"Thank you. I had some wine for lunch and I'm riding the bike, but I'm sure that'll be a zestful *digestif*."

She handed him a crystal thimble, and poured herself a glass.

"Do you have anything to tell me?"

Priest sat down.

"I do. You've heard about Alex Duthie, I suppose?"

"Yes, of course. It's on the radio. In the papers. He was on the Sicily trip with Fergus."

"Murdered by his own gate," said Priest.

"Another sick joke."

"Yes."

"When is this going to stop? I've had a call from the poet Horace Venables. He was an old friend of my husband's. I've never heard him talk in such a manner. He was on the edge of hysteria. He is sure he is about to be murdered."

"What makes him think that?"

There was a message on his answering machine in Spanish and he thought it might be an invitation to a festival. He got someone to translate it for him, but it wasn't. I wrote it down for you. Look: *'Death comes knocking with a ring that has no stone on it and is on no finger.'*

She handed him a scrap of torn off envelope.

"The original is underneath. I don't know any Spanish but Horace spelt it out for me."

Priest studied the paper.

"It's Pablo Neruda. The Chilean poet. *La muerte llega a golpear con un anillo sin piedras y sin dedo.*"

"From a poem?"

"Yes."

"Is Horace right to be worried?"

"I don't know. It could be yet another joke."

"Jokerman?"

Priest drank a little more *slivovica.*

"They found a puppet in Barnaby Brown's cabin with its strings cut. Should that make us laugh? Of course Brown might have planned his own disappearance. People do."

"Is that likely?"

"It's not a question of likely or unlikely. It's a question of motive. Why engineer your own disappearance?"

"Perhaps if you knew a murderer was pursuing you...? Fear?"

"My own publisher asked me this morning if *I* wasn't afraid of being murdered."

"Are you a poet as well?"

"I am."

He drained the crystal thimble, looked at Vesna Diver, who was sitting with her legs tucked up on the sofa opposite him, then pulled out the folded sheet bearing his poem and handed it across. She opened it and read it. Priest watched her as she laid the paper to one side.

"I'll have to read that again when I have more time to think about it."

He rose, walked over to the parrot's cage and drew his fingernails along the bars and the parrot regarded him, put her head on one side, ruffled her neck feathers and said: "*Klinge klinge kleines Frühlingslied!*"

"A diligent pupil!"

"I wish you could unteach her. She's been saying that all week."

He turned back to look at Vesna.

"Were you able to reassure Horace Venables?"

"Nothing I could say could calm him."

"Your husband, Brown and Duthie were all on an Italian trip together. Venables was not of that party was he?"

"No."

"His new book is a great success, apparently."

"*Stray*, you mean? My husband helped him with that sequence. He went through the manuscript in detail and then Horace came down for the weekend and they spent the whole time talking about it. Then Fergus phoned Horace up one evening and told him the book had been taken on by Dolan & Swainson."

"Your husband arranged that?"

"Yes. Didn't you notice it's dedicated to Fergus?"

"As a matter of fact, I did."

Priest turned his attention from the parrot and walked over to the window, staring out. After a moment, he said:

"The reason I came was to tell you that I believe I have found a buyer for your husband's papers who will be prepared to offer far more than the British Library or that university in Atlanta, but I don't want to disclose who it is at the moment."

"That's wonderful news."

"Whenever you're ready someone will come out to assess the material."

"I'm very grateful for what you're doing, Victor. And I know you'll find out who murdered Fergus."

"I suppose I should go," he said.

She stood in the sunlight, watching him from the porch as he donned a black crash helmet and pulled down the visor. The engine of the big machine crackled and he rode away up the street into the afternoon brightness.

*   *   *

The *Krazy Tee Kozy* was and is just off the A26 near Tonbridge. Victor Priest made a wide-circling entrance onto the wide forecourt of the café on his Harley Davidson. The scattered groups of bikers watched his arrival and one or two walked over to admire the machine. He stood chatting for a while, removing his helmet, and locking the bike. Then he began to walk towards other groups of bikers who were standing around their machines. One or two greeted him. They were old acquaintances. The conversation was of cylinders, valves, clutches, and torque.

For half an hour or so, he moved from one group to another, chatting and commenting on the bikes on display, and then entered the café itself.

A woman in a white overall behind the counter was splashing out mugs of tea from a big metal teapot.

"Tea, darling?"

"I'll have a mineral water, if you don't mind."

He paid, taking the plastic bottle and the styrofoam cup, and crossed the big dining area to a table near the window that was just being vacated. The café was full. The face of a suited newsreader mouthed silently from a big television screen on the wall. Priest sat down and put the plastic bag Ackroyd had given him next to the bottle of water. Through the window he had chosen to sit close to, he could see the activity outside. He opened the bag and drew out a copy of *Birds, Beasts and Flowers* by DH Lawrence. It was an impeccable copy of the first edition of the book, complete with dust wrapper, published by Martin Secker. Inside, someone had written *For Sylvia, with love B*. Underneath the writer had added *London, October 1923*.

Who might B have been? Who Sylvia?

He read again poems he knew very well. The spell of the first edition he held in his hands brought him closer to the author.

You tell me I am wrong.

Who are you, who is anybody to tell me I am wrong?

Someone concluded the telling of a joke and two men and two women sitting nearby began to laugh with abandon. They would go quiet for a moment, look at each other, and then burst out laughing again.

He smiled across at them; the waves of mirth were coming his way. He thought of Jokerman and drank his water. Jokerman was an illusion. It was an apparatus, and once you had constructed an apparatus, you were more or less committed to making it work. Priest focussed his mind on Venables, summoning up a picture of the man he had seen give readings at one or two festivals – a rather eager-to-please, insignificant sort of man. He pondered. Supposing he were to alert Joe Biggs to the threat Venables had received? But Biggs could hardly mount a round the clock bodyguard watch; he would have no idea how to go about such a thing.

A waitress in a black dress, wearing a frilly white coronet in her hair, slapped down a tray of food.

"Bangers and mash, darlin?"

"Absolutely not."

"Oh. Sorry, love."

She picked up the tray and wandered off looking for her customer.

He returned to the book:

Ours is the universe of the unfolded rose,

The explicit

The candid revelation.

Drowning the babble and repartee in the café, the volume on the TV set was turned up. The second half of a football match between Tottenham Hotspur and Manchester City was just beginning. A City player dribbled through the Spurs defence and scored a goal at the same moment as the Spurs goalkeeper barged him, and he went down. The commentator's jabbering voice rose to a hysterical pitch. The fallen player was shown in close up. He could not get up; his knee was twisted. Men in track suits carrying a stretcher ran onto the pitch. There were shouts from the customers in the café. The player was pounding the turf with his fists.

The match restarted, and Priest leaned back in his chair. He took out his notebook and sat watching it. Every now and then, pricked by something the commentator said, or by some surprising remark from a member of the crowd in the café, he jotted down a quick phrase. The game headed towards a draw, but in the final minute, a Tottenham player rounded three defenders and cracked a shot home that nearly burst the net. The final whistle went. Tottenham Hotspur 4, Manchester City 3.

The sound on the TV set was turned off. The commentator and a few football pundits began a long, silent inquest on the game. People got to their feet and gathered their belongings.

From outside, came the explosive roar of large motorbike engines kickstarting into life. Bikers and their pillion passengers were starting to leave. Priest looked down at the Lawrence book, which lay open on the table:

When the skies are going to fall, fall they will
In a great chute and rush of débâcle downwards.

Chapter 13: *The Celtic River*

Damian Krapp got off the 205 bus at *The Angel*, at the beginning of City Road, and was almost knocked down by a dreadlocked child on a push-scooter. Was a near-miss a good omen before entering a cemetery? He'd had another telephone call that morning from the Welshman, Robert Rees, who had asked Krapp to meet him at 4pm at William Blake's grave. In the past, Krapp wouldn't have thought twice about ignoring such a cranky invitation, but two days previously *The Boot*'s solicitors had informed him by mail that a wealthy patron named Robert Rees wished to make a substantial donation to the magazine provided that Damian would agree to meet the said Robert Rees and agree to certain conditions. This had been followed up by today's phone call. Krapp had tried to find out what the meeting would entail but Rees would say nothing until they had met. After putting the receiver down Krapp had realised he didn't know where Blake's grave was. Rees's number had not appeared in the display on his telephone, so it was not possible to call back. Calling Eric Lemmon, into the office, Krapp asked him to look on the internet. It turned out the poet was buried in Bunhill Fields, near *The Angel*.

The sky was grey and there was a penetrating drizzle which his broken-winged umbrella was directing into his collar. Why had he left the warmth of his office? Money? The possible salvation of *The Boot?* The magazine had enough funds to see them through the Spring and Summer issues; after that there would not be enough money to pay the rent on the premises, let alone the printer. Subscriptions, despite all his best efforts, had not moved up since he had taken over the editorship. At least they had not gone down. He was not prepared to have the magazine become, as the jargon had it, 'user friendly'. He did not believe in encouraging the writing of poetry in people who would be better off learning to play an instrument or doing yoga. In his opinion poets were made by the severity of the obstacles that were placed in their path. Indeed, Krapp was proud of his own role as an obstacle. He was a scrupulous editor.

At the same time, he loved the magazine and was desperate to save it. If the Welshman was serious this offer could be the solution to the magazine's problems – but what would Krapp have to offer in return? And why couldn't the man have come to Tavistock Square instead of this ridiculous pilgrimage to the grave of a barmy poet? Krapp detested the oracular strain in poetry and Blake, he thought, was responsible for a lot of it.

He found Bunhill Fields and trudged across gravel, dodging pools of water, until he came to a small headstone. *Here lie the remains of the poet and painter William Blake,* it read. *Born 1757, died 1827.* Bloody hippy, thought Krapp. Give him Wordsworth any day. And where was this man Rees?

"Did I keep you waiting?"

Krapp spun round and found himself confronted by a red-bearded man in an oilskin coat and a sou'wester. He looked like a North Sea trawlerman.

"Rotten day isn't it?"

"What's the point of meeting here, Mr Rees? We could have met in my office."

"But how would I have known there wasn't someone listening in another room?"

"This is all very conspiratorial."

"What's conspiratorial about meeting at the grave of England's most celestially-inspired poet? Did you know that on the afternoon of his death Blake burst out singing due to the joy of the things he saw in heaven? I'm sure he is poet-in-residence up there."

Damian Krapp swallowed.

"Do you think we could go to a pub, perhaps? Somewhere dry?"

"*The Angel*?" said Rees. "It would be appropriate."

"I don't care what it's called. I just want to get out of this rain."

They walked back up City Road in rain augmented by wind strong enough to blow Krapp's umbrella inside out, breaking another rib in the process. He flung the useless thing into a litter bin attached to a lamppost. His wet hair became slicked back to his skull, and his woollen coat was not even shower proof. By the time they reached *The Angel* he was soaked and shivering.

The pub was almost empty, it being early evening. They found a quiet corner and Damian spent some time taking off his coat, shaking it with vigour, and dabbing at his face and neck with a handkerchief.

"You look to me as if you need a drink, Mr Krapp."

"I'll have a vodka. A *Grey Goose* if they have it. Make it a double."

When Rees returned with the drink and a sparkling mineral water he placed them on the table, then took off his wet oilskins, which he dumped on the floor. He sat down opposite Krapp.

"You're in luck. Not only do they have your brand of vodka, they also have quite a range of mineral waters."

"Is that good?"

"For those who do not touch alcohol, yes."

"I see. Can we get down to business, Mr Rees? I had a letter from my solicitors informing me of your conditional offer. What kind of money are we talking about and what are these conditions of yours?"

"I'm prepared to fund *The Boot* for two years – let's say to a tune of £200,000. The whole sum will be paid onto a deposit account to be administered by your solicitors who will disburse the money in regular instalments."

Krapp took a drink.

"What do I have to do for this?"

"Very little. You can edit the magazine as you have been doing, but I want the next issue to carry a special feature, say 20 pages, on a poet I particularly admire whose light is under a bushel. This will include a representative selection of poems and an introductory essay. I will be responsible for the entire contents of this feature. All remaining editorial decisions will be yours."

As he listened to Rees's voice, Krapp noticed something about its pitch and intonation. It seemed fluting and over-emphatic somehow, as if the man was acting a part.

"Who is this poet?"

"You won't know the name, and you won't find out until you receive the material."

"So this person has never published in *The Boot*?"

"No."

Damian reflected. Was Rees trying to make him the laughing stock of literary London? What if this poet of his was embarrassingly awful? Would it be another of these second-hand William Blakes? Was that why he'd been brought to the grave? The thought occurred to him that it might be Rees himself who wanted to get published. If so, it was a lot of money for vanity publishing - but it *was* a lot of money.

"Are we speaking about your own work, Mr Rees? Is this the special feature you have in mind?"

The Welshman's face was serious:

"I will disclose nothing at this stage. You may rest assured that I value this poet highly. The work is exceptional."

"That's what you say."

"I do say."

"Whoever it is, you do realise, Mr Rees, that this is not an easy decision for me to take. Let us suppose that your favoured poet is, in my opinion, without literary merit – then all my other editorial decisions are discredited."

"My protégé is an angel of the poetic line. Would you like another drink?"

Krapp took out his handkerchief again and mopped at the rainwater that was still trickling down his face from his hair.

"I'll have another of these."

Rees disappeared to the bar, returning with another double *Grey Goose* and a cup of tea.

"What do you do for a living, Mr Rees? Where does this money come from?"

"I am the director of a company called *Storm,* based in Aberystwyth. We manufacture oil-proof clothing and other protective garments. We export all over the world. Quite a Welsh success story."

Rees gave a huge smile.

"And where does your interest in the arts come from?"

"Do fish swim? I'm Welsh."

Damian stared:

"Are the Welsh all so passionate about the arts that they will give out large sums of money to support it?"

"If all of them had the money, they would. The Celtic river runs deep, Mr Krapp. Its song is in our blood."

Krapp regarded the long face and flowing red beard of his would-be benefactor. The man had startlingly clear eyes. So the song was in his blood, was it? A man of acumen? A successful entrepreneur? Or something else entirely? He finished his drink.

"You say you are prepared to fund the magazine for two years. Am I to expect regular contributions from this poetic angel of yours?"

"I'm not prepared to say at this stage. Let us say that there will be occasional...er...input."

"What you appear to want to do is take over the magazine. Why don't you start your own?"

"No, no. I have neither the time nor the inclination. Damian, the attraction of publication in *The Boot* is that it is a long-established periodical with a committed readership. That is what I value. Nor must you regard this as a take-over. My own editorial interventions will be modest."

Krapp moved his empty glass about on the table. It was 'Damian' now, was it? He forced himself to come to a decision.

"Very well, then, Mr Rees, I agree – with some trepidation, I must admit."

"Excellent!"

The Welshman took a folded document from his inside pocket and spread it out on the table.

"I have a contract here for us both to sign. It's just a formality. I hope you have no objection? I will then see to it that the first instalment is paid immediately."

Krapp read through the single sheet swiftly. It contained nothing different to what had already been discussed. There were two copies and both men put their signatures on each.

"Thank you, Mr Krapp. A very successful outcome to our negotiation."

Rees stood up and pocketed his copy of the contract with a flourish.

"The pleasure is mine," said Krapp.

He watched Rees put on his oilskins and walk out into the rain with a brief salute of farewell. Christ, what had he done?

Krapp went to the bar and ordered another vodka. The bleeping of the gambling machine caught his attention and he went over and fed in his small change, winning nothing.

He sat down again. The hands of the pub clock – it was obviously broken – read high noon. When he was back in the office, he'd have to trawl the internet and see what he could find out about Storm Protective Clothing.

* * *

Carrying his soaked coat, which was too damp to put on, Krapp boarded a 205 bus back into town. He threw the coat onto the seat beside him, and struggled to reclaim his mobile phone from a drenched inner pocket. He wiped the instrument dry on his pullover and called Eric Lemmon to find out if Melinda Speling had arrived

"She's not here yet, but you have another visitor."

"Who?"

"Manfred is here."

"Is he? Oh. Tell him not to wait if he's in a hurry."

"Doesn't look as if he is, Damian."

Krapp had really wanted to have a chat with Melinda alone. There weren't many poets he really liked as human beings, however much he admired their poetry. Melinda was an exception. He'd so much looked forward to sitting beside her, watching her read the review of her new book *The Crystal Frog* in the latest issue of *The Boot*. It was a very warm review – not a common occurrence in his magazine – and he, as editor, wanted to bask in her pleasure. He peered out through the rainstreaked bus windows at pavements full of colliding umbrellas. What a day! With Manfred von Zitzewitz leering at them, Damian and Melinda's cosy intimacy would not be allowed to happen. Furthermore, Manfred and Melinda would not get on, he was sure of that.

He got off the bus and stepped into a puddle, but he was past caring. He crossed the road and went up the narrow staircase and into the office to find von Zitzewitz in the editorial chair, with his boots on the desk, flicking through the issue that had come in from the printer that morning. Without greeting von Zitzewitz, Krapp spread his coat over a radiator to dry, took off his pullover and laid that next to the coat, then removed his shoes and crimson socks and put the socks next to the pullover. His wet things began to steam slightly.

"What kind of poetry is this, Damian?" said von Zitzewitz. "Here, let me quote:

> *It is no night to flap your wings in,*
> *the bells you steer by are toneless as the deep.*

Is this a monologue by a bat? Why do you subject the reading public to this kind of stuff?"

Damian ignored von Zitzewitz and went out of the office and

into the small washroom off the landing. He towelled his face and hair and dried his feet, then combed his hair, ran the towel around the inside of his collar and re-knotted his red tie. Somewhere or other he had a spare pair of socks. He went back into the office, lifted von Zitzewitz's legs clear of the desk, opened a drawer and found the dark blue socks he kept for formal occasions.

"Do I get an answer to my question?"

"You'll be meeting the author shortly, Manfred. Why don't you ask her? Or, on second thoughts, maybe you'd better not."

"She's coming here? Am I sure I want to meet her?"

"Suit yourself. We have a rendezvous."

"Oh, a *rendezvous*, Damian? Is that what it takes to get into your magazine?"

Eric Lemmon put his head round the door.

"Melinda's here, Damian. She's coming up."

Von Zitzewitz got to his feet as a slender woman with frizzy auburn hair, wearing a light plastic raincoat and towing a trolley suitcase, entered the room. Von Zitzewitz's characteristic expression of frowning disapproval changed on seeing her to one of surprise and admiration.

"Hello, Damian!"

"Melinda, darling!"

Krapp went over and embraced her, kissing her warmly on both cheeks. He turned to von Zitzewitz and introduced them. She shook Manfred's hand with gusto.

"I'm so glad to meet you. I've always thought your reviews were the most perceptive and honest of all!"

"Ach!" said von Zitzewitz, who had been unprepared for such effusiveness.

"There's so much back-scratching goes on today. Nobody is prepared to say what they really think. Sometimes you wonder if they *do* think."

"Ach!" said von Zitzewitz again. "Thank you. Such warm words. I wanted to review your latest, but Damian said no."

Too bloody right, thought Krapp. If you had done, she'd have got a very different review. Hoping that von Zitzewitz had other plans for the afternoon, he suggested that in view of the rain they should repair to *The Slug and Lettuce*, which was very close by. This suggestion did not produce the required refusal from von Zitzewitz however, who announced he would be delighted to spend time drinking with Melinda Speling – what better way to pass an unconscionable afternoon? Damian reflected that he needed, as Ron was always telling him, to learn how to tell people to fuck off. He was good at saying no to poetry submissions, why was he so limp in the social sphere? Von Zitzewitz swept up her bag and led the way downstairs. Damian shook his head and followed, his hand resting on Melinda's shoulder. It was only a few yards to the pub, and they ran through the rain and found a seat inside, near a window. Damian and Melinda sat opposite one another and she appraised him, smiling.

"You look good as ever, Damian."

"I got very wet this afternoon," he said. "I think the rain got through to my bones."

"Oh? Does your office leak?"

"Don't be silly, Melinda. I went to meet someone and they wanted to meet in a park."

"I'll have a *Becks*," said von Zitzewitz.

Krapp went to the bar, irritated at the man's gall. Was it a particularly German custom never to be the first to buy a round? Melinda had ordered a *Flame of the South*, and as he stood at the bar watching the ritual of the cocktail being shaken, he heard her clear voice saying:

"I suppose everyone is talking about these awful happenings. Fergus and Alex dead, presumed murdered. It's unbelievable. Did you know them, Manfred? But I do know that Barnaby Brown is alright. No one can kill Barnaby. Did you ever meet him? He's so vital. Like his poetry."

"Ah, his poetry..." said von Zitzewitz.

The barman gave Krapp his change, and the editor navigated the drinks back to the table as fast as he could before Manfred had time to embark on one of his long, critical demolition jobs.

"You really think Barnaby is alive?" asked Damian. "Are you suggesting he's gone into hiding, or something? He couldn't have thought anyone was out to kill him, could he? Why would he want to vanish like that?"

"I don't know Damian!"

"You do believe he's alive, then?"

"I know he is."

"How do you know?"

"I just know."

Krapp shrugged and drank the bitter lemon he had ordered. He had a distinct feeling that a cold was coming on.

"Crisps, Damian!" said von Zitzewitz. "Salt and vinegar. Could you get a packet?"

Krapp hesitated, looked at von Zitzewitz, stood up again and returned to the bar. He drummed his fingers on the bar top while waiting for the barman to notice him, feeling like an errand boy, and listened with mounting annoyance to Melinda extolling the haiku, confessing her own inability to produce anything meaningful with the form, and lauding the work of von Zitzewitz as being truly *exceptional*. Krapp threw down some coins for a packet of crisps and returned with them, tossing them on the table. Manfred tore open the packet and offered them round. If there was one thing Damian disliked it was crisps. He turned to Melinda:

"What's this trip you're undertaking? "

"I'm flying to Bratislava on Monday, Damian."

Von Zitzewitz interjected:

"Oh, you're going to Slovakia, Miss Speling? You seem to go everywhere. Didn't I read in the papers that you were in Sicily with Fergus Diver and Alex Duthie?"

"Yes. *And* Barnaby. Not surprising is it that David didn't want me to go on this trip? After Bratislava I have to go to Prague, Leipzig and Berlin."

Von Zitzewitz pursued his enquiries:

"David?"

"That's my husband."

"Are you not fearful? This maniac appears to select his victims in transit."

Damian reached across the table and held her hands.

"Who says it's a man, Manfred?"

Melinda smiled at Damian, withdrew a hand and stirred her cocktail with the little flag that was stuck into a cherry.

"I have to go," she said. "They didn't give me an option."

"Is it the British Council?" asked Damian. "Are they holding you to your contract?"

Melinda nodded.

"What about enemies?" asked von Zitzewitz. "Did you make enemies while you were in Italy?"

"Of course not. Other people make enemies, not me. It was all wonderful. I just don't understand it."

"Did you all get on?"

"Of course."

"I heard about how well some of you got on," said Damian.

He regretted having said this, as he saw tears form in Melinda's eyes. He stroked her arm.

"Sorry. That was tactless of me. I'm sure you'll have a good time."

Melinda wiped her eyes with a handkerchief, prodding a slice of peach with her beflagged cocktail stick. Damian brought the new issue of *The Boot* out of his bag and handed it to her.

"The latest issue for you."

"Thank you."

"Your poem is in there."

"I know."

"As a matter of fact," said von Zitzewitz, "I was reading it by chance in the office just now..."

Before he could launch into a critical discussion of the poem, Damian used his editorial skills to guide the discussion along different channels. They talked about the candidates for the new Ern Malley prize, which earned Manfred's scorn, and about a new radio programme which was going to be serious, and would allow poets to read their own poems and not have them read by incompetent actors. A discussion would follow the readings. Manfred, who was scheduled to appear on one of the early shows, lauded the fact that breadth and scope were to replace the sound bite.

"I'm sorry Manfred," interrupted Melinda, "it's been wonderful to meet you, but I must be going. I promised to spend the weekend with my sister in Hertford, I'll be coming back on Monday to catch the plane to Bratislava, then Prague, then Leipzig, then Berlin. I must be mad to take this kind of trip on."

She slipped her copy of *The Boot* into a side pocket of her trolley bag and stood up.

"When you're in Berlin, don't miss out on seeing Norman Foster's dome on the top of the Reichstag," said von Zitzewitz. "A glass dome over the political process. It's very apt, I feel. Just what we in the poetry world need. A glass dome so everyone can look in."

Melinda gave both men a rueful smile, then stooped and pecked Damian on the cheek. They watched as her trim figure hurried off.

"A rather special woman," said von Zitzewitz.

"I know."

"Was it completely ethical, Damian, to get her lover to review her book?"

"Who told you he was her lover?"

"Jemima Lee."

"They weren't lovers to my knowledge when I commissioned the review. They may not even have known each other at that stage. It's your round, Manfred."

"Is that bitter lemon you're drinking? Very wise."

Von Zitzewitz harvested Damian's glass, preparatory to going to the bar. Then something struck him, and he leaned towards the editor:

"It occurs to me that only two of the people who were on a reading trip to Italy are still alive. Should they not be concentrating on staying out of harm's way?"

Damian frowned.

"That's a not nice, Manfred. Really. Not nice at all."

Von Zitzewitz rose and strolled towards the bar.

Chapter 14: *The Wellest Dude*

Horace Venables stood gesticulating at the counter of Hampstead police station. The woman constable was very patient with him.

"How can you be sure this is a death threat, sir?"

"Haven't you been reading the newspapers? Poets are being murdered up and down the country? Some of your colleagues must be investigating this. I'm a poet, and I'm next."

"How can you be so certain, sir?"

"Look, look, this message was left on my answerphone. It's in Spanish, but this is the translation. See!"

He pushed forward a piece of paper on which he had transcribed: '*Death comes knocking with a ring that has no stone on it and is on no finger.*'

"Yes, I see. Why do you think it is a death threat?"

"Isn't it obvious. Death is going to come knocking for *me*!"

"Yes sir. It's not actually, er, obvious, sir, if I may say so. I can understand your anxiety, sir, with these homicides going on. Give me your details and I will contact the investigating officer who will get in touch with you."

"But I need protection now!"

"I assure you, sir, we'll send someone round as soon as we can."

She smiled and Venables, feeling rejected, scurried out into Rosslyn Hill. What was the point of trying to explain? If you couldn't see it now, you never would.

It was still raining, although it had eased up in the time he'd been in the station. Then he noticed the street had been blocked by police cars with their blue lights flashing, and an ambulance, and two policemen were putting red and white tape across the road. He saw in the gutter a crushed motorcycle helmet and a pool of blood. Immediately he felt a mounting panic begin to overwhelm him. He couldn't breathe. His heart accelerated. He felt he was falling from a dizzying height; he felt he was dying. He looked around for someone to help him but everybody was focussed on the scene of the accident. He had to get to hospital, and luckily the Royal Free Hospital was just down the hill. He tried to go one way but his legs took him the other. Concentrate, he told himself. Get to a doctor. You know the way. Hurry.

Finally, he staggered in through the glass doors of Casualty and went straight to the nurse at the desk.

"I'm having a heart attack."

"Do you have chest pains?"

"Yes, yes. Do something quickly."

"Sit over there and I'll call a doctor."

He tried to sit down but was immediately on his feet again, holding his chest. He paced around, aware of people staring at him. A young man in a green shift came over to take his name and address but Venables could hardly give the information. Then a doctor in a white coat arrived, a stethoscope hanging from his neck.

"If you come into this cubicle, Mr Venables, I'll examine you."

The doctor listened to his heart and took his blood pressure, then shook his head.

"You're not having a heart attack, Mr Venables. It's a panic attack. I realise it must feel like a heart attack but I assure you it isn't. You'll be all right."

"Really? Really? But I feel so..."

"I can assure you there is absolutely nothing wrong with your heart. There is no arhythmia and your pulse is strong."

"Thank God. Thank you doctor. Thank you."

"Is there anything particularly worrying you? Was there something that happened to trigger this?"

"Blood on the street, doctor. I've just walked by the scene of an accident."

The doctor gave Venables a soothing look of understanding.

"And I've received a death threat."

"A threat? Have you told the police?"

"I've just come from there."

"What did they say? Have they taken your details?"

"Of course they've taken my details. What use is that? My details won't save me."

"I mean are they investigating?"

"Investigating? What is there to investigate? Someone wants to kill me!"

He looked at the doctor with a 'please-save-me' expression.

"Couldn't you keep me in, doctor? Admit me as a patient. Find a bed for me!"

"I'm terribly sorry, Mr Venables, but we are very short of beds. We can't admit people who've had death threats. That's a job for the police."

"They have no sense of urgency, doctor. It could happen tonight."

"What is your occupation, Mr Venables?"

"I'm a poet."

The doctor folded the stethoscope and slipped it into a pocket. "Oh, I see."

"I'm not making this up, doctor."

"No, of course not, but I'm sure you'll be all right. I'm sorry, I have other patients to see to. Rest on one of those chairs out there for at least half an hour, before going home. Try and breathe deeply and slowly. I'll have the nurse bring you a prescription for some herbal sleeping pills. And make sure you take it easy tonight."

"Take it easy? How?"

The doctor gave him an apologetic look and left the cubicle. Venables walked back into the waiting room and sat down. He'd wait for the pills. He was safe here. Nothing could happen with all these people around. It annoyed him though that they all seemed to be staring at him. In particular, a grey-haired black orderly was staring and smiling at him. Venables felt angry. Stop smiling and staring, he thought. Or stare and smile at someone else. Suddenly the man walked over and sat down beside him.

"Man, I'se been watching you. You'se the wellest dude I'se ever seen in this place."

"What?" said Venables.

He got up and walked out into the damp air of Pond Street, then straight to his flat, whose proximity to the hospital had been grounds for his moving there in the first place. At least it had stopped raining. As he reached the steps that led down to the basement, he noticed a small car parked just outside with two large black dogs barking at him from behind the windows. No wonder they were annoyed, he thought, being shut up in a small space like that. Some people shouldn't have pets.

He hurried down the stairs to the basement and was glad to hear the miaowing that always greeted his return.

"Calm down, Emily. I'm back."

Unlocking the door he went in and picked up his old, blind cat, holding her to his chest and stroking her till she purred and he began to calm down. Thank God he had Emily. Originally she had belonged to his wife, but Alison could hardly have taken her to Australia. Anyway, that bastard Chubb hated cats. How could Alison have fallen for a man who felt like that?

He put Emily down and gave her the rest of the tin of sardines he'd had for lunch. She bumped into the table leg on her way to the saucer, but eventually got there, with a steering hand from Venables.

"Not bad, this brand, is it, Emily? Has anybody phoned while I've been out?"

He went into the sitting room and saw there was indeed a winking red light on the phone, and two messages showing. He pressed the button, anxiously. The first was from the publicist at Dolan & Swainson, asking if he'd be free for a reading the following month. The second contained the sound of an open line for a minute, with no words spoken, and then the click as the connection was broken. Oh, my God, what was that? He sat down on the settee. First Fergus, then Brown, and now Duthie. But he didn't belong in their company, did he? Fergus and Duthie had both been confrontational and outspoken. They had written harsh reviews. They had not concealed their contempt for what they considered poor work, and had of course made enemies as a consequence. As for Barnaby Brown...His flamboyant readings and popularity, especially with women, had naturally excited jealousy. Rumour had it that he'd had affairs with quite a few of his female followers, some of them married, and there would be betrayed husbands somewhere in the offing. But what had he, Horace Venables, done to provoke possible assassination? He had led and was still leading a decent orderly life. He had been terribly injured by his wife's leaving him, but he had recovered to write his best poems ever, and had been taken up by Dolan & Swainson into the bargain. Who could possibly begrudge him that?

Vesna Diver had said very kind things to him on the phone the previous day, after he'd had that horrible Spanish message translated. She'd tried to tell him it meant nothing, but he knew it was a warning; someone wanted to kill him. Later on she'd phoned him back with the information that it was from a poem by Neruda. Why Neruda? He'd never met the man, and he'd certainly never been to Chile. It was all very unsettling. Vesna had suggested he come and stay, till he felt better, but he had declined. Fergus had been his best friend; it would have been too painful to be in Fergus's home without him.

Emily came clumsily into the room, seeking Venables out, found his shoe and jumped up onto his lap. He stroked her ears.

If only Alison were here. She would have known what to do. But she was gone forever. And the invitation to Australia had seemed to be the start of such a promising upturn in his career. Alison had been so pleased for him. He had been terribly nervous before going. The day before his flight, he had eaten a kipper for breakfast, and a bone had stuck in his throat. With Casualty just across the road, he thought it would be a simple matter to have the bone extricated, but it had turned out to be a more than usually busy day at the hospital, and he had waited eight hours before being seen. And then the doctor had told him the bone had dissolved. Alison was highly amused.

"Typical, Horace," she'd said.

He'd so wanted her to come with him, but in the event it had all gone very well. The invitation was to the Adelaide Festival Writers' Week. His reading had been attended by an unbelievable crowd of 700 people, and afterwards – ah, if only he could go back! – he'd signed copies of his books for an hour and ten minutes. Then he met his nemesis. Bruce Chubb had come up to him and said: 'My Australian writer friends were telling me you were good, Mr Venables, and now I've heard you read I know they're right.' A big man, tanned and smiley, his thick arms bulging from a T-shirt with the message *Save Antarctica* on it, and that friendly directness Venables now knew was a mask for treachery and deceit. They'd exchanged addresses and Chubb had phoned up before a visit to London, asking if he could stay a few days. A few days that had lasted three weeks. Three weeks of that suntanned, athletic, joke-telling bastard in a drizzly London November. No wonder Alison had been captivated. Returning to his home in Pond Street unexpectedly early one afternoon, Venables had entered the flat, and assuming no one was in, he'd gone upstairs to have a nap. He had opened the bedroom door and there they were. Venables nearly cried at the memory. He had closed the door and left the flat.

This was eleven years ago and it still hurt. With Alison's leaving everything started going wrong. The only woman he'd had a relationship with subsequently had turned out to be mentally disturbed.

They'd been having a few slight arguments, and one day he opened his wardrobe to discover his suits had been neatly razored down the seams – he tried to put one on and it fell into heaps of fabric on the floor. The worst thing that had happened was that he'd dried up – eight years, the longest and most painful interregnum of writer's block he'd ever known. Towards the end of it he was taking down his old books from the shelf and looking at the poems in them disbelievingly – had he really written them? He'd felt sure he'd never write again. Then one day he'd almost sliced off the top of his thumb, so it was merely attached by a hinge of skin, and he'd rushed over to the hospital, holding his wound in a bloody dishtowel. They'd put a temporary dressing on it, and while he was waiting to have it stitched, a nurse came by selling raffle tickets to fund a new oncology wing. The prize was a week on an Adriatic island. He'd bought ten tickets, and won.

The island was called Brač. Arriving by ferry and installing himself in a small and cheerful hotel, he'd picked up a detailed map of the island from the Tourist Information Office and begun to explore the interior. He'd wandered through olive groves, forests of Aleppo pine, and vineyards, with vistas to the blue Adriatic wherever he looked. On his first day a stray dog had attached itself to him. Wherever he went on that island the dog was with him. When he sat in the harbour bar in Bol, drinking the fine local white wine, the dog lay at the foot of his table. When he strolled along the pier eyeing the young women who walked by, arm in arm, the dog ran after them and barked, making them laugh. When he took the bus up the mountain to begin a long ramble, he had to buy a ticket for the dog as well. When the ferry left from Supetar to take him back to the mainland, leaving the mongrel on the jetty, whining, he knew he had to write about it all. This was the beginning of the poems that would eventually make up *Stray*.

As soon as he'd returned he had tentatively shown his notebooks to Fergus who, delighted that his friend was writing again, had warmly encouraged him. Then Fergus had helped him shape the sequence and had brought him to Dolan & Swainson. Was he going to follow Fergus into the grave? Perhaps it would have been safer to have stayed blocked.

He got up and went to the answerphone, listening again to the message in Spanish. It had to have come from the person who was committing these murders. And it meant Venables was next, didn't it?

But what kind of murderer was it that went around quoting lines from famous dead poets? Poetry and murder were opposites. They had nothing to do with one another. What was going on?

Emily had gone to sleep on the settee. She slept a lot now, poor old thing. Sitting down next to her, stroking her somewhat patchy fur, he decided that, despite everything, he needed to take his daily walk over Hampstead Heath. Abandoning one's routine meant giving way to the forces of evil. He'd wrap up warm. Maybe a pint or two in *The Flask* on the way home would also help.

He put on his duffel coat and went out. The dogs were still in the car. Their owner was a criminal and ought to be reported, he thought, as he set off down the street in the direction of Hampstead Heath. It had turned cold and blustery and he pulled his hood up over his ears. He walked down to the station and turned left up the hill onto the Heath. He made for Hampstead Ponds. Two boys, about 15 years of age, were standing by one of the ponds as he passed, the taller holding a tabby cat, stroking its ears and neck. The other boy was laughing. What a curious thing to do, thought Venables, taking your cat for a walk. He stopped as the boy held the animal up by the scruff of the neck and hurled it towards the centre of the pond. With a piercing screech it flew through the air, a kicking ball of fur, and fell into the dark, cold water with a plop. Venables was appalled. What a terrible thing to do to a cat!

A voice inside told him to remonstrate with the boys but they were hulking youths so he thought better of it and hurried onward through a small wood, the yowl of the cat still in his ears. What was it in human beings that made them torture animals? He was guilty, too, was he not? Had it not been an act of cruelty to have discarded the stray he had adopted on the island? It lived on, though, in the poems he hoped would make his name. Did that make amends for his desertion? Probably not.

It looked like rain again, but not just yet. There were very few people about. He always took the same route across the Heath, going in the direction of Parliament Hill. He liked to stand up high with a view over London, watching the kites. It gave him a sense of perspective. Since he'd found his muse again, the lines of a poem would sometimes come to him as he stood there. It had been the right thing to do, to come out like this, he was already feeling better.

It had been the right decision to live close to Hampstead
Heath. Without Alison's legacy, of course, they wouldn't have been
able to afford it. And since then, prices had gone through the roof.
After they'd first moved there, from a semi-detached in Osterley right
under the flight path into Heathrow, he'd published a whole collection
of poems about the Heath, its environs, villages and little communities.
Hatless in Hampstead he'd called it. It had been translated into Japanese. What on earth would the Japanese have made of it?

He climbed Parliament Hill and stood at the summit, gulp-
ing deep draughts of London air. Wordsworth's line 'Earth hath not
anything to show more fair' came to him – except, of course, it had
been written about an inferior London spectacle. Far below, he saw
a tall woman braced against two dogs that were heaving at a leash.
The woman looked as if she were having difficulty controlling them.
He laughed. Stupid dog owners. He never tired of enumerating their
faults. All human laziness, folly and self-regard was encapsulated in
the quirks and quiddities of dog owners; you only had to observe them
to see. Now feeling extremely cheerful, he turned and descended the
hill, walking back in the direction of Hampstead and the pub. He could
already taste that first gulp of *Winter Warmer*.

Near the bottom of the hill, where the Heath ran parallel to the
road, was a children's play area with a notice that adults unaccompa-
nied by children were not permitted to enter. There were no children
or adults about, and going through the play area was a short cut that
Venables often took. He went through the little gate and stopped by
the skeleton of an ancient Fordson tractor that had been placed there
for children to play on. Community helpers had painted it in bright
colours, but the paint had not deterred the rust.

A movement slightly higher up the hill attracted his attention.
Venables opened his mouth. It was the woman he had seen earlier. She
was bending down, unclipping the leash. Two large black dogs hurtled
downwards toward him. Why were they running in his direction? He
was amazed to see them leap the fence in unison and come straight for
him. He was too astonished to move. One of them buried its fangs in
Venables' leg. He roared out in pain and tried to run but the other dog
leapt for his arm, unbalanced him, and he fell over onto his back. Immediately, the two dogs went for his neck and face. His last sensations
were the stink of dog breath and the excruciating pain of dog teeth

tearing his flesh.

Chapter 15: *Cats*

Joe Biggs hopped naked from the daybed and crossed the room to the telephone. He picked up the instrument, looking back at the mop of tousled red hair on the pillow and, hoping she wouldn't wake and say something in a loud voice, he said:

"Joe Biggs. *Artcrimes.*"

"Good morning, Joe. I'm sorry to wake you so early. I thought by phone would be the best way to do it. You wouldn't have wanted me to arrive in the office, would you?"

As if Priest had actually entered, Joe looked around the room.

"Oh. Yeah. I mean no. Sorry, guv. I…"

"Never apologise, never explain, Joe. I don't expect you'll have read the papers this morning? The poet Horace Venables was torn to pieces by some singularly vicious rottweilers on Hampstead Heath yesterday afternoon. Apparently the dogs belonged to a woman. A passerby witnessed the attack. "

"Blimey!"

"Blimey indeed. Perhaps you could get over to the crime scene and sniff around. See if there's anything to be seen."

"'Course, guv."

"Check the papers online to find out where exactly the assault took place. You have my mobile number. I've had to change my plans today, and at the weekend I'm flying to Berlin, so mind the office for me, will you Joe?"

"Yeah, guv, but…"

"She seems a very unusual girl. My congratulations. Enjoy."

The phone clicked off. Biggs rubbed his unshaven chin. Unusual girl? How the hell did Priest know she was there? There had to be a webcam somewhere. How much had he seen? It had been quite a night. Frank had told him Scots women were fierce but Joe hadn't believed it. As for the piercings and the outrageous jewellery - he'd christened her Naily. No, she said, my name is Janet Dunbar. You're Naily, he'd said. Got nails sticking out all over you. Then there'd been more rumpus.

He stalked around the office looking for a camera. Where the hell was it? Maybe there was more than one? His employer had sounded amused; there'd been no reproach in his voice. A *very* unusual girl. Yeah.

Biggs went into the kitchen and plugged in the kettle. He'd been a bit worried about bringing her back to Priest's office. They'd had such a good chat on the train. Fed up she couldn't find a job in Glasgow, angry at her parents, she'd decided to try her luck in London. It turned out she didn't really know where she was going to stay. She had someone she vaguely knew in Dagenham, but it was pretty late when they got in, and suddenly he'd found himself offering Priest's daybed. They'd had a few more drinks, talked a lot, and one thing had led to another. He'd rung his mum to say Priest had wanted him to stay in the office to keep an eye on it. Well, he had kept an eye on it.

He went over, put the palm of his hand on her spiky hair, and pressed down gently.

"Wanna cuppa tea?"

She blinked and sat up, shrugging off the bed clothes, yawning and stretching. He watched the bird tattooed on her left breast move with her. Her skin was perfectly white.

"Aye. Whit time is it?"

"Half nine."

"Oh Jesus. When's yir boss due?"

"He knows, Naily. He's got a webcam or something in here."

"Oh Jesus."

Biggs went back to the kitchen, found a teapot and made some tea.

"Milk and sugar?"

"Aye."

He carried the cups back and passed one to Naily, who was now sitting up in her bra and panties, swinging her legs on the side of the daybed.

"Wi had the lights oot. He couldnae seen much."

"What about this morning? The blinds were up."

"Will he fire ye?"

"Didn't sound like it. He's off to Berlin so he won't be around for a bit. I gotta do a job for him. Investigate something. You wanna come?"

"Investigate whit?"

"Another poet's been murdered. I gotta go take a look at the scene of the crime."

She held the cup with both hands, sipped at the hot drink and giggled.

"Aye. Ah'll come wi' ye."

Joe switched on the computer and checked through the online editions of the newspapers. There were full reports of the attack on Venables, with photographs and white arrows showing the location of the murdered poet at the time of the assault, the children's play area, the position of the only witness, and a dotted line to show the direction the woman had apparently taken after the attack, her dogs back on a leash.

Showered and dressed, Joe and Naily climbed on to the Lambretta and rode in the direction of Hampstead. Naily, who had never in her life been south of the Scots border, wanted to know if they could go via Buckingham Palace, but had to content herself with glimpses of Russell Square, Euston Station, and Camden Town.

They came to a stop near the murder site. The police had erected yellow signs calling for possible witnesses. There were quite a few people milling about, but nothing to see. The area of the children's playground had been marked out of bounds by police tape and the only people inside the area were a fat man in a trench coat, and two uniformed officers. The fat man was gesticulating and talking and the two officers were inspecting an ancient tractor in rainbow colours.

Joe and Naily walked to the edge of the play area and joined the line of people looking across the barrier of red and white tape.

"Nothing much doing here, Naily. They said this guy was a resident of Hampstead. Wonder where he lived?"

"Horace lived in Pond Street," said a middle aged woman beside them. "He was a poet, you know. Another one gone. What do people have against poets?"

"Did you know him, ma'am?"

"Of course I knew him. He was my neighbour. The thing is, who will look after Emily? I tried to get in there this morning but the officer at the door was extremely rude."

"Is his wife ill then?"

"Emily is Horace's cat. She'll be terrified with all those policemen tramping in and out."

"Do you know the address, ma'am?"

"Number four Pond Street. Are you with the newspapers

young man, or with the television?"

"We're investigators," said Joe. "Private, like. You know."

"I'm sure I don't. But if you can catch the monster that did this you have my blessings."

They located Pond Street without difficulty. A uniformed policeman was standing on the pavement outside Venables' address. Joe considered the terrain and explained what they were going to do. At first, Naily wanted no part of the plan, but Joe embraced her, whispered to her, and tickled the inside of her ear with his tongue.

"Yir mad, Joe Biggs."

They walked along the row of shops near the railway station and found a large cardboard carton outside a grocery store. In a side street, they located a ginger cat sitting on a house wall. Naily stroked it, then grabbed it by the scruff of the neck and dropped it in the carton.

"One more for luck," said Joe.

But there were no more cats to be seen. They returned to Pond Street, Naily carrying the carton. Joe approached the policeman outside Horace Venables' house.

"This number four?"

"Yes."

"Venables?"

"Yes."

"From the RSPCA. We gotta pick up a cat."

The policeman peered into the cardboard container. The ginger cat looked up at him. He looked at Naily.

"You got some ID?"

Joe clapped his brow.

"Walked miles to find this place. ID's in the van. It's back there up the hill."

"'N this cat's heavy," added Naily.

"Well. I don't know..."

The policeman fingered the walkie talkie that was attached to his lapel.

"We just wanna pick up this geezer's cat," said Joe. "Straight in and straight out."

"Yeah? There *is* a cat in there. Real ancient moggy. Probably needs feeding."

The officer went to the front door, took out a key and opened it.

"I have to stay here. Cat was last seen downstairs. Leave the front door open."

They went inside, discovering the stairs that led down to a large kitchen and sitting area. Venables' cat was asleep on the settee, but lifted its head as they came in. Naily sat down beside it.

"Joe! The puir old thing is blind."

"Well, we gotta take it with us now."

"Aye, she's Emily awright! Hir name's on hir wee collar.'.."

"See if you can find something for her to eat. I'm gonna have a quick look round."

He went in to what had to be Venables' work room. It was lined with poetry books, and the desk, which was equipped with an old typewriter, was piled high with notebooks, manuscripts, and scribbled drafts. He walked back into the kitchen where Naily was trying to persuade the cat to get off the settee and eat some *Whiskas*. The ginger cat in the cardboard box could smell the food and was miaowing.

"She can't see, Naily."

"She kin smell, can't she?"

Emily had pricked up her ears at the sound of the other cat. She got up, felt for the edge of the settee with a paw, slithered onto the ground and padded across to the food bowl. Joe picked up the yellow piece of paper the cat had been sitting on.

"Look at this," he said, examining it. "Telephone message!"

He went across to the telephone, pressed the answerphone button, and heard a male voice speaking in Spanish. The voice held no inflection or expression and the brief message it gave seemed, as a result, to contain considerable menace. Joe disconnected the little answerphone and dropped it into his pocket.

"Mr Priest will be interested in this, Naily. Let's go!"

"She's eatin'!"

"Well put her in the box with the other cat. Put the food in as well. That copper is going to be suspicious if we hang around here."

Naily picked up Emily and deposited her in the box. The two cats looked at each other. Joe picked up the bowl of cat food and placed it between them. They began to eat.

"Great. Let's go."

They nodded to the policeman on the door, showing him

the two cats in the carton, and walked down the street and round the corner. They returned the ginger cat to its wall and it miaowed, flicked its tail in the air and disappeared under a privet hedge. Joe was all for releasing Emily into the wilds of Hampstead Heath but Naily was shocked by his callousness.

"Wuid ye feed the puir creature to the foxes? That's cruil, Joe. Reelly cruil. Wi'll hae to take her wi' us."

"What'll the guvnor say?"

"Ah dinna care."

With the cardboard box perched between them, they rode back to Lambs Conduit Street. In the Artcrimes office, Joe sat and contemplated the message Horace Venables had received before his death.

"Weird. Someone talked in Spanish on the phone, and someone else wrote it down and wrote a translation underneath."

"Whit's it say, Joe?"

"Something about death not having a finger."

He remembered having seen a book by Venables somewhere. On a shelf above the desk in the little office, he found a copy of a volume entitled *Stray* and stood near the window reading it. He mused on a coincidence of dogs – in the book, at the death. Against some of the poems, in the top right corner of the page, were neat little pencil marks.

"Funny how Mr Priest gives little ticks to all the poems. I guess three ticks means he likes it a lot, two less so, and no ticks means...well, I dunno what it means."

"No ticks is whit you get at schuil."

"I better ring the guvnor. Tell him about this answerphone we nicked."

Joe dialled Priest's number and related the story of the RSPCA inspectors.

"You got an office cat now guvnor."

"So long as it doesn't moult over the furniture, Joe."

Biggs described the strange telephone message he had found, but Priest seemed to know all about it.

"I took the answerphone, guv. Thought we could do a voice analysis."

"Very good, Joe! How shall we do that?"

"Dunno, guv. Thought you'd know."

Priest laughed.

"We haven't got a voice to compare it with. Or have we?"

"Guess not, guv."

"What other lines of investigation shall we pursue, Joe?"

"Not sure guv. What about this Manfred von Wossname geezer? We ain't talked to him yet."

"Good thought. See if you can find out where he lives. I'll be in touch."

Priest hung up, and Joe looked at Naily

"He knew about the telephone message. How did he know that?"

She shrugged. Biggs got up and began to search again for webcams. Where the hell were they? Was the guvnor a voyeur, or was it just the normal kind of security you'd expect of a man who investigated art crimes?

Returning to the main office, he saw that Naily had stripped and was lying naked on the bed.

"C'mon, we'll gie him somethin to watch," she said.

Chapter 16: *The Dart of Love*

Melinda Speling's sister Alice lived some distance outside Hertford, in the countryside. Her difficult husband was absent and the sisters went for long walks. They talked a great deal about Alice's marriage, and not so much about Melinda's. They explored solutions to Alice's problems, philosophised, made each other laugh. Not once did they turn on the TV or look at a newspaper. Alice Speling seemed immune to the lure of news media; her animals and her garden occupied all her thinking time. Melinda allowed herself to surrender to pastoral pursuits.

But on a grey, wet, windy Monday morning, sitting on the train into Central London, she found herself brooding again on the homicidal maniac who was decimating Britain's poets. Normally she would have been buoyed up at the start of a journey. She loved travelling. She and David had conferred for a long time, however, about whether this time she should go or not. Then the news had come through of Alex being murdered in that bizarre fashion. She had phoned up the nice man at the British Council and told him she was pulling out of the tour. The nice man stopped being nice and told her it was too late for that now: the venues were booked, the publicity was out, the editorial contacts had been arranged, the university lecture confirmed.

Not long after that, David had wandered into her room bearing a letter. Although the address had been typed, and the postmark was London, it didn't look official. She opened it and read half a page of typescript that had been signed with his characteristic flourish: Barnaby Brown. She read it through, dazed, not quite understanding. Then she had looked again at the date and the date on the postmark. He was alive! She read it again. It was quite simple. Someone had tried to kill him, but he had had a lucky escape. He knew now who it was that was trying to kill them, and why. He would explain everything and they would meet in Berlin. He knew she would be thinking about pulling out of the tour, but she should go ahead with it. He was staying at a hotel in London under a different name. Their adversary was extremely dangerous; they should not meet until she was safely abroad. She should carry on as if nothing had happened. On no account was she to go to the police, there were reasons for this which he would explain. He would be in touch.

She thought for a moment, then handed the letter to David. It wasn't a love letter, of course, but it made Barnaby's feelings for her clear. Dear David. He understood her as no one else did. It wasn't that he encouraged her relationships with other men; their union could in no way be described as an open marriage. In fact, they were devoted to one another. They had met during Freshers' Week at university, and remained inseparable throughout the three years of study. David had written all her essays for her. Their fellow students considered them as good as married; shortly after finals they had allowed people's opinion of them to become fact.

After graduation, and the registry office wedding, they had played together in an end of term dramsoc production of *As You Like It*. She had played Rosalind and he had played Jacques. Then they had flown to Mallorca. On a balcony overlooking the Mediterranean, David had made a confession.

He did not really enjoy sex. He considered it an interruption. It was true they had had a sex life of sorts over the previous three years, but...He had gazed out over the moonlit water...It had been an effort. Well, if the stories of Melinda's friends were any comparison to go by, she had already understood that. It hadn't bothered her. He was gentle, comforting and solid. She could not imagine a life without his support. He had looked at her with his long, lugubrious face, and quoted Jacques: *I can suck melancholy out of a song as a weasel sucks eggs.*

Since that time, she had felt justified in taking advantage of any non-threatening sexual opportunities as came her way, and had always confided her brief flings to David. Sometimes the flings turned into more prolonged romances, but her husband had never failed to be there for her when heartbreak struck, as it always did. She had never contemplated leaving him. Barnaby was a bit different. He was not married and saw no reason why they should not be more together. She had chosen to go to Iceland rather than be with him on the course in Suffolk because she had wanted to test her own independence. Or rather, the strength of her bond with her husband. It had not been easy.

David frowned at the letter for a long time before putting it down.

"I think it's a matter for the police, despite what he says."

"But what shall I tell them?"

"Show them this."

She had argued with him. Barnaby's letter contained a suggestion that by going to the police she would make matters worse. Barnaby knew what this was all about; they did not. She would have to meet him, talk to him. She had to understand what was going on.

David had laid his hands flat on the table and stood up.

"I'll get back to my trains, then. Saturday service. *'Tis but an hour ago since it was nine, and after one more 'twill be eleven.*"

David had a quotation for every situation. He touched the peak of his railwayman's cap in an ironic salute and went back to his shed. She sat on in the kitchen, looking at the clock, and remembered more of Jacques' speech: *and so from hour to hour we ripe and ripe, and then from hour to hour, we rot and rot, and thereby hangs a tale.*

Perhaps she should have stayed in Shanklin. It was safe there. Nothing ever happened on the Isle of Wight. How could it? There was nothing *to* happen.

Once in town, she put up her umbrella, made a brief call on her publisher near the British Museum to collect a few extra copies of her book, and then bumped her little trolley suitcase towards the Piccadilly Line. At Holborn Station a blind busker was playing 'Blue Skies' and she dropped a twenty pence coin into his cap. Maybe it would bring her luck.

She began the long descent on the escalators, staring moodily at the partly undressed women advertising lingerie. When the train came in it was half empty, and she boarded and found a seat. The train did not depart immediately however but remained humming at the platform with its doors open. She looked at her watch, hoping there would be no hold up. You could never be sure that the London Underground wasn't going to fall apart. After five minutes of waiting, she began to wonder if she shouldn't change her plan and go to Paddington to get the Heathrow Express. Then the doors closed and they were moving. She settled back in relief.

At the airport she fought her way through the crowds, and was furious to be held up at security when the X-ray machine detected her nail scissors inside her toilet bag. She'd meant to take the scissors out, but forgot. She pleaded with the security man, explaining they were a gift from her husband. The man was implacable. 'No sharps,' he said. Her scissors joined a heap of confiscated weapons of mass destruction. Then she was through all the checks and into the waiting area.

She went to *Le Sandwich*, bought an egg mayonnaise roll and had just found a place to sit down when she saw on the screen that her flight was boarding. Leaving behind at least half of the tasteless roll, she trudged off to find Gate 51. A sign told her it would take 10 – 15 minutes to get there, so she quickened her pace a little. After a short delay at the gate, she boarded the plane and found her seat. Before putting her bag in the overhead locker, she thought to extract the new issue of *The Boot*. Then she waited while two chubby boys about ten years old moved out to let her in to her window seat. They were identical twins and she had always found something creepy about the idea of twins, let alone a pair who looked exactly like Tweedledum and Tweedledee, but the mother, who was sitting across the aisle, declined Melinda's offer to swap seats. She shrugged and began to strap herself in. As the plane took off, she opened *The Boot* at the contents page, looked for her own poem, and was extremely surprised to read, under 'Review Section': 'Barnaby Brown is moved to admire *Transparency* by Melinda Speling'.

Why hadn't Damian told her? She'd had the magazine all weekend and had not even opened it. Barnaby was the last person she would have expected to find reviewing the book. He'd never said a word to her about it. It was his usual elegant, concise writing and it captured the essence of her poetry with complete understanding. She stopped after the first paragraph, feeling slightly breathless and murmured his name to herself like a mantra. She read on: *'Transparency' is delightfully agile. Speling's themes are the old ones – love, creativity, spirituality – treated as if for the first time, and all permeated with a delicate earthiness.* The last sentence brought tears to her eyes: *If I lose this book I will buy another.* She stared out the window at the clouds.

"Are you crying, miss?"

The twins were staring at her.

"No," she said. "I have a slight cold."

"I think you're sad, miss," said the same twin, the one nearest her.

She said nothing, and tried to read some of the other contributions to the magazine, but couldn't concentrate. The drinks trolley arrived and she chose a tomato juice. The food trolley came but she didn't want anything. The cloud cover below the plane disappeared and she looked out of the window at the towns and fields of Europe far below. Then she became aware that the twins were trying to grab each other's sandwich, giggling at first and then punching each other in the arm in a kind of ritual until the mother intervened. After that, they sat silently chewing, until one of them said with his mouth full:

"We're sad too, miss."

"Oh? Why?"

We had a peacock and it died. The neighbour poisoned it."

"What a horrible neighbour! Why would anyone do that?"

"They don't like us, miss."

She drained her glass of tomato juice, glancing across at the twins' mother who took no notice of this exchange. What would it be like to live next door to these two? They had funny little turned up noses and squeaky voices. She closed her eyes and tried to sleep, but could not shut out an argument that had started up between them about who could run fastest. The litany of 'I can run faster than you', 'No I can run faster than you' sent her into a half-doze that ended as she felt the plane bump down on landing.

Her escort from the British Council, whom she knew slightly, was waiting for her at Bratislava airport.

"Is it alright if we start for town right away? We can talk about the reading in the car."

To her surprise, the British Council man had actually read her book, and made good comments as they sped towards the city. She began to feel better about what lay ahead and, because her escort kept insisting how much he had liked the piece, she started the reading with her favourite poem from the new collection.

The Crystal Frog

From the open door of the tomb
whose dark chandeliers
lit the shroud of cobwebs,
I waltzed out into the air.

Where the skiffs jostled,
where the planks groaned like old men dying,
where the stars fished for fireflies,
I saw the crystal frog.

One hop and it was gone,
leaving a silver chain behind
with which I pierced my labia
and wear, now, when it rains.

Drizzle, my friend, bring it back,
that small amphibian of light.
Jump, little creature, into my shoes
and we'll be one, I promise.

This got polite applause from an audience that consisted of
a dozen or so male members of the Slovakian Writers' Union, and a
sprinkling of employees of the British Council, mostly female. Melinda wondered how much English the Slovak writers understood. She
sat down while an actress in a slinky nightclub dress read the translation in a voice deepened by years of smoking. Melinda sipped water
and watched the reactions of the members of the Writers' Union. They
were smiling and seemed to be suppressing laughter. She got up and
launched into her next poem. There were no further untoward reactions
from the audience until she reached her final piece, a poem called 'The
Green Hammock'. The translation of the poem was read out by the
actress with somewhat grotesque facial contortions and, in Melinda's
opinion, unnecessary emphasis. A number of the Slovaks present
laughed heartily, earning looks of disapproval from the employees of
the British Council.

Walking her to the chosen restaurant after the reading, her
escort explained that the British Council had been badly advised on
the choice of translator. He tried to reassure her that her reading had
been excellent, but Melinda did not enjoy the meal and had difficulty
sustaining a level of interest in the conversation. She was glad to get
back to her hotel room, and called David.

"How did the reading go?"

"The audience thought my poems were funny."

"Never mind, the one in Prague will be better. What's Bratislava like?"

"I haven't seen much of it. I don't think I really want to."

"It'll all go off well. It always does," he said. "Have you heard
anything from Barnaby?"

"No."

"He'll be in touch. I'm sure you can rely on him."

She put down the phone, unconsoled by this remark, and slept badly. A tiring train journey to Prague the next day took four hours and the reading was not a great success either. She performed adequately, but she was already deciding she didn't much like Eastern Europeans. A couple at the back of the room would obviously have preferred to have been in bed with each other. And an elderly woman in the front row who had bulging, old-fashioned lenses on her spectacles had brought a dog to the reading. It was a very well behaved dog, but Melinda became aware, as people moved away from the creature and its owner, that it was flatulent. It didn't help that her lady escort from the British Council, who was also sitting in the front row, kept broadcasting shock-horror looks at Melinda and holding her nose. At least the translations did not cause any mirth amongst the audience, but they were read in a dead voice by a very thin man with a slight speech impediment.

The next day, she gave a lecture on English contemporary poetry to a packed room of Czech students of English. Their questions afterwards were hostile; they preferred American poetry to English, which they obviously considered effete. Had she ever read Bukowski? Yes, she had, but she couldn't write like that if she tried. She did not add: nor would she want to.

Reaching Leipzig, she was met at the station by a British Council driver holding up a card with her name mis-spelt. He spoke good English and she forgave his understandable error. Entering the hotel lobby, she went to the desk for her room key and was handed a long cream envelope, postmarked Berlin. She parked her trolley suitcase by one of the foyer armchairs, sank into it, stared at the type-written address. A Turkish woman was vacuuming the white carpet. Ignoring the din, she opened the envelope and took out a sheet of paper that had been folded into the shape of a paper dart. She smoothed it out and read the message. It was from Barnaby. A few typed lines and his inimitable signature.

> *A ghrá,*
> *A little dart of love for you. All is well. They do not know that*
> *I survived, but there is no knowing how or where they will*

strike, so I do implore you to be careful. Stay close to your
British Council minders, and don't go sight-seeing unless
you have to. We'll meet in Berlin. I'll let you know a time and
place.
All my love, Barnaby

She knew what *a ghrá* meant – my love. But who on earth
were *they?* Why were *they* doing this? What had she done to merit the
attentions of madmen? She glanced around the lobby, wondering if the
young man lolling against a pillar was, perhaps, carrying a knife? Or
a pistol? Would he perhaps, clap a chloroformed pad over her mouth
as she stood waiting for the lift, drag her into the elevator and throttle
her between floors four and five? And what about the desk clerk, who
kept shooting glances at her across the lobby? Had he already sent a
message to accomplices outside who would be waiting the moment she
stepped into the street? Was it time to go to the police? Barnaby had
been insistent that this would be a bad move. Why? Anyway, she spoke
no German. They would think she was mad. Her contact person from
the British Council would be arriving soon. Perhaps she should try and
say something about all this? Then again, maybe the British Council
was implicated? Stranger things had happened.

Holding the envelope, and towing her trolley, she went
upstairs to her room, unpacked, and waited for her minder to arrive.
When he came, the deputy director of the British Council in Leipzig
turned out to be an amiable, pipe-smoking man and Melinda liked him;
he inspired trust. She would be doing the reading in an unusual round
room with extremely good acoustics, and the deputy director was
confident of a decent sized audience. He had been considerate enough
to provide her with a bottle of the local Meissner wine, and after two
glasses she felt much better. He was right about the audience and right
about the acoustics. She decided to read again the poem 'The Green
Hammock' which, after its reception in Bratislava, she had omitted from her programme in Prague, and she began to put it over with
verve.

As she reached the final lines, she became aware of a new
member of the audience sitting at the back, a man with red hair and a
red beard. He looked very like that Welshman in Taormina. What was
he doing here? She had reached the lines

I can hear time everywhere, like a woodworm,
and I want to be stoned like a plum

and fumbled them, needing three tries to get it right, forcing herself to look down at the book and not at the audience. When she had finished, she risked a glance at the back and saw he was still sitting there. Same beard, same eyebrows, same hair. She resolved to speak to him the minute the reading was over. It would remove all her ridiculous fears if it turned out the man spoke with a German accent. As she was introducing her last poem, however, she saw him get up and slip out the door. Afterwards she asked the deputy director if he knew the man who'd arrived late and left early.

"Not one of our regulars, Melinda. Will you have some more wine?"

She wanted to tell him the whole story, but an enthusiastic audience, carrying copies of books to be signed, surrounded her, and the deputy director withdrew, obviously pleased at the success of the reading. She forced herself to chat with admirers, fended off embarrassing questions from a portly professor, and finally, when she was safely delivered back to the hotel, telephoned David.

"You remember that man I told you about? The Welshman? When we were in Sicily?"

"The one who quarrelled with you?"

"He didn't quarrel with me. He quarrelled with Alex and Barnaby. Anyway, he's here."

"Where?"

"Here! Don't be so dense, David. He was at the reading, I'm sure of it. Red hair and red beard."

"Can't be the same person. Lots of people have red hair. You're imagining things."

"You think so?"

"I think so. Have you heard from Barnaby?"

"Yes. We're going to meet in Berlin."

"Thank God for that. You'll be alright. No need to worry. No need to worry at all."

By the time she reached Berlin, the weather had brightened up considerably. It was a sunny day, and at the British Council, they were very attentive. They had set up a meeting with two German publishers who were interested in translating some essays she had published a few years ago, and the afternoon passed, with coffee and cakes, in agreeable discussion, though she was unable to interest them in translating her poems. After they had gone, a woman called Cornelia Kranz offered to show her some of the sights, but Melinda, mindful of Barnaby's warning, didn't relish this idea. All she wanted to do, though she didn't say this, was hide in her hotel room and wait for her lover to make contact. Cornelia seemed disappointed. On no account should Melinda fail to visit the Reichstag, she said. The spectacular glass cupola that had been created by one of Britain's most brilliant architects just had to be seen. Cornelia could guarantee that they would not have to queue. She knew a way to get round it. Melinda was not to be tempted – even though Manfred von Zitzewitz had also strongly recommended she see it.

She took a taxi from the British Council offices to her hotel, asked for her room key and was given a cream envelope. She sat on the side of her bed and read the short message.

I promised to say when and where. Let's meet in the cupola of the Reichstag at four tomorrow afternoon. Barnaby

So she would go to the Reichstag after all. Of course. A very clever idea. She had been told how tight the security was; what could happen in such a crowded place? Melinda rang the Council offices and asked to speak to Cornelia, saying she had reconsidered her kind offer. They made an arrangement to meet outside the hotel entrance the following day at two o clock. She ordered some food from room service, and found that the choice of English language channels on the television was either news or pornography. She turned the machine off and lay on the bed, trying to read *The Boot*, and failing. She had to admit to herself that she was feeling lonely. And depressed. She looked in her handbag for Barnaby's previous letter and re-read it. The paper still bore the creases of its original shape, and she folded it back into a dart and flew it round the room. It flew very well. She retrieved it and flew it again. It glided across her strewn-about things, and went though the door of the bathroom, landing in the bath.

Another of Barnaby's accomplishments she knew nothing

about.

It was still sunny the following day, and the representative
of the British Council in Berlin came early and took her to an Italian restaurant for lunch. He dropped her back at the hotel as Cornelia
arrived, and the two women took a taxi to the Reichstag. Walking
towards the building, Melinda read the inscription above the entrance:
Dem Deutschen Volk. What did that mean? Cornelia explained: To The
German People. The building had an aura, no doubt about that.

Her guide had a special visitor's pass so they bypassed the
tourists and walked straight to the front. Waiting for the glass doors to
open that would admit them to the security checks, Melinda turned to
look back at the long line of people, and saw a woman with two children standing a little way back in the queue. They saw her and waved.
It was the twins from the plane. Then the door opened and they were
going through the checks and taking the lift to the base level of the
cupola.

As they walked up the sloping spiral ramp to the top, Melinda
took Cornelia's arm and held her tight. Her guide looked at her with a
smile of puzzlement. The space under the cupola was warm, the sunlight on the glass dazzling, but Melinda was shivering.

"Is anything the matter?"

"No, no. I just saw something...."

"What do you think of it?"

"It's stunning."

But she wasn't really taking it in. She was scrutinising the
other people moving about, looking for someone with Barnaby's height
and hair. Would he have changed his appearance as a precaution? It
was a very beautiful building - a masterpiece of glass and mirrors.
They walked up to a central area just under the roof of the dome, with
a large flat-topped steel structure in the middle supporting a circular
bench on which two elderly women were sitting. A small party of
Australian tourists was beginning to descend the downward ramp and a
tall, blonde woman leaning on a long walking stick stood by the curved
glass staring out at the brightness. Nobody seemed remotely familiar.

"The architect's idea," said Cornelia, "was to make democracy transparent. If you look down from here you can see right into the
parliament chamber."

"What?"

"It is our history. We can no longer have people deciding what to do with us in secret. You see? This cupola is the perfect symbol. Absolute transparency."

Melinda stared into Cornelia's face. Transparency? Oh God. She had to get out of here, and fast. Once again she took Cornelia's arm and as she did so felt a sharp stinging pain in the back of her neck. What was it – a bee sting? What were bees doing under this glass dome? She felt behind her neck, drew out a tiny feathered dart and looked at it in bewilderment. What was going on?

"Cornelia..." she said.

Cornelia's lips were moving, but Melinda heard nothing. She tried to take a breath but her lungs were collapsing. She knew everything that was happening to her and could say nothing. She looked at the concerned faces gathering around her and tried to broadcast her pain out through her eyes. Just read what is in my eyes, she thought. Now I am in hell. The bright sun in the sky over Berlin came down through the glass and enveloped her.

Chapter 17: *Old School*

In the breakfast room at the Hotel Adlon, Victor Priest gave his attention to the newspapers he had ordered, a copy of the Berlin *Tagesspiegel* and the *Frankfurter Allgemeine Zeitung*. On the cover of the *Tagesspiegel* were a portrait of Melinda Speling, and a stock photograph of the cupola on the Reichstag. Priest read the report and turned to the *FAZ*. News of the British poet's murder had been squeezed into a column on the right hand side, and there was a different picture of Mrs Speling and a photograph of a jowly man from Scotland Yard.

Priest took his smartphone from his pocket and switched it on. Through the internet connection he could see the Artcrimes office on his display. Two heads, side by side, were fast asleep on the daybed. Priest drank some of his green tea, and dialled the London number.

"Good morning, Joe."

"Morning, guv. What time is it?"

"An hour later than where you are."

"Yeah?"

"I am in Berlin where it is half past seven am. I wanted to let you know that there has been another poetry death. The newspapers are reporting that Melinda Speling collapsed and died yesterday afternoon at about four pm in the Reichstag."

"Heart attack?"

"Unnatural causes, I fear."

"Well, you're in the right place, guv."

"That's true. However it looks as though Scotland Yard is here in all its pomp and majesty. And I have business afoot that precludes intimacy with the *Bundespolizei*."

"Sorry?"

"What I'm doing is not quite legal, Joe. I shall not be consorting with the flatfeet."

"Shall I come to Berlin?"

"There are important things for you to do at home. You mentioned there were two women together with Duthie and Brown in Italy. Let us assume Melinda Speling was one. Who was the other? I take it you have not yet interviewed Manfred von Zitzewitz?"

"No."

"I am very curious to know why he came to Diver's reading."

"OK, guv."

Priest slipped the phone back in his pocket and sat brooding for a moment. His reverie was interrupted by the waiter, who returned with a beam of accomplishment on his face to serve up a pair of commendably improvised kippers. Priest acknowledged their arrival with a furrowed smile and turned his attention to fish.

*　　*　　*

At five minutes before noon, he walked through the stone gateway to the Soviet War Memorial in Treptower Park, looking up and reading the words that appeared in both Russian and German: *The Homeland Will Not Forget its Fallen Heroes*. He passed down a wide alley of trees and turned right into a broad avenue that led up to two gigantic kneeling figures, one on either side. He observed the bronze hammers and sickles mounted on the stone bases, but his gaze was drawn to the colossal statue of a Russian soldier on the far side of the memorial, almost two hundred metres away. It held a sword in one hand and clutched a child in the other.

Moving a pair of compact binoculars from left to right, he traversed the open space in front of him. At the foot of the statue of the Russian soldier stood a tiny figure, holding an attaché case. The only other figures moving through the landscape were an old man with a walking stick, and a woman who held his arm. Priest let the glasses move back and forth, making sure no one else was in sight. The figure at the base of the statue had to be Eddie Stollberger, the man Priest had come to Berlin to meet.

An old friend had been responsible for setting up the meeting. He was worth the retainer Priest had paid over the last fifteen years. The friend's unrivalled knowledge of the treasures that corrupt officials had secreted away had come in handy more than once. But this latest prize threatened to put all those previous discoveries in the shade. If it were true that Eddie Stollberger had a cache of hitherto unknown Kafka manuscripts, it would have been worth walking to Berlin to get them.

Priest went down the steps and walked the rectangular length of the mass grave of Russian infantrymen who had died taking Berlin in 1945. To his right was a series of carved tableaux depicting vignettes of battles – marching troops, terrified women clutching babies, firing squads – all the dismal panoply of war. Priest kept his eye on the figure under the statue, who had begun to make his way down the steps towards him. The man had been observing Priest's progress across the almost deserted memorial. The sunny weather of the previous day had vanished. Grey clouds and a touch of mist had rolled in. Only a few crows were hopping to and fro.

The man drew close and Priest was confronted by a gaunt, elderly individual with grey hair, glasses, and a beaky nose. He was wearing a Russian style winter jacket with a high fur collar.

"*Herr Priest?*"

"*Sie sind Eddie Stollberger?*"

"*Das bin ich.*"

They continued speaking in German. Stollberger asked to see Priest's passport, opened it at the photograph page, contemplated this for a moment, and then looked back at the Englishman.

"You speak excellent German Herr Priest. Where did you learn it?"

"I went to school in Hamburg."

Stollberger handed Priest back the passport.

"May I also see your air ticket?"

Priest nodded, took the ticket from his inside pocket and handed it to the German. An opera programme fell on the ground, and Priest bent to pick it up.

"You like the opera, Herr Priest?"

"I saw a good production of *Fidelio* last night at the Staatsoper."

"Ah yes, it was always a favourite there in the old days."

Stollberger glanced at the air ticket then handed it back. Priest put the air ticket and the programme together and put them away. Turning up the collar of his coat, he said:

"I am anxious to know what you have in your briefcase. Shall we go and discuss this out of the cold wind somewhere?"

"There is a Gasthaus quite close."

Stollberger added in strongly-accented English: *I have murder hunger!*

Priest smiled at the German idiom. He wouldn't eat much because he was looking forward that evening to a leisurely dinner at the Paris Bar near the Bahnhof Zoo and keeping a lookout for which-ever celebrities might also be dining. Nor did he think the area looked promising as far as restaurants were concerned.

The two men walked back to *Am Treptower Park* and stood waiting for the traffic to let up so they could cross the road.

"You chose a striking place for a meeting, Herr Stollberger."

"I had to choose a place where I could see that you came alone."

Ever the Stasi, thought Priest, as the man led the way across the road and into a *Kneipe* that bore the name *Destille*. It was like leaving a time machine and entering a bar of the sixties. The presence of two gambling machines couldn't dispel entirely the atmosphere of the former GDR. The L-shaped room had dingy brown-panelled walls and dirty net curtains on the windows. There were coat hooks all around at about shoulder height. Priest imagined beery congregations of the comrades on cold winter evenings, with heavy fur coats hanging every-where.

The two men took off their coats, slung them over chair backs, sat down and consulted the menu. There were only five items to choose from and none, thought Priest, looked promising. An extremely fat man entered the restaurant, glanced at their table, said *Mahlzeit* and went to the bar at the far end of the dining room. The proprietress, a bony woman in a pink shift with platinum blonde hair and black horn rimmed spectacles, stood beside Priest with a notebook poised in her hand.

"*Was darf's denn sein?*"

Priest went for the safest option: two frankfurters with mustard and a bread roll. He would have had one if one had been on offer, but they always came in twos. Eddie Stollberger ordered chicken livers with apple and onion rings, fried potatoes and vegetables. Deciding not to order wine in this establishment, Priest opted to join Eddie and ordered beer.

"Herr Stollberger, I need to ascertain that this archive is genu-ine. Do you have it all with you?"

"I do. Perhaps you would like to see the Berlin diary first. You will recognise Kafka's very distinctive handwriting, I think."
He rooted in his attaché case and brought out a small blue hard-backed notebook. Priest opened it and under the date January 23, 1927, read

the entry:

Plumbing noises all night. Throbbing elbow.

The handwriting was unmistakable, but a skilful forger could easily manage that. The paper and ink were another matter – as he knew only too well. He took out a magnifying glass and a small silver torch from a chamois leather bag in his pocket, held the torch under the paper and ran the glass over its surface.

"This looks to me like Viennese paper. I don't think it's German. I'm afraid I can tell nothing about the pen used, although the ink has a green tint that is very interesting. It could just be the ink made by the renowned *Grazer Tintenfabrik* – that particular green was a colour they developed for the Emperor."

"Why would Kafka use the Emperor's colour?"

"He was a good Habsburger."

"If that's true, Herr Priest, he goes down in my estimation."

Priest said nothing and flicked to another page of the diary, near the end.

D rubbed back all night. Delayed for appointment. Young girl stalking a crow in the park.

He handed back the diary, and asked to see the other manuscripts, but they were interrupted by the arrival of the food. It was not the only thing that arrived – two of the drinkers at the bar at the end of the room – they had obviously been there for a long time - came unsteadily towards their table. Stollberger replaced the diary in the attaché case.

What was that you were doing?" asked the first man. "Were you trying to set that page on fire?"

"Where are you from?" asked the second.

"Iceland," said Priest.

"Iceland," said the first man. "He's from Iceland."

"No wonder he was trying to light a fire."

"*Verboten*," said the first man. "It's *verboten* to light up in here. No fire raising."

His companion laughed and waved his glowing cigarette in the air, blowing a thin stream of smoke from his nostrils.

"Enough," said Stollberger. "Leave us please. We have important things to discuss."

The blonde proprietress came towards them:

"Leave my customers in peace."

The two men went back to their beers. Priest nibbled at a sausage, thinking that frankfurters were much better in Austria. The slurping noise with which Stollberger was relishing his chicken livers irritated him profoundly. He put extra mustard on the next bite. He was anxious to inspect the rest of the material, and as soon as his fellow diner had cleaned his plate he indicated as much. Stollberger dipped into his attaché case and thrust a single, faded sheet of typescript into the Englishman's hand. Priest read the unmistakable opening sentence of a Kafka story the world had not yet seen:

It was an abominable thing, thought Lieutenant B, to be taking one's submarine down through the cold waters of the North Sea the day after marriage to the beautiful Luise.

Stollberger took back the sheet and replaced it in his bag. A look of satisfaction flickered across his features.

"Kafka is his own country, is he not?"

"Yes, and an exile in it, too. It looks authentic. Let me see more."

Stollberger hesitated, and looked around the room. The two smokers had returned to the counter and were talking in low tones to the proprietress. He took out the bulk of a faded typescript on yellowed paper and handed the lot to Priest. It was a story bearing the title *A Curious Invention*. Priest took the pages and studied them, again using his magnifier and the small but very powerful light.

"My guess is that this story was written, or a fair copy was made, on an *Amata* typewriter. They were designed in Vienna in the early twenties, though only a thousand or so were built. A very distinctive typeface."

Stollberger stared in astonishment.

"How can you tell such things? It is just typewriting."

"I've specialised for a long time in examining the authenticity of twentieth `century literary documents, Mr Stollberger. I have partic-ular expertise in the matter of German historical documents. If they'd come to me I'd have told them straightaway that the Hitler diaries were a forgery. And of course you cannot pursue such a specialism without knowing about the means of production - typewriters have long been a study of mine."

Stollberger took a long draught from his beer, then produced a letter from his inside jacket pocket and handed it to Priest, who perused it with a slight smile, then examined it more closely using the magnifier.

"A letter welcoming you into the Young Pioneers," he said. "Well, well, well!"

"The ideas of those times are still with me, Herr Priest."

"This letter was typed on a *Fortuna*, I see, from the *Fortuna - Werk VEB Stuhl*, about 1946. One of the first typewriters of the German Democratic Republic. I'd guess the letter was written in the late nineteen fifties and that a carbon copy was made at the same time."

"Absolutely amazing," said Stollberger.

"That machine will still be working if it has not been tossed on a scrapheap. When ten computers in a row have become obsolete, those old things will still be able to type a letter."

He leafed through the other manuscripts, reading a paragraph here and there, assuring himself that this was indeed an authentic treasure trove. Handing them back to Stollberger, he asked:

"Ok, how much?"

"I am asking five million euros."

Priest laughed.

"I'm sure you are. I will give you one million."

"You are not serious, Herr Priest."

"I am. The Bodleian in Oxford will not offer you anything without certain guarantees regarding the provenance of this material. And you cannot try to sell it in Germany because if you do you will end up in prison."

"Ah, but there are many private collectors, Herr Priest."

"Go ahead then. Try. I'm offering you one million now – cash. It is a substantial sum of money, Mr Stollberger. I can get it for you in 24 hours."

Stollberger slowly raised his empty glass and waved it in the direction of the waitress. He sat in silence, rubbing his neck, staring at the headlines of the *Berliner Morgenpost* hanging on the wall. Priest flapped his hand at the illegal cigarette smoke emanating from the drinkers at the bar.

"In 24 hours?" Stollberger asked.

"Yes, I can do that very easily."

"I will settle for two million."

"I prefer the purity of uneven numbers."

"What?"

"There's an integrity to a round million, don't you think?" Stollberger's face was perfectly blank. He considered this.

"How about three million?"

"Come, come, Mr Stollberger. Let us not annoy the shade of Kafka by haggling."

Stollberger covered his face with his hands and was silent for a while.

"Alright, Herr Priest. Where shall we meet?"

"Do you know the Grunewaldsee?"

"You speak of West Berlin. I know of it. I have never been there."

"There is a *Jagdschloss,* a hunting lodge, on the southern side of the lake. Do you have a car?"

"Capitalism requires it, Herr Priest. I never owned a private vehicle before."

"No doubt you made illegal use of state property."

"I resent that, Herr Priest. I supported our government, and I was not corrupt."

Priest said nothing. Looking towards the bar, he saw that the proprietress was now engaged in deep colloquy with the fat man who had entered earlier. Priest took Stollberger's glass and his own and walked up to the counter, putting them down with a sharp clack. Without raising his voice, he complained about the slow service and ordered two further glasses of Berliner Kindl. The proprietress apologised and immediately began to draw off the beers. One of the smokers slouched on barstools, whose back was towards Priest, turned around and said in a drink-muddied voice:

"Iceland? Can you pay for your beer?"

"No," said the other smoker, "Iceland is broke."

The nearest man sprawled towards Priest so that his chin was practically on the bar and said:

"Go back to Iceland."

"I will," said Priest.

He told the proprietress not to bring the beers, that he would carry them, and brought the drinks to the table. Stollberger was staring in front of him, twisting the wedding ring on his finger.

"My father was a lifelong communist. It was better he died before the change."

"I suppose you might consider us a symptom of the change, Mr Stollberger. *Prost!*"

Stollberger placed his glass on a beer mat, but did not drink.

"In fifty years, Mr Priest, everyone will live under communism. The way we live now, there is not enough to go round."

Priest looked at his watch.

"You may be right. However, for the moment we have capitalism. Appropriately enough, you will find in the courtyard of the *Jagdschloss* a bronze sculpture of a wild boar being brought down by snarling dogs. It is just in front of the hunting museum. There is a bench nearby. Please be sitting on it at 2pm, tomorrow afternoon."

Stollberger frowned.

"Is that why you have chosen this location? A hunting museum?"

Priest smiled.

"No. Not at all. I chose it because watching television in my hotel the other day, I saw it featured in an old Edgar Wallace movie starring Klaus Kinski."

Stollberger picked up his glass and drank. When he put the glass down the foam had left a small white moustache which he wiped off with the back of his hand.

"*Two* million," he said.

"I thought we had an agreement?"

"We don't yet."

Priest watched the smokers at the bar. One of them had half collapsed off his stool and was trying to get up, while the other made contemptuous gestures towards him. The fat man and the proprietress were once again in conversation, but both were watching the two men as they talked.

Priest stood up:

"My offer stands at one million, Herr Stollberger. I have no doubt the material is worth more than that, but how else will you guarantee that its provenance will be kept secret? It is I who will take the risk of selling it on further. Your name will appear nowhere."

He started to put on his coat:

"I will be there at 2pm as I said and I will have the money with me. You will have to decide for yourself whether you wish to complete our agreement."

He turned to go, then on an afterthought spun round and added:

"I will obviously have to verify that what I receive from you will be what I have just seen. And I will not come alone, Mr Stollberger, although you will not be aware of my companions. I hope you will not be tempted to think I would make an easy target."

"*Großer Gott!* Herr Priest. I would not have you think I am a thug! I have a family, Herr Priest. I am not corrupt. Those of us who worked for the GDR have to live on pitiful pensions. Our jobs were taken away from us. They tried to destroy our ideals and aspirations. I am only trying to redress the situation as best I can."

Priest nodded.

"Two pm then, Herr Stollberger? *Bis morgen!*"

He swung open the door and walked out into the chill air.

* * *

His old friend Anthony Galvin-Stone was occupying a comfortable armchair in the Café Tucher on Pariser Platz and reading a British newspaper interview. Priest peered over Galvin-Stone's shoulder at the large photograph of Inspector George Dobson of Scotland Yard above the columns of text, and by way of announcing himself read aloud the headline printed beside Dobson's fleshy face:

"CASE OF THE BLOWPIPED POET!"

Galvin-Stone swivelled around. He was a man in his mid-sixties with a tanned, somewhat creased face, and abundant thick white hair that was tied at the back in a snood. He wore a dark, Italian suit, camel loafers, and no tie.

"Blowpiped?" asked Priest, sliding into an adjacent chair.

"That's what it says. Killed with a blowpipe tipped with cu-rare. Good to see you, Victor."

"It's been a while."

"Ten years at least."

They regarded each other smiling.

"How would you smuggle a blowpipe into the Reichstag?"

"It says here that a tall blonde woman was observed by an Australian tourist lifting up her walking stick and holding the end against her lips. You don't normally do that with a walking stick, do you? And you'd need the pipe to be long, wouldn't you, or you couldn't guarantee your aim?"

"A rather far-fetched way to go about killing someone, isn't it?"

"When I was at M.I.6 we had even more elaborate scenarios for dispatching villains. So did the villains, by the way."

Galvin-Stone considered Priest, who was holding a leather case across his knees.

"You look as if you've just won the lottery."

Priest patted the case.

"In a sense I have. Eddie Stollberger came up trumps. I wasn't sure he would, but he did."

Galvin-Stone folded the newspaper and put it on a nearby table:

"So it *was* the real thing? Eddie is a good man. Once a communist always a communist. He deserved to get a windfall for his old age. What did you pay? Five million? Kafka must be worth at least that. Come to think of it, I'm hoping for a windfall, too."

Priest gestured towards the British Embassy on the other side of Pariser Platz.

"I'm amazed you're still in the business, Anthony. How come they never rumbled you?"

Galvin-Stone leaned forward.

"Perhaps they guessed. Of course none of us wanted to see the GDR disappear, so in that sense we were all pulling together."

"How did you manage to get back here, to Berlin? I'd have expected them to send you somewhere like Venezuela."

"I pulled a few strings. But there's not much going on at the moment. I stay in touch with a few old comrades. Discreetly."

Priest took out a brown envelope and pushed it across the table.

"The windfall," he said.

Galvin-Stone pocketed the envelope without opening it.

"Do you want an *Apfelstrudel* with cream?"

"I'll just have a double espresso. What do you think of these poet murders? Had you ever heard the name Melinda Speling before?"

"No. I asked the Ambassador yesterday and he hadn't heard of her either."

A very tall waiter, a young man with jet-black brilliantined hair and an ankle length, wrap-around white apron, took their order for coffees with a smile and attempted to persuade them to order strawberry pancakes, which both men declined. Priest leaned back in his leather chair and pointed out that the latest actor to take on the role of James Bond was escorting a beautiful woman to a window table.

"Look who's just walked in, Anthony. Would you say he was licensed to kill?"

Galvin-Stone chuckled.

"He's extremely small, isn't he?"

Priest nodded.

"All the better to hide behind a lamp post."

"Oh we don't hide any more, Victor. We listen to Internet traffic. We hack mobile phones and emails."

"I suppose you're a traitor really, Anthony."

"Depends which side you look at me from," said Galvin-Stone. "It's what they teach you at Eton. Independent thinking."

"*Du bist unverbesserlich.*"

The coffee arrived, together with a plate of very small biscuits, and Galvin-Stone scooped up a handful and crunched them. Priest tasted the coffee and congratulated the waiter on its quality. Galvin-Stone leaned foward:

"Tell me, what are these murders all about? Poets being poisoned and thrown off boats and things. Who's behind it?"

"A thwarted poetry lover, perhaps? You'll be interested to hear that I've been asked to investigate these murders by the widow of the first victim, Fergus Diver."

"*You* have? Wasn't Fergus Diver the fellow who tried to read a poem on the Berlin Wall? Is he dead?"

"Dead as Milton."

"It caused a diplomatic incident. Why are you doing this?"

"Fergus Diver's widow asked me."

"I see. And what have you found out?"

"Precious little."

"I seem to remember that you used to write poems. Do you still indulge?"

"It's not an indulgence, Anthony. It's a necessity."

Suddenly James Bond and his lady friend raised their voices. Priest and Galvin-Stone turned to get a better look, and most of the clientele also turned their heads in that direction. The woman, noticing this, fell silent. Galvin-Stone raised his eyebrows and grinned. Priest, however, was thinking of something else:

"Have you encountered this policeman from the UK?"

"Dobson? Yes. I have to offer him every facility. He's very angry about the German police. He says they aren't cooperating. I'd say there was a language problem."

"I'd really like to know if he turns up anything interesting. He probably won't confide in you, but if you do hear anything..."

"Of course, Victor. Shall we pay? I have to be getting back to the office."

Priest held Galvin-Stone's arm. A violent altercation had broken out between James Bond and the actress. She threw a cup of coffee in the film hero's face, jumped up and walked out of the café shouting something that was obviously obscene in a language that was neither English nor German.

Galvin-Stone leaned over and murmured in Priest's ear:

"Bang, you're dead!"

Chapter 18: *Model Trains*

"*Poison Dart Kills Fourth Bard*," said Biggs. "*Poetry star Melinda Speling dies in Reichstag.*"

"Whir's Reichstag?" asked Naily.

"It's in Germany. Shut up and listen. *Police were hunting a mysterious blowpipe assassin in Berlin last night. Husband David Speling says: 'I just want this madman caught.*"

He held up the newspaper to show the poet's photograph, and also a picture of the poet's husband.

"It says she died in the arms of her sobbing companion, Cornelia Kranz. How about that?"

"Ah wanna die sobbin' in yir arms, Joe Biggs."

"Listen. While you were snoring your head off, I phoned up the British Council to find out who the two women poets were on that trip to Sicily. It turned out to be this Melinda Speling and a woman called Jemima Lee. Guess who's next for the high jump?"

"Rabbie Burns."

He swatted her with the newspaper.

"Get dressed, Naily. We got work to do."

He stood up and flicked on Sky News while Naily wandered into the bathroom. The story of Melinda Speling's murder in the Reichstag was the number one item. Her husband, David Speling, interviewed by a young reporter outside his house in Shanklin, said that his wife's death was a great loss to English poetry. He'd had a bad feeling about the trip, he said, and so had his wife. There were details regarding it that he could not reveal. Inspector Dobson, interviewed at Heathrow en route for Berlin, warned that Scotland Yard was now dealing with a serial killer of poets.

"Oh yeah?" said Joe.

Dobson had a high-pitched cockney voice that was at odds with his corpulent figure. Any poet, he said, who had benefited from the patronage of the British Council and enjoyed foreign travel as a result, would be at particular risk. Poets who felt their lives were in danger should immediately contact the police.

"We gotta go to the Isle of Wight, Naily."

She appeared at the door of the bathroom, her head shrouded in a towel.

"Widja say, Joe?"

"We gotta talk to this David Speling guy. He knows stuff he can't reveal."

"Do ah wanna go to the Isle of Wight, Joe?"

"You prob'ly don't."

"Whit about Emily?"

"Put some food and water down, Naily. Get your jacket on."

They took the 505 bus to Waterloo and bought tickets to Portsmouth. From there the ferry trip to Ryde took half an hour, and they caught a bus along the coast to Shanklin. Biggs had not quite resolved the problem of how they would find the exact location of David Speling's house, but the sight of two large TV vans outside a house not far from the port gave the answer. They wandered in its direction and stopped at the gate. A whole crew was in there – there would be no talking to David Speling for a while.

"Let's git sumpn te eat," said Naily.

They turned around and walked down to the pier to gaze at the sea. Naily pointed towards a large pub called Standall's Cave.

"Yeah, why don't we have a couple of beers as well? Might give us some ideas."

They sat in a bar festooned with nets, seashells, starfish and bosomy mermaids.

"Whit you gonna ask aboot, Joe?"

"About that trip to Sicily. Did his wife get to know any Sicilians? Did she or any of the others have a run-in with the mafia?"

"Whad wuid poets be doin' with the mafia? That's daft."

"Well, what would you ask?"

"Thi Irish feller had'n affair with one of them women, didnae?"

"You think this is all about sex?"

"If yuir wife was off with three guys, and she wis shagging 'em all, yuid want to kill the lot of 'em, wuidn't you?"

"There's no way she was shaggin' 'em all."

"Sez you."

"Yeah. We gotta talk to Mr Speling. Drink up and let's go."

By the time they reached Speling's house, the TV vans had departed. They rang the bell but there was no answer.

"He's gotta be here. If he'd gone out we'd have seen him."

"Mibbe hi's gone to the pub with the TV boys."

"Would you go to the pub if your wife had been murdered?"

"Yep."

Biggs snorted and tried a side-gate which led along the house to a garden in which there was a long ramshackle shed. From inside the shed came a long-drawn out whooping sound. Naily grabbed Joe's arm."Dinna like the sound of that, Joe. Let's gie this a miss."

"Now we're here we're gonna knock."

Biggs took out his *Artcrimes* business card and held it ready, then rapped on the patched-up shed door. After a long delay it opened. A bushy haired man of medium height peered out. He was holding a railwayman's cap in his hand. Behind him they could see and hear miniature trains whizzing along a spaghetti tangle of model railway tracks.

"Were you at the front door? I do apologise. I've just had some TV people here and I thought they'd come back. I really didn't want to talk to them anymore."

Joe slid the business card back into his pocket.

"Sorry," he said. "Not a good time then? We came about your model trains?"

David Speling looked briefly at Biggs, then let his gaze dwell considerably longer on Naily.

"I'm afraid it's sold," he said.

He took in Joe's puzzled expression, and said:

"The rolling stock. I sold it a few weeks ago. Is that not what you came about?"

"No. We was talking to some guy in the port and he said you had a fantastic layout. Naily and I, well, we're down here on holiday. We're both into model trains and we was hoping maybe you'd let us see your set up."

David Speling's face showed pleasure and relief.

"Of course! Do come in. You probably think a grown man playing with trains is rather odd, but it's the only thing that takes my mind off the horrible present. There you are!"

Joe and Naily stepped into the shed and watched the trains speeding along on different levels.

"Musta taken years to build this up," said Joe.

"Puire dead brilliant," said Naily.

They walked around the edges of the installation admiring

and commenting on the detail of the miniature landscape. Naily was entranced with the orderly way in which Speling's paints and materials were stacked on shelves. She sat down at his work desk and began to paint a plain balsa wood sheep. Joe tried to stop her, but Speling held him back.

"You're really very adept, Miss...?"

"Janet Dunbar."

Joe said he was sorry for not having introduced himself. Speling shook his hand and patted Naily on the shoulder.

"David Speling," he said.

He was obviously impressed by her speed and dexterity.

"I'd love to have you come and help me, Janet. Why don't we go and have a cup of tea and you can tell me about *your* railway."

Biggs knew nothing about trains, other than that they served dodgy, overpriced sandwiches and were always late, but Naily began talking about different classes of locomotive, wheel arrangements, gauges, livery and the problem of finding space for a model installation if you lived in a very cramped flat. Joe followed them out of the shed and into Speling's house.

"I'm lucky," said Speling as he served them cups of tea. "That shed is perfect for my requirements. Just the right size and shape."

Joe waited for a lull in the railway conversation.

"What was it with all them TV people?" he asked finally. "They putting your layout on telly?"

Speling, who had been talking animatedly up to that moment, put down his tea cup.

"I don't know if you've read the papers, but the poet who was murdered in Berlin yesterday was my wife. You've heard about all these killings? You've heard someone is murdering our poets?"

Naily's expression tried to convey shock horror. Joe was laconic:

"Couldn't not hear about it."

"Well, yesterday they murdered my Melinda. They just...no reason...she never hurt anyone...they just."

His voice began to break up.

We've come at a bad time," said Joe. "We'll go."

"No," said Speling. "You mustn't. It's a relief to talk to normal people."

"Joe's not normal," said Naily. "Dinna talk to him."

Speling shook his head.

"I don't expect you're poetry readers? My wife, Melinda, was a very special person. Lively, talented, and original. She travelled a lot, you see. Poets are always going off on tours and things. And of course they meet people. Who was I to claim all of her? They're saying what killed her was a poisoned dart. Hard to believe, isn't it? But that's what they're saying."

He sat back in his chair and was silent. They watched him. A tear trickled down his cheek. Naily got up and put a hand on his arm. He looked up at her with a grateful smile and fished a handkerchief from his pocket.

"It's all been a bit much. These TV people… My goodness. Would you like some more tea?"

"Nae," said Naily. "We're guid. Ta fir askin."

"Would you like to see a photograph of her?"

"Aye, we wuid."

Speling went upstairs, and Biggs looked at Naily, who shot her eyebrows up and down. He stared around the room. On the wall was a photograph of the Japanese *shinkosan* speeding over a high bridge. An old station sign on the back of the door bore the name *Adlestrop*.

Speling came back down the stairs with an album. Joe and Naily stood behind him as he sat down and began to leaf through it, going through university days, their wedding day, and birthdays. The most recent pictures were from Italy. Melinda in Milan. Melinda in Rome. Several pictures showed a laughing Melinda with her arm round a man with flowing black hair that Joe identified as Barnaby Brown. Group pictures showed another two figures he recognised, Fergus Diver and Alexander Duthie. There was a thin woman he had never seen before.

"Who are they all?"

Speling pointed, naming them.

"Them three been murdered," said Joe. "Diver, Brown, Duthie. It was in the papers."

"Yes," said Speling, looking up. "But it seems the murderer didn't kill Barnaby Brown. Melinda was going to meet him in Berlin."

"Oh yeah? I thought somebody pushed him off a boat? Isn't he supposed to have drowned?"

"He wrote a letter to Melinda telling her he'd escaped some-how. He didn't say how. He said he knew who the murderer was."

"Blimey. S'pose you told the cops about it?"

"I didn't as a matter of fact. I've not seen any policemen, though I did get a phone call. I've been inundated with these news people, but I haven't told anyone actually. You're the first."

"Who's she?" asked Joe, pointing at the thin woman.

That's Jemima Lee. Something odd about this red-haired fel-low, though. Actually, I don't think he is a poet. He's a Welshman."

"Obviously not a poet, then?"

"No, I didn't mean that. His name was Robert Rees. I remem-ber that Melinda said he had a violent argument about something with Alex Duthie and Fergus Diver."

"Violent?"

"I don't mean physical. Just very…well…passionate. Me-linda thought he might be gay. She said he was a bit over-attentive to Barnaby Brown, if you see what I mean. He just happened to be in the hotel where they were staying. Funnily enough he turned up at her reading in Leipzig the day before she was murdered. She phoned me to tell me about it."

Joe went back to his chair. Speling, with his eyes half-closed and his shoulders shaking, closed the album. Naily took it from off his lap and placed it on a coffee table near Joe. She took Speling's hands in hers and pulled him to his feet.

"Whit d'you know aboot live steam?"

Speling looked surprised and then interested.

"It's amazing what *you* know about model railways, young lady."

"Ah grew up wi' a brother. Mr Speling. Whit he didnae know about model trains wisn't worth knowing. And I *like* 'em. There was one o' they steam locos in yir shed. Cuid you make it go for me?"

Speling looked at Joe.

"Would you like to see…?"

Joe got to his feet. Speling went through the door first and as Naily followed him she jabbed her finger in the direction of the album on the coffee table. Joe opened it, slid out one of the group pictures depicting Robert Rees and Jemima Lee, and followed them to the shed. He watched with interest as Speling filled a water tank in the tender of what Naily announced was a Mallard class locomotive, and heated it up with a tiny immersion heater in the tank. As the water came close to the boil, the engine began to move. Biggs watched it circle, pistons pumping, emitting realistic steam sounds. Naily and David Speling were definitely bonding, he thought. But they would have to get a move on. He tapped his wristwatch, and David brought the train to a standstill. Asking them how long they planned to stay in Shanklin, he begged them to return. He had enjoyed their conversation. It had been a real pleasure to meet them. He thrust a magazine into Joe's hand.

"You'll find some things about my wife in there. It's the latest issue," he said. "I don't want it. Not my kind of thing."

He accompanied them to the gate and kept waving as they walked down the slight hill.

Aye, hie's wavin still," said Naily, turning back.

"Poor sod."

＊　　＊　　＊

Waiting for the bus back to Ryde, Naily said:

"Wi did awright, Joe Biggs. Guid ye didn't come the detective."

"Yeah. You did good too. Never knew you was a train spotter."

The bus took them back to the port, and from Ryde to Portsmouth they spent most of the time on the deck of the ferry watching seagulls. Joe tried Priest's mobile number several times, but couldn't get through. At Portsmouth station, Naily grabbed Joe's arm and pointed.

"Lookit that, Joe."

A display table of books with *Two For Three* stickers on them held copies of books by familiar names: Fergus Diver, Barnaby Brown, Horace Venables, Alexander Duthie and Melinda Speling. There were photographs of the poets. The books were piled high, and a number of travellers were browsing.

They walked on past a news stand and this time Joe took hold of Naily's arm and pointed. The evening paper was carrying a large picture of a muscular youth in a colourful one-piece body suit with the letter **B** on his chest. The youth's fist was pushed forward in front of him and he was heading upwards towards the clouds. Either a bolt of lightning was striking his fist or else his fist was emitting lightning. The newspaper headline read: **Who Is BardSlayer?**

Joe bought the paper and they walked up the platform looking for a quiet carriage. The train was half empty. They found a seat with a table.

"Whit's it all aboot?"

Joe studied the front page.

"Something on the internet. BardSlayer! Blimey. Looks like these poet murders are giving people ideas."

"Mibbe it's the murderer?"

Dunno," said Joe, reading further. "Some new super hero. You can track BardSlayer's movements using GPS. Why would you wanna do that?"

He folded up the paper, put it on the seat next to him, and began to jot things into his notebook. Priest would want a full report. Naily took off her shoes and socks, put one foot up on the table and started painting her toenails green. He looked up.

"You ain't gonna be able to get to the bar like that."

"The bar's that way, Joe Biggs. Ah'll have a sandwich."

He didn't move but sat completing his notes. Then he turned to the copy of *The Boot* that David Speling had given him. It was head-scratching stuff. He tried to read Barnaby Brown's review of a new book by Melinda Speling - *love, creativity, spirituality – all permeated with a delicate earthiness.* Did that mean Brown had been shagging the lady? Biggs took up his phone and pressed redial.

"Joe here," he said

"Glad you called," said Priest. "I have been speaking to a medical colleague here. Mrs Speling died a very unpleasant death. Curare paralyses and then suffocates. The victim is conscious while this happens and cannot communicate what is happening. Death is slow to come."

"Strewth."

Biggs looked across at Naily, whose forehead was wrinkled with concentration as she dabbed with a brush at her toenails. He told Priest about the photograph and the letter Mrs Speling had received from Barnaby Brown.

"We must conclude, then, that Barnaby Brown is still alive and may be in Berlin?"

"Yeah."

"And Robert Rees may be in Leipzig, or indeed here in Berlin? Or he may have been a figment of Mrs Speling's imagination?"

"What exactly did she say about him?"

"Said she thought he was gay. I gotta photograph of him so he ain't imaginary."

"Hmm. What about the other woman who was in Sicily?"

"She's in the same picture. Her name is Jemima Lee."

"Scan the photograph and email it to me. If this perpetrator is not apprehended, the entire poetry establishment will soon be dead."

Biggs realised he wanted Priest to come back and take charge. He felt as if he was holding the reins of several horses that were all trying to go in different directions.

"You seen this BardSlayer stuff in the papers?"

"I have. There will always be someone willing to exploit a tragic situation for their own sinister and possibly commercial ends."

"Yeah, guv."

"I will delay my departure, Joe, and travel to Leipzig. It may be easier there to locate the tracks of this Robert Rees."

Joe was startled as another fast train going by in the opposite direction made a kind of explosive snapping noise. He looked out of the window at the blur. Then it was gone.

"OK. There was something else in the papers yesterday. Something about a blonde woman with a blowpipe. A tall blonde woman."

Priest said nothing.

"Couldn't be the lady that was on that ferry with Brown, could it?"

His employer's voice held an ironic inflection:

"The 'right piece of stuff', you mean?"

"Yeah."

"It seems I must look out for a reincarnated Barnaby Brown, a red-haired Welshman and a dishy blonde. You're keeping me busy, Joe. Make sure you stay alert too."

Priest ended the call and Biggs tapped his chin with the phone. Naily was now absorbed in a magazine. He looked out of the window. Who needed sheep? He was glad when at last they were running past yellowed brick housebacks and he glimpsed familiar streets below a bridge.

*   *   *

In the *Artcrimes* office, he found further copies of *The Boot* arrayed
on a shelf, and took down a few samples. Leafing through them, he
noticed that here too Priest had distributed ticks to the poems. In one
or two cases, poems had been disapproved of by having lines drawn
through them with a ruler. He sat scratching his ankle. Some bloody
insect, probably in Speling's shed, had bitten him.

Naily was lying on the daybed, stroking a purring cat, and
turning the glossy pages of a magazine.

"If I scan that picture Speling gave us into the computer,
Naily, can you download it onto this mobile and send it to the guvnor?"

By way of reply, he got a yawn.

Yeah, he thought. He scanned the group photograph of the poets in Sicily, leaving it up on the monitor, and noted down the address
of the editorial offices of *The Boot*. 52A Tavistock Square wasn't very
far from Lamb's Conduit Street. He looked at the name of the editor
and laughed aloud. Telling Naily he wouldn't be long, he walked up
Southampton Row, and into Tavistock Square, stopping in front of a
brass plate that bore the words *The Boot, established 1952*. He rang the
bell and a voice crackled over the entryphone:

"Yes?"

He cleared his throat.

"I'd like to speak to Mr Damian Krapp on a matter of importance."

.   "Who is this?"

"I am Joe Biggs from *Artcrimes*."

There was silence for a moment and then the door clicked
open. Biggs climbed the narrow stairway and was greeted by a willowy
young man who showed him through into the main editorial office. A
stout, balding individual in a corduroy suit, wearing a green, v-necked
pullover and a black and white bow tie, was sitting at a desk reading a
typed manuscript.

"Oh. Hello. You're Joe Biggs? Do come in and sit down."

Biggs proffered the *Artcrimes* business card.

"From *Artcrimes*? You're famous! Amazing how you recov-

203

ered that stolen Lucien Freud. To what do I owe the pleasure...? You won't find any stolen paintings here."

"Yeah. Actually it was my guvnor found the pictures. Victor Priest. I'm his assistant."

"Victor Priest. Yes, of course. Well, Mr Biggs, what's it all about?"

"Murder."

Krapp placed the page he was holding on the desk.

"God. Yes. These ghastly poet murders. Soon I'll have no contributors left. What does all this have to do with your organisation?"

"My guvnor was asked to investigate by a Mrs Diver. I suppose you knew all those poets who went to Sicily?"

Krapp considered Joe with benevolent care.

"You seem very young to be a detective, Mr Biggs."

He sat back in his chair.

"Barnaby Brown and Fergus Diver were mainstays of this magazine. Melinda Speling was my favourite contemporary woman poet and a dear friend of mine. She was here in this office just a few days ago. I am devastated. Simply devastated."

Joe said nothing.

"Can I get you a drink? I was thinking of having a vodka."

"Oh. Yeah. Thanks."

Damian Krapp went to a small cupboard, took out a bottle and two glasses, poured out drinks, and handed one to Biggs.

"You ain't had any submissions from Barnaby Brown lately, have you?"

"Yes. He sent us a poem recently. Before he was murdered."

"You didn't get none *after* he was murdered?"

"What?"

"I mean, he might be still alive."

"Thank God! No. We've heard nothing. What makes you think...?"

"You ever hear of a bloke called Robert Rees?"

Krapp sat down with a thump.

"What did you say?"

Biggs fished in his pocket and handed the photograph to the startled editor.

"This geezer."

"Good God! I know him!"

"Yeah?"

"I met him for the first time a few days ago. He has offered to be a benefactor to the magazine. How did you get this?"

"He was in Sicily with all them other poets in the picture. That's where that photo was taken. I got it from Mrs Speling's husband. What do you know about him?"

"I know he runs a business manufacturing protective clothing called *Storm*. Based in Aberystwyth."

"You meeting him again?"

"Almost certainly. He is investing money in our periodical."

"Can I give you my mobile number? Would you call me when you're meeting him? I'd like to talk to him."

Krapp looked doubtful.

"Why? Is he suspected of something? Could he be...dangerous?"

"Might be."

"Should the police be informed?"

"Not enough to go on for them."

Krapp seemed agitated.

"I'm not sure about this. It's all very disturbing."

Biggs pondered the editor's chaotic desk for a while.

"Are you a poet, Mr Krapp?"

"Of course I am. A minor poet, perhaps. I wouldn't let my own work into the magazine though."

He gave a high-pitched laugh.

"The thing is," said Biggs, "this murderer is out to get poets, and you're one of them. You could be running a risk meeting Rees. Suppose you let me know when you're meeting him next and I tag along in the background? Then I'd be there if you needed me."

Damian Krapp appraised Joe Biggs' sturdy frame.

"I'll think about it," he said.

Chapter 19: A *Spirit Creature*

In the dream he was lying in the jungle and a tremendous downpour was crashing through the leaves. Bill Gerard-Wright opened his eyes to see the brownish stain on the ceiling through which the rain was leaking onto his forehead. The pillow underneath his head was damp. He rolled clear of the drip and got out of bed.

Through the window he could discern the rain-smudged outline of the mountain. It had been very kind of the Gareth Hopkins Foundation to offer him a residency in the poet's own cottage, perched on the edge of a Welsh lake, in a village which had a population of twenty in winter but which in summer swelled to two thousand or more. It was not summer, however, and it seemed to have been raining for the entire three weeks since he'd arrived.

He looked gloomily at the untended and waterlogged garden. He was only here because Penny had got the house. With her money she could afford lawyers. Losing his home on top of having been dropped by Dolan & Swainson – Jesus, he'd published four books with them, all very well received – had seemed to be the decisive punch that had concluded his hopes for the future. Then he'd run into Aaron Hopkins for the first time in years.

Hopkins had been Gerard-Wright's original editor at Dolan & Swainson and had left the firm in disgust at what he saw as their high-handed treatment of poets. The old man had made him a very serious double offer – a residency in Gareth Hopkins's former home, and publication by his esteemed new imprint, The Hopkins Press (good paper, proper typesetting, scrupulous editing) and a decent emolument to go with the residency. How could he have refused all that?

He shivered. The cottage was not very well heated, and what heat there was escaped through the ill-fitting windows. He put on two sweaters, the last a heavy, hand-knitted one he'd bought in Ireland, made himself a cup of tea and went and sat in the room he had designated as his study, looking through his previous day's work. There was to be a reading in two day's time at the village church that now belonged to the Hopkins Foundation. He wondered what kind of an audience he could expect, given that the Foundation's local supporters were notoriously conservative, and there weren't even many of them. He hadn't made many friends, or indeed even drinking partners, in the village. In the last two days he'd run into a man down by the lake shore who had offered to give him a run round the lake in his motor boat, but there was something ingratiating in the man's manner that put him off and, politely, he had declined the offer.

He realised he wasn't concentrating on his poem, and he shuffled the sheets together and fastened them with a paper clip. It had taken him ten years of his life to reach Canto 8 of his epic poem *Drawn with a Willow Brush* and Aaron was urging him to complete it in time for publication next year but Gerard-Wright didn't know if he still had the horsepower. He'd hoped that the new surroundings would galvanise him; they hadn't, quite. He would read some sections of the long poem on Wednesday evening, but at the risk of disappointing Aaron he would read mainly short poems.

He looked out the window. Did it ever stop raining in Wales? He watched a pair of beaming ramblers in yellow rainwear head off up the mountain track past his house, and wondered what they got out of it. Rolling a spliff, he lit up and inhaled, thinking again about Penny. She knew about his financial situation; she could have been a bit generous. When she'd inherited all that money and they'd bought the house overlooking the bay, he'd thought he had finally found a place he could settle down in. But it was her place, not his, and the sea breezes hadn't been enough. He'd started travelling to do readings again, and residencies abroad, meeting with fierce opposition from Penny. It had all fallen apart.

A noise beyond the window caught his attention. A donkey in the neighbour's garden was trying to pull a yellow shirt off the washing line, its lips curled back over huge teeth. He began to laugh. Maybe this place had its entertainments after all. The housewife came running out into the garden and started whacking the donkey with a broom.

The donkey emitted a tremendous hee-haw, galloped round the garden, jumped over the little stone wall into his garden and went straight past his window.

He opened it and leaned out.

Some critter," he called.

"That was one of our local wild donkeys. They're terrible."

She pointed to the gate into her garden.

"We always keep that shut," she said, "in case they get in. I saw someone down there earlier loitering. I wonder if they let it in on purpose."

He eyed the housewife and blew out more smoke. She was about forty, and wearing a simple house shift. Her dark hair was tousled and wet from the rain. She came through the little gate that separated their two properties and approached his window, smiling.

"That was a jenny. A female. They're not dangerous unless you really annoy them. They roam all over the mountain here. You can hear them when they bray. They sound like foghorns."

"Oh, that's what it was. I thought it must be boats on the lake."

"I expect you must be the new poet in residence. Mr Gerard-Wright?"

"Call me Bill. Does it ever stop raining here?"

"It's easing off."

She held out her palm to feel the rain.

"What's your name?"

"Sally Green. I'm glad the house is occupied again. Are you going to put that donkey in a poem?"

"Might do. Are you interested in poetry? I'm giving a reading on Wednesday. Why don't you come along?"

"I just might. If I can persuade my husband. See you around, Bill."

She smiled again and went back into her cottage.

There's always a husband, he thought. He went to look for his old battered boots that he'd thrown into a corner. His trench coat was hanging on a hook in the hall. He put on his trilby, grabbed his eagle-headed stick and marched out into the damp air.

The L-shaped lake reflected the sullen, overcast sky. He noticed that the wooded island had some kind of ruined tower on it. Big birds were flapping above the trees. What were they? He'd have to buy binoculars. If he walked into the village he ran the risk of running into the man with the motor boat and he wasn't in the mood for conversation, but he didn't want to go up the mountain. He was a man for the flat. Should he walk clockwise or widdershins around the lake? Today, he decided, he'd go against the clock.

*   *   *

Aaron Hopkins was waiting at the village church. Gerard-

Wright had decided to arrive an hour early for the reading in order to procure himself a drink before supplies ran out. Judging by the number of bottles lined up on the table, he needn't have worried.

Hopkins handed him a glass of white wine, and said:

"Have you met Robert Rees? He's a true fan of yours."

The poet regarded a familiar figure, a tall, slightly stooped, red-bearded man in a sand- coloured suit. His red hair was combed in waves.

"I'm so pleased to be hearing you read. Would you mind signing this for me?"

To Gerard-Wright's surprise, he was handed the long out of print City Lights edition of *Trainsmoke*.

"Oh," he said. "You're the man with the motor boat. How long have you known Aaron?"

"A couple of days," said Rees, beaming. "I hope you're going to read the *Totem Pole Chant*."

"I wasn't actually. It's too long."

"The true poetry *aficionado* is never deterred by length, Mr Gerard-Wright. That amulet you're wearing, does it come from your Navajo period?"

Long tapered fingers took hold of his lucky wolf's paw that hung on a rawhide thong round his neck. The red beard came much too close for Gerard Wright's liking. He drew back.

"I don't like people messing with my stone."

"I'm sorry. We don't want to upset the spirits, do we?"

Gerard-Wright had long been resigned to the fact that one couldn't pick one's admirers.

"Is it OK to smoke, Aaron?"

"Outside I'm afraid."

He took a fresh glass of wine, nodded to Rees, and headed out into the churchyard. The rain had held off, though it was a cloudy evening. A few people were starting to arrive. He stood some distance away from the church door, perched his wine glass on a gravestone, and began covertly to roll a joint. He wasn't going to give them that damn chant. Why did they always want to hear the old warhorses? He lit up, took a deep drag, and stared at a cloud in the shape of Australia.

"But soft! Methinks I scent the evening air."

He spun round.

"I was wondering if we might have a little chat, Bill?"

"Sorry. I need a little space to prepare myself for the reading."

"Of course. I shan't disturb you further. Wow them, Bill."

He watched Rees lope back to the church entrance, and sucked again on his joint, remembering a pretentious French Canadian poet he'd flattened in a bar in Montreal. He still recalled that right hook with deep satisfaction, and the sound of shattering glasses that followed. He turned back to contemplate the headstones scattered across the church precincts. What kind of reading would it be? He never knew how they would turn out.

As it happened, it was one of those average to middling readings you did a lot of. Then came the ordeal of question time. An elderly man asked was there any connection between the displaced Navajo people and their all-but-submerged culture and the suppressed culture of Wales towards which the official dominant culture of the United Kingdom so grossly condescended? Gerard-Wright was relieved when Robert Rees interjected:

"I think your question is out of order, sir. It raises political questions that have no substantive bearing on what we have just heard. I'm sure we all noticed that Bill read no work from his Navajo period this evening. He wanted to show us new work. Personally, I want to thank him for a really splendid reading."

This got applause from some quarters and the elderly man looked discomfited and sat down. Gerard-Wright went over afterwards to thank Rees for his timely defence. His admirer divested a bottle of its brown paper wrapping and held it up.

"Would you care to share this with me later in my hotel?"

Bill looked at the label, said yes, then turned to find Aaron and was introduced to several more elderly residents of the village. Of Sally Green there was no sign. People said their farewells and drifted off. He signed a small number of books. Eventually, Rees came over to him and calling goodbye to Aaron, they set off for Rees's hotel, walking along the lake shore. The rain had ceased and the moon silhouetted the ruins of the tower on the island.

"Doesn't that remind you of Caspar David Friedrich?"

"Who?"

"He's my favourite German romantic painter."

"I don't do romanticism."

They drew close to the water and stopped, listening to the plash of wavelets on the grass bank, and the gentle thump of a few moored boats against a jetty. The air was clean and fresh. Up on the hillside just above the village, a few dark shapes moved to and fro.

"Have you met the local donkeys?"

Gerard-Wright squinted at the moonlit hillside.

"Yeah. I have."

"I seem to recall you once reading a poem about a donkey?"

The poet said nothing. What was Rees thinking of? He couldn't be thinking of that occasion at the Cheltenham festival, could he? It was just what the fucking Cheltenham festival had deserved. But, no, Rees couldn't have known about that.

With a long drawn out cry, an owl floated from behind the village and headed across the water to the trees on the island. Rees indicated they should walk on to the hotel. Apart from the light on the front steps, there was no one about. They pushed open the door and went up to Rees's room, where he opened a bottle of vintage brandy. They clinked glasses and settled themselves into chairs.

"To your reading tonight, Bill."

"To romanticism!"

Gerard-Wright tasted the cognac. It was good.

"You've had a long career, Bill. What is it that drives you? What makes you write?"

Here it comes, he thought. Once an admirer had cornered you, all they wanted to talk about was your work. He took another reflective drink, and said:

"Gotta do something to fill the days."

"Come, come. Give me a proper answer. How do you get that openness into your work?"

The funny thing was that though he could always predict the questions, he never really had a pat answer.

"Maybe it was the time I spent in the States in my twenties. I dunno."

"Ah yes, America. Those wide open spaces. They haven't quite accepted you in your own country, have they?"

Gerard-Wright laughed.

"They don't know where I fit."

"It's the problem they had with Shelley. Did him no harm in

the long run, did it?"

"I don't give a fuck about that reputation stuff."

"Don't you? Really?"

"What I do care about is getting a poem right, and doing a reading that gets it across loud and clear. Not like tonight."

"It was fine, Bill. Perhaps not as good as the one you gave in Toronto last year? Do you remember the response you got to 'The Wigwam of the Baroness'? Why didn't you read it tonight?"

Gerard-Wright blinked. This birdish man had been in Toronto as well? He was a bundle of surprises.

"Gotta vary the programme, Bob."

"Would you mind reading the poem now?"

He did mind. He didn't do private shows, not even for people who bought him drinks. He sat back, shaking his head and drained his glass.

"Enough for one night," he said.

He put the glass down on the floor and made as if to go. Rees jumped up, picked up the glass and refilled it.

"It's an infant of a night. We must nurture it."

He held out the glass to Gerard-Wright, who took it with a show of reluctance.

"I promise to be a brilliant audience, Bill."

The poet sighed, pulled his leather bag onto his lap and fished out a number of battered and stained paperbacks. He wasn't even sure, now, which book the poem was in. He shuffled through them. Robert Rees said:

"*Blind Alleys.*"

"Oh, yeah. That was where it was. He found the book and the page, took a drink, stroked his moustache, cleared his throat, and read:

The Wigwam of the Baroness

It was yellow when she bought it
but the crowshit soon put paid to that.
Then the crows built their nests
in the fork-tree roof.
The baroness addressed her lover:
'Antoine. Those crows! Can't you

do something?' But Antoine
was kissing her neck. 'I like
crows,' he said. 'They bring
good luck. The inuit call them
spirit creatures.' He unbuttoned
her blouse. 'Fact is, I was once
a crow myself.' He buried his face
in the warmth of her skin &
she heard his muffled caw.
A louder caw came from above
& she felt the wind of wings.

Rees applauded.
"Magnificent."
"Just a strange little poem. No big deal."
"Yes, it is strange. Like so much of your work."
Gerard-Wright leaned forward and put his glass down on the circle-stained hotel table.
"Enough about poetry. You wanna hear a story about a donkey?"
He made a performance of telling his story of the donkey, the yellow shirt on the line and the housewife.
Rees smiled. Yes," he said. "They're all over the place. There are probably some sniffing around this hotel as we speak. Another drop?"
Gerard-Wright nodded and Rees topped up the glass.
"I suppose they go in packs," the poet said.
"Wild donkeys don't have the herd instinct that horses do. Have you ever asked yourself why they're so loud? The braying, I mean,"
"Never have."
"It's because they forage far and wide on unpromising ground and sometimes lose contact with their fellow donkeys. They need to be able to bellow a bit so the rest of their pack can hear them."
"Is that right?"
"And of course they have big ears."
"You're not serious are you?" said Gerard-Wright, laughing.
"That is an evolutionary fact," said Rees. "Take some more of

the nectar, Bill."

Gerard-Wright topped up his glass.

"What fascinates me is that island out on the lake," said Rees. "Are there any donkeys out there?"

"I don't think so. I walk round the lake every day and I've never seen any. They'd have to be able to swim to reach it."

"Oh donkeys can swim. All equine species can swim. Are there any human beings living out there?"

"Doubt it. Just a ruin."

Rees, who had not drunk much so far, tasted what was in his glass.

"It seems to me a pity that an island like that should only be inhabited by herons. I could imagine myself living on that island."

"Who'd want to live on that? You'd need to row to the pub."

"Well, of course, if you did live there, you'd need company. Donkeys, perhaps."

"Yeah? What kind of company is a wild donkey? All they're good for is biting you, kicking you, and eating your best shirts. I think I need a spliff."

He rolled one adroitly and offered first toke to Rees, who declined. Taking a deep inhalation, Gerard-Wright directed a jet of smoke at the smoke alarm on the ceiling. Rees ran to the bathroom and came back flapping a towel.

"We'll all have to go and stand outside, if you do that."

Gerard-Wright began to laugh uncontrollably.

"I can just see you on the back of a donkey swimming to the island."

"Can you, now?" said Rees, swinging the towel. "Well I could think of a drier way of getting a donkey over there."

"Yeah. Build a bridge."

"No, no, no. I have a motor boat. If we lassoed one of these creatures, we could tow it out to the island."

"We *could*?"

"Imagine the villagers waking up to see a donkey braying back at them from the island tomorrow morning!"

Gerard-Wright, who had had a vision of a donkey with Sally Green, naked, on its back, was gasping with laughter.

"I wanna see you ride a donkey, Bob."

"We have to catch one first."

"Yeah? Where you gonna get a lasso?"

"A mooring rope would do."

"Do you know how to throw a rope?"

"Yes."

"Have you any idea how strong these creatures are?"

"They're no stronger than horses. You can lasso them."

Gerard-Wright got to his feet.

"I wanna see you rope one of those beasts. Don't expect me to do anything if it runs away with you."

Rees went to the window and looked out.

"Why don't we? It's nearly dawn. Let's go"

Christ, the guy really meant it. The place was waking up at last. Laughing and shaking his head, he followed Rees out.

*   *   *

A crow watched from a tree as the silhouettes of two men moved quickly up the hill. One of the men was carrying a coil of rope slung across his shoulder. The other was carrying a stick. They approached a small group of donkeys. Some were asleep on their feet, others were lying down. The crow left its branch and circled, cawing. The first man twirled the rope around his head a few times and flung it in the direction of one of the donkeys. The rope settled around the creature's neck and the man pulled the rope tight. The donkey emitted a terrific hee-haw, and the other donkeys woke. From higher up the hill came another answering hee-haw. The second man whacked the lassoed donkey's rump with his stick to set it galloping, and the man holding the end of the rope pursued the donkey down the hill. The other man fell to his knees, laughing, but got up as he realised the other donkeys were advancing towards him, braying and snorting. Then he too turned and ran after the first man.

The crow flew high over the road leading down to the lake. The lassoed donkey had come to a dead stop and was refusing to budge. The two men were pulling at the rope and shouting at it. The man with the stick hit the donkey on its nose and the animal turned round and kicked him hard so that he fell into a hedge. The donkey then turned and galloped towards the water with the other man running behind, still holding the rope. The crow alighted on the church steeple. It observed the other donkeys charging loudly down the hill in pursuit of their lassoed brother. The sun was coming up on the village.

The man who had fallen into the hedge climbed out of it and caught up with the other man at a loping run. From the church steeple, the crow had a good view of the two men tying one end of the rope around the donkey's neck to the stern of the boat. They jumped in and the first man started the engine and cast off. As the motorboat moved out from the jetty, the lassoed donkey gave a piercing howl and dug in all its heels. The engine of the motorboat roared. The donkey, with its legs thrust stiffly in front of it, was tugged towards the water. It screeched, fell into the water, and was forced to start swimming. The remainder of the donkey pack came thundering up to the water's edge and stopped. They keened a choral hee-haw in the direction of the swimming donkey, but none set off in pursuit.

The crow rested a while, preening its feathers. The boat made progress towards the island in the middle of the lake, towing the donkey behind it. The crow flew off again over the water and landed in a tree on the island, near the shore. It watched as the boat beached and the two men tugged the braying donkey on to the island. As soon as it was on land it began to kick out with its hind legs. One of the men grabbed the stick off the other man and began to beat the donkey repeatedly with it. The other man shouted and waved his hand in the air, walking backwards away from them. The man who now had the stick, and was still holding the rope, released it. The donkey catapulted towards the stickless man and kicked out at him with its hind legs until he fell. As he tried to get up the donkey kicked at his head with its front legs, then bit him in the neck. The man lay still on the ground, and the other man ran to the boat and set off over the water. After standing there for a few minutes, snorting, the donkey lost interest and began to eat a thorn bush.

The crow flew down and landed on the ground beside the fallen man. It hopped onto a trilby hat. There was not a single twitch from the man. The crow hopped nearer and onto the face. It plucked out a still warm eye. The other eye stared up at the sky, waiting its turn.

Chapter 20: *One, two, three, four...*

Gordon's Wine Bar in Villiers Street was packed. A rather overweight, balding Indian man, holding up two glasses of wine, pushed through tight groups of chattering drinkers. He was aimed at a table at the far end of the low-ceilinged room.

"Excuse me!" he called. "Excuse me! I am a danger to you with these glasses!"

Manfred von Zitzewitz sat alone at the table, watching this performance.

"Do you have to make such a song and dance out of everything, Tambi?"

Kumar sat down and placed the glasses on the table.

"It's so unexpected to be sitting in this wine bar with you, Manfred. Let us clink!"

Von Zitzewitz raised his glass somewhat and Kumar dinged his own against it.

They drank. Very little light was getting in through the filthy window above the table, but the German didn't mind this. He liked a place where one could be private in a crowd. Whenever he had reason to meet someone he had important business with, this was his preferred venue.

"What's all this about Damian selling out *The Boot*?"

Kumar leaned forward, breathing garlic. The German, squeezed into a tight corner, pressed himself back in his chair. Tambi wore the look of one who has revelations to make. He had gone to the offices of *The Boot* one evening bearing poems for the Sri Lankan section of the next issue, and found Damian Krapp sitting in front of a half-finished bottle of vodka. The editor had been in a mood to unburden himself of a problem. A Welsh businessman called Robert Rees had approached him with an offer to fund *The Boot* - £200,000 over two years. All Krapp would have to do in return was let Rees have twenty pages of his own selection in the next issue. Damian had looked apologetic and told Kumar that the Sri Lankan section would unfortunately have to be held over until a later issue.

"Naturally, Manfred, I erupted like Vesuvius. All my hard work!"

Krapp had kept insisting it was a good deal. It would put *The*

Boot's finances in order for the foreseeable future. Kumar had asked what the twenty pages would consist of but it was one of the conditions of the offer that no one should see them until they were ready to appear.

"What an interesting publishing decision!"

"*The Boot* will be holed below the waterline, Manfred, and will glug to the bottom."

"Glug it will. Is Damian seriously proposing not to read any of these twenty pages before they appear?"

"Yes, apparently they will go straight to the printers. Imagine what might be in them?"

"We don't have to imagine. It will be dire."

"It could be dangerous. What if it's sacrilegious, blasphemous? All of us connected with *The Boot* might have a fatwa issued against us."

"I think this is simply some wealthy amateur versifier who wants to see his pathetic drivelling in print."

"I hope you're right."

Von Zitzewitz said with emphasis:

"We cannot allow this to happen."

"It is happening, Manfred. Damian has signed a contract."

"Then he must tear it up. This is what we are going to do. You will phone up half the members of the board and I will phone the other half. We will solicit their agreement that Damian Krapp is to be removed as editor if he allows this thing to go through. I know everyone will agree with us. Poppy certainly will. Then we confront Damian."

Kumar giggled nervously.

"Damian will break a bottle over our heads. Our blood will spill."

"No he won't. Damian is a mouse-lover. There will be no blood. Let us get going on this. Mobile telephones are useless in here. I will go upstairs and call Poppy and Mark Dolan. Then you can call Jemima Lee and Stanislaus Green."

Von Zitzewitz pushed brusquely through the crowd and went up the narrow stairwell, keying in the number of his editor, Mark Dolan. The publisher was horrified to hear what Krapp was doing and agreed immediately that he would have to be stopped. Poppy Irving told him his call had not even been necessary. She would back him all the way. He returned to the table, giving Kumar the thumbs up, and the Indian left, reappearing after a while with fresh glasses of wine and the news that Stanislaus Green was astounded at Krapp's perfidy and was completely on their side. Jemima Lee was unavailable but Kumar had left a message.

"Will we do the deed tonight, Manfred?"

"I think so. Knowing Damian's habits – especially with a new issue looming – he will be in the office late. Drink up and we'll go over there."

They left the wine bar, walked up Villiers Street to the Strand and hailed a taxi.

There was a light still on at the offices of *The Boot*. Kumar rang the bell and the door opened on the buzzer. Damian Krapp was surprised to see visitors at such a late hour, and startled and upset to hear their ultimatum.

"We have no money," he objected. "What is the alternative?"

"I would rather see *The Boot* die than be desecrated," said von Zitzewitz. "And there is an alternative. Protest. We must get up a petition, speak to politicians, write stern letters in our own defence. We must let the world know."

"We must make the Arts Council change its mind," added Kumar.

"We did protest," said Krapp. "It didn't work."

"It was too half-hearted. Anyway, you have no option if you want to continue as editor. The board is unanimous, except for Jemima, and she will certainly join us."

Damian sat quite still. He looked haggard. The two men stood watching him for a moment or two, then they bade him goodnight, went down the stairs and out onto the pavement. Something made von Zitzewitz look up at the window and he saw Krapp staring down. He wasn't looking at them.

Clearly, on the night air, von Zitzewitz heard the rhythmic chanting of two girls skipping, and caught the words of their skipping song:

> *One two*
> *Freddy's coming for you*
> *Three four*
> *Better lock your door*

*   *   *

When his visitors had gone Damian Krapp went to his cupboard, took out his bottle of *Grey Goose*, and poured himself a glass. He brought this to the window where he stood, deep in thought, for a while. If the board was against him he would have no option but to tear up the contract. God knows how *The Boot* would survive without the Welshman's money. Maybe something else would materialise. Or maybe he was completely wrong. Maybe poetry in the modern world was doomed. Lots of people would write it, but no one would read what they'd written because there would be no means of judicious dissemination. Editors like himself were brontosauruses. Or was it brontosaurii? There would be the internet of course, but that was a cloaca. With no critical standards left, drivel could become classic. It already probably bloody was.

Two girls skipping on the pavement below attracted his attention. They were singing something but he couldn't pick out the words. He turned and went to the telephone.

He looked on the contract for Robert Rees's number but it wasn't there, then he remembered Rees had given him a card with a mobile number on it, and warned him not to show the number to anyone. Typical of the very rich, he had thought, always protecting their privacy and scared stiff of the less well off. He found the card and dialled the number.

There was no answer and no possibility of leaving a message. He let it ring for a long time and hung up. Then almost immediately his phone rang. He picked up the receiver and heard the stagey Welsh voice.

"Damian. How nice to hear from you."

"We need to talk."

"We *are* talking."

"Yes, but something's come up that I need to discuss with you."

"Well, let's discuss it."

"I'm afraid I'm going to have to rescind our agreement. The board will not back me."

"But we have a contract."

"I know. I'm very sorry. I have no option. Perhaps we can come to some other arrangement about publishing your twenty pages of poetry?"

"What other arrangement?"

"You could let me see them, for example."

"Out of the question."

"That's the problem. The board cannot go along with my publishing something I personally have not selected. I am after all their chosen editor. If this work is as good as you say it is we should be able to select it together, and that will remove the problem."

"Mr Krapp, what you select for your magazine corresponds to an idea of taste to which I do not adhere. You would be incapable of recognising the quality of this work."

"Well, that's that, then."

"No, that's not that. I consider the contract binding. You will be hearing more from me."

The phone cut off and Krapp listened to static through the earpiece. He poured himself another drink, put the bottle away again, and sat down at his desk. He hadn't liked the Welshman's tone at all. He might be in need of protection. What had he got himself into? Should he phone that Joe Biggs fellow from *Artcrimes*? Krapp rummaged in the papers on his desk for the card Biggs had given him and found himself staring at the obituary of Bill Gerard-Wright he'd clipped from *The Times*.

What a good thing it was that the man could not have known either the time or the means of his surcease. It hadn't been an appropriate death, but what was an appropriate death, anyway? He contemplated his own mortality for a moment, then drained his glass, turned off the lights in the office, and made for home, where Ron was cooking lasagne.

*   *   *

The phone rang and Naily handed it to Biggs. He looked at the number in the display, pressed the green button and clicked on the loudspeaker so that Naily could listen in.

"Morning, guv."

"Good morning, Joe. You've heard the news?"

"Yeah."

"I'm admiring your wall chart."

As the news of the murder of Bill Gerard-Wright made the headlines, Biggs had been in the process of turning Priest's office into a replica of every police investigation bureau he had ever seen on television. On one wall he had pinned up pictures of the murdered poets, and all those associated with them. On another he had put a blown up picture of Robert Rees, and a profile of an imaginary woman, with a photo of a scorpion brooch inset beside it. He had drawn diagrams that showed the timeline of events in the case of each murder, and had jotted down every known sighting of Rees.

"You'll need a picture of Gerard-Wright," said Priest. "There's a good one in *The Telegraph*."

Biggs considered his wall pinnings. He looked at Naily.

"Where you got them cameras, guv?"

"You must forgive me, Joe. When I installed a surveillance system some years ago I did not intend to pry on your love life. I had no idea when I employed you that you would take up residence in the *Artcrimes* office."

"Sorry Mr Priest. We was planning to find a place together, but what with all these things you got me doing ..."

"I understand."

"Beats me where you put 'em though."

"Ah. So you've looked?"

Priest chuckled.

"In the meantime, I think it would be as well if you took down that picture of the ridiculous youth in coloured tights."

"BardSlayer, guv? Don't you think we should see what it's all about? I mean, it's gotta be connected. The people doing this could be murderers."

His employer sounded suddenly angry.

"Somebody is cashing in, Joe. Somebody is making a mockery of this pogrom of poets. It isn't funny. I hardly think you can attribute multiple homicides to a comic book character."

"OK, Mr Priest. I'll take it down."

"Have you spoken to Jemima Lee?"

"No, guv."

"Manfred von Zitz..."

"No guv."

"What news of Robert Rees?"

"I talked to this Krapp guy. The editor of *The Boot*. Looks like Rees is putting money into the mag. I don't think Krapp trusts Rees. He's gonna phone me if Rees wants to set up a meeting."

Priest said nothing for a moment.

"I think it's time we did something, don't you Joe?"

"Like what, guv?"

A citizen's arrest, perhaps? We can't be certain Rees is behind all this, but suspicion mounts up does it not?"

"Sure does."

"Let me know if Krapp calls you. It's time for action."

The phone clicked off and Joe looked at Naily.

"Well, if you ask me this BardSlayer character might have something to do with it."

Naily, holding Emily in her arms, moved to stand in front of Joe's wall display.

"Whit's that, Joe?"

"Scorpion brooch. Viola Walsh was wearing one on that ferry boat."

"Where dja git the picture?"

"Googled it. Dunno if it's like hers. But it's a scorpion alright."

Naily transferred her attention to BardSlayer. He was always depicted in the same dynamic pose, cape flowing, hair streaming back, fist flung forward, as he jetted through the air like a rocket.

"Who's doin Mr BardSlayer, eh?"

She took down the illustration with one hand and gave it to Biggs.

"Search me."

He fumbled in his pocket, drew out a small BardSlayer figure and stood it on the table.

"How many you got, Naily?"

"Ah found two."

BardSlayer was popping up everywhere. He was sprayed on walls. He disfigured election posters and advertisements (or improved them, depending on your point of view). He fluttered down from high buildings in origami shapes. If you sat down at a restaurant table, there'd be a plastic replica tucked into your napkin.

"What I don't get is how he can appear overnight all over the country."

"If it's the murderer doin it, Joe, Thiz gotta be a lotta murderers."

"Yeah."

"Does yir Mr Priest think yir gonna catch this killer all by yersel'?"

He looked at her.

"We got work to do, Naily. Put the cat down. We gotta go an' talk to a guy called Manfred von Zitzewitz."

On Joe's Lambretta, they weaved through the traffic towards West London. Von Zitzewitz lived in Putney. At one point they ran into a traffic jam that had been caused by motorists stopping to look at a gigantic mural on the blank side-wall of a building. BardSlayer was streaking skyward dangling a longfaced, shabbily-dressed and expostulating creature by the collar. Underneath the picture in looping italics was the caption: *Gotcha!*

As Joe weaved through the columns of vehicles, Naily hugging him tight, he shouted into the slipstream:

"Guess that's a poet he's caught!"

"A whizz of a sprayer, Joe! Ah know talent when ah see it!"

In Holmbush Road, Manfred von Zitzewitz opened the door.

"Oh, yes. *Artcrimes*. We talked on the phone, did we not?"

He led them down a narrow flight of stairs into a large kitchen. Von Zitzewitz seemed anxious. Had his life been threatened? On a long wooden table was a laptop, some papers, a plate with buttered toast and a boiled egg in an egg cup. He explained that he usually worked as he ate. He knew about the reputation of *Artcrimes* and was glad they were involved. The police were useless. If these homicides were not brought to a halt soon, citizens would have to mobilise. He would consider forming an association of vigilantes. It wouldn't be at all surprising to learn that a government cull of artists was behind it. Subsidising art was a drain on the exchequer. Get rid of impecunious poets! Save money! Von Zitzetwitz was contemptuous. Was Joe Biggs a poetry reader? Von Zitzewitz suspected not. As for Naily...? Would they like some tea? Actually, he'd just run out. And there was no milk. Yes, he'd been to Fergus Diver's last reading, but not because he had the slightest interest in Diver's work. He had gone to Diver's reading in order to kill time before catching the late train back to London. And a very boring reading it had been too. He had not stayed until the end.

A man in a deerstalker? Yes, indeed. Very bushy and red haired. The man had been a latecomer, like himself. Of course, the way Diver had died...Dreadful. Appalling. Had they seen the news about Bill Gerard-Wright? One of the let-it-all-hang-out school. Words, words, words. Von Zitzewitz himself had been conducting a one man campaign for brevity now for forty years. Was anyone listening? He doubted it. Yes, he had met Gerard-Wright a few times. They had read together once at the Cheltenham Literature Festival. An improbable pairing, but that was the way festival organisers worked. Their reading had been scheduled at the same time as a talk from the UK's most popular politician, who had just declared war on everybody. Naturally the audience all went to hear the idiot. Von Zitzewitz had found Gerard-Wright in the empty yurt where they were supposed to do their reading, smoking marijuana, drinking beer, and scribbling furiously. He was writing a broadside against the politician, lambasting him for everything he stood for. It was extremely ribald. In every scene in which he appeared, von Zitzewitz recalled, the politician was doing something unspeakable with a donkey. Amazing how fertile Gerard-Wright's imagination was. At least in respect to what you could do with a donkey. In the event, they had had an audience of twelve and Gerard-Wright had read his poem aloud with glee to cheers and applause. It wasn't a *poem*, you understand, said von Zitzewitz. He himself had not read any of his haiku that evening and had thereby forfeited his fee. But it had seemed right to do so.

"Don't suppose there was a guy in a deerstalker in the audience, was there?"

Von Zitzewitz stopped talking, put a spoon into what now must have been a cold egg, and took a mouthful, with toast.

"It was rather a long time ago," he said.

"Anyway," said Joe, "if you think about the murder, it sort of explains the donkeys, doesn't it? Question is: who was in the audience?"

Von Zitzewitz chewed slowly.

"I see what you mean," he said.

He had seemed agitated at the start of their visit, and was even more agitated as they were leaving. They asked if there was anything the matter.

"Something most definitely is the matter," said von Zitzewitz. "But don't worry. It has nothing to do with these events. It has to do with the future of a magazine with which I am intimately connected. Anyway I, as a mere haikuist, do not feel threatened by this maniac."

They rode away, leaving him standing on the pavement.

Chapter 21: *BardSlayer!*

Jeff Pratt was lonely at school, played no sports, and lived in a house by the sea. Often he saw the bards and their tearjerkers. The bards would recite poems to crowds. A creature holding a jug would pass among the people collecting their tears. The bard would drink down the tears and harangue the crowd: kill those who do not love poetry! Seek them out and kill them! *The crowd would disperse, looking for victims.*

Jeff was immune to these recitations. They did not make him weep.

One day a grey-haired man spoke to him near the beach. He suggested he should show Jeff a cave. Jeff was glad someone was taking an interest and went with the man. In the cave, the man sat on a boulder and said:

"I am not all I seem."

It was dark in the cave. The boy looked at the man's bushy eyebrows.

"My real name is Osip. I am three thousand years old."

The boy looked back towards the entrance to the cave. It was a long way off.

"I am here to save humanity from the bards. I have great powers. You are the one I have picked to help me. Come here."

The boy didn't move.

"You see those steps?"

Jeff looked and saw stone steps leading down. He could hear the sea roaring below.

"You will descend those twenty steps. When you reach the slab at the bottom you will let three waves break over you. On the third wave you will utter the word Kazilta! *You will become BardSlayer and share my powers with me."*

The boy looked into deep grey eyes. He was fed up with being a nobody. He went down the steps and on the third wave he shouted Kazilta! *Suddenly, he was no longer puny. He wore a yellow body suit with a black cape. The letter* **B** *was written on his chest. He made a fist, thrust his right arm forward and flew over Middletown-on-Sea. He saw his mother in the garden, reading a book of poems. When he returned, Osip was waiting.*

"You will help me destroy the bards," he said. "We must free humanity from their toils. Starting with your mother."

Ace Comics was five storeys up in an awe-inspiring building. Suzy had picked out his suit, the shoes and the tie, and they gave him courage. He was met by a genial man in shirt sleeves called Fred Saunders.

"Follow me," said Fred.

Saunders led the way through a long *atelier* where young men and women sat before tilted boards, drawing intently, colouring in, or gossiping in low tones over mugs of coffee. At the end of the workshop, they entered a carpeted area. The doors of a number of offices stood open; they were all empty. Glass doors opened into a meeting room. Seven people were sitting round a rectangular table and they looked up smiling as Fred Saunders ushered him in and introduced him.

"Here's the man we've all been dying to meet: Daniel Crane!"

All of those present began to rap the table with the ends of their pencils, or rulers, or fists, whatever came to hand. It was like a twenty one gun salute, and Daniel acknowledged it, modestly.

He laid his portfolio case on the table, drew out an illustration and held it up.

"Er, this is BardSlayer," he said.

Appreciative laughter. Smiles. Goodwill. He had a receptive audience. Ordering the nerves in his stomach to stop fluttering, he began to explain the idea behind BardSlayer.

"It was…What was it?"

The story that adjusts itself. The story that responds to its audience. The story that liberates itself. The story that frees its readers, also. The story that brings down the walls of its own prison. No dictation!

He stumbled over his words. He knew the ideas were all coming out in disjointed bits and pieces, but as he explored his theme he sensed he had the goodwill of his listeners. He delved into his bag for drawings, mock-ups, models and passed them round. As he was talking, his gaze wandered to the panorama windows. Stick-like figures were scurrying across a bridge. A very short while ago, he had been one of those citizens down there.

He needed to keep focussed. Concentrate!

After the presentation, he sat down. Eight people were looking at him. Most probably they had decided he was a complete fraud.

Leo Lopez, the art director at Ace Comics, a heavily built, balding man in braces, stood up:

"We're getting fantastic feedback, Daniel. And another thing! Tell him Fred! Make the boy happy!"

Fred Saunders grinned:

"We have a movie tie-in for this, Daniel. They have put money on the table. A lot of money. There's been great competition to get the rights."

For a moment there was silence; they were all looking at each other. Then a babble of questions and answers began that nearly overwhelmed him. Where had he acquired his computer skills? Who made the models? How had he managed to motivate so many people to join in the fun? Did he think the BardSlayer project would usher in a whole new genre of collaborative storytelling. What other surprises did he have up his sleeve?

At the end of the session, Leo came up to him and put a copy of the first issue of *BardSlayer!* into his hand. The colour reproduction was fantastic; the issue had already sold out and was reprinting. But the comic book was an artefact. BardSlayer was already in cyberspace. He had, as they say, 'gone viral'. He was out there. The art director gave a short speech about orchestrating the collaboration of thousands of digitally-inspired illuminators. Yes, he had called them 'illuminators'. Then he turned to his staff, made a short speech of thanks and asked if anyone had any more questions. With smiles and nods to Daniel, most of the group left the room.

A young woman who had been sitting to his right, and who had not spoken until then, asked:

"Where did you get the idea, Daniel? Did it have anything to do with these murders of poets we keep reading about? I mean, do you hate poetry or something? The way you depict these bards, well, they're evil...?"

He finished packing away his material and clicked his portfolio case shut. "They're supposed to be."

"The thing about them is," she said, "they're not bards. I mean they're not poets at all, are they?"

"No. They're false poets. They're false artists. They pretend to be poets in order to destroy poetry."

"So you like poetry really? BardSlayer wants to save the world for poetry?"

"That's a good way to put it."

Fred Saunders showed him out of the building. It was a pleasant morning – a few clouds, a light breeze, the sunlight held warmth – and he decided to walk along the river. Suzy, he knew, would be sitting beside the phone waiting to hear how it had gone, but he wanted to savour success all by himself for a while.

There was a little park along the embankment and he went in and sat on a bench. Two young men were setting up deckchairs in front of the bandstand, and one or two band members were warming up their instruments for a lunchtime concert. He leaned back, closed his eyes, and let the sunshine play on his face.

It had been cold on the cliff. The drowned village had exerted an irresistible pull. He'd been so keen to spend a week in Barnaby Brown's company at the Tamlyn Trust, and then, watching the activity that was going on there, he'd had the sudden feeling it was all wrong. It wasn't real cordiality he'd witnessed, but smiles of treachery. Would-be poets. Rivals for the hand of the muse. All nurturing evil thoughts towards one another. Was he really expecting people like that to listen to his epic poem?

He'd moved closer and closer to the edge of the cliff. The villagers under the waves had been beckoning to him. He felt giddy.

Then he'd become aware of someone sitting next to him.

"Are you alright?"

"What?"

"You're not depressed are you? A couple of months ago we had a suicide here."

"I just wanted to see if I could see the submerged village."

"There's nothing to see. Anyway, it's getting dark. What's your name?"

He told her, and asked for hers. It was Suzy Tallis. She wanted to know what he was doing there and he told her about the Tamlyn Trust. Oh, poetry, she'd said. She'd been surprised people still wrote it. Nobody read that stuff, did they? Daniel asked her if she'd read any at school and she told him she'd never attended one. Her father was an inventor who built thermo-couples for industry. Her father was a genius. Naturally he despised schools, governments and religion. Geniuses do. He'd been their teacher so there'd been no need for school. Wasn't it getting a bit cold, and shouldn't they move somewhere warm?

Daniel stretched his arms along the back of the bench. He opened his eyes. The band had taken its place on the stand and was warming up with *The Dambusters March*.

Sunlight flashed on the bright metal of trombones and cornets placed on the ground. Attracted by the music, people were starting to occupy the deckchairs.

How shocked she'd been to learn he was planning to spend the night under the stars. He should stay with the Tallis family. They had more spare room than they knew what do with. As they walked towards her house, she had asked if it would worry him that her Mum and Dad were nudists? She herself was an anarcho-syndicalist. What politics was he? She was interested in men at the moment, but later on she thought she would become a lesbian. She really wanted to have an affair with an older, intellectual woman. A Simone de Beauvoir sort of person. Her brother Jake was at Art College and she'd like to go to art school, too, but Jake had had such terrible fights with their father about going there that she didn't feel she could face it. Fights with Dad, that is. Then she'd asked him:

"Do you kiss?"

He was taken aback by this question and asked:

"What do you mean?"

She demonstrated.

When the kiss was over, he realised he had left his bag with his books and his epic poem on the top of the cliff and announced his intention of going back to fetch it. Suzy had put her arm around his waist:

"I don't know if you noticed, Daniel, but it's dark already. Mum is making a stew and Dad has to have his meals on time. Why don't we eat first and go back for it later? Has it got your name on?"

"All over it."

"It'll still be there. Don't worry."

He never had gone back for it. She had conducted him round the side of a vast redbrick Victorian villa and into a very hot kitchen, where his first glimpse of Mrs Tallis was a woman wearing an apron and nothing else. A rosy bottom and long, greying hair.

Don't mind me," she'd said. "I'm usually like this. Are you a waif and stray? Suzy collects them."

"Daniel will be staying tonight," said Suzy.

"What a nice name. Daniel. You can put him in the second spare room."

"He can sleep with me."

"I hope that's alright with Daniel."

Mrs Tallis took a pot from the stove and looked at him:

"She's very forward. We should have sent her to school."

Daniel laughed aloud at the recollection as the band crashed into a brassy waltz. He had eaten supper with the family, meeting her brother Jake, and Suzy's preoccupied father, and later that night he had lost his virginity. Suzy had been very matter-of-fact about it; a great burden had lifted. The following morning, she had taken him into what she called the art room, where Jake sat at a big easel, working with great concentration. Daniel, peering over his shoulder, learned that Jake and Suzy were collaborating on what they called a graphic novel. Comic to you, Daniel, Jake had said. They needed a villain and Daniel had picked up a fine brush and sketched a long-faced man in a rumpled suit, with voluminous bags under his eyes, a big wet-lipped mouth and Charlie Chaplin style too-big shoes for flat feet that pointed right and left. Underneath, he wrote *Bard*.

Was there something grim in that depiction that suggested the features of Fergus Diver? He was amused by his own cartoon. All morning they had talked and drawn pictures for one another. His skill at drawing was something he'd been able to do since he was a child; he was surprised to find that Jake and Suzy loved the speed with which he could do it. And how good it had been not to be a virgin anymore. He could not stop embracing her, just as the Tallis family embraced him. He had come for a night and stayed. By the end of the week, he was glad he had left his epic poem on the cliff.

The poet murders were discussed at breakfast. Mr Tallis thought one poet less was good for society and took himself off to the laboratory. Jake shouted after him: 'Dad, since when do you approve of murder?' and looked at his mother with an expression that read 'Dad's hopeless.' Mrs Tallis found this funny. Suzy revealed that Daniel had

had pretensions to become a poet. Jake was not impressed. How can you do anything with words? he'd asked. Words are so vague. What image do you get if I say tinker, tailor, politician, crook? It's all a blur, isn't it? But if I *draw* you a tailor...

That morning, Daniel had drawn BardSlayer. He thought Bard-Slayer should have great intelligence, but should be trusting where he should have learned not to be. Jake agreed. Super heroes had to be god-like, but like all the gods, they had to have a special weakness, a point of vulnerability. Yes, said Daniel. A fatal flaw. He drew a wise-looking senior citizen. This is Osip, he said. BardSlayer's weakness would be that he derived his strength from Osip. When the old man grew tired, BardSlayer would turn back into the insecure weakling, Jeff Pratt. That was the moment the Bards could defeat him.

Mrs Tallis had expressed surprise, some weeks later, that Daniel was still there. Other waifs and strays, it seemed, had been fairly rapidly evicted back into waif-and-straydom. But he felt adopted. He'd got used to seeing Mrs Tallis wander in and out of the conservatory with no clothes on, and George Tallis, equally naked, descending the stairs with one hand on the balustrade and a book in the other. Daniel himself preferred to stay dressed; he couldn't quite get used to Jake and Suzy's unconcern about mere garments.

A burst of clapping broke into his reverie. The band had launched into *Entry of the Gladiators*. Some youths drinking bottled beer nearby raised their bottles and cheered. Daniel looked at the beer drinkers and noticed that, sitting on top of a green waste basket and held in place by a clip, there was a tiny, painted bard. He got up and plucked it off the wire mesh. It fitted nicely in his palm. This particular model was fashioned out of some sort of bendy plastic. Its blubbery red lips seemed to be on the verge of reciting something. He could imagine the audience getting up and shuffling towards him, muttering Kill! Kill!

He went back to the bench, collected his portfolio case and set off across Embankment Bridge towards the Festival Hall, stopping at mid-point to secure the bard to the bridge parapet. People would have to be keen-eyed to spot it; all you could see were two green hands, clinging on. Pity he didn't have a tearjerker in his pocket. Where there were tearjerkers, there was always a bard.

They owed the models to Jake and his art college friends. As the story began to evolve, Jake started to make designs and pass them to his friends, who set up little tableaux in public places – like nativity cribs, said Jake, except of course everyone knew *that* story. Enterprising colleagues buried models and artefacts at locations to be discovered by using satellite coordinates revealed on the internet. The models were made of any material that came to hand – clay, wood, tin, plastic. They created treasure hunts. People all over the country teamed up to track down caches of BardSlayer material hidden at coordinates posted on the web.

As he entered the Festival Hall, Daniel wished he'd brought a bard or two in his pocket. He felt like going upstairs and parking a few models in the room where he'd been a participant in Barnaby Brown's workshop. That would give them something to think about. He'd had Barnaby's last collection in his pocket the day he met Suzy, and he'd made the mistake, later, of showing it to Jake. What withering contempt that had elicited! Things that Jake thought dishonest or affected got the full laser beam of his scorn; he found much to discommend in Barnaby's poems.

"Up his own arse," he'd said, throwing the book down.

The Royal Festival hall was busy; Daniel bought a sandwich and a coffee and sat watching people come in and go out. He recalled the weird Welshman, Robert Rees. What kind of a stunt had *he* been trying to pull? Daniel had been unable to track down anyone of that name, in or out of academe. As for the magazine *Storm*... It now existed as an evil organisation in the bardic empire, headed by the villainous plotter Herbert Sore.

He had kept Barnaby's book, and still read and re-read the poems. He didn't agree with Jake's estimation at all. Sometimes he felt sad to have abandoned that particular vocation: poet. The problem was that poetry was like bat communication. If it were possible to talk to a bat and the bat could speak English, it would still be very hard to understand what the bat was saying. How could a human being grasp bat problems? His own poems were bat poems. He knew that. Daniel nudged his specs back up his nose, sipped his coffee and decided that a truly genuine poet was one who chose not be one. Like himself. Like Rimbaud.

Well. It was good to have thoughts, even if you didn't have the faintest idea where they were leading. He finished his coffee and went into one of the roomy Festival Hall toilets. It was empty and there was a broad expanse of unsullied wall. He pulled out one of his sprays and in a few strokes drew BardSlayer coming in to land, feet first, cape flowing upward in the slipstream of his descent. He left the toilet and walked out on to the terraces overlooking the Thames. A string of barges was slowly chugging past going downriver.

Graffiti had been part of the campaign from the start. Bards appeared on walls, uttering threats and a day or so later BardSlayer would appear in attack mode. He had evolved into the world's most popular super hero. In the sphere of cyber space, BardSlayer asked for friends and offered to lend his powers in return; he had no difficulty in finding friends. The bards were false artists bent on destroying authenticity. They had been hired by politicians to depress art and destroy real human communication. The only way to save humanity was to have everybody take part in the story that would redeem the planet. That was the whole point.

He took out his mobile phone.

"Suzy?"

"Hello, Sweetie, where are you?"

"I'm standing by the river, near the Festival Hall."

"How did it go?"

"What?"

"The presentation, silly."

"Oh. It went very well. I've got a copy of BardSlayer! – the comic - in my bag. They think there's going to be a film."

"Fantastic! I love you!"

"I love you too!"

For a while he stood watching the slow revolutions of the London Eye, and the barges moving in long lines along the river. Then he went back inside, bought another coffee, sat down, and began to write in his notebook.

It was always a long journey to the Kazilta Stone. Osip would cross the bridge of ice, pass under the frozen waterfall, and walk into the dark mountain. Reaching the magic boulder, he would lie upon the glittering slab and in a few hours he would awake, refreshed and full of the energy he needed to continue the struggle.

But trees were down. Ferry boats were not plying the rivers. Avalanches clogged mountain paths. This time the journey had ex-

hausted him. Near the bridge of ice, Osip saw a pair of clownish shoes jutting from behind a tree. He saw, reflected in a pool, a long face behind his shoulder that vanished when he turned.

If the long faces stopped him reaching the stone, humanity was lost.

The bards were multiplying, but wherever they appeared BardSlayer would swoop down and fly them, kicking and screaming, to the Black Hole. He would let them fall, and watch them vanish into the cosmic abyss. He patrolled the planet without cease. Now and then, he would be Jeff Pratt for a day and sit with his mother drinking tea in her kitchen. Then Osip would transmit an urgent message and Jeff would become BardSlayer again. His mother would quietly put away the tea things.

On a platform in a town square in Australia, a bard stood up to recite. As he recited, the crowd grew wild and set off towards Nooky Bend with the bard leading them. There were some young people in Nooky Bend who, without hope of reward, had set up a commune to explore new forms of art. BardSlayer saw the homicidal mob enter the precincts of the town and march towards the commune. In a trice, he flew down and collared the bard. As he was lifting his howling captive through the air, he felt his powers fail. He fell to earth. The bard jeered and scurried off.

Alone in the main street of Nooky Bend, stood a boy. Kazilta! he called out. Kazilta! he called again.

Osip lay sprawled on the ground. He could go no further. The entrance to the dark mountain was very close, but unreachable. All around he sensed dark shapes gathering in.

The inhabitants of Nooky Bend had taken refuge in their houses. Jeff Pratt saw a pair of clownish shoes jutting from behind a street corner. Reflected in a shop window, he saw a long face atop a rumpled suit that vanished when he turned.

"Kazilta!" he shouted. Nothing happened.

How would he save humanity now?

Chapter 22: The Deep Song

Victor Priest was wearing a grey tweed coat that hung open to show a blue silk suit with a barely perceptible yellow stripe, soft Italian shoes and an art deco tie. He looked very different from the last time she had seen him, in motor cycle leathers. She drew back to study him, looked at his face, and thought she saw lines of strain around his eyes. She took his hand and drew him over the threshold.

"It's good you're here, Victor," she said. "Inspector Dobson has just left."

"I know. I saw the car and waited. I hope he was not presumptuous. I decided that with a police driver outside he wouldn't be."

"Come through into the living room, Victor."

"No," he said. He had come to take her away. He hoped she had nothing planned, and that if she did she would cancel it. He had good news for her and he wanted to take her to his house on the coast, cook her a meal, and celebrate the occasion.

She asked him to wait in the hall and hurried upstairs. She changed and stood in front of the bathroom mirror brushing on make up. She found a blouse she had bought some time before and not yet worn, and a pair of new shoes, put on her favourite green skirt and came back down the stairs. He was standing in the hallway looking up at her. She took her best coat from the hall cupboard.

"Do you live far away, Victor?"

"By distance, yes. By speed, no."

He was right about that. Then, as they approached the house by means of a winding, steep-climbing lane, she gave a cry. Priest's house stood at the highest point above a cliff overlooking the sea. It was a grey stone, Edwardian building with a slate roof, bay windows on the ground floor, and a conservatory at the back. They drove between two stone pillars topped with griffins and the wheels of the Porsche crunched over gravel and came to a stop. As she got out of the car, she found she was looking down a stairwell into an illuminated swimming pool by the side of the house. It seemed huge. Not Olympic-sized, perhaps, but very big for a domestic installation. The water in the pool was absolutely still. And inviting.

"May I confess something, Victor?"

"Confess all."

"I was junior Jugoslav champion in the 100 metres freestyle. And I have a gold medal to prove it."

"Really? Perhaps we should have a swim before I start cooking."

"I'd love to. I used to go twice a week to the municipal pool, but since Fergus died I haven't been."

They went up a flight of stone steps to the house, and the door was opened by Priest's housekeeper. He instructed Maddy to show Vesna around and disappeared into the kitchen to make some preparations for an early dinner. She was shown a spacious library, a billiards room with a full-size billiards table, an elegant sitting room with French windows and a log fire. They looked at the upstairs rooms, including Priest's study. There were corridors and more corridors, and a flight of back stairs. Maddy explained it was easy to get lost in the house and led her down into the kitchen. Priest was doing something at the stove.

"Thank you Maddy," he called. "No need to wait around. Mrs Diver and I are going for a swim."

The housekeeper departed. Vesna and Priest went down stairs into the pool.

"Oh," she said.

He raised his eyebrows.

"No gear?"

"No."

He nodded.

"Then we won't bother."

She watched as he stripped off and laid his clothes over the back of a white recliner by the pool. Though he was certainly forty years old or more, and she had even noticed a grey hair or two amongst the blonde, he had an athletic body like those of the young men she had known on the swimming team. He ran naked to the edge of the pool, dived in, and began to swim a powerful crawl. Without hesitating, she took off her clothes and followed him into the water.

They swam for about half an hour, racing each other back and forth, demonstrating different strokes – Priest could do a ludicrously over-achieving butterfly stroke that had her laughing till the tears came – and they then started playing water polo, throwing the ball and chasing after it. When they climbed out, Priest took big sauna towels from a cupboard and she wrapped herself in one.

"Sauna?" he asked.

"No thank you, Victor. I don't really like them."

She contemplated her wet hair in a mirror.

"What am I going to do about that?"

"There's a changing room over there. You'll find everything you need."

As she went in, she wondered how often Victor Priest had visitors. Putting her clothes on a chair, she dried her hair, combed it, and got dressed. There was expensive perfume in an elaborate bottle and she used some of it. She looked at herself in the mirror. Perhaps she was a bit older than Priest, but she had kept her figure. Fergus had always employed heavy irony on the subject of her swimming and gymnastics. He was a man who had considered his own body an encumbrance to be borne with, but he had been proud of her at festivals because she knew how to look good in clothes.

There was a tap at the door.

"I'm going upstairs, Vesna. See you in the kitchen."

"Alright."

She sat for a while in the comfy chair that had been provided in the changing room and thought about Priest. He had to be enormously rich to own this house. How come he lived on his own, as he appeared to? Were there no women in his life? At one moment in the pool, they had collided as they raced for the ball, and she had felt his arm grip her waist. He had held her hard against his body for a moment, and then released her. When they got out of the pool she had seen very clearly, and he had made no attempt to hide the fact, that he was aroused.

She thought again about Fergus. Their sex life had been dormant for at least five years. Eventually they had taken to sleeping in separate bedrooms and she had been relieved to be away from his snoring. It wasn't that Fergus had lost all interest in the opposite sex. She knew that he was conducting little affairs, but they seemed to be mostly verbal, conducted by letter or email, or clandestine phone calls. At least, he thought they were clandestine. It was quite possible that Vesna had known what Fergus was going to do before Fergus knew himself.

Well, Fergus was dead. Perhaps it was time for her to wake up and do something else with her life. She left the changing room and went up the stairs to the kitchen, breathing in unexpected, smoky aromas as she neared the control centre. Priest turned round as she entered. He was wearing an apron with the words *Dobro dosli* on it, in cyrillic, the Serbian for welcome.

"Where did you get that, Victor?"

"I bought it on the internet. I thought, seeing as I'm cooking a Serbian meal, that it would be appropriate."

He indicated the dishes on the sideboard

"*Gibanica* to start with. I have made it with real Serbian *kajmak* and the strudel dough is my own. Paul at the Trocadero in Paris showed me how to make it. I have a chilled Ilocki *Traminac* to go with it. I know Ilok is just across the border in Croatia, but we'll ignore that. Did you know the wines from Ilok were the glory of the Hapsburg empire? Then we'll have a little fish soup, *alaska corba*, and to follow that I've grilled you some home-made *cevapcici,* made with three different kinds of meat, and the main course is roast quail with rice. I've found an excellent *Prokupac* to drink with it. We'll finish with *savijaca sa visnjama*, sour cherry roll. How's my pronunciation?"

"Terrible, Victor. You surely don't expect me to eat all that?"

But he did. Each course was light and cooked with the military aplomb of a Karadjordjević. They ate the tiny individual cheese strudels he had made – they were so light, they floated down your throat – and moved on to the soup. Priest talked with enthusiasm for a while about the work of Kafka, but she had never read Kafka, and noticing this he moved on to other themes. As he was serving up the *cevapcici*, with strips of roasted and marinaded pepper, he said, almost with a note of apology in his voice:

"The University of Nagoya have offered $800,000 for your husband's papers. I am very sorry I could not persuade them to go to the million I'd hoped for but it is still a very good price. Do I have your permission to accept their offer?"

"That's amazing, Victor, how can I thank you?"

She sat back in her chair, looking at him. Such a sum would completely secure her future. How had he done it? She hadn't expected her husband to be worth so much. The truth was, she hadn't really expected his poems to be worth anything at all. A terrible feeling of disloyalty swept over her. Fergus was hardly in the grave. She dropped her fork, with a clatter, on the plate.

"Is anything the matter?"

"I'm sorry."

She dabbed at her eyes with a paper napkin.

"Not the roast peppers is it? I put some chili in the marinade."

"No, no. These *cevapcici* are so perfect, Victor. I've never eaten anything like this in England. My mother couldn't have made them any better."

She cleared her throat with vigour. Victor regarded her with intense sympathy.

"It hardly seems to right to call them meat balls, does it? They're not even balls. More like sausages."

She couldn't help it. She started to laugh.

"When I began to study how to make *cevapcici,* I realised that in fact it was quite a science."

He parodied the mannerisms of a TV chef.

"It's the mixing of the meats, the *marriage* of the paprika and garlic. And then you see you need this little indoor charcoal grill that imparts just the right smoky flavour."

"Enough, Victor!"

"Soul food really, isn't it? Are you ready for the roast quail?"

She was laughing hard and held up her napkin to cover her mouth. He leaned forward:

"More *Prokupac*?"

Her laughter subsided. She nodded and he refilled her glass. Drinking wine, she watched him as he got up to dish the quail onto a plate.

"Do you think Fergus was worth that amount of money?"

"Ah."

Priest sat down again at the table and began to portion food onto fresh plates.

"The value of poetry is hard to gauge, Vesna. Attaching a price to an oeuvre is a difficult thing to do."

"Yes, Victor, but do you esteem my husband's work as much as that price would imply?"

"Oh, I'd say he was undoubtedly one of the best of the current crop."

"The best of the current crop? That sounds less than enthusiastic."

"People are trapped in their time, Vesna. May I quote you Li Po: *No one understands now. Those who could hear the deep song vanished long ago.*"

"I'm not quite sure I follow you, Victor."

He smiled and said nothing.

"You know," she said, "you remind me of Tomica?"

"Tomica?"

"We were on the swim team together. You have a look of him."

"I do?"

"And some of his passion."

He smiled.

"What happened to Tomica?"

"In the war. He died. He was at Vukovar. I don't know what he was doing and I don't want to know."

They ate in silence for a while. When the quail was finished, Priest placed dessert on the table and sat down, indicating she should help herself. As she sawed off a slice of sour cherry roll, he said:

"You engaged me originally to find your husband's murderer."

"I did. And have you?"

"I have. His name is Robert Rees. Does the name mean anything to you?"

She shook her head.

"He passes himself off as a Welshman running a business out of Aberystwyth, but there is no such company, and certainly not in Aberystwyth. He has an accomplice by the name of Viola Walsh."

She looked at Victor, suddenly worried. Surely it couldn't be one of Fergus's...?

"The attractive blonde you mentioned?"

"The very same."

Vesna stared down at the sour cherry roll down on her plate. Was he telling her a *woman* poisoned Fergus? How and why did that have to happen? She fought back a feeling of panic.

"Have you told the police, Victor?"

"I'll tell my assistant tomorrow to report our findings to Scotland Yard."

She was silent. Priest realised she had finished eating and began to clear away the things. He suggested they should move into the drawing room, where there was a fire. He brought a bottle of *Vil-*

jamovka, cold from the fridge, and two thimbles to drink from. She did not sit down but stood staring out of the windows at some lights out on the sea.

"We will catch this assassin very soon. Don't worry, Vesna."

She turned round. He had been approaching her with a glass in his hand, but he put the glass down and embraced her. He kissed her and she felt herself responding, but drew back. She could feel the strength of his desire and smiled an apology. He did not insist. They sat down in armchairs at opposite sides of the fire.

"On the strength of a recent rather successful business transaction," he said, "I have bought a property in New Zealand, in the south island. I was thinking of going there for a month or so. Would you feel like accompanying me to the Antipodes?"

She burst into tears.

He came across to her, stroking her hair. Then he pulled her to her feet with gentle strength and embraced her once again. Once again, she disentangled herself, looked up, and stroked his cheek.

"Victor. This is too much at once. You're very kind. I really...I really think I should go home now."

He was looking at her with admiration. Why had he picked her? She wasn't used to men looking at her like that. She knew that she had better leave. If she drank any brandy, she would spend the night here in Priest's house.

"So soon? It's an infant of a night."

"I must go," she said. "Thank you so much for your kindness, Victor. The meal was truly wonderful. But I must go."

He stood for a moment without saying anything. Then he said: "I'll get the car keys."

*   *   *

Van Ackroyd had settled down to watch *The Blue Room,* JJ Moon's celebrated late show about the arts, and Moon himself had just walked on to the studio set in white canvas shoes, a cream linen suit and open-necked blue shirt and crossed his legs in the famous blue chair, when the doorbell rang. Ackroyd groaned, got up and opened the front door.

"Victor! What a surprise!"

"Hello Van. I'm not disturbing you am I?"

Priest walked in to Ackroyd's living room. He seemed agitated, and Ackroyd handed him a glass of red wine.

"What brings you here so late?"

"I couldn't settle. Too many things on my mind."

It was very unlike Priest to visit unannounced. No doubt the small leather document case he held was significant, but he wasn't the kind of man who turned up on the off chance you might be at home – especially not when he had literary treasure to reveal.

"What are you watching?"

"The JJ Moon show."

Moon was introducing the programme. Apart from the livid birth scar down one side of his face, the several-times broken nose, and the patchy hair of an alopecia sufferer, Moon was also ugly. Indeed he made a thing of it.

Priest regarded the TV set. The presenter was employing the jovial patter that was the preamble to all his shows, but with less levity than usual. Tonight's subject was the serial execution of the best poets of the United Kingdom, and the unholy interest in the art form this had awakened in the population at large.

Moon had produced a cardboard cut-out of BardSlayer and was holding it aloft.

"And what about this phenomenon, ladies and gentlemen. What does *this* have to do with poetry?"

Priest sat down.

"Van? What is that?"

Ackroyd shrugged and said:

"It must be an advertising campaign, though I don't know what for."

"Pretty crass, don't you think, when real poets are being killed?"

Priest sat back in his chair and put the leather case on his lap. Moon was introducing his first guest, Anita Bellows. A short-haired woman in a long black dress walked over to the blue sofa. Two tiny black monkeys dangled from her ears.

JJ Moon flashed his crooked teeth:

"Anita, why is this happening to poets?"

"Our very existence, JJ, is a challenge to the way of life most people prefer to adopt."

Moon nodded.

"Would you see yourself as the conscience of the nation?"

"This is absurd," said Priest.

Moon made a signal and lights came up on a stage in another part of the set. The shuffling rhythm of a reggae band began to fill the studio and applause greeted Manny Lascalle, the Trinidadian dub poet. He launched into a performance of an elegy called 'Murder Riddims'. Behind him the steel drummer created bendy waves of sound.

"For God's sake turn that racket down," said Priest.

Ackroyd would have liked to go on listening, but he heard a note in Priest's voice that made him turn down the volume. Priest got up and put his leather document case on a sideboard. He opened it and took out a manuscript, handling it with great care. Then he turned to Ackroyd, holding it up.

"Take a look at this, Van."

Ackroyd put down his glass and walked over to inspect it. He scrutinised it, then pulled out a drawer and took out his magnifying eyepiece, running it over the script.

"My God Victor. I hear the true voice of K. And the paper and type looks authentic. What did you pay?"

"It came cheap."

Ackroyd whistled.

"How did you get away with it? You could retire forever on the proceeds from this. You know you won't be able to offer them for auction without certification of their origin?"

"I'm hoping you'll find one of your millionaire private collectors for me. They don't care where things come from."

Ackroyd returned to his seat and felt for his glass with his hand. He raised it to Priest and drank. What was Victor not capable of pulling off? Ackroyd knew he would have no difficulty selling the manuscripts. As for the price that could be attached to them...? They'd be hammering on Ackroyd's door when they knew Franz Kafka had come back from the grave. Priest was still standing by the sideboard, arranging the material in his document case. He looked tired.

"You've not been overdoing it, have you Victor? Are you still embroiled in that murder enquiry?"

But Priest did not reply. He had turned to watch the silent

mouthings of Manny Lascalle. He bent down and turned up the volume control on the set.

> - *De teef of de hound*
> *Bring de poet down*
> *De kick of de mule*
> *Make de poet a ghoul*
> *Dey killin poet-tree!*
> *Dey killin poet-tree!*

"This is grotesque," said Priest.

As the song concluded, Moon pressed a button on the console beside his chair, the studio darkened, and the face of Melinda Speling was projected on to a screen. In a very measured way, she began to read a poem called 'The Green Hammock.' There was an intent hush whilst this film was in progress. After the reading, Anita Bellows jumped up and began to clap, leading the applause from the audience.

"You see?" she cried. "A spirit speaking from the sky! What a loss to poetry!"

JJ Moon, pleased with the reaction he had provoked, motioned for quiet and turned to his two guests:

"I can see that poem got to you both. But Melinda Speling is dead. So where does that leave us? Where does poetry go from here?"

He turned back again.

"And that, ladies and gentlemen, is the question we have for you today."

He bent down and produced a large placard from underneath the blue chair and held it up for all to see. In fluorescent blue writing, it read:

WHITHER POETRY?

Ackroyd emitted a huge guffaw. Priest jumped up, turned off the volume again, and began to pace up and down. Then he stopped. He apologised once more for disturbing Ackroyd so late. He had come to talk about many things, and somehow the TV programme had distracted him.

"I had vowed it would never happen to me again, Van. But it has."

Ackroyd understood immediately what his friend was talking about. He offered more drink, coffee, a late repast, what would Victor like? But Priest seemed dashed and forlorn.

"Did she turn you down?"

"No. But don't you see, Van, this is going to ruin my plans."

Ackroyd didn't see. What plans? If the lady had not said no, there was hope. There was always hope. He assumed that Victor was talking about Fergus Diver's widow. Was he right? Priest did not respond. Well, was there some other diva on the horizon? Ackroyd was not judgmental. He merely wanted to know.

Priest stopped pacing.

"You're a good friend, Van. I brought you something. I suspect this will be even more of a surprise than Franz Kafka."

He opened his case again, took out a document wallet, and handed it to Ackroyd. There were about eighty sheets of A4 paper in the wallet, held together by a rubber band. The top sheet announced, quite simply: *Lunar Conspiracies*. Underneath was the author's name. Ackroyd gave an exclamation:

"Victor! This is amazing. There must be seventy poems here. It's a book!"

"I hope so, Van. It was a long time in the making. Though the new ones came quickly. Very quickly."

Ackroyd leafed through the pages and started reading.

"No, Van. Don't read them now. It's late. I must be going."

Then Priest was gone. Ackroyd sat down and looked at a brief epigraph Victor had put at the front of the book. He read:

> *under the mucus of slubbed clouds*
> *stalks and gleams from each*
> > *sprained tantrum*
> *a spell chaffered by black trees*
> *their genital shadows plucked by*
> > *tasselled winds*
> *as the auguries that we revere*
> > *are immunised*

"Yes," thought Ackroyd. "Yes!"

Chapter 23: *An Irregular Contributor*

Damian Krapp had expected that calling another emergency board meeting at short notice would present great problems, but all barring one of the board members had immediately agreed to come. It was Jemima Lee who presented a problem.

On the telephone, Tambi Kumar had explained:

"You see, Damian, she is sure she will be the next one."

Jemima was holed up in her tenth floor flat on the Byker Wall in Newcastle-on-Tyne, watching every news bulletin. She had not been out of the flat for nearly two weeks and had arranged for food to be delivered.

"She is beleaguered, Damian. Completely beleaguered."

"So how are we going to persuade her to come down to London?"

"It will be very difficult, Damian, to get her to take a train."

The briefest of glances at Tambi's review of her most recent book told him why train travel would not seem opportune. The first paragraph of the review began:

Reading The Metro Suicides I was thrilled by the way Jemima Lee has captured so exactly the hold underground transport systems have on our imaginations. Is it because they are so deep in the ground, halfway to Hades? Which of us has not stood on a very long escalator thinking we are not coming back up? The subject of the poems in The Metro Suicides, is, yes, suicide, but these poems somehow manage never to be depressing. The deaths that repeat themselves there make up the bitter zest of sweet life. I remember back in Delhi in 2002 waiting on the platform for the very first train on the new underground system to draw in. The shininess of it! It seemed to be commanding me to plunge!

His reading was interrupted by Eric Lemmon, who poked his head round the door and grinned.

"Guess what, Damian, there's a lady obituarist to see you."

"A what?"

"Wait till you see her."

Was Lemmon making fun of him? He didn't want anything more to do with obituaries, or people who wrote them. He pulled open the drawer of his desk to check that his snubbie was still there.

He hadn't wanted to have a gun but Ron had persuaded him – he'd acquired one from an East End acquaintance and insisted that Damian keep it in the office in case that threatening Welshman showed up with malicious intent. They'd driven out into Hertfordshire and gone into a field. 'You've got to practise with it', Ron had said. 'Try not to hit any cows.' He'd blasted off a round, quite surprised by the kick the little pistol had. 'That's enough, Ron had said. 'Ammunition's expensive'.

What would he do if Robert Rees really were standing there menacing him? Would he be able to pull a trigger? He closed the drawer and looked up as a tall, blonde woman entered, smiling. Eric Lemmon standing behind her said:

"This is Viola Walsh, Damian. I'll leave your travel bag by the door, Mrs Walsh."

"Thank you, Eric. Hello Mr Krapp. I hope you don't mind this intrusion."

"Well, I do have a board meeting today, but it's not for two hours."

He stood up and thrust forward a hand.

"What can I do for you?"

"I don't know if you managed to read my obituary of Melinda Speling in *The Guardian?* And of Barnaby Brown and Fergus Diver in *The Times?*"

Damian took in his visitor's elegant business suit. She was appraising him carefully, her head held slightly to one side, her green eyes fixed on his.

"Yes, I did read the obits. I'm afraid I didn't notice the name of the author."

He motioned to her to sit down. She did so, crossing her legs and adjusting her skirt.

"Why would you? The names of obituary writers vanish; the fame of their subjects burns on."

Her voice was quiet, rather deep, beautifully modulated. Krapp listened in fascination as she began to murmur:

Eheu fugaces, Postume, Postume..."

"Horace," he began. "My Latin isn't..."

"How the years go by Postumus, alas how they pass by. Horace doesn't actually say it in the poem, but it is true isn't it that although we all know we're going to die, none of us can really believe it?"

Damian wasn't quite sure how to take this. Viola Walsh looked like a competent female business executive. Why was she sitting here quoting stuff at him he definitely didn't want to hear? He had a very important meeting coming up and he needed to get clear in his head what he was going to say to the board members.

"All the obituaries I've had to write lately have been as a result of homicide, Mr Krapp. I daresay you've noticed, but in case you haven't there have been six murders of poets to date. All were put to death in a way that reflected the matter or the manner of their poems. Now we have Bill Gerard-Wright, kicked to death by a donkey."

Damian sighed.

"Yes. Donkeys. What on earth did Gerard-Wright have to do with donkeys?"

"We don't know," said Viola, "what role donkeys may or may not have played in his private life."

"I suppose not. May I offer you an espresso? I've got a new machine designed for astronauts."

"Thank you, that's very kind, but I've had three already today."

A large sandy-coloured retriever that had been lying quietly under the desk woofed.

"Don't mind Boris. I'm looking after him for my partner. He's completely harmless."

"He's very big. He must take a lot of feeding."

Damian nodded.

"I've brought a fourpack of *Cesar* lamb and chicken mix. That should keep him happy."

"Sounds like a feast. Did you say you were having a meeting? My colleague at *The Observer* mentioned you might be."

Damian bent down and patted Boris:

"What colleague is that? Do you mean Stanislaus?"

"Yes. Stanislaus. This afternoon, then?"

"Sorry?"

"Your meeting?"

"Oh. Yes. At two. What brings you to see me Mrs Walsh? What can I do for you?"

Damian eyed the vodka bottle, which he had left out on top of a filing cabinet. Was it good form to offer strange women a drink in the middle of the morning? He was beginning to find that any dealings with people he didn't know required lubricant.

"I'm working on a piece about these killings. It's a philosophical piece, really, an extended meditation on the relationship of an artist's work to the artist's own death. Does death complete an invisible pattern begun in the artist's earliest years, a pattern not in any way consciously observed by the artist? How does Thanatos, the brother of sleep, announce himself? I was wondering if *The Boot* would be interested in publishing it?"

"How extended?" asked Krapp.

Boris got up, tail wagging, and laid his snout on Viola Walsh's lap. She stroked his head and tweaked his ears.

"There's a nice boy," she said.

"What length is it? Would it be more than twenty pages? Funnily enough, I have a gap of that length to fill in the next issue."

He remembered that he had promised to give the space to Tambi's Sri Lankan selection, but this was more appropriate. *The Boot* would have to take notice of these terrifying goings on.

"I can shape it to twenty pages."

"When could you have it ready?"

Viola Walsh looked at her watch, and then seemed embarrassed.

"Oh, in about a week?"

"That would be fine. We still have a week before I finalise the issue."

Viola Walsh stood up.

"I must be leaving, Mr Krapp. I'll send you the article as soon as I've checked through the draft."

Damian Krapp watched her move to the door. Boris got to his feet and followed her. She turned and fondled his ear.

"You are a handsome fellow. What a pity you have to be cooped up in this nasty office. Goodbye Mr Krapp."

"Yes. Goodbye."

Krapp didn't care for having his office described as nasty. Untidy yes, but not nasty. Before his visitor could make a clean exit, however, the door opened and Manfred von Zitzewitz walked in. The two did an awkward little dance in the doorway.

"I had no idea Damian had such a charming visitor. Manfred von Zitzewitz is my name."

He bowed and clicked his heels.

"Pleased to meet you, Mr Von Zitzewitz. Viola Walsh. I'm a journalist."

They shook hands.

"Mrs Walsh is an obituarist," said Damian. "She has written pieces on Melinda, Barnaby and Alex Duthie."

"You've cornered the market, then?"

Von Zitzewitz looked pleased at his own remark. He continued: "The only time journalists show an interest in poetry is when death strikes a practitioner."

"Oh. I wouldn't say that."

"Ah. What would you say, then?"

Her self-possession seemed to wobble for a moment.

"Herr von Zitzewitz, I was on my way out. Such a pleasure to meet you. However briefly."

She looked once more at Damian Krapp and went out of the door. The German followed the departing visitor down the stairs with his eyes, then turned to Krapp with eyebrows raised.

"Who was *that*?"

"I think you upset the lady, Manfred. She's writing a piece for me about the murders."

Damian caught sight of the elegant black travel bag which Eric Lemmon had placed by the door.

"You made her forget her bag," he said. "I expect she'll be back for it. Then I think you should apologise."

"Your wish is my command, as always."

Boris woofed again, went to his water bowl and made loud slurping noises.

"Will the dog be writing a piece for you, too, Damian?"

*   *   *

The latter stages of Jemima Lee's progress towards London in an express bus were relayed by mobile phone to Damian. Tambi Kumar had agreed to take the train north and fetch her back on the bus, on condition that his travel costs came out of the petty cash. It was the only way they had been able to persuade her to come to the meeting and Damian was full of thanks when Tambi, followed by a very pale Jemima, came up the stairs and into the meeting room.

"Jemima, my love! How are you?"

"Dreadful. My spine aches and I'm expecting to be shot any minute."

"I keep telling you," said Tambi, "so long as you keep away from railways, you will be fine."

The board-members arrived and filed into the meeting room one by one.

Stanislaus Green was the last to mount the stairs, out of breath and leaning heavily on his stick. Eric Lemmon dispensed tea and biscuits to those who wanted it. They took their places around the table. As Eric wheeled his little trolley out of the door, Boris padded in and lay down at Damian's feet. Krapp cleared his throat.

"First of all, regarding the funding proposal and its conditions... I think you all know about that. I have bowed to the wishes of this board and I have torn up the agreement with Robert Rees."

"Which you shouldn't have made in the first place, Damian," said von Zitzewitz.

"Well it's now null and void. God knows how we will keep going."

"If there's no one left to write poetry," said Mark Dolan, "we may not need to."

Damian directed a sombre glance at the publisher. Dolan's comment had provided him with his cue:

"I would like to propose that the next issue of *The Boot* be a memorial issue. It will only contain poems by the dead poets, or elegies on them, and celebratory essays about them. This will be an obituary issue. We will run a black border around the cover, and a fine black line around the margins of each page."

Manfred von Zitzewitz gave a groan that caused Boris to look up and growl.

"And bound with a black ribbon, I suppose?"

There was a murmur from the others.

"Manfred's right," said Poppy Irving. "You could give away a free wreath with every copy. What's the point?"

"How do the rest of you feel?" asked Krapp, looking at Green and Kumar.

"I'm all for a memorial issue," croaked Stanislaus Green.

"And the black border would lend it an appropriate gravitas."

Boris got up and gave a loud bark which caused amusement.

Damian patted the dog and said:

"Quiet, Boris."

"Tell us exactly what you propose putting into this issue," said Mark Dolan. "Will it be previously published poems, or new work? And who's going to write these essays?"

"Well, I have a number of contributions on file from those poets who have been victims of this holocaust. Unpublished poems. I have been profoundly touched to receive for the first time a contribution from the legendary and reclusive SJP Ramsbottom – an elegy to all of them called 'Anthem for Doomed Poets'."

"Good God, is he still alive?" said Stanislaus Green. "I interviewed him for *Osprey* magazine in 1951."

Damian acknowledged this comment with a smile.

"Stanislaus, I know you are writing something on Diver. I have already received essays on Melinda Speling and Barnaby Brown. I am commissioning essays from others."

Boris had begun whining. He stood, with ears pricked up. Taking no notice, Damian continued:

"And the *pièce de résistance* will be a 20 page essay dealing with the philosophical implications of the murders by Viola Walsh. A very skilful piece by her on Melinda Speling was in *The Observer* this weekend, and some of you may have seen her obituaries of Barnaby Brown and Fergus Diver in *The Times*."

"Twenty pages?" cried Kumar. "Those aren't the pages which were reserved for my Sri Lankan anthology, by any chance?"

"We obviously have to hold those over, Tambi. They aren't germane to the issue, are they?"

By this time Boris's whining had got louder, and he had gone over to the door, which he was pawing. He kept looking back at Damian Krapp.

"I don't know what's got into him. He's never like this," said Krapp.

"May I ask," enquired von Zitzewitz, "what the philosophical implications of murder might be? There is no philosophy in murder. It is brutal idiocy. *Basta!*"

"I have to say," said Tambi, raising his voice, "that I object

254

most strongly to this. I promised these Sri Lankan poets their work would be in the next issue."

"You have no right to promise anyone anything, Tambi. You're not the editor," said Poppy Irving.

"Tambi, this isn't the moment," said Mark Dolan. "It's a serious matter we have to..."

Boris began to howl, and Manfred von Zitzewitz began to laugh with ironic exaggeration. Exasperated, Damian got up, opened the door and called to Eric Lemmon to take the dog out for a walk. Eric clipped a leash onto Boris's collar, but the dog refused to move, and kept looking back at Krapp. The howling grew, as Eric tugged at the lead and dragged Boris across the floor to the head of the stairs. The board members watched this little drama and looked at each other.

"I'm sorry," said Krapp. "This is very unusual behaviour for Boris."

"Can I come back to the plans for the issue – not what's not going to be in it, but what is?" said von Zitzewitz. "Can we at least dispense with the black border?"

"No," said Damian resolutely. "Why should we?"

"Because it's vulgar, it's in bad taste, it's inappropriate, sentimental and exploitative."

"How do *you* honour *your* dead?" said Mark Dolan.

"With words. That's what poetry boils down to. It's not about cenotaphs, and ceremonies and stupid black borders. It's about what you say and how you say it."

"This is not the right time to be squabbling," said Stanislaus Green.

Tambi Kumar thought it was *exactly* the right time to be squabbling, or to put it more precisely, time to consider matters such as the breadth and diversity of the magazine, an issue that the Arts Council had raised but which had not been gone into, and which led directly to consideration of the vital, absolutely *vital* portfolio of poems he had assembled from neglected Sri Lankan poets. His tirade was brought to a halt by an equally lengthy contribution from Manfred von Zitzewitz, who was sorry to have appeared, perhaps, lukewarm on the matter of introducing poets from far-flung corners of the former British Empire, and who, even now, wondered what *genuine* interest there might be in the reading public for Sri Lankan poetry, but who considered such a project at least more *viable,* yes, viable was the word, than some pseudo-philosophical ruminations from a woman whose charms he would have thought Damian Krapp, at least, would be resistant to.

"I am fed up," said Tambi Kumar. "It may interest you to know that, although it comes from India, I do not like tea. I am going in search of that vodka bottle I know Damian keeps in his office."

He jumped to his feet, knocking over his chair, and made for the door. At that exact moment, a timing device sent an electric current between two points, and detonated the six kilos of semtex in the black Gucci bag that Viola Walsh had left behind. The explosion burst a gas main causing it to send a fireball up through the rotting timbers of the elderly building. It blew the roof into the air and sent flames leaping towards the sky. Then the entire building slowly caved in. When the dust, flames and smoke had died down there was nothing left of 52A Tavistock Square except a gigantic pile of rubble.

Chapter 24: *Two Boots*

Joe Biggs took five or six issues of *The Boot* off the shelf and sat down to study them. The poems in the issues had been awarded Priest's customary ticks. As Joe flicked through the pages, it struck him that there were only a few poems that had been awarded the magical three ticks, and they were all by poets that had been murdered. He did a further cross-check and noticed that every single one of the murdered poets had been given three ticks, at least once.

"Naily, do you realise that it's the poets that Priest rates most highly that have been murdered?"

"Do you think he's daeing it?"

"The guvnor? Don't be daft."

He went to replace the issues on the shelf and watched in dismay as the entire stack slithered sideways and off the shelf on to the floor. Behind them were three neat piles of pamphlets, multiple copies of the same three titles: *The Auguries*, *The Shaved Log* and *The Underwater Light*, all by Victor Priest, and published by The Odic Press. He examined a copy or two. The paper was of beautiful quality. None of the poetry books Priest had given him to read had had production values to match these. Even the print seemed different, better somehow. They were little artworks in themselves, whatever was inside them.

Why hadn't the guvnor told him he was a poet? Now that Biggs thought about it, it was logical – how else to account for such great interest? But how come he hadn't seen Priest's name in any of those issues of *The Boot* he'd looked at?

Flicking through the first pamphlet, he saw that it was much shorter than the kind of poetry book Priest had been lending him, just a few pages, really. Not a bad idea, Biggs thought – he wouldn't want to wade through three hundred pages of poetry. He tried to read the first poem in the booklet.

"Hey, Naily, you wanna hear a chunk of the guvnor's poetry?"

"No!"

He read a few sentences aloud.

"Sounds sex-starved to me."

"You reckon?"

"Yeah."

Biggs returned the pamphlets to their place, picked up the copies of *The Boot* that had fallen on the floor and put them back where they'd come from. He contemplated the drawers below the shelf and then opened one. There were piles of manuscripts inside and he took a few pages out. They had all been rejected by a variety of magazines, and Priest had listed and dated each rejection as it came in. Biggs put the manuscripts back and opened a piece of grey folded paper. It was a letter from Dolan & Swainson Ltd.

Dear Mr Priest,
Thank you so much for submitting your manuscript. I have read it with great interest – rarely do I come across writing of such a judicious nature. There is not a word out of place. However, I kept wanting it to engage more with the world we wake up to. I realise that your avoidance of obvious subject matter is a deliberate strategy, but because of this Dolan & Swainson *is not the publisher for you – however much I regret coming to this decision. I am sorry to be so obtuse.*
Yours sincerely,
Mark Dolan

Joe folded the letter and replaced it in the drawer.

"There's loads of rejections here, Naily. Mr Priest couldn't get his poems into magazines. And that big publisher Dolan and Swainson turned him down too."

Naily had brought the teapot, cups and biscuits into the room and set them down on a table. She squatted on the floor and poured two cups of tea.

"Yi know that scorpion you wis tellin me aboot? Wis it sompn like this?"

She opened her fingers to reveal an amber scorpion.

"Looks like a wummin's brooch disnit? What's Victor Priest daeing with somethin like that?"

"Where did you find it?"

"Ah thought to make the bed, Joe, so ah moved it. The brooch wis on the carpet underneath."

Biggs took the scorpion and inspected it.

"Christ," he said.

The ground shook. There was the sound of a tremendous explosion and they felt an ear-shattering reverberation. It had come from somewhere not too far off. They looked at each other and Naily jumped up. There were shouts from outside and then alarm bells. They ran down into the street and stared up at the sky. A cloud of smoke mixed with dust was wafting their way. There were hundreds of people in the street, pouring out of shops, pubs and offices. Naily started to cough.

"Let's go back in, Joe. I cannae breathe in this."

"Hang about. Look where it's coming from. Let's go see what happened."

Walking towards Southampton Row, they realised a major disaster had occurred. The wailing of fire engines, police cars and ambulances was everywhere. Traffic had come to a standstill. People were blowing their horns and getting out of their cars. As the pair rounded a corner, a policeman prevented them from going any further. Over his shoulder, they could see a hole where once the building had been that had housed *The Boot*. Firemen and police were combing through the debris. A huge crowd had gathered.

"Jesus, Naily. The whole building's gone!"

A policeman prevented them from getting any closer.

"Hey, that's Damian Krapp's assistant over there with a dog," said Joe.

But Eric Lemmon did not recognise him.

"Don't you remember me?" asked Biggs. "I came to see Damian Krapp the other day. You let me in."

"Oh? Oh? Yeah."

"What happened?"

"What happened? You can see what happened. Damian is dead. They're all dead. All except me – and Boris. Boris saved my life. If Damian hadn't asked me to take Boris for a walk, it would have been me as well. Now they won't let me back in there."

"No," said Biggs. "There isn't a there to be let back in, is there?"

Lemmon looked at him, then at Naily, then back at Joe.

"Who are you again?"

"Joe Biggs, *Artcrimes*, remember? Private detective."

"Yeah," said Eric.

He leaned against a wall, then slithered down and sat on the pavement, with his knees drawn up. Boris nudged against him, whining.

"Yeah. I did let you in, didn't I?"

He rubbed the dog's head and began to moan. Joe and Naily crouched down beside him.

"Whit wis it? Wis it a bomb?"

"God knows."

Eric stared at the punk girl.

"Who are you?"

"I'm wi' him."

She jerked her thumb at Biggs.

Eric related the events that had led up to his taking the dog for a walk – the arrival of the board-members for the meeting, his preparing tea and biscuits. He'd heard raised voices but Damian had told him it might be a difficult meeting. Then Boris had started howling – maybe the quarrel had upset him – and Damian asked him to take the dog out. He'd just gone into the park when the bang happened.

"I still can't believe it," he said.

"Wis it a gas main?"

"How should I know if it was a gas main? It was Armageddon."

"Who was at the meeting?" asked Joe.

The dog was growling and whining alternately. Naily was whispering into Boris's ear and stroking him. Lemmon offered her the lead to hold and buried his head in his hands. A forest of legs and backs grew around them on the pavement as the crowd of gawpers gathered, straining to see what was going on beyond the police cordon. Eric began enumerating the board-members who'd attended.

"Did Mr Krapp have any other visitors today?"

"No. I don't...Oh, yes. One."

"A tall red-bearded man?"

"No, a woman."

"What did she look like?"

"Blonde. Tall blonde."

"Do you know what she wanted?"

"No idea. I know she forgot her bag."

Biggs emitted a half-whistle.

"What was this lady's name?"

"She did say. I'm sorry. I can't remember."

"Viola Walsh?"

"I don't know. She had a suit on. One of those business lady types. Here, boy!"

Naily was squatting cross-legged on the floor, and holding Boris's head, soothing him with long, slow strokes. At Eric's call, the dog got up and moved back close to Eric.

"I think maybe that bag she left had a bomb in it," said Joe.

"I had it in my hand. I put it by the door."

"The dog knew. He saved your life."

There was a cry. Pushing through the crowd, distraught and dishevelled, a short man with jet black hair tied behind in a snood and sporting a goatee, threw up his arms over the little group on the ground, kneeled down and embraced Lemmon in a tearful hug.

"I thought everyone was dead! Thank God you're alive! Where's Damian? Where are the others?"

"They were all inside, Ron,"

"The house is destroyed. There's nothing left. Was Damian in there?"

"Yes, Ron. Fuck it. He was."

"What happened? Was it a gas main?"

"I dunno Ron. I'm so sorry. Look. Boris is still alive."

The dog barked and began to lick Ron's hand.

"It was a bomb," said Biggs.

Ron released Eric and turned:

"A bomb? You can't be serious. Who'd plant a bomb at *The Boot*?"

"A nutter," said Naily.

*   *   *

They went up the stairs to the *Artcrimes* office. Joe tried to look at the room again as if it was the first time he'd seen it. Was there anything else to find out? He stood, undecided, in the middle of the room.

"Waddaya think, Joe?"

"It's weird, Naily. Is there some connection between Viola Walsh and the guvnor? How did that scorpion get in here? Mr Priest don't wear no brooches. And if there is a connection, and he's involved, why would he investigate himself, if he was? Why employ *me?* Don' make sense."

The tea pot with the tea they had not drunk was still on the table. He poured himself a cup. As he lifted the tea cup to his lips, he heard the front door click and the tread of his employer on the stairs. Joe got up quickly, looking round the room. What had he moved that he shouldn't have done? Priest entered, holding a small case and looking grave.

"Good afternoon, Joe. You've heard the news?"

"We heard the bang," said Joe. "We just been there."

"So is everybody else. Central London is one solid traffic jam. It seems the offices of *The Boot* were completely destroyed. I trust everything's well?"

Priest looked around at the wall of pictures Joe had pinned up, and then at the newspaper clippings. Naily appeared in the doorway of the kitchen.

"Ah, you must be my assistant's assistant. What do you call yourself?"

"Janet Dunbar."

"Dunbar? I'm delighted to meet you."

He took her small hand in a firm clasp. His gaze fell on a small clothes drier in the corner of the office on which a number of underthings were drying.

"My little office *is* a bit cramped. Is that tea you've made?"

Priest sat down on the daybed and Naily brought an extra cup and served it.

"Did you say you went to inspect the damage in Tavistock Square? This is very cold tea."

"Yeah. Today they had a visitor. A blonde woman. She left a bag behind. What's the odds that was Viola Walsh and the bag had the bomb in it?"

"What *are* the odds, Joe?"

Biggs began to expound his theory. There had to be many people involved. How else account for the growing frequency of the killings, and the fact that they occurred at great distances from each other – Berlin, Wales, London? He had also given thought to the motive behind the murders. In his opinion, poems would be an excellent method of delivering encrypted messages. If you were conducting industrial espionage, what better way to communicate complex information? You'd need an environment that would be above suspicion. Added to which, nobody *reads* poetry books. And if anyone did – well they wouldn't understand it anyway.

Priest began to laugh.

"So these messages would be hidden in plain sight? Ingenious. But why would poets be conducting industrial espionage?"

"Well, they wouldn't, guv. But if you're a poet you ain't gonna make any money. Are you? So if somebody says: 'put this in your next book and make it look like a poem and I'll give you fifty grand', you're gonna do it, aintcha?"

"And...?"

"And then you want more money or you're gonna tell the cops. So the spies kill you."

"I see. You mean all these murdered poets were killed because they were blackmailers as well as couriers for a spy ring?"

"Yeah."

Priest buried his face in his hands, massaging his temples with the tips of his fingers.

"How do you turn industrial information into a poem, Joe?"

"Dunno, guv. You're the poet."

Priest gave Joe and Naily an intense scrutiny.

"What would these perpetrators have to gain from blowing up a poetry magazine? "

"I reckon Krapp went back on the deal, guv."

"What deal?"

"I reckon this geezer Rees wanted to give money to the mag because he wanted to put messages in it."

Priest stood up, holding his cup and saucer, and drained the teacup.

"You might be right," he said.

He carried his empty cup into the kitchen and Naily and Joe heard the tap run.

When he appeared again at the door, he was drying the cup.

"However, one doesn't normally blow up a potential business partner out of pique. Or does one?"

He looked down. A plaintive miaow had attracted his attention. Emily had bumped into his shoe on her way across the room. Priest smiled at Naily.

"Mr Venables' cat I presume?"

He was about to bend and tickle Emily's ear when his mobile telephone rang.

Pulling it out of his pocket to answer it, he retreated again into the kitchen. One half of the conversation that followed was clearly audible. Priest's voice became confiding and gentle. He was reassuring whoever it was on the other end that everything was all right. He had actually just heard the news himself, and it was terrible, but he was sure it would very soon be all over. They were getting close. He would come to her house in the late afternoon tomorrow. Was that alright?

He said what had to be a name twice, and his voice caressed the name. Then Priest came back into the room.

"Couldn't help hearing that bit about getting close, guv. Are we?"

"Well, we don't know where to find our elusive Welshman, but I think Ms Viola Walsh can help us. We need to talk to her, Joe."

"Yeah. How do we do that?"

Priest handed Biggs a business card. It was on satiny paper and printed in distinctive gold lettering. It read Viola Walsh, Obituarist. There was a street name and number, and the name of a town: Aberystwyth.

"Where d'you get this, guv?"

"I was very struck by the fact that a tall blonde woman was seen in the Reichstag at the time of Melinda Speling's murder. I spent an hour or so telephoning the hotels in Berlin and asking if I could speak to Viola Walsh. It turned out she stayed at the Inter-Continental. The hotel makes a practice of collecting the business cards of guests. That's how they compile their mailing lists."

Priest sat down and asked Joe if there was still some of the cash left he had given him. They could no longer stay in the office. If they wanted to, they could find a hotel nearby and leave their things there. However, as soon as possible they were to drive to Aberystwyth, find a place to stay, locate the address on the business card and keep it under observation. As soon as they sighted Viola Walsh, they were to phone Priest and he would come immediately.

"You can take my car," he said.

"Blimey. Your Porsche, guv?"

"No. It's another vehicle I use sometimes. Time is of the essence. Would you like to collect your things together? I'd be grateful if you could also take the cat."

Naily and Joe gathered together what they had strewn about the office and they went down into the street, Naily cradling Emily in her arms. Priest's vehicle was a big Mercedes saloon and he had displayed the blue handicapped card in the front window.

"Think you can drive it, Joe?"

"Sure."

"It's getting a bit long in the tooth, I'm afraid. The boot lock is jammed so you'll have to put your things on the back seat. When you have a moment, see if you can lever the boot open. The engine is in good shape. It's a powerful machine. Will you go straight to Wales, or will you find a hotel here first?"

"Joe looked at Naily.

"We'll go straight there, guv. Phone you when we get there."

"Excellent. *Bon Voyage.*"

*   *   *

Joe drove several streets away and stopped the car.

"What was all that about?"

"He's up to sompn."

"Yeah, what's he playing at?"

"Who wis he talkin' to on the phone?"

Joe reflected.

"When he hired me he said it was because Fergus Diver's widow wanted him to investigate her husband's murder. Was that her name he was saying? Vesna?"

"Mibbe."

Biggs reached forward, took hold of the blue wheelchair card for handicapped people and examined it. There was a picture of a very old lady and the name Elizabeth Jane Priest. It was valid for the year. He threw it back and tried to open the glove compartment of the car but it was locked. The ignition key did not work in the lock. He took a penknife from his pocket, leaned across, and picked the lock open.

Naily bent forward, stretched her hand inside and took out a pistol. She handed it to Joe without expression. He felt further inside the compartment with his right hand but found only a service book and a map of the greater London area. There was no navigation system in the car. He sat back in the driver's seat, examining the pistol. The breech opened and Naily gave a little exclamation.

"Is that loaded?"

"Yeah. Wonder what's in the boot, Naily?"

"He said it was jammed."

"Yeah."

Joe got out of the car and tried the key in the boot lock. It turned uselessly. Naily joined him and they stood looking at the back of the car.

"Gotta get it open, the guvnor said."

"Whit if it's a bomb?"

Joe laughed.

"Why would it be a bomb?"

"Mibbe Viola Walsh wore an amber scorpion and mibbe it ended up in Mr Priest's office. Mibbe we know that Mr Priest is a poet, though he don't tell anyone he is. Mibbe a whole poetry magazine got blown up because of it. Mibbe ah just gotta funny feelin."

"I gotta funny feeling too."

Biggs kicked the back tyre of the Mercedes, then took his phone out and dialled a number.

"Frank? Yeah, I know. I'm sorry. Been real busy. You still at work? Gotta favour to ask. OK if we come round right away?"

They drove east through the City towards Wapping. Frank's day job was at a garage, and he came out of an oily shed underneath a railway arch, wiping his hands on a filthy rag. He grinned at Joe, gave Naily a considered once-over, and looked at the car.

"Nice wheels. What's it all about, Joe?"

"Can't get the boot lid open. Lock is bust."

"That all?"

Frank took the key off Joe and tried it, then went back into the shed and came out with a tyre lever. Naily took hold of his arm.

"The whole car's mibbe a bomb."

"You what?"

Frank looked at Joe.

"Is she for real?"

Biggs shrugged.

"Just supposin' it was a bomb, Frank, and openin' it with a tyre lever was designed to make it go off, how else could you get it open?"

Frank looked at the car, and drew his sleeve across his brow, leaving an oily trace. Without a word, he went back into the shed and procured a length of cable and an electric cutter. He clicked the plug of the cutter into the socket attached to the cable and drew an imaginary line with his finger across the top of the boot lid.

"Make a hole here. No problem. Your car, is it?"

"No."

"Gonna make a mess."

"Be my guest."

There was a horrible screeching sound, and sparks flew. Naily covered her ears. Frank cut a large rectangular hole in the upper part of the boot lid and peered in.

"Fuck me," he said.

He went back into the shed and came back with a powerful torch. One after another, they gazed in. Some kind of electric appliance was attached by wires to the hinges on the boot lid. Next to it was a tartan carry-all, zipped up. There was a yellow car jack secured to the wheel arch. Otherwise the boot was empty.

"Betcha that's a bomb," said Naily.

"Looks kinda funny," said Frank. "Where d'you get this Merc?"

"Belongs to the boss. He said to get the lid open."

"You offended 'im, 'ave you?"

"Not so far as I know."

Frank sighed. He was a car mechanic, he said, not a bomb defuser. In the movies, you took a pair of cutters and sliced through a wire. In the movies, you didn't know whether it was the red wire or the blue wire that made the bomb harmless. You had ten seconds left so you took a guess and it was always right because it was the movies and a girl was waiting. He didn't have a clue which wire he should snip, but he could see where a battery was connected and maybe if he cut the wires nothing would happen? And maybe something would.

"We cuid go stand behind that big truck over there," said Naily, pointing.

Frank handed the cutters to Joe.

"Yeah. We'll go and stand over there. Here y'are, Joe. You can do the cutting."

Biggs peered into the boot lid hole.

"Which wire?

"Take your pick."

Naily gave a cry and rescued Emily from the back seat. As she and Frank hurried away, Joe put the torch in his mouth and focussed the light on two AA batteries that were connected by wires to the hinges and to the small parcel wrapped in plastic. He puzzled over this constellation for a while, then felt Naily tugging at his arm. He took the torch out of his mouth.

"What?"

"Gimme a kiss, Joe."

"Blimey, Naily. I'm busy."

"Gimme a kiss, Joe Biggs."

He looked down at her face.

"I ain't gonna blow myself up, you know."

"Ah cuid help you, mibbe?"

"No. Where's Emily?"

"With Frank."

"Go and look after her."

She squeezed his arm, gave him a searching look, and walked away across the yard. He turned back to the hole in the boot of the car, aimed the torch, and taking a deep breath, reached in though the hole and snipped the wires between the batteries and the parcel, and then the wires to the hinges. He took the torch out of his mouth again, bent down to pick up the tyre lever where Frank had dropped it, and broke open the boot. He lifted out the tartan holdall and unzipped it. He took a blonde wig and a woman's skirt from the bag, put on the blonde wig, held the skirt across his belly and wiggled his hips.

"How about that?" he shouted. "How about *thaaaaaaaat!*"

Naily and Frank were walking back towards him across the concrete. They stopped to watch the performance. Joe dropped the skirt, threw off the wig, and peered into the holdall again. This time he took out a red wig and a deerstalker. He clapped them on his head.

"Yeah! Take a good look! The bomb I was carryin went off and killed me. Yoo hoo, look at me! I'm a dead fuckin Welshman! I get paid three hundred pounds a week for being a dead Welshman. I just love gettin blown up. It's my vocaaaation!"

Joe was shouting and his voice echoed under the railways arches. People emerged from some of the other premises to see what was going on.

"Hello everybody! I'm a dead Welshman! I love to kill poets. See this car? It blew me up and killed me, so I stole it from Victor Priest. I stooooole it!"

He pointed at Naily.

"Look at her! She's dead too! Do we look dead to you? She's a dead blonde! Hallo everybody! We're deceased! We're de-ceeeeeeeeeeeeased!"

As he shouted, he danced. His rant was clapped and cheered by the impromptu audience.

Frank and Naily approached him, and Biggs said in a normal voice:

"*Why* we was killin poets is anyone's guess. But evidence is evidence, ain't it?"

"I ain't got a fuckin clue what you're on about," said Frank.

Chapter 25: *The Flight of the Scorpion*

She looked through her wardrobe and found clothes she hadn't worn in a long time. It had been a beautiful day; the sun had shone for most of it; now she would dress for the evening. In front of the mirror, she eased a cream silk blouse over her hips, then stood sideways on to the glass inspecting her figure.

She went downstairs to the kitchen. The newspaper open on the table was still announcing news of the blast at the offices of *The Boot*. She had known some of the people it had killed. They had been friends.

And Victor said he knew who the murderer was.

She went through into the living room, took the parrot out of her cage and sat down on the couch, the bird on her wrist. She stroked the feathers, murmuring:

"Would you like to have a holiday in New Zealand? I wonder if they let parrots in?"

The parrot put her head on one side. Vesna got up and went to the window, the bird still on her wrist.

The light was changing from a brilliant brightness to a dusky, golden glow. She became aware of the throb of a powerful motorcycle. There was a narrow lane running along the bottom of her garden and she saw a man clad entirely in black leather with a black helmet weave his way to her garden gate. He stopped, dismounted and bared his head. It was Victor. Why had he chosen to come in the back way? She put the parrot back in her cage and went out on to the lawn to meet him.

"I'm so glad you came."

"I'm very glad to see you."

He drew her into a powerful embrace. She could feel the smooth leather that encased him. It creaked. Why should she feel guilty about holding him? Why should the length of time you spent in mourning be a measure of your fidelity?

"Let's go in out of the garden, Victor."

He took her arm and they walked into the house. He went into the hall, placed his helmet on a small table and removed his leather jacket. Then he sat down and slid off his boots, before peeling off the close-fitting leather trousers. Underneath he was wearing a beige jacket and a light blue shirt. He had brought a pair of leather slippers in a small carry-all.

"I like your transformation act," she said.

She watched him walk back into the living room and go over to stare at the bird. The parrot remained silent, eyeing him.

He turned to face her:

"You've read about this bomb?"

"It's terrible. I knew most of those people. Damian Krapp was often a guest in this house! I suppose it's the end of his magazine as well?"

"I would suppose that too."

She went over to the cage, put her hand in and the parrot hopped once more onto her wrist. The parrot's little black eyes glittered, regarding Priest.

He enunciated with great care:

"Bread and butter pudding!"

The bird made a guttural noise and ruffled her neck feathers. Vesna laughed.

"I don't believe you're ever going to teach her to say that."

"You may well be right. Why don't we sit down, I have a lot to tell you?"

She sat down on the couch and Priest pulled up an armchair.

"Some time ago a young man persuaded me against my better judgement to give him employment at *Artcrimes*.. His name was Joseph Biggs. I didn't know that he was a poet. He seemed to me to be an ordinary young man from the east end of London. In fact, he was an unpublished poet who harboured a homicidal grudge against what he conceived to be 'the poetry establishment'. He felt his work deserved publication, but it was rejected everywhere. He made individual approaches to poets – most of those, I assume, who have been killed – but he was given no encouragement. He came to me, I suspect, because of my somewhat hidden reputation in the poetry world, and possibly because he thought I might provide him with new contacts."

"This is bizarre, Victor. Did he propose to murder his way to publication?"

"Some idea of that sort may have possessed his diseased brain. He wanted, perhaps, to clear the field for himself. He had an accomplice in all this, his girlfriend, a young woman called Janet Dunbar.

I assume she was taken in by his paranoid delusions. In her case, too, there is a question of mental stability. She was from Glasgow I believe. Yesterday afternoon, they stole my Mercedes and I have not seen them since."

"But what about this man Rees? And the blonde woman?"

"Mr Biggs and Miss Dunbar are extremely professional when it comes to disguise. Very clever. Biggs and Dunbar were nothing if not accomplished actors."

"*Were*? Are they dead?"

Priest blinked.

"Oops. Wishful thinking, my dearest. It's getting dark. Shall I draw the curtains?"

The sun had gone down as they talked and the room was dim. He got up to draw the curtains and the parrot left her wrist, fluttered to a standard lamp and perched there.

"It's incredible, Victor. All these cold blooded murders just for…just for…?"

"For poetry? I'm afraid that seems to be about the size of it. Do you let her fly everywhere?"

"What? Oh, she's used to being out of her cage."

Vesna got up and went over the lamp, inviting the bird to hop back on to her arm. The parrot was in no mood to go back into her prison, however. She flew to the back of an old-fashioned wooden chair in a far corner of the room. Vesna turned and felt Victor take her in his arms. He was kissing her hair, her cheeks, her neck. She could feel his hands tight against her back. Then he was undoing the buttons on her blouse, pulling her down onto the rug, his whole weight was on her. The prolonged ringing of the doorbell made her open her eyes. He was looking at her with a question on his face. She shook her head; she was expecting no one. But the doorbell continued to ring. They waited. Its plangent noise provoked the parrot to retaliatory squawking.

"Maybe your bike is blocking the back lane?"

He shook his head.

"Maybe it's Inspector Dobson? Perhaps they've caught your suspects."

He propped himself on one arm.

"In that case, you better answer it. But do up your buttons first."

She got up, adjusted her clothing, went through the hall to the front door and opened it.

"Mrs Diver?"

She saw a young man with a mod hairstyle in a red and white striped jacket, carrying a tartan holdall. Next to him stood a punk girl in a shiny leather jacket and ripped miniskirt. She had drawn elaborate black crow's feet on herself that expanded outwards from her eyebrows.

"Yes?"

"Do you have a visitor called Victor Priest? We'd like to speak to him."

Vesna called out:

"There are some people to see you, Victor."

What business could this peculiar couple have with Victor? She watched his customary self-assurance vanish as they were shown into the living room.

"Good evening, guv," said the young man.

"What do you want, Joe?"

"We want you to turn yourself in."

Vesna watched as the young man dropped to his knees and unzipped the holdall which he'd placed on the carpet. He drew out a red wig and a red beard and arranged them on the rug.

"Have you been watching the news, lady? Maybe you've seen this fellow? The police are looking everywhere for him."

She could sense tension in the air but she still had no idea what was going on. The punk girl was watching her to see how she would react. The young man reached into the holdall again and drew out a woman's blonde wig. He placed that next to the red wig on the floor, and added a strange looking brooch where the woman's lapel would have been, if there'd been a woman.

"They want to find her, as well."

The young man pointed at Priest.

"Two people, but only one man. Him."

Vesna looked across at Victor who was standing quite still, contemplating the young man. Then she looked down at the contents of the bag the visitor had arranged on the floor.

"Are you going to tell us your name, young man?"

"Joe Biggs, ma'am."

"Biggs? I know about you. I know what you have done. Why have you brought these things here? You killed my husband. Are you now going to try and kill us?"

The parrot left its perch and flew across to take up its old position atop the lamp. The young man flinched as it brushed past his face.

"*Amalia, the fatal courtesan!*" the parrot cried.

"What's Mr Priest been telling you, ma'am? It was him that tried to kill us. He told us to take his car and booby-trapped it with a bomb. He put these wigs and things in the car so when it blew up the cops'd find them along with us and conclude we was the murderers. I brought these disguises to prove the pair the cops are after don't exist. That's Robert Rees over there. He's Viola Walsh, as well. Victor Priest killed all those poets. He killed your husband."

"What nonsense are you talking? Mr Priest is a friend of mine. He is a detective."

"Yeah. He commits the crimes he investigates."

She stared at Victor. He seemed amused. There was a strange smile on his lips, and he wore an expression she could not interpret. He was looking straight at her, examining her reactions to these accusations.

"Can you give me one good reason," she said, "why he would do such things?"

"Dunno, ma'am. He must have had one."

Vesna felt the room swirling round her head. Victor's face fragmented into pieces. Her legs would no longer support her, and she felt herself falling. She lost consciousness for a moment. When she opened her eyes she was lying on the sofa. Victor was saying:

"I'm not turning myself in. What are you going to do about it, Joe?"

"I'm gonna make a citizen's arrest, guv."

"I'd like to see you try."

Vesna saw the young man take a step forward and grasp Victor by the arm.

Then the room exploded. Priest took hold of the young man's wrist and threw him across the room. The lamp toppled over, sending the parrot into paroxysms of shrieking and flapping. The young man picked himself up, dropped into a boxing crouch and jabbed at Victor. As if by magic, Priest caught the punching fist in two hands and performed some kind of asiatic throw. This time the young man hit the wall. The punk girl cried out: 'Don't!' but the young man was on his feet again, swinging wildly at Victor. The punk girl took a pistol from her handbag, pointing it with both hands. 'Don' yi fuckin' move or ah'll blow yir head off!' she cried. The young man stopped swinging. Victor stared at the punk girl.

"Dunbar," he said. "*Timor mortis ne conturbat me.*"

With extreme coolness and deliberation he walked over to the punk girl, took the pistol from her hands and tossed it onto a chair. Then he slapped her hard and she fell across Vesna. The young man advanced towards Victor and received two fast blows to the head. His head snapped back and he fell as if he'd been shot. Victor was like a professional boxer, only faster, more controlled. The punk girl was whimpering. Victor stooped and set the lamp to rights. He stood for a moment regarding Vesna on the sofa, then went into the hall and reappeared carrying his motorcycle gear which he began to put on. The young woman slithered to the floor and crawled across to the young man, cradling his head in her arms.

"Joe, baby," she crooned. "You alreet, baby?"

She looked at Victor.

"Yi cuida killed him."

"It takes a lot to kill a person."

"Yi'd know aboot that, wuid'n you?"

Priest zipped up his jacket. Vesna watched him bow in her direction.

"Goodbye, my dear," he said. "*Lebewohl.*"

He turned on his heel, walked to the French window and disappeared into the dark of the garden. The young man climbed to his feet, holding his head.

"Where'd the bastard go?"

For answer they heard the loud roar of a motorcycle engine. Vesna saw the young man beckon to the young woman and together they ran out of the room. She heard the motorbike thunder off, then she heard a car starting up and driving away. Everything went quiet. She lay on the sofa and watched the parrot preening its feathers and recovering its composure.

*   *   *

"He's gonna be difficult to catch," said Joe.

The shops were shut and the streets of Lewes empty as they sped through the town in pursuit of a weaving red tail-light. She tried to find the socket for her seat-belt, looked at Joe, hunched over the steering wheel of the Mercedes, and wondered if he could cope with fast driving. Catching Priest wasn't worth losing your life for. It was madness to be driving at this speed through a town. An old man on a pedestrian crossing had never hobbled so fast, and she saw his stick waving in the air as they flashed by.

As they cleared the town she looked at the speedometer and saw they were doing 90. Her mad cousin Donald used to drive like this whenever he came home from the oil-rigs. She wasn't usually a nervous passenger, but when Joe went wide on a tight bend and lights flashed blindingly into the windscreen, and there were foghorn blasts from the hooter of an oncoming truck, she said a quick prayer.

They went through a patch of woodland and then they were on a straight road, empty except for the tail-light of the motorbike ahead. It was a clear night and she could see that the moon was almost full. What would they do if they did catch Victor Priest? Joe was no match for him. They had the pistol, but she doubted whether either of them would dare to use it. She'd already proved once this evening that she was no use at plugging people. Christ, she'd only got on that train to London thinking there might be a job at the end of it. And now where was she? Where was Victor Priest going? And what was his plan? Would she end up mangled in the wreck of the Mercedes, or would she be murdered by Victor Priest?

"Joe, this is crazy. Wir never goin' to catch him. And even if wi dae, what good'll that be? Hie'll shoot us."

"Shootin' ain't his style. It's too ordinary. He's gotta stop sometime."

"An' when hie daes, whit'll ye do then?"

The green light from the dashboard tinted Joe's features. His lips were tightly compressed.

"There's a car-jack in the boot. I'll use that. I'm not takin' on Victor Priest again without something in my hand."

"I doan like it, Joe. I really dinnae."

Road-signs flashed by and she saw the name of a town in the

headlights. A fox ran across the road, making Joe swerve. There was a vicious scraping noise on her side of the car as they ran alongside a hedge. She ducked away. For a moment she thought Joe had lost complete control of the car – it slid from side to side, but then he brought it back into line.

"Loose gravel on the road, Naily."

"Gie up, Joe."

She stared at the speedometer as the needle climbed even higher.

"We'll catch him."

Sure enough the tail-light ahead seemed to be getting closer, but then as they came over the brow of a hill it had vanished, and Biggs braked sharply.

"Where the fuck has he gone?"

Naily staring out of her passenger window caught a glimpse of a red light through hedges.

"Ah think he's goon doun that wee road, Joe."

Biggs wrenched the wheel, and with a screech of tyres, he directed the heavy vehicle in pursuit. The road was narrow and twisty, and he had to slow down, but not enough, Naily reflected. If there was something coming the other way there would be a head on collision. They climbed a steep hill through pine trees and then the road flattened out. Naily had an instinct that the sea was very close but she couldn't see it. She wound down her window a little. She could smell it.

The moonlight showed moorland without any trees, just a few clumps of bushes. The motorbike was clearly visible about a quarter of a mile ahead. Suddenly Naily saw it leave the road and take off over the moor.

"Fuck'n hell, whit's he daein' noo?" she said.

Biggs accelerated to the place where the motorbike had left the road and slammed on the brakes. They saw a narrow stony track leading off across rough ground and glimpsed the helmeted rider standing up in the foot-rests of the bike, bouncing his machine over the stones like a motocross ace.

"I can't drive along that," said Joe.

"Hie's headin' fir the sea," said Naily. "I bet hie's got a boat doon there."

"Come on, we gotta run."

Naily got out of the car and watched as Joe ran round, yanked off the wire that was securing the boot lid shut, and took out a car jack which he hefted in his hand. She doubted that even with this would he be any match for Priest but she said nothing. They began to run along the track. They passed a ruined caravan with shattered windows. Huge pylons were strung out across the moor. The cables hummed in the moonlight. She didn't like the country at the best of times, and this was super creepy. Running on stones wasn't easy, either – how Joe managed in his Chelsea boots was a mystery, but he wasn't complaining. Thing about the countryside was: she always got the feeling something horrible was going to leap up and attack her. She slowed down, feeling as if she couldn't get enough air into her lungs, but Biggs shouted at her to carry on.

The beat of the motorbike's engine dwindled. What was Priest doing now? They stopped by the edge of a cliff. Priest was riding his machine down what seemed an impossibly steep path. Up to the right, loomed the shadow of a large, unlit villa. Far below they could see a small jetty with a boat moored to it. And out on the water, in the middle of a natural harbour, the black shape of a seaplane sat in the moonlight.

"Look, Joe! He's gotta a fuck'n plane."

"Let's get down there. Come on, hurry."

Joe Biggs sure didn't give up easily, she thought, running after him down the slope. The path here had even more loose stones, and several times she slipped and nearly fell. Biggs was well ahead of her, bounding goat-like over the rough terrain.

By now, she saw, Priest had ridden to the end of the jetty, and had dismounted. He was standing gazing back at them in his black leathers, looking in the moonlight like some kind of ancient warrior. The sight of him gave her the shivers. She hoped Joe wouldn't catch up with him. Priest, she was sure, would have no compunction about killing his former assistant.

In a cascade of stones and sand, she fell headlong, ripping her black tights and scratching her knees. Getting to her feet she saw that Biggs had already reached the jetty and was running along it, brandishing the car jack. In the boat, Priest was trying to start the outboard motor. She saw him bend and tug the starter cord several times but heard no responding clatter of an engine. Just as it seemed Joe would get there, the engine kicked into life and the boat purred away across the calm water, with Priest standing up at the tiller, waving. Biggs came to a dead stop. Thank Christ, thought Naily.

Limping slightly, she went on down the path. By the time she reached the jetty, Priest was already clambering up into the plane. She walked to where Biggs was standing, staring out over the moonlit sea and she took his arm.

"Och, let him go, Joe. You didja best."

"I very nearly got him, fuck it!"

"I'm glad you didnae."

"I thought you wanted him caught," he said and looked at her. She said nothing.

The engine of the seaplane roared into life, silvery light flashing off its turning propellers. It taxied across the water to the far side of the little bay and turned to face the horizon. The engine noise grew to a scream and the plane began to move fast towards the open sea. It lifted off, banked steeply, and came back directly towards them, flying straight overhead, and waggled its wings. Printed on its underside they saw the single word: *Scorpion*. The plane was so clearly visible, she thought she could see the pilot's face at the cockpit window. No, that had to be an optical illusion. The plane was silhouetted for a moment against the moon and then it was gone.

*   *   *

Search for Poet-killer Continues
(*The Times*, Tuesday 23 March 2012)
Police hunting Europe-wide for the De Havilland Canada DHC-3 seaplane in which the collector and art crimes investigator Victor Priest disappeared on Saturday evening have reported no sightings. Weather conditions were good at the time and there have been no reports of aviation mishaps. The plane was briefly tracked by air traffic controllers over the English Channel and then vanished from radar screens. Victor Priest has been identified as the serial killer who perpetrated a campaign of ruthless executions of poets and their associates. Thirteen murders were committed. In order to carry out his evil programme, Priest, who is a master of disguises, pretended variously to be a redhaired Welshman, or an eye-catching blonde. Ironically, it has emerged

that Priest was investigating the murders he himself was committing.
No flight report was filed. Priest and his aircraft seem to have disap-
peared as completely as Amelia Earhart in 1937. At a press confer-
ence yesterday, Chief Inspector Dobson of the Yard said that if Priest's
intention had been to fly the Atlantic the sharks would have had him by
now.

Chapter 26: *Cognac*

The effigy of WB Yeats had been moved to a corner of the shop and was wearing a wide brimmed black hat. Some of the book tables had been removed, and folding chairs had been set up in the space that was left. Piled high on a table by the door were copies of the long-awaited book that was to be launched in the course of the evening: *Lunar Conspiracies* by Victor Priest. Next to them was the beautifully produced edition of Priest's pen and ink sketches of his victims: *A Gallery of Poets*. It was the biggest venture Van Ackroyd had ever undertaken, a coffee-table sized book, and he had been taken aback at its success. It had sold hugely, four thousand six hundred copies to date. He surveyed his preparations for the reading. What a pity Priest would not be there to do justice to his own poems – Ackroyd would have to read them himself. Still, he had been very familiar with Priest's style of delivery and felt reasonably confident he'd be able to put the poems across. He was nervous; his palms were sweating. Maddy came out of the kitchen and with a smile handed him a glass of white wine. He drank it off at a gulp.

There were still a couple of hours to go before the reading started, but he was surprised to see that small groups of people had gathered on the pavement outside. Some of them were pointing to the large poster with a photograph of Priest that he had put up in the window. Before the full details of Priest's homicidal spree had emerged, Ackroyd had successfully managed to negotiate the sale of the Kafka manuscripts to the Arab multi-millionaire and poet Sheikh Badr al Din. At this very minute, the rare pages would be under glass and adorning the walls of the Golden Palace on the northernmost of Dubai's Palm Islands in the Persian Gulf. Naturally, the sale had been conducted privately, and away from the glare of publicity, with the help of Ackroyd's confidential go-between, Sydney Trent, another ex-alumni of the International School in Hamburg. *Sydney, du warst erster Klasse,* Ackroyd had told him on the phone. *Das ist eine fantastische Summe!* He'd had most of the money paid into Priest's Swiss bank account, keeping back a reserve on a separate account in England. Ackroyd also learned that, Priest had managed, just before being unmasked, to sell, through Christie's in New York, the Eliot translation of a canto from Dante's *Inferno*. If Priest was still on the planet he would not be in need of money.

Ackroyd himself had unearthed the sketches of the murdered poets. When the TV news began to contain reports of his friend's disappearance and his possible implication in the murders, he had driven over to Priest's house. He wanted to arrive before the police did, anticipating that they might confiscate all kinds of valuable material without having a clue as to what it was. He also needed to make sure that Maddy was taken care of. He had known Priest's housekeeper for many years, and was very fond of her.

In the airy study overlooking the sea where Victor wrote, Ackroyd had found a portfolio containing the sketches. He'd been startled. It had been years since he'd seen this side of Priest's artistic talent; they were miracles of the macabre. Priest had depicted each poet in his or her final throes - Melinda Speling, for example, her right hand clasping her neck, the lucency of her eyes envisioning the approach of death, Alexander Duthie gazing up in horror at the hammer and sickle that was about to nail him to the ground, Damian Krapp's face flying off into fragments. It was worthy of Goya. Maddy had helped him stash the sketches and a good number of drafts and rare books into the back of his ancient Ford, and as he had driven away he had nearly collided with a police Range Rover that was coming fast from the other direction.

The money he had put into the reserve account had been more than sufficient to ensure the quality of the book production matched the quality of the drawings. He had taken care of Maddy by buying her a small terrace house in Deal. Ackroyd was by no means wealthy, but he could afford to have her come in and clean twice a week. There was an added benefit in that Victor had taught her to cook some of his favourite dishes. She had made no comment on the sketches, or indeed on her ex-employer's astonishing career as a mass murderer except to say that Mr Priest had always been good to her and she had never had any cause to complain.

Ackroyd watched her setting up a drinks table. She had placed buckets of ice on the floor, and was pushing bottles of white *Chateauneuf du Pape* into them. She had put on a little white coronet and a white apron so that no one would mistake her for a poetry lover.

He picked up a copy of *Lunar Conspiracies* and flicked through the pages. The money had also been enough to cover the cost of producing the poems. When he had started to go through the manuscript Priest had given him, he had been amazed to see how many poems there were that he had not seen before. They were of rare beauty. The Odic Press had previously only published pamphlets in small numbers and had never ventured into commercial publishing before, so this was the perfect book to move into another league with. If only Priest could be here.

Had Ackroyd voiced this last thought aloud, many eyebrows would have been raised. Victor Priest had made a cull of a goodly portion of the UK poetry establishment; full details of his campaign of elimination were only now just beginning to emerge - the meticulous strategy that lay behind it, the quick change disguises. How many other identities had the man assumed? Had Van known the real Priest at all? Would he show up tonight in another disguise? It would be just like him to stand there in the crowd with a sardonic grin, watching a mere bookseller blunder through the reading of those carefully-wrought poems.

However much Ackroyd might have deplored Priest's orchestrated fugue of assassinations (and of course he did, he most certainly did), it had definitely put a rocket-booster under poetry sales. He was very hopeful for the success of *Lunar Conspiracies,* and if the sales of the sketches were anything to go by, it ought to be a runner. He'd been surprised when the BBC phoned up to ask if they could send someone to cover the launch. When two television vans drew up outside the bookshop, he had gone forward to greet them, but three burly technicians carrying cameras, lights and microphone booms had come bustling into the shop, more or less ignoring him, and started reorganising everything. Ackroyd became extremely irritated. His irritation, however, turned to effusiveness when JJ Moon, himself, came in, holding out his hand and grinning. This would really put the book on the map.
It certainly had, and within half an hour it was impossible to move for the crowd in the shop. When the reading started, Ackroyd realised that what he had planned as a small, intimate poetry launch had turned into something quite different. The white wine had run out and practically all copies of both books had been sold before he even climbed on to the improvised platform to begin his recitation. He had rather hoped that he could have turned the whole affair over to the professional skills of Moon himself, but JJ had declined saying he was there merely to film some footage of the event and catch its atmosphere prior to put-

ting together an edition of *The Blue Room* on Priest.

Ackroyd tried to give the poems their full weight in his reading of them. There was a hush of concentrated attention in the room, disturbed only by a person with a hacking cough. As Ackroyd concluded the title poem, a tall stack of books toppled over. The audience sighed as if in recognition of this mystical event. At the end there was no applause for a while, just silence, and then a slow-building and very prolonged clapping. The remaining unsold books were snapped up and Ackroyd took orders for further sales. If it continued like this he'd have to order a reprint immediately. Now that Dolan & Swainson was Dolan-less, the Odic Press might be on the way to becoming Britain's premier poetry publisher. But there was no wine left, and he was hot under the TV lights, and bothered by all the questions and requests for signatures. He refused however to sign Priest's name, but rather reluctantly put his own in the volumes that were thrust under his nose. He'd never taken so much money in a single day, and he lost track of who had paid what and how much change was due. He was very conscious of JJ Moon observing the chaos and wondered how much of it would turn up on *The Blue Room.*

A portly man in a raincoat approached him, asking for a copy of the book, but there were none left. The man introduced himself as Chief Inspector Dobson of Scotland Yard, and Ackroyd remembered having seen his pudgy face on television. He insisted on giving Ackroyd his card and demanded that the book should be sent to him as soon as it became available again, on the grounds that somewhere in its lines might be clues as to Priest's whereabouts. Ackroyd retorted indignantly that Victor Priest was a serious poet and didn't write acrostics, but this cut no ice with Dobson. He wanted the book to be sent on in the next few days.

Before Van Ackroyd could finally close the door of the shop, he had to deal with a very persistent last customer. This was an ancient individual in wire-rimmed glasses who was full of praise for Ackroyd's reading, and wanted him to participate in a series of poetry events at the Kent Marshes Poetry Society. Ackroyd identified the man as the cougher. In between enthusiastic and laudatory splutters, the elderly gentleman buried his face in a flaglike white handkerchief and gave vent to appalling laryngeal explosions. After several exchanges at cross-purpose, Ackroyd realised that the man appeared to believe he was actually addressing Victor Priest. Without bothering to correct this misapprehension, Ackroyd made some vague promises and shooed the man out of the door.

He went to the back of the office, sat down at his desk and pondered. There was a bottle of fifty year old reserve cognac in a cupboard and on an impulse he got up and fetched it. He took two brandy glasses from his desk drawer, put one on the other side of the table and one in front of himself. He poured liberal measures into both and held up his glass.

"To you, Victor. Your work is out there now. People are reading you at last. How do you feel?"

Ackroyd got up, walked round the desk, sat down and picked up the second glass.

"Vindicated."

Ackroyd took a swig, then went back and took a swig from his own.

"They all want to kill you, Victor."

He sat for a moment, then got up and moved to Priest's imagined chair.

"They all want to write like me, but they won't be able to. The song I hear is deeper than the grave."

Ackroyd took a swallow and returned to his chair.

"Is that where you are, Victor? In the grave?"

He emptied his own glass and went around the table again to finish what was left in the second glass.

"Ah, that is an excellent question."

THAT'S LIFE!

An Anthology of Contemporary British and Irish Poetry

Compiled and edited by J.J. Moon

Anita Bellows

TO EMPTINESS
(from ' Eros in Handcuffs')

I am emptied now
of all but my own hollow fog.

We were lost today
taking the route past the barbershop
translating the rocks
on the way.

You walked ahead, carrying
Leonard Fitzpatrick O'Toole.
I called to poverty in the sky.
He was heavy, I know.

Lucinda I have reached
the secret sexual place of placelesness.
Your wisdom unshaves me..
Each little follicle is so alive.

And the minutes are husbands
dropping us into the diminuendo of a drop
whose droplesness
will last until we drop it.

I am emptied of all
but my own wet drainage.

Barnaby Brown

TO ASH AGAIN

The urn turned upside down,
emptied out the ashes
and rolled away. The wind
grabbed each ash flake,
swooped it into the sky,
swirled it across the sea,
over fish, through gulls,
and on the other side
the ashes came together
to form the reborn man
who stole a bicycle,
pedalled up a mountain
and into a rushy tarn
where he drowned,
while the urn floated
across that same sea,
rolled across sand, fields,
then up that mountain, as trout
heaved the corpse out,
lightning bolts blasted it
to ash, which the urn ate,
then turned upside down…

The Day I Met the Merman

I was on Tory Island. I'd gone there
at the invitation of the King, who wanted
to paint me lolling in a wreck
with blue seaweed in my hair.
So I arrived seasick, to be marched
to the far end of the island, beyond
the lighthouse, and down to the rocks
where a juicy wreck waited, still
displaying splotches of its erstwhile

blue. And asleep in there we found
the merman! I can tell you, the King
was fit for tying, till I pointed out
what a fine subject for a portrait
the merman would be. *I don't do
portraits*, he snapped, *only seascapes!*
'This fellow is a denizen of the sea'
was my reply. And indeed, he looked
like a huge blue salmon with blond hair.
I hopped in beside him, waking him,
wondering why the King wished to
paint me, as I was hardly a seascape.
The merman appraised us both,
wagging his tail. He cleared his throat
and sounds flew out of his mouth
I'd never heard before, yet I knew
what he was saying – he was advising me
to swap my feet and legs for a tail
just like his, as one day I would drown.
Then he slithered into the water and
swam away. The king threw the seaweed
wig at me and bade me put it on.
He took out his paints and brush, but
before he began, he handed me a hipflask
of brandy. *After thon scaly blue fellow,
I think we deserve a good slug*, he said.
And his painting hangs in the island hotel.

Fergus Diver

THE SKELETON OF THE GIRAFFE

Wired high, its neckbones reach
the ceiling in a graceful anglepoise.
Below the framework of its carcase stands
a teacher with a mob of boys:

'See the lines its backbone makes?
Perfect balance! Nature is an artist.
Imagine it: the veldt, the wandering giraffe
browsing trees, its neck an alpinist.

No doubt you've seen them standing
inscrutable and silent at the zoo,
but thirty miles an hour is what
giraffes can do if lions pursue.

That, boys, is a chassis. Is it not?.
Imagine you could roam a prairie,
a fleet-foot, polka-dotted galloper,
foraging and having sex and being bony!

Alas, the males have sex with other males.
They neck for hours, then mount to climax
and Africans with rifles mow them down
and sell their hides for useless artefacts.'

A FIGURE RISING FROM THE CARPET

From the enigmatic, flat position I arose
Forming exceptional patterns, circle upon circle
I thought of heavy-nippled girls raising their eyebrows
And lifting their bushy smocks higher and
I possessed a vision of the big obedient dark continent of time

I speak the language that wears no clothes
I go about my stone task with grimy muscles

How apparent it is to those who stare!
I am all consonants and no vowels
Nothing you can make a word with like
oo aa oo aa eeeeee

THE POISONED

They came to the city with laurels on their mind.

Fedelini met Beatrice – she
of the stygian hair, the twisted, luscious mouth,
a leopardess, a rapier in her plackets.

Perciatelli acquired great estates and vineyards.
They found him head down in a barrel of Barolo, and fished
a single rabbit's foot from his throat.

Ciriole was always dressed to kill. What he did,
who he consorted with – this was a mystery.
He was found in the gutter, his windpipe slashed.

Mafaldine became a General. His *condottieri*
put the Duke of Savoy to the sword. Castles in Ferrara
burned. He was hanged to great applause.

The *chiromante* smiled upon Stringozzi.
She saw great estates and herds of water buffalo.
He was stabbed in a brawl at Gornito's.

Their dreams were salted down like anchovies.
The only one who prospered was Elicoidali.
He took what he wanted. Made sure he kept it.

But was it their minds she poisoned -
Amalia, the fatal courtesan -
Not for her, not for laurels, not even for themselves
Did they die.

Alexander Duthie

THE STUPENDOUS QUESTION

I write to unclog the pure fount of omnipotence
And release into the sky the radiant awareness
The white barge on the river of Egypt bearing the queen of victory
Beyond the main deep, beyond the continental shelf
Towards the abyss where the questions lurk

I see the woman from elfland who tantalises me
Stripping herself naked for her living-death lover
With his belching braces and his glowing face and his stained vest
Let her hold to him as eternity clung to Boethíus!
Man's extinction is next...! We must not flinch!

I hear them still, the men gathering at the pit head,
Low-voiced in the dark, the glow of their fags, their helmets lit,
Waiting for the lift that will carry them down, down
Like sweat-stained Persephones into the coaly vaults of Dis!
And they interest me not – only the higher brain centres are real!

BAD CONSCIENCE

I should have gone to the shipyard in Govan
and asked the men to weld me a suit of steel
with hinges to allow me to walk and kneel
at the altar of industry, hearing the Great Hymn
to Stalin explode in my head like a bomb
and the blinding clarity that results therefrom.

They claimed I was the grindstone workers' bard.
With posters and placards they named me the one
poet who spoke the truth, who favoured the sun.
Why could I not, then, consummate their regard
with more convulsive poems? I should have gone
instead of moving here and turning into stone

Bill Gerard-Wright

A SINGLE FEATHER
(from 'Trainsmoke')

That Apache headdress suits you.
I like the way the fire haunts your tepee,
I like the yellow glow in your eyes.
Think of me as gone, think of me as gone,
down to the bottom of the canyon.
You'll never hear the wind as close as this.
You'll never taste moonshine mescal.
A single feather, that's all –
the ghost of an eagle in the sky,
& blood on the agave's leaves.

THE WIGWAM OF THE BARONESS

It was yellow when she bought it
but the crowshit soon put paid to that.
Then the crows built their nests
in the fork-tree roof.
The baroness addressed her lover:
'Antoine. Those crows! Can't you
do something?' But Antoine
was kissing her neck. 'I like
crows,' he said. 'They bring
good luck. The inuit call them
spirit creatures.' He unbuttoned
her blouse. 'Fact is, I was once
a crow myself.' He buried his face
in the warmth of her skin &
she heard his muffled caw.
A louder caw came from above
& she felt the wind of wings.

Poppy Irving

AN ESSAY ON CHIMNEYS

I love the word 'chimneys'.
They tower red in my mind.
I am taking a train to my mother's
with the novels of Bennett in a bag.

When I heave my parcel
onto the kitchen table,
my mother exclaims:
"You have brought *Lord Raingo!*"

(ii)

She points to the window.
Controlled explosions are levelling
my chimneys.
"I hate History," I say.

"Do not regret the destruction of our town," she says.
"It is the infamy of testosterone.
Do they not know what occurs
when we raise these builded pinnacles!"

(iii)

I return home by train. The idea of glory
has been scratched in the glass of the carriage window
by some vacant yob whose idea of art
is violence, unremitting, and crap in execution.

Through rivers of houses and mortal fields, we speed
toward the Arnold I have left behind.
And far away I see the hills
like psychic turnstiles.

Damian Krapp

AS THE PODS CLONE

Wordsworth, thou shoulds't be living at this hour,
thy fog-enhrouded alpinism power
is what we need. Thy doctorly and firm
prescriptions against the horrid worm
that turneth inspiration's pencil blunt
and burroweth through passion with a grunt
are indispensable if we are not to die,
and never see the rocketship of poesy fly.

From a peak we need to glimpse the bards
happy-horned and leaping, vale to vale.
Instead we see a shuffling to the microphone
of men who've come to read their poems by train.
Theorists in minivans go up the pass
and suffocate the rabbits with their gas.
Vicious critics stamp the last true poet's toe.
Wordsworth, hast thou nodded off, below?

Tambi Kumar

IDENTITY CRISIS

Are you the black fellow
with ear-bashing music
under your rainbow hat,
chanting words that add up
to nothing at all, strumming
an invisible, unheard guitar?

Or are you the white bugger
with heart-galloping music
under your striped vest
yodelling words that add up
to everything that exists,
and banging a tin can?

Oh, the confusion you create,
black fellow, white bugger,
singing of corkscrewed love.
Can you not be one or the other?
Can you not be your own man?
Or should I eat a famished bird?

THE ONE-EYED PHILOSOPHER OF KATMANDU

The more a man wants, the less he gets –
so said the One-eyed Philosopher of Katmandu
over hot goats' urine and baked goat turds

that spring day I bumped my mountain-bike
up those steep, twisty roads to his green hut
camouflaged with lurid, sticky green creepers.

A bespectacled parrot was his sole companion,
and it chanted at regular intervals: *Death comes
to those fools who are never expecting him.*

The philosopher took out his glass eye to rub,
then replaced it in its socket. Typical of a bird,
he said, to be so sure of great death's gender.

I myself, he continued, know nothing about it,
beyond the fact it's a clifftop, and we all must
take the bewildering step off the edge into space.

And you, my young poet, he said, addressing me –
Be sure in your scribing to speak of that space
and nothing else, and then you may get everything.

Manny Lascalle

MURDER RIDDIMS

De food dat he eat
Put death on de plate
De boat goin on
Let de poet drown
De swing of de gate
Spell de poet's fate
De flight of de dart
Put poison in de heart
De teef of de hound
Bring de poet down
De kick of de mule
Make de poet a ghoul
De blast of de bomb
More poets gone
Dey killin poet-tree!
Dey killin poet-tree!

> *Dit dat dibbydat dubba dubba dum*
> *Dit dat dibbydat dubba dubba dum*
> *Dey am killin poet-tree*
> *For dey do not like to see*
> *People doin poet-tree*
> *Dit dat dibbydat dubba dubba dum*
> *Dit dat dibbydat dubba dubba dum!*

SAXOPHONE MAN

Saxophone man, he come,
bright red hair, orange suit,
yellow hat wid parrot feather,
smile so big like de sun.

He go walkin' up de street,
stand at de fountain and play.
De crows comin' to hear dat man.
De children run to him.

Me go slow, limp after,
always back of de line
listnin' to notes bend
dancin' to sad tunes.

Den Saxman take a walk,
he walk fast, still playin'.
De children run after.
I try to keep up, but no.

Over de bridge dey go.
Over de bridge dey tumble
down to de harbour
to de pier's end.

When dey get to de water
de splashing start like crazy.
Up ahead I see dem.
One by one dey all jump in.

Music stop like dat, man!
Saxman he go runnin'
off to de woods by de ribber.
He never be seen again.

Jemima Lee
(from 'The Metro Suicides')

4th METRO SUICIDE

She was small and curly haired,
and her shoulder bag held sheet music.
The red-haired boy kept staring at her,
and she moved like a python,
slithering through the crowd.
Would she crush the world and eat it?
The red-haired boy followed her.
It was Tuesday. She'd just had breakfast.
Smiley, smiley, flashed the sun.
A nun winked at a transvestite
who turned away, muttering German.
How much sunshine could the world take?

NOWHERE

She'd lost her appetite,
her vagina was closed,
and a moth beat at the pane.
On the floor, a beetle
teased out its life until she ended it.
The crunch echoed in her blood.
How she hated this town,
the black and white scarves,
stupid bridges and trains,
chips with everything
and very fat men.
The pubs were louder than
gunshots in the night.
The cinemas showed shite.
She took out a muslin
and spread it over her face.
It was cool under there.
It was a place to hide in.
No one would find her.

RUARI MACLEOD

A Garden

I too had a garden once. I'd hear the hinge
scrape on the gatepost, and welcome
the loud boys with leaping buckets
who'd swagger onto the grass. I'd buy
their mackerel and listen to their jokes.

There were clouds up there in scaldy blue
drifting over the tenements, and their
pram-pushed babbies who'd always bawl,
whether the clouds dropped rain or no.
I tried to devise a system to include them –

clouds, babbies, boys – even the rats that
skittered around the garden, squeaking.
What now can I cram into my stanzas?
The dogskull I dug up behind the dahlias?
That oar that had rotted into the ground?

A. D. Penfold

BUST

The sculptures were all blue.
In my head was a Roman bust.
I woke up and tried out my voice –
I heard the cry of parrots.
What could have caused this change?
I was lost in a mad museum.

Life in a cracked museum
teaches you how to be blue.
I pondered the nature of change,
how civilisation goes bust
and all one is left with is parrots,
mimicking the rational voice.

They said I had a good voice,
cool as a vast museum,
a tone that could silence parrots,
a speech that was darker than blue,
a mood that took flight on a bust-
ed wing and a prayer for change.

But how to accomplish change?
I wished for a woman's voice
or even better, a woman's bust,
and feared the end of my museum.
A terrible fanfare blew -
the sound of a thousand parrots.

I was lost in a jungle of parrots,
struggling to make a change.
Though trapped in walls of blue
I summoned an antique voice.
Flames engulfed my museum.
I knew my flush was bust.

Everywhere boom and bust,
the fierce cries of parrots.
All time went up in that museum.
Ash lay thick on the Exchange.
Traders with loss-making voices
turned the air poisonous blue.

Change a card and bust.
Voice the triumph of the parrots.
Let the whole museum burn to blue.

Victor Priest
(from 'Lunar Conspiracies)

LUNAR CONSPIRACIES

The throbbing leveret of my hand
tenses toward your glacial hair.
What grudge shall bear my tide onward
to the amphora filled with kisses –
be-silvered oracles of syllables,
the spoors of aristocratic snails?
I am building my church in your shadow.
Crazed mosaic of trouble,
bewildered pledge of the last explorer,
scythed prophecies, lunar conspiracies –
the god is swimming to shore.

THE AUGURIES

Under the crypt of the toadstone
before thought curls to the
                              wisp of a must
where *can* becomes *will*
                    subjugated by effluvium
the grey heron immobile at dawn
under the mucus of slubbed clouds
stalks and gleams from each
                              sprained tantrum
a spell chaffered by black trees
their genital shadows plucked by
                         tasselled winds
as the auguries that we revere
                         are immunised

THE ROCOCCO JUMP

My sensual equerry knows
blood is the rain of lost adventure.
The breakthrough renegades
have crashed the orifex in veils of doubt.
Under the leaping hounds of storm
I set up demon stalls,
lounge on tilted shadows.
I roam as blind as jasmine dust beneath
the coloured breath of fortune.
Let me hunt down the lanes of disconnection.
Let me wrest these bones from stillness
and kiss the shudders of my meaning

Amelia Quirk

F'AIRY ST'ORY

I saw a wicked old lady with a yellow turban
Beating her husband to death with a fan
And I said: "Ventilator! Why do you belabour so the soft
                                        umbrella of your aviary ?"
And she, with a smudgy riposte: "I flail the Persian of evening,
                        I embroider the marmite of souls..."

And I, to the old gentleman, who was dust by this time, his
                        cummerbund a saffron swarm of gnats:
"Is it not, in the mortgage of your life, a red tiger to a candlewick
To endure such wheelchairs of shoe leather, such
                                        whistling paellas of gloom?"

And he, from his bathtub of might-be's, his bombed
                                        armageddon of lies:
"Poet, in your scaffolding of ironweed, your knowledgeable
                                        saddlebags of grunts ,
How can'st thou presume to penetrate this birdcage of impalpable
                uppercuts, these feather-smacking horsehoes of woe?"

I saw a villainous tram driver digging a pit for the victims of his oil
I saw how he treadled the girls of the rail with terrible fists
And I saw the gooseberry river and memory's bridge with its
                                        sunshine and lingerie
I saw the languid goats of the apocalypse chewing the feet of the poor

And I wept...

Melinda Speling

THE CRYSTAL FROG

From the open door of the tomb
whose dark chandeliers
lit the shroud of cobwebs,
I waltzed out into the air.

Where the skiffs jostled,
where the planks groaned like old men dying,
where the stars fished for fireflies,
I saw the crystal frog.

One hop and it was gone,
leaving a silver chain behind
with which I pierced my labia
and wear, now, when it rains.

Drizzle, my friend, bring it back,
that small amphibian of light.
Jump, little creature, into my shoes
and we'll be one, I promise.

THE GREEN HAMMOCK

A tearful wasp rustles at my ear,
trilobites munch in the apples
and the clock tower founders
through the quiet gramophone of the leaves.

Gravity is dying in its gaiters.
The long white body is laid out to swing
where the shadows flush
deep dark cisterns of the German mercy.

The boots it wears are a thoughtful rhapsody
like the cluck of blackbirds
or the swan-feather sheen of my boots
over my crossed-leg destinations.

Beneath the holes of murmuring string
the cool mole gropes.
A lullaby throws rocks at me,
but they are only falling pears.

Let this knot unravel
the breathtaking sister of my knees.
I can hear time everywhere, like woodworm,
and I want to be stoned like a plum.

Horace Venables

GIFTS
(from 'Stray')

I have a leaning fig tree
I would like to give to you,
a crooked vineyard and an olive grove
high above the sea.

I give you quercus ilex, myrtle.
My dog will bark a greeting.
Where cisterns swarm with dragonflies
we shall contrive a meeting.

Beneath the shadow of a pine,
lovers come to learn
the taste of crunchy juniper
and watch the eagles turn

Take this berry, sweet and dry.
Lie upon this sunny stone.
Let me embrace with words again
the one I could not own.

NOT CRICKET

The girls who ran towards me
when I was young came running
across invisibly green parks
calling out: *Howzat! Howzat!*

Today those shouts
seem blind as sightscreens.
We played love with a straight bat.
Fielders sat calmly in their dinghies, fishing.

Those girls.
They were like boundaries.
They were like scoreboards.
They were like smashed pavilion clocks.

Nowadays
the hard red balls
and the sound of willow meeting leather
make me feel utterly sick.

Manfred Von Zitzewitz
four poems from 'Bastard Zen'

RESCUE

The one-armed sailor
handcuffed to the drifting boat
attempted to wave.

OCCUPATIONAL HAZARD

The postman hammered
at the door of the castle
trying to get out.

MISSED

Snorting and stamping,
the bull tried to extract its
horns from the barn door.

GLAD

The white stallion
galloped along the runway
to meet the airplane.